SALT OF THE EARTH

by

Mark Allan Johnson

Inspired by historical events, this novel contains fictitious characters, places and circumstances.

For the Boushey Family—

Past is not always prologue

Hickory Hill

Part One

One

~~1846 Equality, Gallatin County, Illinois

"Damn government," John Hart Crenshaw said, his face turning scarlet as the cravat he had neatly knotted before staining it with gravy dripping from his biscuits during breakfast. He crumpled the letter he was reading into a ball and threw it at the fireplace. It fell short.

"John," Francine Taylor Crenshaw said, raising her voice as if to scold a child. "You don't want the doctor to bleed you again."

"The government is already letting my blood, Sina," John said, bending over with a grunt, a gold button popping from his brocade vest. He picked it up from the Persian rug, retrieved the letter and dropped it onto the fire Cyrus had lit before John and Sina rose from bed. It erupted into flames. He took the poker and stabbed at the logs as if to assure the letter's total annihilation. He slammed the poker into its stand and slipped the vest button into his watch pocket. Patsy could sew it on later.

"They say I haven't paid taxes. What kind of fool pays taxes?"

Sina kept her tongue. When John was in one of his moods, she would retreat to help Patsy with her chores.

Sometimes her husband ranted against his enemies who were plotting his downfall with the wicked ways of Lucifer's Legion; other times he sank into a deep melancholy that robbed him of speech as he sat in his leather chair by the river rock fireplace, watching the flames consume cords of logs that Cyrus had split.

"They desire to force me into relinquishing my salt works."

"I do not understand business matters, John, nor do I wish to. I have a home to keep."

"Damn government," Sina heard John repeating as she withdrew into the kitchen.

"Is Mr. Crenshaw in one of them moods?" Patsy asked. She was peeling apples, careful not to break the strip of mottled skin that rolled down from the paring knife like an uncoiling spring.

"Lately he's always in one of his moods, Patsy."

"If I had a man, I'd tell him not to be actin' such a child. You think havin' a man is worth the trouble, ma'am? I been without so long…"

"Mr. Crenshaw wants dumplings for supper tonight," Sina said, interrupting. She preferred Patsy not bring up the man who had become like a father to her children after their own father, Silas, had been sold. Rueben was a slave from Kentucky, legally leased and brought across the Ohio River to John Hart Crenshaw's salt work

Zeke Stubbs, John's overseer, rode Rueben hard from the start. There was something about Rueben that Zeke despised. Rueben carried himself with too much pride. Too much dignity. Zeke was infuriated by the way Rueben said, "Yes sir." It didn't sound like he meant it. There was a glint in Rueben's black eyes that said he thought he was Zeke's equal. One day while Rueben was hauling brine to boil down in the iron pots, Zeke accused him of being lazy. The way Rueben looked at Zeke caused him to crack his skull with the heavy riding stick he called his persuader. Since Mr. Crenshaw's salt works were just across the Ohio River from the slave state of Kentucky in the supposedly free state of Illinois, Zeke assumed every nigger was plotting an escape farther north towards Canada and away from the slave south. Rueben hit the ground dead.

"Mr. Crenshaw do like his dumplins'," Patsy said.

"I'm riding down to the salt works," John said, entering the kitchen.

"You startled me, John," Sina said. "You never come in the kitchen."

"I have business that needs my attention," he said. "Dumplings tonight?"

"If you are not gone all evening attending to business."

"Not if there are dumplings," he said, lightly kissing Sina on the cheek.

"John," Sina scolded, blushing, pushing him back.

"You know how I like my dumplings, Patsy? Not too doughy."

"You never complain 'bout my dumplins', Mr. Crenshaw," Patsy said with a grin. "There be apple pie, too."

"Your dumplings and pies are the best in all of Gallatin County," John said, heading for the front door, whistling.

"Something on your mind," Patsy?" Sina asked. "You look sad."

"You seen my girls, ma'am?" Patsy asked. "Now that Beulah be with child she need to learn how to make dumplins'."

"I have never seen two young ones so close as Beulah and Betsy," Sina said

"That be true, ma'am. But sometimes they be so different I almost forgets they be twins...." Patsy's voice trailed towards tears as she retrieved a can of lard from the pantry.

"Go look for them, Patsy. I'll start the dough."

"Yes, ma'am," Patsy said, untying her apron and hanging it on a hook beside the kitchen door. "They probably be out under that old elm talkin' like they do. Just lost track of time. They can't be far."

~~~

All men are not created equal, Zeke Stubbs thought, and it made him laugh when he heard that the man who wrote that all men were created equal was a slave owner. No one Zeke knew believed a white man and a nigger were equal. Niggers brought good prices at auction, but that was because they worked like mules, or they were young girls with wide breeding hips or Mammies who suckled like swollen milk cows. More animal than human, Zeke thought, and no schooling or fancy clothes would make them anything more than dressed up monkeys.

Gallatin County sat on the southern tip of Illinois where it narrowed as the Ohio flowed into the Mississippi on its run to the Delta. Across the Ohio was the slave state of Kentucky, home to horse breeders and traders in human flesh. It was true that Kentucky was losing its appetite for the Peculiar Institution, not out of divine revelation, but because Blue Grass country held fertile ground to grow the crops that made slaves an expensive luxury. But Kentuckians could still broker the Negroes they did not need without question or conscience that had come into their possession and ship them down river to the Deep South where King Cotton's hunger for strong backs was growing more insatiable, or legally lease them across the river to the free state of Illinois.

Besides the gold he shared with Mr. Crenshaw from each sale, Zeke felt he was doing a duty by returning the niggers to their rightful condition. He remembered the travelling preacher from his boyhood, his arm raised as if to grasp St. Michael's flaming sword, roaring, "Slaves, obey your earthly masters with fear and trembling." It was in the

Bible. It could not be much plainer. Zeke was doing the Lord's work.

~~~

"I require the bill of sale," John said.

"I ain't never cheated you, Mr. Crenshaw," Zeke Stubbs said, struggling to rein in his stamping roan. The horse threw its head back, snorted and knocked John's broad-brimmed hat into the mud before stomping it flat.

"Deliver these niggers," John said, nodding towards two dark-skinned girls, one pregnant, huddling on the bed of the farm wagon, attempting to use thin shawls against the rain that had been steady since sunrise, "sell them for no less than I have instructed and you'll get what's coming to you. Attempt swindling me and you'd have a better chance escaping the hounds of hell."

"You ain't nothin' if not a hypocrite, Mr. Crenshaw, talkin' about God all the time. You are about as holy as a muleskinner."

"I have skinned many a mule in my time, Mr. Stubbs," John said. "I am not above skinning a thief."

"You forgot your hat," Zeke said, his roan circling it like a cutting horse herding a calf.

"Get these niggers to the landing," John shouted, his face reddening. He mounted and reined his horse towards Hickory Hill, feeling exposed as rain fell, plastering his thinning hair flat to his hatless head. Cyrus would have hell to pay if he hadn't kept the fire stoked.

"Get that sorry excuse for a horse movin', George," Zeke barked at the man in wagon's driver seat. George's crow-black face revealed no trace of white master. "Got to meet the flatboat at the landin' before dark."

"Yes sir, Mr. Stubbs," George said, clucking a command and shaking the reins. "Come on, Sally. You heard what Mr. Stubbs said. You got a dry barn waitin' when this job be done."

"George!" Zeke bellowed. "Break an axel on that wagon and you'll carry the niggers to the river on your back!"

"Ain't my fault, Mr. Stubbs. It be easier for Sally to be pullin' a sled through this muck," George said.

"Use the whip," Zeke nearly screamed.

"I ain't never used no whip on Sally and I ain't about to begin now," George replied, realizing too late Zeke would probably take the whip to him later for his insolence.

The wagon's wheels found little traction in the slop that had been a passable road before the downpour began. The rain was not letting up and Zeke's anger turned to rage as he watched the wagon slide sideways towards the ridge, the left rear wheel buckle under and the rim and spokes snap into kindling. The terrified horse struggled against her harness while her thrashing hooves could not prevent the wagon from slipping over the river embankment.

"George!" Zeke yelled. "Save the niggers!"

The wagon lodged against a young stand of birch that bent towards the river under the wagon's weight. George jumped from the wagon seat and began unbuckling the tangled harnesses that tethered the frantic horse to the wagon.

"The niggers!" Zeke hollered. "Forget the horse. Get the niggers."

George pretended he didn't hear. If it meant a lashing, so be it. He wasn't going to let Sally suffer.

"Whoa, Sally," George said, unbuckling the last rein. "You be free now, girl."

Released from the wagon, the mare struggled up the bank, dragging its straps and buckles like jangling lengths of chain. Zeke dismounted and grabbed the horse's collar, guiding it to the road where it stood fetlock-deep in the mud, too tired to rear or bolt in fright from the cracks of lightning and rumble of thunder.

George climbed into the wagon bed after seeing Sally was safe. The two girls were lying against the side that had tilted to a precarious angle. One of the girls clutched the top rough-cut board; the other girl clung to her.

"Girl", George said, reaching out his arm. "Grab my hand."

The pregnant girl stared at George, her fingers dug deep into her companion's shawl.

"Dammit, girl! Let go of her and grab my hand!"

She continued to stare at George, her eyes dry and huge. The wagon shifted, jerking closer to the river. The girl blinked and slowly reached out her arm. George strained to reach it. Their fingers touched and stretched to interlock. He pulled hard while still hanging onto the tilted, rain-slick boards of the wagon side. The pregnant girl was surprisingly light. He hauled her up, careful to protect her belly that held a profit Mr. Crenshaw would personally whip George for losing.

"My sister," the girl pleaded.

"She gonna be just fine. I get you up to the road then I go back for her," George said.

The girl hung on George like a terrified child. He struggled up the embankment, reaching the road without falling. The girl wouldn't let go.

"This is the one I want," Zeke said, grabbing the girl by the arm and dragging her towards his horse. "Should get double the price at the river. The other one ain't worth the trouble."

"I ain't gonna let her die any more than I was gonna let Sally get hurt," George said, looking up at Zeke with undisguised hatred.

"Look at me like that again, boy, and you'll be stretched out in the nigger graveyard next to Reuben."

A sharp crack interrupted Zeke's tirade. The wagon hitched down the embankment as one of two young birches that had braced it snapped. The wagon hesitated until the second birch uprooted from the saturated soil.

"Betsy!" the pregnant girl screamed. "My sister!"

She broke free from Zeke and ran back to the river, slipping and falling into the mud, crawling towards the edge.

"If anythin' happens to her," Zeke said to George, "you will answer to Mr. Crenshaw."

George got to her just in time to see the wagon jerk and tumble into the rain-swelled river.

"Betsy," the pregnant girl sobbed.

"I's sorry about this, Miss Beulah," George said, kneeling to put his arm around her shoulder. "Mr. Stubbs said I'd be sold down river, too, if I didn't take you and Miss Betsy to the landin'."

"Hush, George. It ain't your fault." Beulah said. "Betsy's gone to a better place."

She gently lifted George's arm from her shoulder and stood. She walked back to Zeke who had mounted his horse.

"You take that useless nag back to Hickory Hill," Zeke said to George. "Tell Mr. Crenshaw that you lost his wagon and one of his niggers. I'm takin' this one to the landin' and get every ounce of gold I can for her and the piccaninny in her belly."

Zeke reached down and yanked Beulah onto the horse's rump behind the saddle.

"You go back and tell Mr. Crenshaw what you done, boy," Zeke said, turning to George. "And you tell him I'll get his gold like he wants. Maybe more."

Zeke dug his heels into his horse's flank and yanked the reins towards the road. Beulah gripped Zeke's rain slicker with all the strength she had left as the horse struggled down the muddy road towards the landing.

George clucked for Sally. She shook her head, the harnesses jingling like sleigh bells. She came to George's soothing coaxes.

"We goin' home, Sally," George said, grabbing her collar and swinging up on her slick back. He squeezed with his thighs and pulled the loose reins up. "You know the way."

Horses know where there home be, George thought. A melancholy washed over him, cold as the rain that saturated his thin coat and brought shivers with each wind gust.

"Git up, Sally," George said. "Go home. You know the way."

~~~

The flatboat was tied up to a makeshift mooring; a kerosene lamp hanging from a pole attached to the squat cabin threw a dancing patch of light on the splintered planking, exposing wide gaps.

"You be careful goin' out to the boat," Zeke said, lowering Beulah from his horse's rump. "Don't want you fallin' through and gettin' washed out to the Gulf like the other nigger."

"Betsy," Beulah said.

"A Christian name don't make a nigger nothin' more than just a nigger."

"She be my sister."

"Keep walkin' to the boat," Zeke said, dismounting and looping the reins around the end of the railing that looked as rickety as the dock. The wind swayed the branches of a willow hanging over the river bank back and forth in time to the clanking kerosene lamp on its pole. Something was making Zeke feel uneasy. "Keep walkin'. I'm right behind you."

Beulah wrapped her wet shawl tighter as she cautiously stepped over one gap in the dock and then another. She didn't care about herself, but she loved her baby. She had already named her unborn child, confident that, by the way he kicked, it was a boy. Beulah knew the child's master would change his name, but her baby boy would always have the name she gave him, even if he never heard it. When Seth got to heaven, that's what Jesus would call him.

A dark figure stooped out of the flatboat's cabin and into the lamplight. He was aiming a Kentucky flintlock at Zeke.

"I was told two niggers," he said. "You tryin' to pull somethin'? Crenshaw said you might."

"Lost one to the river. Lost the wagon, too. That nigger driver's fault. Lucky you got this nigger. Better luck, she's got a pickaninny in her belly. Might say it's two for the price of one."

"Or two for the price of none," the man said, pulling the squirrel gun's trigger. The hammer's flint sparked the gunpowder in the pan that exploded into flash and smoke. The round ball hit Zeke just above his right eye. He stood motionless with a look of shock, as if a field slave had slapped him across the face, then fell, plunging through the shattering rail and off the dock into the river. A red halo spread around his head as he floated face down into the swirling current.

Beulah had fallen to the dock, pulling her shawl over her head, curling on her side to protect her baby. To protect Seth. She felt a boot kicking her in the back.

"Into the boat, nigger," the man was hollering, poking her with the spent flintlock. Beulah could still smell the powder. "Got a surprise for you."

Beulah struggled to her feet and stumbled towards the cabin. The man with the squirrel gun took the kerosene lamp from its pole and pulled back the canvass door. Inside, Beulah could see another man sitting on a bench at a rough-cut table, smoking a pipe. In the corner what looked to be a pile of clothes was moving. The man with the pipe pulled it from his mouth and pointed with its stem towards what looked like a rag pile with a toothless grin.

"Your surprise," the man with the squirrel gun said, lifting the lamp to expose a face in the pile of rags.

"Betsy," Beulah said, too weary to show the joy she felt. "I knowed you be alive."

"She drifted up against the dock hangin' onto broken bits of a wagon," the man with the pipe said.

"Figured she must be one of the niggers Stubbs was bringin', " the man with the Squirrel gun said.

"So why you kill Stubbs?" Beulah asked, kneeling to put her arms around Betsy.

"Mr. Crenshaw said Stubbs was a no good sneak thief who deserved worse than a bullet in the head, but that it would do," the man with the squirrel gun said.

"And we get Stubbs's share," the man with the pipe said, relighting it with a long wooden match scratched across the slivering table.

"Y'all think you can trust Mr. Crenshaw?" Beulah asked. "He stole me and Betsy from our mama."

"We ain't no niggers," the man with the squirrel gun said, gently hanging the rifle on wall pegs above the table. He gave the stock a caress as if putting a child to bed. "Mr. Crenshaw gave his word."

Mrs. Crenshaw gave her word, too, Beulah thought. She promised that me and Betsy would never be sold, Beulah remembered. She promise that we would never be taken away from Mama. She gave her word. Now Beulah wondered if her word was any better than Mr. Crenshaw's. But that had never been Beulah's experience. Mrs. Crenshaw had always protected her and Betsy against Mr. Crenshaw's temper like when she chipped a china saucer or scorched his best Sunday Shirt with an overheated iron, knowing that his way of punishment would be a shaving strap. Or maybe the Mrs. Crenshaw has no idea we been kidnapped, Beulah pondered. Maybe she be in the dark as much as Betsy and me on this boat, now that the man with the squirrel gun took the lamp and closed the canvas door. Beulah held her sister tighter as the boat began to rock, moving away from the dock and out into the river that flowed south, strong and steady as the rain that had returned to beat on the cabin's roof.

Two

"Delicious," John said, stabbing the last perfectly formed and firm dumpling from the gilt-edged platter with his fork.

"Take some chicken," Sina said.

"You know I can't abide boiled chicken. Tasteless," he said, filling his mouth with more seasoned dough.

"Mrs. Crenshaw like my chicken," Patsy said, carrying another platter of dumplings in from the kitchen.

"Then there will be plenty for her," John said, motioning Patsy towards his plate, raising his fork.

"I think you've had enough, John," Sina said, "You popped a button off your vest this morning."

"The thread was weak," John said. "Just one more? I'll save the apple pie for breakfast. You were more permissive with the children when they were young."

"I do not believe in the rod."

"I do. You may share the rest with the help, Patsy," John said, taking one dumpling from the platter she was holding. "Especially the chicken."

"Thank you, sir. They be happy."

"Where did you find your girls, Patsy?" Sina asked.

"I ain't yet, Mrs. Crenshaw. It be gettin' late and I be afraid for them. They never be out after dark before.

They be good girls, always do their chores, even if Betsy moans all the time." Patsy said, biting her lower lip to hide its trembling.

"See if Mr. Stubbs can help you find the girls," Sina said.

"Zeke is doing some business for me," John said. "He won't be back until tomorrow. Ask Cyrus to help you look."

"George would be better," Patsy said. "Cyrus don't see so good after dark no more."

"George is with Zeke. Won't be back until tomorrow."

"I am worried, John," Sina said. "The sun is down..."

"Tomorrow," John insisted. "Cyrus can help look in the morning, after first light."

Sina looked at Patsy. Patsy took the meaning of the concern in her eyes. Mr. Crenshaw was done talking about her girls. Patsy had to search for them on her own, later, when everyone was asleep, no matter how dangerous it might be. Without her girls, Patsy didn't care if she was kidnapped by Night Riders and hauled back to Louisiana. Cutting cane would just be God's punishment for losing her girls.

~~~

Patsy was shivering, but not because the rain had soaked through her thin shawl and cotton dress. And not out of fear for her safety. She accepted the cruel fact she would be easy prey for the Night Riders before she left Hickory Hill in search of her girls. She knew the chances anyone of her color took being out after nightfall, freed or not. That meant nothing to the men who knew her worth in the Memphis Slave Market. Patsy was shivering for Beulah and Betsy. And for her unborn grandbaby she had prayed would come of age in a land that had forsaken slavery and indenture and all ungodly forms of servitude. All men were created equal, she had heard a preacher preach when she was a child. She liked those words and was certain the preacher meant that women were equal just the same. Patsy's hope had grown with the size of Beulah's belly. And though she knew that Beulah's condition would make her a ripe fruit for the Night Riders to pick, Patsy refused to believe that Jesus would let her girls be captured and chained and floated downriver to the auction markets of Memphis to be sold alongside strings of Missouri Mules.

~~~

"Quit your cryin', Betsy," Beulah said. "You too growed up to be actin' like a baby. Mama would whup your bottom."

"I ain't no child," Betsy said.

"Then stop actin' like one. You is my twin. We's the same age…"

"Shut your mouths," the man said, packing fresh tobacco into his pipe from a cow skin pouch. "Ain't gonna be no nigger uprisin' on my watch."

"Jim," the other man called from the deck. "Get your ass out here you lazy son of a bitch and grab a pole before we run aground."

"I ain't your nigger, Frank," Jim said, pulling the canvas door back, then turning to scowl at Beulah. "I think them's plottin' somethin'."

"You afraid of two unarmed Negresses? They gonna knock you out and steal your corncob?"

"But I'm good enough to man a pole."

"You finally said somethin' I can agree with," Frank said. "There's that island up ahead. I've got the tiller. Take a pole and start heavin' starboard into the current and away from the rocks."

"So, you need my help?"

"I need your help," Frank admitted.

"You be good little girls," Jim said to Beulah and Betsy. "And stop that goddam blubberin'." He pulled a wooden match from his shirt pocket, struck it with his thumbnail and lit his corncob.

"Jim!"

"Alright. Alright. Keep your britches on."

Frank could barely see the island's outline downstream, but he was familiar with its treacherousness from his frequent trips delivering human cargo and he knew where the river sank and surged over submerged rock, not quite rapids but nearly as dangerous for flatboats. He pulled the tiller hard to port. The island was coming up faster than he anticipated.

Patsy had not found Beulah and Betsy under their talkin' elm, one of the few elms at Hickory Hill that had survived the last outbreak of Dutch disease, when she had begun her search before she served dumplings to Mr. Crenshaw. She also knew the girls were not in the servants' cabin, since she had searched there after the supper dishes were done and Mr. Crenshaw was asleep in front of the fire. Her girls had been taken, of that Patsy was certain. And she was also certain that their first destination would be the landing on the river where flatboats docked to load before floating south to sell her girls. Patsy had no plan and little hope, just a blind determined grit to save her girls from cruelty worse than Mr. Crenshaw ever dispensed to the stubborn and the disobedient with his horsewhip.

Patsy knew life could be worse. She had been born into the sugar country of Louisiana, stooping to scoop up the cut cane, carrying it to the sugarhouse for grinding in the smothering heat when she was still a child, plantation failures sending her from field to field like a packhorse with an straight back and good teeth.

"What you doin' out here this time of night," George said, pulling Sally to a halt. The rain had been slowing for the last hour, the clouds cracking enough to expose a handful of stars and a lopsided moon. George could see it was Patsy, looking up at him with a cold countenance. "There be Night Riders…"

"They took my girls," Patsy said. "And Beulah be with child."

"I know she be," George said, sliding down from Sally. "Now let me help you up, Miss Patsy. Ain't right for you to be walkin' in this slop. Now where your shoes be?"

"The mud took them," Patsy said. "Used to walk on sugarcane stubble, when I was a child. Got tough feet."

"I's sure you does," George said, taking Patsy by the waist and lifting her up on Sally's back. He took the reins.

"You just grab Sally's mane and hang on tight. She won't mind. She be slippery with sweat and rain."

"You know where my girls be, George?"

"Now why would I know that," George said.

"Mr. Crenshaw said you was gone with Mr. Stubbs on business. What kinda business? Where be the wagon?"

"You ask too many questions, Miss Patsy. I's just a livery nigger. All I knows is horses."

George pulled the reins tight and began walking Sally.

"Now you hang on tight to that mane," George said. "Won't be long for we get home."

Patsy felt despair seizing her throat. She would let it hold sway until the morning when making biscuits and churning butter would soothe her hurt heart with familiar chores. Maybe my girls will be at Hickory Hill, she thought, waiting for me with a story of why they were so late and missed supper. She will scold them for worrying their poor old mama. She will threaten them with no supper. Then she will hug them, feed them and put them to bed. Beulah might be having a child, but she was still Patsy's baby.

~~~

"Shove harder, you bastard!" Frank yelled at Jim. The river roaring over the rocks that ringed the island drowned out his command.

"What?" Jim yelled, turning to look at Frank who was motioning with his head towards port while pulling hard on the tiller until he feared the old wood might snap.

"Shove off the rocks!"

Jim jerked around, jabbing the pole against a river-smoothed boulder, leaning in with all the strength he could muster. The pole slipped from the rock. Jim fell hard to the deck, the pole torn away in the torrent. The flatboat followed the pole into the rocks, rising up and rolling Jim back against the cabin, cracking his head on the pine boards. Blood ran from his greasy hair. The flatboat fell back and began making a full turn in the churning current. The rocks caught the tiller and threatened to catapult Frank overboard. He lifted the tiller, waiting for the flatboat to point downriver, then sank it deep into the water, following the flow away from the rocks, away from the island and southwest towards the junction where the Ohio mingled with the Mississippi. He would concern himself with Jim as soon as the flatboat settled into a slow drift.

Betsy's sobs had turned to weeping until the flatboat slammed against the rocks, shocking her into silence like an open-handed slap.

"You stay right here," Beulah said, releasing herself from Betsy's trembling embrace. "It be quiet now."

"Maybe they both washed away and drowned."

Beulah began crawling toward the cabin's canvas door.

"Beulah!" Betsy cried.

"Don't you start bawlin' again. My shawl is wet enough."

Beulah pulled the canvass door back far enough to see one man standing, clutching the tiller. He looked grim.

He did not move. It looks like the river be steering him, Beulah thought. He did not notice her as she stood, leaned out and saw the other man lying against the cabin wall. There was blood in his hair and blood on the deck. She could see his chest heaving and hear his raspy breaths. He was still alive.

"Girl," Frank said, releasing one hand from the tiller to wipe his face. "Get back in the cabin."

"You think I would jump in the river and swim to shore? You think I would leave my sister behind? Your friend, he be bleedin'. You got bandages?"

"Don't need niggers playin' doctor. Jim'll be all right, soon as he wakes up.

"I can help. My mama knows all about healin'. She learned it from her mama. Her mama come from New Orleans."

"You keep your voodoo away from Jim. And don't you go stickin' him with pins."

Beulah reached under her skirt and began tearing her one good petticoat into strips.

"He bleed to death less I stop it," Beulah said. "You want him be dead?"

"No. Weaklin' that he is, I need him to help get this flatboat to Memphis. Patch him up, if you can."

Jim began groaning. He opened his eyes. A look of horror washed over his pale face when he realized one of the nigger girls was wrapping cloth around his head.

"She's tryin' to kill me," Jim shouted, sitting up and ripping the bandage from her head.

"You're bleedin'," Frank said. "Now, you can bleed to death or let her dress that wound. Don't really matter to me."

"What wound?" Jim asked, looking puzzled.

"God almighty," Frank said. "You about as dense as them rocks that near put us on the bottom of the river."

"Rocks?"

"Like the ones you got rattlin' in your head."

"The island," Jim said, beginning to remember. "That's right. My head hurts."

Frank shook his. "Sit back down and let her at least stop the bleedin'. Don't want no slippery blood on my deck. Someone might get hurt."

Beulah picked up the strip of cloth Jim had torn from his wound and began wrapping again.

"Not too tight!" Jim complained.

Beulah stifled a reply, remembering what her mama had said, that being disrespectful would only get you the whip. Tonight it wasn't the whip she feared; it was the marketplace in Memphis, and the cotton fields of Mississippi, or the sugarcane fields of Louisiana. She also feared for Betsy who did not share Beulah's fortitude and had always leaned on her sister, even though Betsy was older, born five minutes before Beulah. Now Betsy really needed Beulah to lean on. She just hoped she wouldn't collapse under her weight.

Three

Salt. A gift of life from dead seas; offering for Egyptian gods; Homer's divine substance; vital trade commodity to the seafaring Phoenicians; preserver of food or destroyer of crops for Romans to spread on conquered and burned Carthage fields. Greeks bought slaves with salt and Moorish merchants traded salt for gold, ounce for ounce. The Bible warned that the Salt of the Earth remains valuable only until its saltiness is lost and then must be thrown out and trampled underfoot. Spilled salt is tossed over the shoulder to hit the Devil in the eye and salt is taken in grains when the tales get too tall.

While the glaciers melted after the last Ice Age to open paths to a new world, Mastodon and Wooly Mammoth were drawn to this saline swamp. Later Buffalo traces led to the lick where herds shouldered the earth into the shape a half moon, their long trails guiding the Old World immigrants to the brine that they boiled in clay pots, their scattered shards discovered by those inflicted with Manifest Destiny, American settlers who displaced the misnamed Indian, the French and the English with ambition and the labor of the bought, the leased and the kidnapped.

~~~

"Christ," John shouted. "This fire needs to be hotter. I'll be laid out in my parlor before this brine boils down."

"Yes sir, Mr. Crenshaw. We needs more wood."

"Then cut more."

"We is runnin' out of trees."

"What's your name, boy?"

"I's called Arthur."

"Well, boy. I don't care if you've got to go to Kentucky for firewood. Do it. Make this fire hotter."

"Yes sir, Mr. Crenshaw. The boys is cuttin' what they can."

Hollowed-out logs ran brine miles from the wells to the iron pots, felled trees joisted into wooden pipe, elevated and sloped to flow like Roman aqueducts. The smell of fresh-cut timber mingled with salty steam. The bubbling black pots lined the edge of a dwindling stand of Slippery Elm, White Ash and Oak. Muscular Negroes worked the sparse woodland. One Negro angled his axe into the trunk of a White Oak with the precision of a railroad worker pounding down a railroad spike with his nine-pound hammer. Two Negroes buck-sawed trunks into rounds and one Negro split the rounds with wedge and sledge into logs to stoke the fires for the pots. The process had continued for years, consuming forests like Moses' locust devouring Egypt's wheat, all for the sake of salt and profit.

"Near done with this stand of trees, Mr. Crenshaw," Elias said, riding up beside John. Elias was leader of the work gang, a slave leased from Kentucky who had proven his loyalty enough to be trusted with a horse. John liked Elias, as much as he could like a Negro. He followed orders, kept any opinions he might have to himself and got a good day's work out of the other darkies without resorting to the whip. Elias would have made an excellent overseer, if he had been white. "We gonna need more pipe to run to the next stand, Mr. Crenshaw."

John was lost in speculation. His empire of salt was crumbling. His land leases were about to expire. He never did own the salt works. It was the shrewd businessman who used other people's money to get rich, he would boast when times were good. Or in his case, other people's land. But the shrewdest man knows when to cut his losses, John thought. Now that the government wanted back taxes, it might be time to look for another line of work. Or at least an easier way to make money.

"Mr. Crenshaw?" Elias repeated.

"No, Elias. No need to find more trees to cut. When that stand is committed to the flames, I shall be done with salt."

"Why you say that, Mr. Crenshaw. Salt be your life. There be more trees on that ridge over yonder. Just need to run more pipe and move the pots..."

"Too costly, Elias. The wells are getting deeper, the pipes are getting longer and I'm getting older. I am tired."

"What you gonna do, Mr. Crenshaw? What we gonna do?"

Boiling down the brine for salt was backbreaking work. Wells had to be dug, wood had to be chopped to feed the fires and when the trees ran out, wooden pipes carved from logs run farther to carry the brine from wells to the next source of wood. The process continued for years. But it could not go on forever. John leased slaves from Kentucky since no white men in Gallatin County would stoop to mining salt, for any wage. It had always been a relief to John that no self-respecting white man would take the job since all he needed to provide for his darkies were clapboard cabins and weekly rations of corn meal and molasses, lard and peas, greens and flour and maybe bits of meat for Sunday. It was the system that had made and sustained fortunes. But now skyrocketing costs and the fact that salt works in states like Ohio that were blessed with a more abundant and accessible supply were undercutting his prices. John had increasingly turned to the kidnapping of darkies and selling them into slavery to afford keeping his property and reputation as a family man and upstanding Methodist Elder intact. Yes, he had been indicted and tried for illegal slave trafficking in the past, but he knew that no evidence or hearsay could sway juries or judges who shared his belief that the darkies should be thankful for their captivity. They should be thankful that civilized Europeans had brought them to a new continent that offered salvation for their childlike souls. Left in the jungles, they would be damned to the eternal fires of hell. Even when drifting down the Mississippi to be sold for chopping cotton or cutting sugar cane they were on the road to heaven. Yes, the darkies should be grateful.

"What we gonna do if you give up the salt, Mr. Crenshaw?" Elias repeated, recognizing this was one of those times Mr. Crenshaw would float off into thought. Elias grew fearful when Mr. Crenshaw started talking about selling his salt works because Elias knew that being a leased slave from Kentucky, he would be up for auction alongside the iron boiling pots, and mules. Mr. Crenshaw could be harsh, a bad mood meaning the whip for not keeping the fires burning, but Elias would rather chance a lashing from Mr. Crenshaw than tempt the wrath of a cotton field overseer in Mississippi.

~~~

"Quiet now, boy," Elias whispered to Chief, the chestnut quarter horse with two white diamonds decorating his nose Mr. Crenshaw had allowed Elias to ride and groom. Chief nodded, taking the bit and bridle with a quick snort. Elias tossed the blanket and saddle over Chief's straight back and began to adjust the belts and buckles. "We is goin' for a fine ride, Boy. A fine long ride."

Elias led Chief towards the barn door. He unlatched it and pushed it open slowly enough to keep the rusted hinges from creaking. The sun had set hours before, but the swath the Milky Way splashed across the sky was enough before the moon rose to show the smoke curling up from the fire he had left burning in his cabin's river stone hearth at the bottom of the rise. Zeke Stubbs was most likely patrolling Hickory Hill's rolling acres with the doggedness of a bounty hunter, with the urgency of a battlefield sentry, catching sleep as catch could, always on the lookout for runaways, Hickory Hill's or fugitives from across the river who believed they had reached the emancipation of a Free State. Zeke had hunted them as much to keep the darkies in their place as for the money. Zeke's desires were few—an occasional bottle of rye and a pouch of tobacco to roll. Women were not worth the trouble. Doing the Lord's work, reminding niggers of their place in this Christian world, that was what Zeke once told Elias he had been put on God's green earth to do. Zeke loved his work with a passion of a missionary preaching to Hottentots, with the glee of a Mountain Man finding a wolf in his bear trap, attempting to chew off its foot.

Elias walked Chief out of the barn, shutting the doors with the gentleness of his mother's hands applying a cool cloth to his fevered brow. He mounted and scanned the sky.

~~~

Elias sat on his mother's lap as she gently rocked on their cabin porch. She pointed to one flickering light in the blackness, "That be the North Star, Elias. Someday you follow that star. Someday you be free."

"Free?" Elias asked. He had heard the word whispered like a secret among the men who lived in the cabins that lined the Kentucky farm's hemp field. But he had never heard his mother say the word before, or any of the other women or girls. It must be a man's business, he thought. Maybe he was too young to ask.

"You gets to it by followin' that star," his mother said in a soft voice.

"They all look alike," Elias said. "How do I know what star to follow?"

"See that drinkin' gourd over there?"

"No."

"There," she said, turning his head with her hands. "Right there."

"I see it," Elias said. "It be upside down. All the water spilled out."

"Hush," his mother said, quieting Elias' excitement. "See how the handle points to the North Star?"

"I see it," Elias said with the delight of discovery.

"Hush now, Elias. This be our secret. That star never moves. It always be there, waitin' for you to follow. When you do, Elias, you be free."

~~~

Elias nudged Chief gently with his boots. His horse was showing signs of the weariness Elias had been fighting for hours. His desire was to surrender to the fatigue that was overtaking him like a feverish delirium. When he allowed himself to shut his eyes and nearly fall from the saddle in sleep, Chief had stamped and snorted until Elias jerked erect. Sleepiness was startled from him by the sudden fear of being lost until he remembered he was following the North Star, pointed to by the bent handle of the drinking gourd.

"Keep goin', Chief," Elias said, adding a soft prod with his knees. "We can rest when the sun come up."

The night remained clear and the moon, waxing to harvest, rose brilliant over a low hill. Elias urged Chief away from the old buffalo trail he had been following all night. The swelling moon was driving him towards the cover of thick woods along the Saline River. Even if he had slipped Zeke, there would be other Night Riders, especially now that the rain had passed. All the white folks Elias knew complained about the weather, pining for sun during seasons of rain or praying for rain when the sun came out to make them sweat. Now that the rain had stopped and the Night Riders could be coming like cattle to sweetgrass. Elias steered Chief into the dense stands of elm and ash lining the riverbank. Chief protested at the underbrush, tugging back towards the trail. Elias leaned over to cluck and soothe, stroking Chief's neck to assure him this was the best way. But the way to where, Elias did not know. He had never been this far north and he was not sure how far north he needed to go to be free. That was one thing his mother never told him.

Elias sat up straight. He pulled back the reins, keeping Chief steady and still. He could hear horses on the buffalo trail ahead and two men talking. He caught the glint of moonlight reflecting from their oiled dusters. Night Riders. He could see them through the trees, but they were not looking down at the soft trail to see the tracks that would have led them into the woods. They were not searching the moonlit land or listening for any telltale signs of the horse that Night Riders sent by Mr. Crenshaw would have known Elias was riding. They were arguing with a mounting anger about a woman named Lou.

"You are one son of a bitch, Ethan. If I see you cozyin' up to Lou again..."

"You'll do what, Amos?" Ethan asked. "You ain't got the gumption to step on a roach..."

Amos pulled back his duster, exposing a long-barreled Colt. Ethan drew the rifle from his saddle and struck Ethan under the chin with its butt before Amos could draw his revolver, knocking him from his horse. Amos fell hard to the muddy trail. Ethan slid his rifle back into its saddle holster and dismounted, pulling his own Colt and pointing it at Amos' belly.

Elias released the tension on Chief's reins, giving them a gentle flick, prompting him farther into the woods and away from the trail where Amos and Ethan were using the Lord's name in vain. The shouting stopped. There was a short silence, then the telltale crack of a pistol shot. Elias was tempted to turn back towards the trail now for Chief's sake, sure that no Night Riders would be tracking him tonight. But he was still not taking any gambles. He could see the North Star glimmer through the treetops and he could hear his mother's voice in the wind that rustled the autumn leaves into falling. You be free, Elias. You be free.

Four

     Michael Kelly Lawler came to Illinois from Ireland with his father, John Lawler of Queens County and his mother, Elizabeth Kelly of County Kildare, when he was not yet two years of age. He had been born in Monasterevin Town on the River Barrow, bounded by bogland and glacier-melt gravel plains of the Heath, the short grass country of the horse breeder, Kildare's Curragh, home to the Irish Derby and where the British Army set up camp to train for Empire wars, not leaving until the Republic of Ireland won its freedom from the Crown.

     In March, 1816, long before potatoes caught the blight and the Irish starved in the Great Famine while British ships under military guard continued sailing to England with holds of wheat, oats, barley, peas, beans, onions, rabbits, salmon, oysters, lard, honey and butter, the Lawler family, John and Elizabeth and toddler Michael landed in New York. After a brief stay they left for Maryland, Frederick Town, had a girl child, Mary Elizabeth, then immigrated to settle in Illinois, Gallatin County, in November of 1819, where the family was completed with the births of Margaret and Thomas Richard. John Lawler was now a naturalized citizen of the United States of America. He had given Ireland back to the

Irish, all memories washed away by three thousand miles of icy Atlantic Ocean, left behind and buried along the wagon trails on the eight hundred mile pilgrimage into a new world freed from King and the Empire's religion. He bought a farm in 1838 in the Ponds Settlement, the first Catholics in a Protestant territory, helping build a log church and bringing in the first priest to bless and bury generations of Lawlers to come.

~~~

"Father," Elizabeth Hart Crenshaw Lawler acknowledged, opening the front door of the one and a half-story double log house she and Michael Kelly Lawler had named Tara Hall. "Scrape your boots. Ruth just beat the rugs and swept the floors."

"Daughters should not command their Papas," John Hart Crenshaw said, scraping layers of mud from his riding boots on the blade of the scrubber, then finished on the bristle porch mat. He turned to show Elizabeth the soles of his boots, one at a time. "To your approval?"

"Come in, Father," Elizabeth said, opening the door wider.

John felt the warmth of a stoked fire and the homey smell of seasoned meat and bread baking. He looked to see if the bloody crucifix was still hanging over the doorway to Michael's library, entwined with dried palm fronds. It was.

"You used to call me Papa. When you call me Father I feel like one of your pompous priests..."

"Grandfather," a young girl said, running into the room, her long blonde curls bouncing like springs. She wrapped her arms around John's waist.

"Margaret," John said stiffening. 'You are a young lady. Act as such."

"Margaret is eight," Elizabeth said.

"Well old enough to be a lady," John insisted, reaching behind his waist to pry Margaret's fingers loose.

"Grandfather, you are hurting me," Margaret said, running to Elizabeth who hugged her sobbing daughter.

"Ladies do not cry," John said, as if reading from a book of etiquette.

"Margaret is just a little girl," Elizabeth said, blotting her tears with the hem of her white crinoline petticoat. "What is it you want of us, Father?"

"Have you heard from that Papist husband of yours recently."

"Captain Lawler is a faithful letter writer," Elizabeth said.

"He has not been replying to my correspondence."

"Why would you be corresponding with Captain Lawler without my knowledge?"

"My business," John said. "And none of yours."

"He is my husband."

"Your business is the children and the house. If you recall, when I gave you a hundred and eighty acres after your ill-advised elopement, you were living in a two-room house with a lean-to kitchen. The barn roof leaked less. The horses had better accommodations. Your husband's business ability has built your property into nine hundred acres. There are good reasons you do not need to know what requires me to communicate you're your husband."

"Michael keeps me informed of his business dealings," Elizabeth said.

"He is wrong for doing that," John said.

"We are partners."

"No," John insisted. "He is wrong to involve his wife in his business. And you are wrong to allow him to do so. The Papist has made you ill-mannered and insolent."

"His name is Captain Lawler."

"Is that why he volunteered to fight in Mexico? To be called Captain when he returns? If he does return."

"You can be a cruel man, Father. Margaret, go see if Ruth needs help in the kitchen," Elizabeth said, wiping

Margret's last tear. Margaret ran towards the kitchen, looking up at the crucifix as she passed.

"That grotesque display is disturbing," John said. "It is not appropriate for the children. The blood is so..."

"True?"

"Do not interrupt your father. A cross should be simple, a symbol of God's sacrifice. It should not be an object for idolatry. It should not be dripping with blood. This is something for superstitious peasants."

"The peasants Michael is fighting in Mexico?"

John ignored the question and moved on.

"Margaret will begin thinking she's a niggcr, as much time as she spends with the help," John said, leaving the subject of the crucifix for another day. And there would surely be other days.

"She loves Ruth. And I would appreciate it if you respected this household by keeping your foul language to yourself."

"Darkie? Coon? Maybe Smoked Irish?"

"Margaret is half Irish," Elizabeth reminded her father.

John raised one eyebrow.

"Why do you come here to torment me?" Elizabeth asked. "You have other children."

But they are not married to a Papist, John thought, a blustery, blarney-spewing Irishman, only twenty-three when he seduced John's seventeen year old daughter into eloping to bow before the pope, eloping and married by a heretic priest. Elizabeth had been such a good Methodist. Now she prayed to plaster painted saints and committed idolatry kneeling in devotion of marble statues of Mary and rattling beads. Now she asked a man to forgive her sins and believed the wafer she ate and the wine she drank were really Jesus' flesh and blood. Disgusting. And, to make matters worse, she swore to raise her children to be heretics. Try as he might, John could not control his contempt for his second oldest daughter for choosing the wrong religion. He had long ago resigned himself to the fact that Elizabeth, her husband and children would all burn in hell. But it didn't mean he had to approve. However, Michael Kelly Lawler was a successful hardware merchant, farmer, lawyer and business associate, when he wasn't off fighting Mexicans. John had made a side bet with a Romanish devil, and it had proven to be very lucrative.

"I love Michael," Elizabeth said.

"You are under his cunning spell," John said. "He uses that same Irish charm on judges for land deals, same as when he's talking farmers into marching with him to Mexico. I know how persuasive he can be. He can sell water to a drowning man, and in so doing has increased my fortune. Increased your family's fortune."

"For the love of money is the root of all evil," Elizabeth quoted 1 Timothy.

"Evil? Making an honest living is evil?"

"Money isn't evil," Elizabeth said. "Worshipping it is. Honest? That is blasphemy."

"Blasphemy? You do not have the right to use that word, Elizabeth. You are having another child with that Papist…"

"Captain Lawler," Elizabeth asserted, rubbing her swelling belly that held the proof of her love for Michael, and Michael's love for Elizabeth. Michael would be gone for the birth and baptism, but Elizabeth felt safe with Ruth who was as proficient at birthing babies as she was baking bread. With each child, Elizabeth's father had demanded that only Dr. Hastings should bring a Crenshaw into the world, as he had Elizabeth. But Elizabeth was of a different mind, full of beliefs that her father would like to have a judge declare illegal. Allowing a nigger to help birth a Crenshaw would be the first case on the docket.

~~~

Elizabeth went to her husband's desk in his library. Growing up, Michael had only been able to attend school in short sessions until he left in his middle teens to help on the family farm. But he could read, and he read voraciously. His father encouraged him to read when not in school. Michael's library was filled with books bound in maroon leather, backs broken from frequent readings. There were books of English poetry, volumes of Shakespeare, books on the birds and trees of Illinois, books on weather and plane geometry and Irish history. And one bookshelf dedicated to books of the law from which he drew his knowledge of individual rights and the ways of commerce.

Elizabeth rolled the top of the desk up. The pigeonholes were filled with neatly folded papers and ledgers. On the desktop was a flagon filled with steel-nib pens, a bottle of India-ink and a stack of letters, sent from Mexico, bearing the postal marks of stops along the way, addressed in Michael's precise hand. Elizabeth picked up the top envelope and pulled out the folded letter, the one that had arrived last week, the one she had only read three times. She was going to read it for the fourth.

Darling Elizabeth,
As before, I have no intention of detailing the deeds of the war in which I am now engaged. War is a man's duty, even as I am aware of your feelings about the fairer sex being endowed with the same rights as men. It may be that sometime in the future women will be given the vote, but they will never, thank God, carry arms or go to war or do the other work only men are preordained to do by temperament and constitution. Thomas Jefferson wrote that "all men are created equal", he did not designate the descendants of Eve. I do, however, believe that the laws of a just God include Negro men as endowed with the same rights as White men. Those testifying to the Christian faith

cannot deny that Jesus preached kindness, foremost to his enemies, to the leper and the lame, even if your father argues that Africans are so inferior they must be brought to God through enslavement because only White men know how to put them on the road to heaven. I am reminded how my own father came to this country with only my mother and me and built the good life of which my family and I benefit. He had grown weary of his treatment, of being considered an interloper living on his kin's land, suffering from the English belief that the Irish were descended from clans that were even inferior to the African slaves cutting sugarcane in Jamaica. But you and I share the same convictions concerning enslavement of any people, even if I fall short of matching your fervor for promoting political rights for women. I send my love to you, our precious children and those yet to be born. I have every confidence in Ruth as midwife and do not allow your father to talk you into permitting old Doctor Hasting to come near you. Doctor Hastings still bleeds your father for the grippe.

Your Loving & Faithful Husband,
Michael

Elizabeth folded the letter and slid it back into its envelope. She loved Michael but could be troubled by his recalcitrance. He fought for the Rights of Man as he saw them in foreign lands, or on his adopted soil, but could be totally blind to the fact that women deserve the same rights as men.

"Are you reading Papa's letters again," Margaret asked, skipping, unladylike, into the library.

"I am," Elizabeth said, rolling the desktop down. "I miss your Papa."

"I miss Papa too, Mama. When is he coming home?"

"When he is done with his work."

"What kind of work is he doing in Mexico? Is he selling plows to the Mexicans?"

"No. He is fighting for freedom," Elizabeth said, surprised that Margaret knew about Mexico, having never told her that her father had been commissioned as a Captain in the Illinois Volunteers, Company G, 3rd Regiment.

"Fighting for the Mexicans' freedom?" Margaret asked.

"For Americans' freedom."

"Why would he be fighting in Mexico for Americans' freedom?"

"I cannot say," Elizabeth said. "It is something men do. You can ask your Papa when he comes home."

"Will it be a long time, Mama? I miss Papa."

Elizabeth slowly shook her head, locking the fingers of her hands under her belly for support. She could feel the baby kick. "Papa will return when the American Army wins."

"What is the prize?" Margaret asked, imagining it would be a gift like the pony her Papa had given her for her last birthday. Elizabeth didn't answer. She stood looking at the gilt-framed paintings of Kildare thoroughbreds on the wall over Michael's desk. She replaced the letter and rolled the desk top down.

Five

"I ain't your mama," Beulah said. "It be time you stop wipin' your nose on my dress. It ain't never gonna dry if you keep wettin' it with your blubberin'. You want me to come down with the consumption?"

"I ain't coughin' on you," Betsy said, a quick anger staunching the sob from her voice.

"Not yet you ain't. But far as I can tell you'd just as soon catch the pox and die. I got no mind for dyin'. My mind is to find a home for my child without slave traders or overseers with whips."

"And where that be, Beulah?"

"It ain't down this river. It be back in the direction we come."

"Hickory Hill?"

"No, Betsy. Mr. Crenshaw just sell us again."

"I do want to see Mama, Beulah."

"You gotta be strong or you die, Betsy. I know you think that be the easy way but I say the Lord ain't ready for you yet. He got plans for the three of us."

"Plans?" Betsy asked, wiping her eyes. "You know what them plans be?"

"No," Beulah said. "Life 'bout figurin' 'em out. The preacher said the Lord helps them what helps themselves. I believe that. I ain't waitin' for Moses to part no sea and lead us outta captivity. We do it ourselves. Now you stop your weepin'. I gotta work on our plan."

Beulah hugged her knees and buried her face in the damp folds of her dress. Plans. That was all she had left. Except for her unborn child, and Betsy. Beulah would do anything for that child. She knew she should feel the same for Betsy, but Betsy was so…No, Beulah thought, Betsy is my sister. Even if Mama spoiled her into stayin' a child, I still do anythin' for her. Beulah sat up, putting both hands to her belly. Well, almost anythin', long as my child be safe.

"You remember Hezekiah?" Beulah asked, lifting her head but not looking at Betsy.

"He worked the salt back a few months? His backside be all covered with scars? His face shiny black like a coal pail?"

"That be him," Beulah said. "We talked from time to time, but not so nobody would see."

"He like you?" Betsy asked. Her crying had finally passed like a bilious fever, leaving her exhausted. She let out a wide yawn.

"We just talk," Beulah said. Being with child, she had no interest in a man's needs, but she was interested in what Hezekiah knew. "Mostly, I just listen. I didn't know then, but Hezekiah might set us free."

"You sick, Beulah? You talkin' crazy. He be just a field nigger."

"But smart. He listened and never forgot. Never forgot hearin' other slaves talkin' 'bout the Underground Railroad…"

"How do a railroad run underground?" Betsy asked, twisting her face in disbelief.

"Ain't no real railroad," Beulah said, grinning. It was the first question she asked when Hezekiah talked about it. "It be people livin' on farms and in towns and cities helpin' runaway slaves hide from the slave catchers and keep movin' on to freedom."

"White people help?"

"Some do. They be called abolitionists."

"Never heard that word. What that mean?"

"They want to free all the slaves. They say slavery be against God's will."

"White preachers say God wants slaves to obey their masters. Negro preachers say that, too."

Beulah didn't feel the need to answer Betsy. She knew what both white and Negro preachers preached that slaves should submit to their owners the way wives do to their husbands. It was in the Bible. It was God's Law. To break any of God's Laws would be a sin and could mean the everlasting fires of hell. But that was not what Hezekiah said. Hezekiah said what men like Mr. Crenshaw did was the sin, keeping Negroes in bondage like the Pharaohs of Egypt did to the Hebrews. Hezekiah said it was time for each slave to become his own Moses. Hezekiah told Beulah about the Underground Railroad and how he had been helped north from the cotton fields in Mississippi, through Tennessee, skirting the markets of Memphis and getting as far as Kentucky before he was caught one clear night at the river's edge, sniffed out by hounds as he attempted to cross the Ohio to Illinois. He was sold to a hemp plantation, then leased to Mr. Crenshaw's Hickory Hill salt works. Beulah remembered each detail. How he said he moved through the night concealed under moonless or cloudy skies, keepin' off roads and trails, listenin' for hounds or horses or loud talkin' Night Riders who did nothin' to disguise their intent out of scorn for what they considered easy and ignorant prey. Niggers were stupid, the Night Riders agreed. And if they tried to swim the river they'd sink and drown, 'cause everyone knowed that niggers don't float, so there'd be no chance of losin' the stench that gives them away, even if their skin hid them in the dark.

"After what Mr. Crenshaw done to us," Beulah said, her cupped hands feeling the baby kick, "he don't deserve to be my master, no matter what no preachers say. He promised Mama he'd keep us together, never sell us, no matter how much he needs money."

"He be the master, Beulah. We his...property. He sell us anytime he want," Betsy said. Her red eyes began welling.

"Don't you do it."

"Don't I do what?"

"Don't you start your blubberin' again. Maybe you don't mind bein' nothin' more than another mule, but I does."

"What you got, Beulah."

"Somethin' Hezekiah give me."

Betsy put her hand over her mouth.

Beulah had leaned back against the rough boards of the flatboat cabin, pulling something from under the skirts of her dress. Sun streaming in through a crack in the canvas door glinted off the blade of a knife she held on the palm of her hand like an offering.

Betsy's hand slid from her mouth. Her eyes grew large. She looked at Beulah then towards the door. Shadows moved across the canvas.

"Shush," Beulah warned, sensing Betsy's fright and realizing her reaction could be loud. Betsy understood.

"Where you got that?" Betsy whispered.

"Hezekiah," Beulah said. "It be a reapin' knife for cuttin' hemp. That what he do in Kentucky before he came to Hickory Hill. He snuck two with him..."

"And he give you a knife? You give him anythin'?"

"Some of Mama's apple pie," knowing what Betsy was asking. "Just pie."

Beulah could smell the smoke from Jim's corncob pipe. It swirled through the doorway as he pulled back the canvass. She slid the knife between her baby-swollen breasts.

"What're you niggers talkin' 'bout?" Jim snapped.

Beulah stared at him until he looked away to Betsy.

"How your head be?" Beulah asked.

"You done a good job," Jim said, reaching up to feel the tightly-wrapped bandage that covered the gash in his forehead, then caught himself. "You niggers talk too much. Well, I guess you can start sayin' your goodbyes. We're landin' soon and we know buyers who'll snatch each of you up quick. Didn't think you'd stay together, now did you?"

Jim laughed as Betsy began to cry.

Beulah tried to stand. Jim lumbered over and shoved her back down. Her head hit the wall of the cabin. She sat stunned. She reached for the knife.

"You niggers keep it down and stay put or the shackles go on," Jim said. "Now say your goodbyes, or whatever mumbo-jumbo you darkies do."

Jim turned towards the canvas door and stopped, striking a match with his thumbnail, attempting to relight his pipe. Still dazed, Beulah struggled to her feet, grasping the reaping knife.

"Beulah!" Betsy whispered, grabbing Beulah's wrist. "You put that knife away! You never be free if you kill a white man. You be dead. Both you and your baby and most likely me, too!"

Beulah was trembling with anger. She tore her arm free from Betsy's grasp with a strength she didn't know she had. Jim's back was still towards her as he dropped the wooden match that burned his fingers. He reached in his shirt pocket for another, struck it and produced billows of choking smoke. Beulah knew just where to drive the knife that would make death silent and certain. Hezekiah had taught her.

"Beulah!" Betsy repeated, taking Beulah by the arm.

"I told you niggers to shut up," Jim said, blowing out the match, stooping to open the canvas door, but not looking back. "Now, shut up!"

"They goin' to split us up, Betsy," Beulah said, continuing to hold the knife as if poised to strike.

"You think of somethin'," Betsy said. "Just put the knife away. Tell me more about what Hezekiah tell you. He sound smart. Just hide the knife, Beulah."

"You right, Betsy. Anger just come over me like a cloud when Jim say they not sellin' us together. I gots to make a plan before that happens. Jim thinks we just dumb niggers. We got to surprise him and Frank. Truth told, they be the dumb ones. I been watchin' them. That somethin' Hezekiah say to do. Watch the white folk. See how they go 'bout doin' things. Figure 'em out. That what Hezekiah say."

"Then what do we do, Beulah? How we both get free?"

"Don't know yet. But I ain't goin' to lose you. Already lost Mama. But I ain't gonna lose you."

Six

Elias was hungry. His stomach was talking and telling him he hadn't eaten for days. There was plenty of water to scoop from feeder streams running into the Little Wabash River, and handfuls of berries he hoped would not make him sick, but he wasn't carrying a gun or even a knife for game and he had seen no farms with gardens or orchards. He was hungry.

Elias had followed the river north by day, seeking the concealment of woodland without trails, not chancing movement after dark, fretful that a Night Rider running low on whiskey money might be on the prowl, especially when the sky was cloudless and the rain remained on the far plains he had heard talk about when he was still in Kentucky.

Elias had overheard the bosses talk of beasts called buffalo and how the Indians used their hides to build houses called teepees, for robes and blankets, their bones for tools and dried dung for fires to cook their meat. Elias also overheard stories of Indians rounded up like cattle, driven west on long trails muddied by tears, across big rivers and gathered together on barren places called reservations that Elias imagined to be like slave pens. But he also heard about Indians who still rode free, roaming the unsettled plains, stalking the buffalo, staying always a camp ahead of the cavalry, waging defiance towards wagon train and homesteader, against prospector, mountain men and their disease.

Chief shook his reins and gave a loud snort. Better than a hound, Elias thought, when it came to sensing danger. Chief came to a halt.

"What is it?" Elias whispered, knowing something had spooked his horse. Elias heard a pistol cock.

"Where're you goin'?" a voice behind Elias asked. Elias turned to see the long barrel of a Colt pointed at him. The hand that held it was black as the face half hidden behind the trunk of a tree.

"Put the pistol down and I might tell you," Elias said with all the bravado he could muster.

The man behind the tree slowly uncocked the Colt, but did not holster it. He crooked his arm across his chest, the gun at ready. "Where're you goin'," he asked again.

"If I knew do you think I'd be tellin' you?" Elias said. He turned Chief towards the man.

"Runaway slave?" the man asked. "Horse thief?"

Elias did not answer. He knew that being guilty of one could mean being captured and sold to worse places than Hickory Hill. The other meant a rope.

"Who're you?" Elias asked. Maybe he could distract the man long enough to make a break.

"Don't matter none who I be," the man said, "other than I be the man holdin' the gun and askin' the questions and you be the man who answers 'em. You runnin' away from Crenshaw, ain't you? Took one of his horses, looks like. He ain't goin' to be too happy, now will he?"

"You work for Mr. Crenshaw?" Elias asked.

"Never called him Mister," the man said, pulling his shirt up and turning to expose a back crisscrossed with healed welts while keeping one eye on Elias. "Called him other names, that's for sure. But never Mister."

"Must've done somethin' to deserve that," Elias said, being mad enough at another Negro pointing a gun at him that he had blurted out in anger what might get him shot, and something he knew to be seldom true.

"You was no better'n a house nigger," the man said. "You might as well been polishin' Crenshaw's boots and brushin' his big beaver hat the way you rode around on his horse, all high and mighty like."

Elias did not want to get into an argument over who had been the most mistreated. He knew he was one of Mr. Crenshaw's favorites. He had trusted Elias with the use of Chief. He had told Elias that if he had been white he would have hired him as an overseer or foreman. Elias felt a pang of guilt when the man showed him his scars. Elias was likeable. Other slaves had accused him of being a bootlicker, but he had never even blacked Mr. Crenshaw's boots. It wasn't his fault if people liked him. But, for men like the one who had just pointed a pistol at him, Elias was a traitor, kneeling to the Massa to avoid the lash, for better food, for a better cabin, for the use of a horse.

"I worked the salt," Elias said.

"I know you did, Elias," the man said, stepping out from behind the tree, tucking the Colt in the rope belt that held up very tattered pants.

"Caleb? Damn! I thought you was dead!"

"Near be," Caleb said, pulling the Colt from his belt and stroking the barrel like a purring cat. "Willy thought he'd caught me runnin' off, but I whupped him upside the head with fire log out by the brine pot pile and swiped his pistol. The runt didn't look like such a big man when he was sprawled out on the ground."

"How long you been gone?" Elias asked, dismounting Chief.

"Lost track of time. But not long after Josiah chopped off Crenshaw's leg. Crenshaw be really mad 'cause you run off with his best horse...'"

"Chopped off Mr. Crenshaw's leg...?" Elias began.

"Tell you about it later. Hungry? Got some food. Not much."

Caleb opened a stained bandana and offered the contents to Elias.

"You eat this?" Elias asked. "What is it?"

"What I could scrounge," Caleb said, acting hurt.

Elias examined the items more carefully. There were limp carrots with very wilted tops, roots that might have been turnips, beets that seemed bled of all color and a half-eaten cob of corn. But the single apple was firm, stippled yellow and red, cool to the touch. Elias' stomach rumbled in anticipation.

"Got shot at pickin' that apple," Caleb said, seeing Elias' eyes fixing on it. "Two barrels of buckshot. But all the old farmer killed was a branch of apples over my head. Got sprayed with the sauce. I shot back. He skedaddled before he could reload. I took his mule for my trouble. He never come back. Think he couldn't believe his eyes. A nigger with a big old Colt. Sure that he thought niggers is too dumb to figure how to shoot a pistol. Then I took his mule, mangy as it is. Better than walkin'. Here. This be my last apple. You take it."

Elias had not noticed it when he was concentrating on Caleb's Colt pistol, but a mule was tied to the tree Caleb had used for concealment. It was just as mangy as Caleb said. Elias accepted the apple and bit into it with the greatest pleasure he could remember since riding away from Hickory Hill.

"Where're you headed?" Elias asked between bites.

"West." Caleb said.

"Thought runaways was supposed to head north," Elias said. "That's what Mama always told me. Go north."

"We is north," Caleb said, picking a carrot from the rag, then carefully folding the neckerchief like the remaining vegetables were jewels in a velvet cloth. "We is in the Free State of Illinois."

"Then what the Night Riders be 'bout?"

"They be 'bout makin' money for the likes of Mr. John Hart Crenshaw. They don't call us slaves. We is leased."

"Slave or leased, mean the same thing to me. Mr. Crenshaw talkin' 'bout closin' down the salt works. That why I left. For a fact he'd sell me down the river to the cotton fields for the money. That why I'm doin' like Mama said, followin' the North Star."

"You be one dumb Negro," Caleb said, biting into the soggy carrot. "Nothin' for you up north but snow and freezin' to death come winter, and that be soon."

"So what you have in mind?"

"West," Caleb said. "We is headed west."

Seven

Patsy was weary. Not the tired that sleep would cure, but the tired that starts in the heart, spreads to the head and imbeds deep into the bones.

"Lord..." Patsy began before letting the prayer drift into the silence of the night. The Lord knew her troubles. The preacher had said He wouldn't give her a burden she could not carry. But her back was aching something terrible and the weight of her two lost girls seemed more than she could bear.

Patsy had slipped away again from her empty cabin after serving supper to the Crenshaws. She knew there was no hope of finding Beulah or Betsy on her own, but Miss Elizabeth might help. Miss Elizabeth had been her favorite of all the Crenshaws' children. She knew it wasn't charitable to like one child more than the rest, but Elizabeth had a spirit that made that impossible.

"What you doin' here after dark?" Ruth asked, opening Tara Hall's front door. "Anyways, you supposed to go round back. Captain Lawler don't like servants tracking mud across the rug Mr. Crenshaw give his daughter for a weddin' present. They have that rug for almost ten years now..."

"Who is it, Ruth?" Elizabeth interrupted. Ruth was known to carry on indefinitely once riled. She could scold with the venom of a spinster schoolmarm.

"It be Patsy. I told her she need to go round back..."

"That's fine, Ruth. I'll make sure she cleans her shoes well before she enters," Elizabeth said, smiling at Patsy who began scrubbing her shoes on the horse-hair mat.

"Still ain't right for her to be knockin' on the front door," Ruth protested. There was nothing that upset Ruth more than help who thought they were better. God put us where we is, Ruth would tell new help, and that's that.

"Thank you, Ruth. I'm sure you have something to do."

"Well, I ain't makin' tea for her, if that be what you thinkin'," Ruth said on her way towards the kitchen.

"Come in, Patsy. Do not pay mind to Ruth. She believes this is her house and we only live in it," Elizabeth said. "Sit by the fire. Any news about Beulah and Betsy?"

"That be why I's here, Miss Elizabeth." Even after she had married Michael Kelly Lawler, Patsy continued to call her Miss Elizabeth. She was Miss Elizabeth when she was born and always would be. "There be no more I can do. Mr. and Mrs. Crenshaw say it be in God's hands. But I say it be in the Night Rider's hands. And in the hands of the boatmen that floats them to the slave markets."

"You know for a fact that the girls were abducted and transported...south?"

"Don't know much about facts, Miss Elizabeth. Don't even know what my real name be. But I feel it in my bones they have been sold down the river..."

"But who would sell your girls down the river, as you say?"

"I's hopin' you might help me find out," Patsy said. What Patsy didn't say was that she was sure Elizabeth's father had her girls kidnapped. He might tell Patsy her dumplings and apple pies were the best, as Mrs. Crenshaw would tell Patsy her children were like family, but Mr. Crenshaw's true mind towards Patsy and her girls, or any Negro on Hickory Hill, was that they were property no different than a brine pot.

"I only wish I could, Patsy. You know how I feel about you and your girls. You are like family."

Patsy stared at the flames in the fireplace that danced and changed colors as they devoured the sawed logs cut precisely to fit the iron grate. The pop of an exploding tree knot brought her back to the living room, to the house of Mr. Crenshaw's eldest daughter, the house built by Elizabeth's husband, Michael Kelly Lawler, Captain of a Company of Riflemen at war with the Mexicans somewhere south of the Mississippi cotton fields where she feared her children were bound. Family, she thought, mulling the word Miss Elizabeth had spoken over and over. Family, Patsy thought. If Miss Elizabeth knew the truth about Beulah and Betsy would admit to it.

"Patsy?" Elizabeth said.

"Sorry, Miss Elizabeth. I's just thinkin' 'bout my children."

"I am so sorry, Patsy. Maybe Mr. Stubbs could assist…"

"Mr. Stubbs be a Night Rider hisself," Patsy interrupted, something she never did with the white folks, afraid she may have said too much. But his was about her kidnapped daughters.

"I am not familiar with that term, Night Rider," Elizabeth replied. A slight annoyance entered her eyes. A wrinkle appeared on her alabaster brow, then smoothed. She smiled at Patsy. "But I have heard there are dangers being out after dark. There are unscrupulous men."

"Yes, Miss Elizabeth. There be bad men everywhere. Have you heard from Captain Lawler?"

"I just received a letter…" Elizabeth began, but caught herself from asking if Patsy would like to read it.

"How the Captain be?" Patsy blurted, sensing what Miss Elizabeth almost asked. She would have declined, not because she couldn't read, since she had learned from other slaves when she was cutting cane and picking cotton, but because slaves were beaten when caught with a McGuffey Reader or even folded pages of smuggled Northern newspapers with articles about abolitionists and free black men who wore brocade waistcoats and beaver hats and conducted business with whites. She had learned that letters had sounds and the sounds had meaning and from the meaning grew ideas that were new and gleaming as the gates of heaven, learned in slave cabins in the light of guttering candles, learned early in the morning before the sun or overseers rose from hard nights of living on steady diets of rye whiskey and town tarts.

"Captain Lawler is in good spirits. He writes many letters keeping me apprised of his progress towards Mexico, the hardships and how loyal his men are to him and the cause."

"I know it not be my place, Miss Elizabeth, but why do men go so far away to fight?"

"Captain Lawler says for him it is because he is Irish, Patsy. And that we are Catholic in a Protestant land."

"Our preacher say Catholics kneel down to statues… Sorry, Miss Elizabeth."

"Captain Lawler has convictions," Elizabeth continued.

"Convictions?"

"He stands up for what he believes. He is a strong-willed man and a fighter."

"So he be in Mexico to fight for his…"

"For his convictions," Elizabeth said. "For his beliefs. And maybe he wants to show Mr. Crenshaw he is as good an American as any English Methodist."

White people do have their peculiar troubles, Patsy thought, and some they seem to make up just to give themselves something to do, like going all the way to Mexico to fight for…convictions.

"My girls…" Patsy began.

"Yes, your girls," Elizabeth said, returning from visions of the Rio Grande that Michael had described in his letters and with such detail she could feel the heat and see the river run slow and wide on its way to the Gulf of Mexico. "I wish I could help, Patsy."

"Ain't your fault, Miss Elizabeth. I knows how it is. I's just hopin'."

"Don't give up hope, Patsy. I'll talk to Mr. Stubbs when he gets back from doing my father's business. He seems to know much about…" Elizabeth stopped, unsure of what to say next.

I ain't ever had much hope to lose, Patsy thought. Not now. Not never. Patsy scolded herself for thinking Miss Elizabeth could help. She might have raised her like her own, but Miss Elizabeth was still a Crenshaw when cornered and Patsy heard in her voice that she felt cornered as a coon up an ash tree surrounded by baying hounds.

"I go see if Mr. Stubbs be back from doin' Mr. Crenshaw's business, in the mornin'," Patsy said. "Don't want nobody to know I's out prowlin' in the dark."

"You are safe in this house," Elizabeth said, glad that Patsy had moved on from talk about Beulah and Betsy, her father and Night Riders. There was no question her father had something to do with the girls' disappearance, and no question that Stubbs was the executioner of her father's will. Elizabeth loved her father as God instructed, but felt locked in his prison cell when he offered Michael land for a house after their marriage and snared him in his business dealings, using Michael's knowledge of the law and his Irish way with words. Elizabeth was well aware of the methods her father employed to keep her within his hold, same as with her mother, who accepted his domination as biblical, to honor and obey, obey being the most important.

"Will Captain Lawler be home 'fore the child be born?" Patsy asked, taking what good there was to be taken from knowing that life abides even as the welfare and whereabouts of the children that had sprung from her were unknown as her destination after death, although the preacher had promised heaven for good servants. But who would she share paradise with? Night Riders and Mr. Crenshaw? If Jesus and his Father were white men, would anything change? And why did she have to fear God? The preacher always said she asked too many questions. It was the Devil putting doubts in her head, he would admonish.

"No, Patsy," Elizabeth said, her eyes confirming her words that her husband was committed to his Company and would be gone until victory was complete. "But then, men only have one thing to do with bringing life into this world."

"That be God's truth," Patsy said, not finishing the rest of her thought out loud, that although men may be mostly ignorant about bringin' life into the world after the act, they sure is good at usherin' it out. "I best be gettin' back to my cabin, Miss Elizabeth. I do thank you for listen' to my woes."

"Patsy..." Elizabeth began with the intention of asking Patsy if she wanted to spend the night, but decided it was not her place. "Be careful.'

"I always is, Miss Elizabeth. "But that not always be enough, is it?"

"If my father asks, you were never here," Elizabeth said, walking Patsy to the front door. She opened it. A gust of wind moved the spaniel curls that dangled just in front of her ears as decoration to her tight bun and lace cap. She kept the curls for Michael who said they made her look like a school girl. "You be careful, Patsy"

Patsy stepped out into the night air, turned to say something to Miss Elizabeth, changed her mind and walked away. There was nothing Miss Elizabeth or no white woman could do for her. She heard the door shut and did not turn around. Patsy was on her own.

Eight

Sina could not sleep. It did not help that John was snoring next to her with the raspy rhythm of a bucksaw being drawn through a felled tree. She was envious. John never had trouble sleeping. On the nights he was not away on business, he would be asleep before she blew out the bedside candle. On other evenings, when he would meet with associates, smoking foul-smelling cigars and drinking brandy in his library, Sina could hear their competing voices from her bedroom growing louder and louder as if volume determined the winner of a debate. She would try to sleep but outbursts of liquored laughter, argument and the occasional fist pounded on John's carved oak desk with ivory inlays would jerk her awake until he came to bed, exhausted, reeking of tobacco, beginning to bucksaw logs while his pillow was still cool. A clear conscience, he would tell her. He had no regrets to bedevil his mind. He had principles and stuck to them like burrs to wool stockings. And when his time came to meet his Maker, he would be able to justify every deed with no fear of reckoning. His conscience was clear.

Sina pulled back the patchwork quilt Patsy had sewn from remnants of her children's clothes, stuffed with goose feathers and warm against the night chill that kept her snug under its weight. Tonight she was restless. Patsy's missing girls played in her mind like the edge of a nightmare at waking. Sina didn't need use of the commode concealed in a walnut cabinet John had shipped by river barge from Cincinnati, hidden behind an oriental screen painted with peacocks, a design ensured to trigger John's crude sense of humor. And when she was forced to, especially when she was with child, she was grateful to her husband that her only choice was not the outhouse that, as her grandmother had told her, was always too far away in the winter and too close in the summer. Sina had heard there was a hotel in Boston that had indoor plumbing, but was sure it would take years for such a luxury to make it across the Mississippi.

Tonight she got out of bed to go to the window. It was clear, a fine autumn night without rain or wind. Through the open window she caught the scent of wood fire drifting up from the servant's cabins. By now the fires would be burnt down to ember, leaving enough heat to last until morning when they would be rekindled for breakfast. She could see the cabins on the rise that began its slope to the river, outlined by the rising moon. She counted one, two, three from the left. That was Patsy's cabin. It worried Sina about Beulah and Betsy. She could only guess what lengths she would have gone to if any of her children had vanished. She tried to imagine the life of a woman like Patsy, but was forced to confess to herself that she considered the Negroes at Hickory Hill more as children or, she felt ashamed for thinking, like pets that gladly did her bidding for food and a few kind words. It was only being Christian to protect them from the harsh cruelties of a world they could never understand while leading them to Jesus and heaven. In this she agreed with her husband. John had pointed out that God must approve since even the President of the United States, James K. Polk, had brought his slaves with him to the White House. Sina did not agree with John that they often needed beatings like disobedient dogs. Kindness was Sina's way. You catch more flies with honey, she would tell John. I'm not looking to catch flies, John would tell Sina and after all, darkies were children that would only be spoiled if the rod were spared. Sina knew when it was best to keep her own council, and God's. She never argued with John, the way Elizabeth did. But Elizabeth was a modern woman. She read newspapers her husband bought and discussed things with him Sina believed only men should trouble themselves with. Elizabeth had children to raise and nurture and one on the way. Where her daughter got the idea that woman should vote, Sina did not know. And Elizabeth was teaching her girls dangerous ideas that would just leave them disappointed and maybe unmarried. What men would want a bride who refused to submit to her husband's commands? God ordained the man head of the household as God also directed slaves to be good servants.

Sina was turning from the window with thoughts of her feather bed when movement near Patsy's cabin caught her eye. A form came up over the rise, outlined by stars that shimmered like gold flakes in a prospector's pan. The form vanished behind the cabin. It was Patsy, Sina was certain, returning from a futile search for her children. It was getting cold. Elizabeth shut the window and drew the heavy velvet curtains. John let out a snort, turned on his side and began breathing steadily but without the rattle. Elizabeth drew back the covers and slipped in, careful not to disturb John. There was much to do in the morning and soon Cyrus would be awake, stacking kindling on the still warm fireplace ash. She put Patsy and her girls out of her mind. If something needed to be done, John would do it. He was head of the household. After that decision, sleep came easy.

~~~

Patsy struggled up the three wooden steps to her cabin's porch, leaning on the rail that bowed even under her slight weight. A jagged sliver stabbed her hand, piercing the palm deep enough to leave a stigmata of blood when she removed the long splinter. She felt no pain. Even more than before, her mind was not on herself, not on her discomforts or deprivations or disappointments.

Patsy had cared for her mother after she collapsed in a Louisiana sugarcane field, felled by a horridly humid afternoon, the left side of her face frozen in a drooping frown, her arm limp as the empty sleeve of a boiled dress shirt. Patsy would feed her mother, dab the drooled porridge from her face, and coax half a smile with her silly antics as she told about the young men who pursued her like a pack of heated hounds. Still her mother faded like the brilliant shades of sunset consumed by smothering clouds. Patsy refused to feel the pain as her mother was lowered into the earth wearing her Sunday dress and wrapped in a patchwork quilt she had made from her master's scraps, buried behind the slave cabins, near the creek shaded by a grove of cypress in an overgrown graveyard marked by stick crosses hammered together with handmade blacksmith nails. Her mother was another loss added to a list that grew like Spanish moss drooping from Southern oaks.

Patsy's master had cared little about the day to day business of cultivating sugarcane on his family plantation after he inherited it from his father, except that the slaves who worked it could be sold when he was running low on poker stakes. Patsy was sold to a Mississippi cotton plantation owner after her mother died to cover a bluff on a pair of deuces her master lost to his inability to hold either a poker face or his bourbon.

Patsy was marched along the roads from Louisiana to Mississippi, roped with other slaves into coffles, trailing behind a white man on a black horse, more than one-thousand steps to a mile, fifteen miles to a day, gawked at by slaves cutting stands of cane that changed to cotton fields as they trudged north, moisture from the Gulf drying into a different Southern heat as they approached their cotton plantation destination.

Patsy was numb, all feeling drained from her body like blood from a gutted rabbit. She saw her feet moving with a slow drag, shuffling up dust that hung in the heat like a dirty mist, but she did not recognize them as her feet, as she did not know the hands she held up to block the brilliant sun, hands that looked old as her mother's when Patsy folded them over her breast and wrapped her in her patchwork quilt. But she did know the sting of the riding crop applied to her legs by the coffle overseer who had doubled back.

"Get them feet movin', nigger," he yelled. "You holdin' up the whole lot. We got miles before you can sit that lazy ass down."

He raised the riding crop again and slashed it across her emaciated buttocks to punctuate his point. Patsy winced, feeling a sharper sting, then stuffed the hurt into a gunnysack of previous pains and buried it in a hole she had already dug. She increased her stride enough to make the white man on the black horse ride back to the front of the coffle, confident he had secured a victory.

Patsy's time at the cotton plantation was not long. She escaped in the commotion the evening her master died, kicked in the head as he showed off his prize racing thoroughbred to supper guests, stumbling, grabbing the Arabian's tail to gain balance, not wanting to spill his glass of brandy. Patsy made her way north alone, knowing nothing of the Underground Railway, although often helped by those who ran it. Patsy's end of the line had come near Equality, in the Free State of Illinois, captured by Night Riders and sold to John Hart Crenshaw to serve his desires at Hickory Hill. But she gave praise to the Lord for the fortune of not being sent back down river to sugarcane or cotton as she now feared might be the fate of Betsy, Beulah and her unborn grandchild.

Nine

Elias and Caleb had slipped the woodland shelter that shadowed the Little Wabash and struck out across the open flatness of Illinois, drifting northwest from one green island fed by streams and rivers to the next, seeking the concealment of tree, scrub and brush when daylight made them conspicuous as raisins in a rice pudding. Caleb was determined to head west and take Elias with him, hiding by day, travelling in the cover of darkness, knowing Night Riders prowled like feral cats in search of field mice, running away from salt and cotton and cane and anything that white men wanted hauled or boiled, chopped or cut, weeded or picked in the blistering fever of a Southern sun or the bitter wind of an Illinois winter.

Caleb told Elias he had heard that out west a man of color was free to make a life from his own sweat. He would not be a cursed beast of burden, owned like the mule he was riding. Caleb said he had argued with the Preachers after plantation meetings that Noah getting drunk and Ham seeing him naked was no reason for all dark skinned men to be forever in bondage. Noah's son just covered him up. Why would God be punishing Caleb for another man's act of kindness? The will of God is not to be questioned, the

Preachers would answer, adding that it was the Devil who sewed doubt. To which Caleb replied, "I doubt that."

"Bet the preachers just 'bout give up on your soul," Elias said to Caleb as they rode through the falling darkness, keeping track of the point the sun had set so their backs would face it as it rose the next morning.

"Preachers said I was hell-bent on damnation and I said even the Devil couldn't think of much worse punishment than haulin' brine and boilin' it down to salt."

"Guess you ain't too religious," Elias said.

"Heard of lot of coloreds prayin' for freedom but seems to me the only freedom we get is what we takes for ourselves," Caleb said.

"Amen," Elias agreed.

Elias and Caleb had been riding for days, always hungry, snaring what they could after they camped for the day in the refuge of what tangled undergrowth they could find, cooking their catch over small fires, Elias doing the roasting, Caleb guarding with his pistol, heightened to every shadow that moved across prairie grass or dappled stands of black walnut leaning over streams, curious shapes formed by sun and cloud. They had moved undetected, skirting settlements while isolated farmyards proved productive for gathering eggs and ranging chickens, scrawny and almost meatless creatures, resembling jackrabbit, all muscle and sinew with little drippings to pop in the fire.

~ ~ ~

Indian summer. Elias had heard the words spoken together first by white folk when he was a child; words that seemed to mean something good. Later he understood it to be lingering warm weather. Not the sultry dog day heat that sheened you with sweat like a racehorse after running five furlongs under an August sun, but autumn days that gave no suggestion of winter, bright days like a balmy evening after supper, sitting on the porch steps, swatting at moths drawn to the candlelight from the open door while fireflies wandered random paths among the stars like swollen Jupiters and Mars.

"How far you think we come?" Caleb asked, rousing Elias from his reverie.

Elias looked up to see Caleb staring at him from the saddle of his stolen mule.

"Don't mean nothin' if we ain't got no idea where we's goin'," Elias snapped.

"I got me an idea," Caleb said. "West. First we cross the Mississippi to that new free state. Iowa, it be called. White man takes Indian land then names it after 'em. Ain't that somethin'? And you don't need to bite my head off. You ain't no field boss no more."

"I was a slave, same as you be," Elias said. He was growing tired of Caleb's endless jabber. Elias knew he was just as ignorant about the world as Caleb, but at least Elias was smart enough not to not let folks know. "And I stole this horse just like you stole that mule."

"What you mean when you said Indian summer?" Caleb asked.

"What?"

"You said somethin' about Indian Summer. Not a good sign when you start talkin' to yourself out loud."

"The weather," Elias said. "Reminded me of when I was a child, down south…"

"I don't remember nothin' 'bout bein' a child," Caleb said. "And glad I doesn't. Only thing you need to remember is where you is right now. You keep slippin' away like you been and you fall off your horse and get trampled, end up with an arrow in your back or hogtied with leather straps trottin' behind a pony."

"I'd heard Indians…"

"All depends on which Indians you run into. Some keep slaves and don't mind ones that is already broke in like we is. Some'll trade you to Night Riders for a bottle of rotgut. Then again, some Indians take runaways into their tribe and even give 'em squaws. Like I said, all depends on what Indians you run into."

Elias was letting Caleb's words flow over his thoughts like runoff from a thunderstorm filling a dry gulch, becoming the soothing drone of his mother's singing as she rocked him on the porch when he was still too young for the cotton fields.

Elias heard what sounded like a mad Blue Tail fly buzz past his left ear. It was not an Indian summer firefly. It was a feathered arrow that imbedded itself in Caleb's right arm, spinning him from his mule. He fell to the ground, still clutching the reins. The mule stopped, looking down on Caleb as if waiting for a command. Caleb struggled to his feet, grabbing at the arrow that ran through his bicep, snapping it off. He threw the feathered shaft to the ground with anger then grabbed and yanked the arrowhead out that still protruded from his arm. The flint edges cut his fingers. Blood flowed red without spurting from his wounds. He attempted to pull his pistol with his left hand. An Indian rode up from behind on a white pony blotched with brown, a drawn bow aiming an arrow at Elias. The Indian was motioning Elias to dismount and for Caleb to remain where he was and take his hand off his gun. They both obeyed

~ ~ ~

"Don't show no fear," Caleb said, clenching his fist to ease the throbbing ache in his arm while Elias bandaged it with strips from Caleb's shirt with the expertise he had gathered at the salt works when leased slaves sometimes chopped their toes instead of the log. One Indian's eyes followed their slightest move as Caleb searched for a less painful position. "They is nothin' but dogs, smellin' if you be scared."

"Hold still," Elias said. He watched the other Indian squatting over the small fire, roasting something that might be a skinned rabbit. He had never been so close to an

Indian before. Most had been pushed west, farther into the plains, away from ancestral lands. But some had resisted; a few stubborn bands had clung to their wandering ways, living off the ever more crowded land with the guile of fugitive slaves, clothed in a hodgepodge of traded shirts and coats and hats decorated with feathers and coins, armed with wooden bows, bartered knives and stolen rifles.

"That be too tight," Caleb said, clawing at the crimson bandage that wrapped his arm.

"Leave that alone," Elias said. "You want to bleed to death?"

"Depends on what these Indians plan to do with us."

"We be dead by now, if they just want my horse. Your mangy mule ain't worth killin' for."

"That one took my pistol," Caleb said, pointing at the Indian roasting the rabbit. The other Indian reached for the knife tucked in his rope belt, pulling it out slowly and inspecting the blade with his thumb.

"Careful who you be pointin' at," Elias said. "They might be dogs, but they be dogs with sharp knives, and your pistol. Any plan for what we do?"

"I been in worse scrapes," Caleb said.

"Any plans?"

"I needs time to think."

The Indian hunching over the cook fire stood and removed blackened meat from the roasting stick. He showed no concern that it had just come sizzling out of the fire. He pulled it apart, offering half to the other Indian. They squatted and ate slowly and with intent, offering nothing to Elias or Caleb.

"They be gettin' rid of us soon, one way or the other. Ain't gonna waste no food on us," Caleb said. "I think we just be ponies to trade for jerky and fire water."

"For once," Elias said, "I think you be right."

One Indian stood and threw bare bones at the fire. They hissed and flamed. He pulled the knife from his rope belt and began to walk slowly towards Elias and Caleb.

Ten

"Ain't seen hide nor hair of Zeke, Mr. Crenshaw," Cyrus said. "Not since, well, can't rightly remember when I seen him last. My memory been givin' me fits lately."

John was glad Zeke was missing. If Zeke returned it would have meant the flatboat slavers had not done their job. It was worth it to John to barter Patsy's girls for ridding himself of Zeke. Zeke had been a renegade, bad as the rogue Indians that scavenged the grasslands, stealing from honest white men who lived by the sweat of their brows. And like those savages, Zeke was a tick on the rump of a lame ass with morals to match. He had been useful for keeping the niggers in line, and selling them when John needed the cash. But Zeke had been biting the hand that fed him and John had lost his tolerance for such flagrant insolence.

"He should be showing up soon," John said, controlling his urge to grin. "Go see if Patsy needs assistance, without her girls to help. She seems out of sorts this morning. Her biscuits were heavy as lead sinkers. And the gravy thin as broth."

"That for sure don't sound like Patsy," Cyrus agreed.

"I'm riding into Equality on business," John said. "Before you help Patsy, go tell Elias to saddle my horse."

"Funny thing, Mr. Crenshaw. I ain't seen Elias neither. Not since, well, there I go again. I ain't seen him for a peculiar length of time."

John felt a sense of foreboding. Elias had acted agitated when John talked about the need of closing the salt works. Elias was a hard worker, for a nigger. And loyal, or at least he had been. The notion that Elias might run away had never crossed John's mind. But if he had run away, and got caught, he'd be headed south to join Patsy's girls in the cotton fields. Nobody could accuse John Hart Crenshaw of favoring one nigger over another. Like children, they required strict parents who were not afraid to dole out righteous punishment.

"Want me to saddle your horse, Mr. Crenshaw?" Cyrus asked,

"No," John said, knowing Cyrus couldn't begin to get a saddle over the back of his horse. Cyrus was good for house chores, helping Patsy and chopping wood, but even then he sometimes missed the round and nearly took off a foot. "I'll do it myself. You go see about Patsy."

"Yes, Mr. Crenshaw," Cyrus said, wondering if Mr. Crenshaw realized there was no way he could lift a saddle with his lumbago. He hoped Mr. Crenshaw didn't. There be nothin' more useless than a feeble nigger with a failing' memory, Cyrus thought. And he would do all he could to keep his house servant position.

~ ~ ~

The road from Hickory Hill to the county seat of Equality wove through low mounds and fields, dotted here and there with trees and shrubs along brooks and streams. John remained alert riding near these thickets that could hide highwaymen as well as runaway niggers believing they were on a road to freedom. Wherever you go, John would tell house servants or field hands who appeared on the verge of running, you take your black skin with you. Don't think you will find freedom up north, or out west. Not in these United States of America, John would tell them. You should feel fortunate that God put you here and not in the heathen jungles of Africa. God made you the white men's burden and charged us to not spare the rod if that's what it takes to save your souls. God demands obedience and so do I, he had told Caleb at the salt works after whipping him for refusing to stand or remove his straw hat. But in truth it was more for the squint of his eyes that said he could kill John, given the opportunity. And now that Caleb was a runaway, John rode with his pistol belt turned for ease of access as he passed the thickets that could conceal a lazy nigger like Caleb.

~ ~ ~

"You look exhausted," Sina said to John as he limped through the front door. He shut it behind him with a weary effort, removed his hat and duster and handed them to Patsy who had appeared from the kitchen.

"I am," he replied. "It was a very long day."

"Got supper still warmed for you, Mr. Crenshaw," Patsy said.

"Not hungry," John said. He sat down hard in his chair by the fireplace.

"Patsy," Sina said. "Find Cyrus and have him help Mr. Crenshaw remove his boots."

John slumped farther into the chair, rubbing his hands over his face as if washing off the soap after a shave. "They want to ruin me," he said.

"Who?" Sina asked, already knowing the answer. The topic of financial ruin had been the side dish with every meal for months.

"The imposters who call themselves businessmen," John said. "Their only business is destroying other's fortune for their own personal gain."

Sina was familiar with John's grievances as she was familiar with the local farmers' complaints about drought that turned to curses at the swelling rivers when the rain refused to stop. As little as Sina knew of business, she did know her husband was as ruthless in defending his holdings as any of the bankers from Equality were intent on acquiring his for financial gain. And she was proud of her husband for being the God-fearing family-provider he was.

"Help you with your boots, Mr. Crenshaw?" Cyrus asked. He was sweating and attempting to disguise a heaving chest. John absent-mindedly raised his foot. Cyrus backed over the leg and began tugging at the boot. It wouldn't budge. Cyrus was panting like one of John's hounds after a coon hunt. If John had not been so tired he would have been angry. Cyrus turned with a look of fright.

"Never mind, Cyrus," Sina said, reading John's face.

"Yes, Mrs. Crenshaw," Cyrus said, struggling to stand erect. When Sina looked as though she might offer help, he waved her off. "I be fine, Mrs. Crenshaw. Just couldn't get a good grip on the leather."

~ ~ ~

"How old do you think Cyrus is?" John asked after Cyrus left the room.

"It is hard to tell. Negroes often look younger than their years, don't they?"

"I hate it when they live past their usefulness," John said.

It was another grouse Sina often heard from her husband. Old niggers were as much a burden as old dogs or a lame horse, but it wasn't acceptable, especially for a Methodist Elder, to put them down. Just how long Cyrus would live, no one could say. With the exception of his lumbago, failing eyesight and forgetfulness, Cyrus seemed healthy, for his advanced years, however many they were.

"Not to be unkind," John said, tugging at his boot and having no more success removing it than Cyrus, "but it would be better for all concerned if he just dropped dead."

"John," Sina scolded. "That is not humorous."

"It was not intended to be," John said, grunting in a final effort that removed his muddy riding boot. He sat back, gathering strength for an assault on the other boot. "Financially, it is time to consider selling off some of the land."

"You always land on your feet, John. No matter how bad things might look."

"Today, things look bad," John said as he leaned to yank the other boot from his swollen foot. It fell to the braided rug with a thud.

~ ~ ~

John Hart Crenshaw liked to play games—Hide and Seek and Blind Man's Bluff as a child and later Chess. He was intrigued by competitions of trickery and dodges, concealment and deception, relying on clever strategies and tricky tactics that often required the necessary sacrifice of Queens and Knights, Bishops and Castles and rows of pawns to defend the King and secure final victory.

John had told the Equality Bankers he had never kept ledgers, except in his head. He did not trust numbers scratched in books. Figures could be altered or blotched to suit another's needs. Numbers could be bloated like a fatted calf to hide thievery or shrunk to the size of a flea to force bankruptcy and sale. Numbers in books were tools for the shifty and the shiftless. But the Equality Bankers had insisted he must be keeping records and John admitted that at one time he did, but the few books that he had kept were all destroyed in the Cypress Mill fire of March, 1842. In the succeeding years he had relied on a firm handshake instead of ink to seal contracts and a strong memory for conducting the business of making salt. Then you should be familiar with the state of your affairs, the Equality Bankers insisted.

The mortgage on your property is overdue and your taxes are delinquent. John argued that he was not delinquent, and that he was insulted by the use of such an ugly word. He was an honorable man, a Methodist Elder. He was an honest man who paid his debts but he did not believe in taxes for they were just a lazy man's ruse to steal from those who had labored to build and maintain their wealth.

"They did not approve of my financial practices," John said to Sina. "They are calling in my mortgage."

"What does that mean, John?"

"Oh. Now you are interested in my business. You could not be bothered when times were good."

"I am concerned about you, John. You do not look well. Just the ride to Equality and back would wear out a much younger man."

"I am far from an old man, Sina. And I will not be defeated by greedy bankers who hide behind the billowing skirts of petty bureaucracy. But that is just my vanity talking. They are doing me a favor."

"A favor? I might be ignorant of business," Sina said, perplexed by John's sudden change of mood from ire to self-satisfaction, "but losing the salt works is…"

"Liberating," John finished.

Eleven

"Seasick?" Beulah asked. "You ain't never been near the sea in your life. How you know what seasick be? We's on a river, not no ocean."

"Old Cyrus. He be talkin' once 'bout his grandpa," Betsy said, lifting her head from her filthy dress that covered a huddle of knees and arms. "Chained in the hold of a ship 'fore it be again' the law to bring slaves from Africa to America. Cyrus say the waves made his grandpa seasick and he heaved the whole trip even if he had nothin' to eat. That be how I's feelin', seasick, even if we be on a river."

She do look miserable, Beulah thought. But Betsy always be complainin' 'bout one thing or the next, her face most the time lookin' like a child ready to bawl.

"I feel powerful sick," Betsy said, each word catching in her throat like bits of underdone meat. "It be the boat. My stomach be heavin' when it rises up and falls."

The Mississippi was widening as dawn gave enough light to make its banks visible. A steady breeze flapped the sail and rocked the flatboat side to side.

"I be the one with child. I should be the one sick," Beulah caught herself repeating her familiar response to Betsy's constant moans.

Beulah did pity Betsy's misery but was unwilling to share with her that the wind-driven rollers were also tumbling her stomach, a stomach already assaulted by kicks from the boy in her belly. Yes, it is a boy, she continued to insist. Girls don't kick like a Tennessee mule. Between the kicks and the flatboat's motion, Beulah struggled to keep the contents of a meager breakfast down. She had willingly accepted her mother's command, that being the responsible one, it was Beulah's place to protect Betsy. If she threw up it would scare Betsy more than the thought of being sold in Memphis, where Jim told her the Auction Market took place. Look for a high bluff, Jim had said to Beulah between pulls of moonshine and working the tiller as they drifted on an easy current the night before. That's where you and your ugly sister will be sold. Now that high bluff was just on the horizon, rising and falling with the swells of the river.

~ ~ ~

Tall embankments rose from the wide river, brooding under low clouds above the rolling water like a high castle wall protecting its citadel from barbarian hordes—the Chickasaw Bluffs, shielding Memphis from the savage floods of the Mississippi. The wind died with the rising sun. Jim dropped the sail then pulled the long tiller hard to port in the drift, slowly turning the flatboat towards the eastern shore. Frank rowed the starboard oar, scolding himself or not hiring another hand for the other oar. But that would have meant splitting the sale of the niggers three ways, he thought. Sharing the sale with Jim was bad enough. Frank rowed harder, digging deeper into the river. This must be what it's like being a nigger, he thought every time he took the oar, or did anything that strained his muscles and put an ache in his back. This was harder work than a white man was born to do. But Frank had plans. First, he would sell the niggers, then sell the flatboat to a trader taking niggers south to New Orleans.

Or, if he couldn't find a buyer for the flatboat, he would dismantle it and sell the timber for cash. Then he would rid himself of Jim, one way or the other, and use both shares of money to buy land. Frank had no intentions of returning to Hickory Hill. He was tired of being Mr. Crenshaw's white nigger, doing his dirty work for a few gold coins, for whiskey, tobacco and a bedbug cot. He'd never own a plantation or sip mint juleps on a wide and breezy porch, but he had the wits to grow and raise enough crop and stock to survive and maybe just a little more. He was imagining the lay of his land when the oar slipped from his sweating hands and was nearly ripped from the rowlock by the waters that swirled around the end of Mud Island, the long peninsula built from the silt where the Wolf River met the Mississippi, sheltering the landings of Memphis from the greedy Father of Rivers.

The rudder was already as hard to starboard as it would go and Jim was doing all he could to keep it there.

"Row harder," Jim yelled back at Frank. "Ain't my fault you can't hang on to the oar."

The flatboat began a slow turn towards the bluffs that had lowered the length of the peninsula from a high wall to a flat mud point.

"We be turnin'," Beulah said to Betsy.

"Memphis?" Betsy asked.

"Likely," Beulah said, holding back the canvas at the cabin door enough to see land glide by. Frank stowed the oar, picked up the long pole, found the shallow riverbed and began guiding the flatboat around the point of muddy earth. Jim was straining against the rudder, sweat running rivulets down his filthy face.

"Grab another pole," Frank yelled.

Jim lifted the long tiller out of the water, secured it and took a long pole down from its brackets on the side of the cabin.

"Shove her around the point," Frank said.

Beulah let the canvass door fall closed. She sat beside Betsy, leaning against the rough planks of the cabin wall. She could feel slivers attempting to penetrate the shawl she pulled tighter against the shivering. She clenched her teeth, determined to ignore the cold and the slivers.

"We be landin' soon," Beulah said.

"Don't let them take me away from you," Betsy began to sob. "You my big sister. Don't let them take me..."

"What you expect me to do?"

"You be my big sister..."

Beulah was weary enough to doze off, awakening as her head fell back and cracked the cabin wall.

"You suppose to take care of me," Betsy said, shaking Beulah by the shoulders. "That what Mama said."

"You seem strong enough to take care of yourself," Beulah said, rubbing her eyes. "We need to figure this out. And I mean we. I ain't your big sister no more."

"What you mean, ain't my sister?"

"Not like you want. I's too tired. I can't take care of you no more. We got to lean on each other, Betsy. That what I mean. Sometimes you gotta take care of me. Time for you to grow up. I got a baby to worry 'bout..."

"Stop talkin' 'bout that baby all the time. I's tired of hearin' about that baby..."

"That what I mean," Beulah said, standing up and going back to the canvas door. "You need to grow up. You ain't the only one in the world carryin' burdens."

Betsy said something, but Beulah wasn't listening. She opened the canvas door and stepped out onto the deck. Frank and Jim were polling towards a dock constructed of what looked like discards from a sawmill. They were too busy to yell at her to get back in the cabin.

~ ~ ~

A red-bearded man stood waiting on the dock. Frank stowed his poll, picked up the bowline and tossed it to the man who pulled it around a dock cleat and tied it off with a hasty clove hitch. The stern-line brought the flatboat snug up against the low landing, leaving only a modest step up from the boat deck.

"The name's Devlin Doyle," the bearded man said. "Mr. Cruickshank instructed me to bring you and your cargo to the market."

"Don't know no Mr. Cruickshank," Frank said. His neck hairs were twitching, the way they always did when something wasn't right. "I always do business with Rolf Torgerson. How do you even know who I am?"

"Mr. Torgerson took sick. He's dead, to be more to the point. Mr. Cruickshank has taken on his business."

"That still don't tell me how you know who I am. Or what my cargo is."

"Memphis is a small town, Mr. McDougal," Devlin said. "When my associates informed me there was a flatboat polling around Mud Island and only two on board to man the sail, the tiller and two oars they told me it could only be Frank McDougal and Jim Stutter, and that you, Mr. McDougal, would be the...spokesman."

Frank had no reply. It was true. His reputation up and down the river was for being what he would call thrifty, like a good Scotsman, being from the McDougal Clan as he was. Jim called him cheap. But Jim was not a Scotsman. Jim was a drunkard.

"Well then, Mr. Doyle. I will bring out my cargo. Then you can lead us to the auction."

"It would be my pleasure, Mr. McDougal," Devlin said, feigning a slight bow.

~ ~ ~

Memphis was the largest port along the Mississippi on its 600-mile run from the Ohio River to Vicksburg. It was also the largest inland cotton port in the world. Its favorable location had attracted human settlement from the Mound Builders to their descendants, the Chickasaw, who first encountered Europeans when Hernando DeSoto and his army of Conquistadors arrived in 1541 looking for gold and a shortcut waterway to the riches of the Orient, but only found the Mississippi River. Camping near the future site of Memphis, DeSoto claimed the land for Spain. A year later he died of fever at the age of forty-five, finding no gold or passage to the Pacific, his possessions at death being three horses, seven hundred hogs, and four Indian slaves. For the next two hundred years the land changed hands from Spanish to French to English before Tennessee was admitted as the 16th state of the Union in 1796. When the Chickasaw Indians sold the land to the United States in 1818, Andrew Jackson and other investors anticipated the potential of a city on the bluffs, naming it Memphis, Abode of the Good. Incorporated in 1826, it became a way station for settlers headed west. But by the 1840's, Memphis was booming with the wealth of the white gold DeSoto never found—King Cotton.

~ ~ ~

"Shackle the niggers," Frank said to Devlin.

"I think we can get the ladies to auction without resorting to irons," Devlin said.

"They are my niggers," Frank said. "I don't trust any of 'em. Man, woman or child. Even a woman carryin' a pickaninny."

"With child?" Devlin asked, looking at Beulah.

Beulah stood on the landing with Betsy who was clutching her shawl. Beulah met Devlin's stare and did not look away.

"Should fetch a better price. But don't think it makes her tame. She's got the fight of a mama bear protectin' her cub, whether they be born or not. Now, put these fetters on," Frank insisted, handing Devlin two pair of linked shackles.

"Sorry, ladies," Devlin said, squatting to place and adjust the shackles around Beulah and Betsy's ankles.

"Make hers tight," Frank said, pointing to Beulah. "I don't trust that one."

"You have made that clear, Mr. McDougal," Devlin said, leaving the shackles loose as he could.

Beulah moved her gaze to Frank. A rage boiled up she never felt, hatred, the color of crimson, a blaze burning behind her eyes.

"No reason to worry," Devlin said, standing and brushing dust from the knees of his trousers. "The ladies are secured."

"Jim," Frank said, keeping his eyes fixed on Beulah's. "You stay with the boat."

"I…" Jim began to protest.

"You stay with the boat. Don't want some buzzards sailin' off the New Orleans with it. I'll sell the niggers and be back," Frank said. "You don't think I'd run off with the money, do you?"

"Of course I don't," Jim said. "Any more than I would."

Which is why you'll never be no more than trash, Frank thought. Frank had plans and Jim was just a festering tooth that needed pulling.

"How far to the auction?" Frank asked Devlin.

"Not far," Devlin said. "We should be there before Noon. The Auction starts at two o'clock to give the Good Gentlemen of Memphis time for an ample lunch."

~ ~ ~

Beulah and Betsy hobbled through the cobble-stone streets. No one paid attention. The sight of two niggers shackled and being lead to a slave market auction was usual as a wagon of cotton being pulled by a team of swayed-back horses to the riverboat docks. That just might be a blessing, Beulah thought. If me and Betsy can get ourselves free, we might disappear into this river of black faces. She had never seen so many of her people. Some had the confident look of freed men of color, other's scurried behind finely dressed Mistresses with items wrapped in paper and tied with string, and still others shuffled, bound in coffles, down the same cobbles, urged on by men in preacher coats and hats and holding short riding whips.

"Stop daydreamin'," Frank said, tugging on Beulah's arm.

"I be movin'," Beulah said. "You is hurtin' me."

"Not like I should…" Frank said, raising his hand.

"You don't want to damage your goods, now do you, Mr. McDougal?" Devlin intervened. "Mr. Cruickshank would be disappointed."

"You're right," Frank said, lowering his arm. "I need every dollar I can get."

"Would you be heading back to…just where did you say you were from, Mr. McDougal?"

"Never did," Frank said. He thought fast to come up with a story he wouldn't forget. "I'm headed to my cousin's sugarcane plantation in Louisiana, after I sell the niggers. I do business for him."

"Oh. I thought you worked for someone in Illinois," Devlin said, knowing it was true, since he had talked to Jim while Frank was discussing fees with the landing agent.

"Don't know who gave you that idea," Frank said, adding no details, always worried someone could use them against him.

"Doesn't matter," Devlin said. He wasn't sure why Frank was lying, but he knew that he was. Devlin didn't like Frank from the moment he set eyes on him. Most of the men Devlin dealt with were less than Gentlemen. Even the Gentlemen were generally counterfeit, yet impressively devious. But there was something more of the Devil in Frank than most men he had met on his travels on the river. And not the brawling demon that lived in whiskey bottles to incite wharf tavern fights over drunken insults. Devlin could smell Frank's foulness like gangrene growing in a wound. Jim, on the other hand, was friendly, if a little slow, anxious to tell Devlin everything he knew, whether he knew it or not. Jim was an obedient mongrel who followed commands and only occasionally snarled between tail wags. Frank, on the other hand, had plans. Serious plans. He did not laugh easily as Jim did. And he kept talk to the bare bones. Devlin could spot a man plotting from the bank on the other side of the river. To make your way in this world, his Da had told him, back in County Clare, don't let anyone know your true mind. Smile. Use your gift with words. Buy them drinks and make the toasts, but keep your mind to yourself. Devlin had taken his Da's advice as his only possession of importance when he left home, besides a cardboard grip strapped with a length of horse harness. The grip held one wool shirt, one pair of wool trousers, one wool long john and one pair of wool socks that still bore the evidence of his late mother's darning skills. It also carried the family Bible. Devlin had not asked permission from his father to take the Bible, but Da couldn't read and spent his days staring at black piles of praties rotting in the field as he nursed glasses of poteen, "little pot", a most potent spirit distilled in Ireland since the 1600s when potatoes were first planted, grumbling that the blight might make this his last batch. Devlin's older brother, Davey, was busy struggling to delay eviction while his younger brother, Finian would not need the Bible since he was in the seminary. Tradition said that all good Irish Catholic families were obligated to sacrifice one son to Rome, something that had pleased Finian's mother, providing her with a peaceful death. Devlin had stashed away enough coins with the family Bible to buy passage to Americay, leaving him with only his wits as anything of financial worth when he docked. After a short stay, he left the teeming streets of Manhattan and headed west, working keelboats and barges down the Ohio and the Mississippi to Memphis. He had no intention of staying. But he had stumbled into a job working for Mr. Torgerson, until his boss was stabbed to death by a customer who claimed he had knowingly sold him a nigger with consumption and arthritic hands. Now Devlin worked for Mr. Cruikshank who knew that pleasing the buyer kept you in business and not gutted by a hunting knife. Devlin was not proud of himself for being in the human bondage business, considering he had lived his life under an English rule that considered the Irish of similar intelligence to the gorillas recently discovered in Darkest Africa. But the job of handling slaves bound for the auction block had provided Devlin with a cot in a flophouse, pub stew, pints and the occasional game of cards, all the time searching situations that would trouble his conscience less.

"What's your name?" Devlin asked the Negress who was with child. He could sense she had a strong spirit like Frank had said. She wasn't yet broken.

Beulah didn't answer.

"Come, Madame. My intentions are pure."

"Beulah," she said, flattered by being called Madame. She had not meant to answer, but she could not help herself.

"Beulah," Devlin said. "Thou shalt no more be termed Forsaken; neither shall thy land any more be termed Desolate; but thou shalt be called *Hephzibah* and thy land *Beulah*; for the Lord delighteth in thee"... Isiah. That's all I remember. Not sure about chapter and verse."

"You be a preacher?" Beulah asked.

"Lord, no," Devlin said. "My brother, Finian, is the one going to be a priest. I'm not the preacher. I liked to read and the only book we had in our house was the Bible. Da always said I was acting like a Prod, reading it all the time. The Book was meant for Ma to write in the names of kin when they were born or died, and the rest was for priests to tell us what it means."

"Wish I could read better. Mama taught me some words, but…" Beulah said, stopping herself, frightened, realizing she was confessing to a crime.

"Now don't you go wishing for things you can't have," Devlin said. "It'll only make you cynical. And I won't reveal to anyone your ability to read. It will remain our secret."

"I ain't never heard that word, Sir. What do… cynical mean?"

"It means that I am showing off. And, I certainly am not a Sir. Call me Devlin"

"I ain't never called no…"

"White man?" Devlin asked as Beulah stuttered to find a word that wouldn't bring the whip.

Beulah nodded, finishing, "…by his first name."

"Then we can break precedence," Devlin said.

"What that mean?"

"That I am an unrepentant braggart."

Beulah liked Devlin's words, even though she had no idea what they meant, unless he explained. She also liked his kindness. It had been a long time since a man had treated her with kindness. She had never known her father and the father of her child was mean as a cornered badger, but she seldom thought of him and practiced pushing those thoughts down deep into the river of memory like a deformed kitten in a burlap sack that required drowning.

~~~

Beulah refused to shiver, even as a gusting wind blew in from the river and through the cracks in the slats of the slave pen wall to move the stagnant air. The only sound was the clink of metal as slaves waiting for auction adjusted their shackles chained to pegs driven deep into the hard-packed dirt floor. No one spoke. Betsy was asleep, her breathing the gentle purr of a kitten. Beulah stroked her hair. She loved Betsy, even for all the trouble she could bring.

The door opened. Light streamed in through the putrid air. A short and stocky man stood framed in the doorway, a riding crop gripped tightly in a pudgy left fist. Beulah could smell him from across the room. As he came closer, the stench grew. If he had ever taken a bath, it hadn't done much good. And, he must have been very fond of onions.

"I brung clean clothes," he said, opening a burlap sack he had carried flung over his shoulder. He reached into the sack handed a dress to Beulah and one to Betsy. They looked coarse as the sack, but clean. He went around the pen, giving clothes to all the slaves. "Mr. Cruickshank always says that clean niggers fetch better prices, so I'll be bringin' in buckets of water. Scrub the skin that shows until it shines. Now, get dressed."

"Can't pull pants up over shackles," a voice in the darkness said.

"Smart boy," the man said, smacking the palm of his hand with the riding crop and turning to the very dark African who had stood to expose his leg chain. "I got the key. I got the whip. And I got men outside itchin' to fill the backside of the first nigger to run with buckshot. You woman just pull off them filthy rags you're wearin'. Don't care if you ain't got nothin' underneath. At auction, the less you wear, the better. The buyers want a good look. They are gentlemen who know what they want. But don't y'all worry. Every one of you, even the ugliest, the crippled or feeble-minded, will be sold by sunset and most be workin' the cotton fields tomorrow after sunrise. And don't go believin' none of them stories about niggers escapin' the pens. Sure, some have tried, but they ain't alive to tell about it. If you're dyin' to be free, we are happy to oblige."

Betsy stared at it the clean dress, confused.

"I can't put this on here," she said. "There be men starin' at me."

"There be men checkin' you out like a farm horse soon enough."

"But..."

Beulah yanked Betsy's dress off over her head. Mama had sewn it, adding the puffy sleeves that Betsy liked. But now it was torn and stained as an old rag Beulah would use to polish Mrs. Crenshaw's silver. Betsy let out a yelp, trying to cover her nakedness. Beulah tugged the clean dress down over Betsy's head, shoving her arms into it like dressing a doll. She looked up at the man with the riding whip. He was grinning at Beulah, waiting for her to change.

"Don't bring no attention to yourself," Beulah whispered. "Don't tempt the whip. We need to be like quiet children no one pays attention to, if we want to be free."

"Free?" Betsy said a little too loud.

"Hush now. You be a quiet child. No more moanin' or weepin'."

"I try."

"You do more than try, if'n you don't want to be pickin' cotton till you die of heat stroke."

"You got plans, Beulah?"

"I will. In time. But for now, hush."

The door creaked open. A man hauled in two full buckets of water, leaving a wet trail. Behind him, another man entered the pen. It was Devlin, carrying towels, washcloths and bars of lye soap.

"One bucket for the men, one for the women. Mr. Cruickshank wants you clean. Teeth and all. If you ain't clean enough..." the man with the whip said, smacking it against his palm, not bothering to finish the sentence.

Devlin brought the bucket to Beulah, then handed her a washcloth, towel and a bar of soap.

"You be first, good lady. Before the rest dirty up the water," Devlin whispered to Beulah.

Beulah looked up at Devlin with seething contempt, refusing to take the washcloth.

"No need for that," Devlin said. "Wash your pretty face."

"So I fetch a better price for your boss man?"

"That is the theory," Devlin said, his face vacant of its usual grin. "But I do know that insolence fetches lower prices and meaner masters who assume they can beat you into submission."

"What be insolence?"

"The way you are acting."

"You want me to…"

"I don't want you to get hurt," Devlin said. "Especially since you are with child."

"How you know that? I's hardly showin'."

"Frank is peddling you like a mare foaling a thoroughbred foal. Mr. Cruickshank has a preference for Negresses with child."

"Preference. I do know what that mean," Beulah said.

"Not what you're thinking," Devlin said. "Two for the price of one. Now, wash that pretty face."

Beulah reluctantly dunked the rag in the cold water, wrung it out and held it over her eyes. She hadn't washed her face since—she couldn't remember when. She dipped the rag into the slop bucket again without wringing it, water running down her breast while she scrubbed her face hard like a mother removing play-dirt from her child's cheeks and ears.

"You missed a spot," Devlin said, the wisp of a grin returning to his face.

"What you care?" Beulah said. She shoved the bucket towards Betsy.

"The better you look," Devlin said, "the better your chances are of being sold to a more refined master."

"All masters be as bad."

"Some are better than others," Devlin said.

"What you know?" Beulah asked, nudging Betsy who had fallen asleep again. "You be white."

"I am Irish."

"That make you special?"

"To other Irish, maybe. But not to the rest of the world. Particularly to our English masters in the Old Country."

"You had masters?"

"Negroes aren't the only slaves in the world," Devlin said.

Beulah felt confused. Whites never talked to her like she was an adult, except maybe Mrs. Crenshaw. Mr. Crenshaw treated her like a stupid child, and Zeke Stubbs treated her like a dumb dog that needed kicks to follow commands. Mr. Crenshaw be about the same, less he want somethin'. Betsy was awake, sprinkling water on her face like dampening one of Mr. Crenshaw's shirts for the flatiron.

"Wash you face," Beulah said. 'You need to look your best."

"Who care what I look like?'

Beulah looked at Devlin. "Wash you face," she repeated. "And any skin that shows. Don't want nobody thinkin' we is trash."

Devlin took the bucket when Betsy was done and gave it to woman behind her. Devlin noticed the sprinkle of salt in her hair and the wrinkles spreading on her face like cracks in old plaster. It wasn't just the years, Devlin knew. Even the young aged early in the cotton and sugar cane fields, far beyond their number of sunrises and sets. But she might have been a house servant, old as she looks and sitting in this pen as victim of a dead master or lost plantation, sold by court order into a more severe servitude. The softness of her hands as she accepted the bucket and the terror on his face convinced Devlin it was the latter. This was a fate he did not want for Beulah.

"Here, my lady," Devlin said. "Get some of that road dust off. I hear there are buyers in need of house servants today."

"Thank you, sir," the she said with a nod, scrubbing her hands and face with an urgency, as if they were covered with the King of Scotland's blood.

Devlin tried not to care, but he knew this woman would not last long picking Mississippi cotton. He hoped for her a genteel plantation house, but left it at that. Devlin had his own stomach to fill.

"Pass the bucket when you're done, my lady. The auction starts soon."

~ ~ ~

The fall sun was sharp and painful to Beulah's eyes as she was lead out of the pen in her clean dress. She had scrubbed herself to a shine and did the same to Betsy without regard to her sister's loud protests. Beulah and Betsy were the first chosen to go on the block. They and been the only young women in the pen and Beulah hoped that might keep them together as twins, strong and healthy and one carrying a child. She could only hope.

"Keep your heads down," Devlin said as he walked beside them. They were unshackled. "Show no signs of arrogance. Get branded as prideful and you will be sold to a trashy rascal out of spite."

"What he say?" Betsy asked, poking Beulah.

"Hush your mouth and look at the ground."

"Why?"

"Keep drawing attention to yourself," Devlin interrupted, "and you'll be picking cotton and being flogged for not picking enough. And you'll never see your sister again. Potential troublemakers are dealt with harshly."

Betsy put her head down.

"Good girl," Devlin assured her.

"I'm not dog," Betsy said, looking sideways at Devlin, still keeping her head lowered.

"You will surely be treated as a dog if you do not begin acting more subservient. Obedient," Devlin added, seeing Betsy's puzzled look. "It is just a game, darling. It does not change who you are. These men cannot take your souls."

Beulah began to reply, then stopped, practicing what Devlin had instructed. Be the obedient little dogs for now, he had said. Run and fetch, but make your own plans, bide your time and your time will come.

Twelve

Josiah swung his double-bladed axe with the ease and precision of a woodsman, producing the ringing sound of seasoned wood as the halves of each quarter fell into two piles to feed the brine pot fires. Balancing another log on the splitting stump, he looked up to see a rider approaching down the salt works road, his horse gingerly trotting to avoid the ruts that had deepened in the last rain. It was John Hart Crenshaw. As he drew closer Josiah could see that his face was more grim that usual. Josiah took a whet stone from his overall pocket, spit on it, and began honing his axe's edge. Elias had warned him something bad was coming, that Mr. Crenshaw's mind was set on selling the salt works. That be why Elias run off with one of the Mr. Crenshaw's best horses, Josiah reckoned. Elias told him he would rather take his chances with the Night Riders than pick cotton down river. After Elias left, Mr. Crenshaw threatened to beat every nigger at Hickory Hill until someone told him where Elias went. Mostly, he was angry about his horse. No nigger had ever run off with one of my horses, he told the salt workers he had gathered around the brine pots the day after Elias disappeared. And what made it worse, he said, was that he had trusted Elias. Treated him almost like a white man. Nothing worse than ungrateful niggers, Mr. Crenshaw said. I give you boys silverware to eat with, he told them, and you stab me in the back with a butter knife.

"Boy," John said as he rode up to Josiah. "Put the axe down. Where is…your Boss Man?"

John would have used his overseer's name, but he couldn't remember it. Since Zeke was gone, there had been one white trash after another overseeing the niggers. All of about the same intelligence, John thought to himself as he watched this nigger closely, his hand still holding the handle of the axe that leaned against his leg.

"He be over by the tree line," Josiah said. "Bustin' up a fight. He do like bustin' up fights. Give him a chance to use his bullwhip. Fancies hisself an artist with a whip. Least that what he say."

"You come with me boy. I have something to tell everyone. Leave the axe here."

Josiah swung the axe and stuck it deep into the splitting stump with a whack that startled John's horse. It pranced backwards and threatened to rear. John's firm grip on the reins held the horse in check.

"Get!" John roared, motioning Josiah towards the tree line.

"You gonna sell us all downriver, ain't you?" Josiah asked.

"None of your concern, boy. Get moving."

Josiah walked ahead of John and his spooked horse. Too much the jittery type, Josiah thought. Not meant for work, just for struttin'. Like Mr. Crenshaw. All bluster and brag, but never dirties his soft pale hands with work. No white man do at the salt works, Josiah concluded. The work be too hard. That's why God created niggers, Zeke had told him. Now Zeke be gone and looks like for good. There were rumors that Mr. Crenshaw had something to do with it, and Josiah believed he did. But the new boss be no better. Bosses might not all look alike, but they do act the same.

~ ~ ~

"You," John yelled at the grubby man snapping his whip back for another lashing of a Negro sprawled in tree line sawdust. His shirt was shredded and streaked with blood.

"Name's Willy," the man said.

"Put the whip down, Willy," John said, dismounting and handing the reins to Josiah. "Tell all the Negroes I want to talk to them. And help that Negro up."

"Nigger'll get up on his own. A bucket of brine-water will see to that."

John learned long ago not to interfere too much with his overseers, unless they started stealing form him. They knew their job and they got work out of the niggers, even if the methods could be cruel, excessively harsh even for John's hardened sensitivities. But he drew the line at damaging his property beyond repair.

"I got two niggers here who spend more time scufflin' than fallin' trees."

"I don't really care," John said, surprised as the weariness his voice. It was beginning to be a chore to keep command, covering the rising resignation of age and too many battles with the bluster that had built his reputation. "Bring all the Negroes here. Now."

"Yes, sir," Willy said.

John watched him call the tree-cutters gather. He was glad that Zeke was gone, but he also knew that Willy was just as crooked and willing to sell his sister for a slug of whiskey and a plug of tobacco. It was only a matter of time before Willy was more liability than asset.

"This is the last one," Willy said, dumping a bucket of brine-water on the Negro he had whipped who was lying face down in the dirt.

Willy grabbed him by the arm and dragged him to the ragged line of salt-workers to face John, who took the horse's reins from Josiah and motioned for him to join the others.

"We's all bein' sold down river," Josiah whispered to the man in the shredded shirt.

"I heard," the bloodied man who had just regained consciousness said, weaving like a drunk as he whispered back. "That be why Willy was whippin' me. He heard me talkin' 'bout it to others."

"Silence," John said, looking directly at Josiah. He knew an insolent nigger when he saw one. Best to get rid of troublemakers soon as possible, John thought. Like Zeke.

"I know you all have heard the talk. It is not a rumor," John began. "It is true. I am selling the salt works and some of my other assets..."

"That mean us, don't it?" Josiah asked.

"Do not interrupt me, boy," John said, meeting Josiah's glare of defiance with an unwavering gaze. "I'm sure you heard this from Elias, that horse thief..."

John held his tongue. He wasn't going to let the niggers see that one of their kind could make him lose his temper. It could only encourage their boldness.

"It be common knowledge, Mr. Crenshaw," Josiah answered as politely as he possibly could.

"The salt works have been sold," John said, regaining composure. "I will have an agent out this week to check on the rest of my...assets. Until then I expect an honest day's labor from each and every one of you. It would be better for all of us if I can tell your future employers you are trustworthy and hard working."

Josiah began to say something, but stopped when Willy stuck him hard in the back with the handle of his whip.

~ ~ ~

The sun had already set by the time Josiah climbed the stairs to his porch. The cabin was dark. No candles burned and no cooking fire blazed.

"Hannah?" Josiah called into the darkness. No response. The hearth was cold. Kindling had been laid but not lit. Panic swept over Josiah like the first chill of a fever. He went to the table and lit the stub of a candle. The bed was still neatly made. The kitchen was clean with no signs that Hannah had begun dinner. The dirt-floor shack was empty. Hannah was gone.

"Hannah!" Josiah yelled, standing on the porch. Nothing. Not even an echo.

"She be gone," a voice said out of the darkness. A man walked into a patch of moonlight. Josiah could see it was Noah, the man Willy had been whipping.

"Gone?"

"My woman tell me two men come just after noon when she be carryin' water back from the well and dragged your woman into a wagon. They headed south, towards the river. Molly hid herself until I come home. Like I could defend her again' agent men in my condition. Anyway, it be your fault I got whipped, tellin' me 'bout Elias and how he run off with Mr. Crenshaw's horse because we all bein' sold down river."

"It be true, Noah."

"And it be true they took your woman," Noah said. "That be your fault, too. She gone because you talk too much"

Josiah flinched at those words. He knew he had been lucky to be with Hannah as long as they had. He also felt fortunate they had never had children to lose, even though he and Hannah had repeatedly tried, since losing children was a sorrow he was not sure he could bear. But now he wasn't feeling lucky. The anger in him rose like bubbles in a pot of brine just before the boil.

~ ~ ~

Josiah brooded all night until the first pale shades of dawn drew him from the hard wooden chair by the fireplace to the door. He could not bring himself to sleep alone in bed without Hannah, having not been separated since they jumped the broom. The years they had been together made him forget his life before her. His new life had begun the day he laid eyes on Hannah, working the vegetable garden, carrying baskets of beans and peas, squash and radishes, mustard and greens. He dared not look at her for long, shuffling past in a coffle with other leased slaves from Kentucky, delivered bound in their chains to a certain Mr. John Hart Crenshaw of Hickory Hill to work his salt in the Free State of Illinois. Laughable, Josiah thought to himself, that, that he be a slave in a Free State and still in chains. But all that fell away as he saw the eyes of the woman carrying her basket of vegetables in a kitchen patch near the road. Her eyes were not those of the defeated. They were clear and steadfast and looked at Josiah as he passed with intention, with the message that even here, not all was lost.

"Boy," said the Boss Man who looked young enough to be Josiah's son, riding up on a horse that looked older than both their ages combined. "Keep your eyes off the women. Your only chance to have one of them is if you work hard enough and Mr. Crenshaw is feelin' generous."

"I weren't lookin'…

The tip of a whip slashed across Josiah's face.

"Shut your black mouth," the Boss Man said, rolling his whip back up into a coil. "March."

Josiah marched, but stole a last glimpse of the woman carrying her vegetable basket. She looked at him. Josiah tried not to be hopeful, but there was something about her that said, "I will be yours. Wait. Wait. I will be yours."

~ ~ ~

"Boss Man madder'n I ever seen him this mornin'," Noah said. "Mad 'bout what?" Josiah asked, standing on the porch of his cabin, rubbing what little sleep he had gotten from his eyes and hitching up the straps of his coveralls.

"Don't need no reason. Just told me go get yo' ass down to the salt works or ..."

"I be tired," Josiah said.

"What nigger ain't?"

"I be tired of it all."

"Now don't you start that runaway nigger talk. You hear? Mr. Crenshaw wouldn't abide by another, after Elias took that fine horse of his and...you listenin' to me, Josiah?"

"I ain't listenin' to nobody no more," Josiah said. "I tried bein' the good nigger, workin' hard, keepin' my mouth shut, and they send my Hannah to hell. I tried bein' the good nigger and they be fixin' to sell me south, to the same hell."

"You hush yourself," Noah said. Panic chilled him like a bucket of cold well water. He pulled a filthy kerchief from his coverall pocket and wiped his face.

"I ain't listenin'," Josiah said, walking down the cabin stairs. "I ain't listenin' to nobody no more."

~ ~ ~

Willy loved his new job. It had been his good fortune to be the only white man Mr. Crenshaw saw the day he rode up to say Zeke was gone, He made him Overseer on the spot. There was talk of what happened to Zeke, that maybe Mr. Crenshaw had something to do with it, but Willy paid it no mind. Other men had come and gone. Willy knew that overseeing salt work niggers wasn't considered a plum job, but he had been treated like a nigger himself most of his life. He was short to the point Zeke would laugh at him as he struggled to mount his horse. His feet turning out made him walk in a way that gave him the nickname he hated, Willy the Duck. Duck, for short. Now that he carried the Overseer whip, he was going to get the respect he felt he had always deserved and never got.

"Where you been, boy?" Willy hollered loud enough for everyone near the brine pots to hear. He reined his horse in a tight circle around Josiah. "Beauty sleep ain't goin' to help you none. You owe Mr. Crenshaw a full day of work. It's long past sunup. Start choppin' that wood, boy."

Josiah bit his upper lip to keep his tongue in place. He burned to say something with the ferocity of the fires that boiled the brine pots. I owe Mr. Crenshaw nothin', he thought, but did not say it. He sold my woman. He keeps me a slave in a state they say be free. I work all day for scraps of food the white man won't eat.

"I ain't lickin' nobody's boots," Josiah said as he pulled the axe from the splitting stump.

"What you say, boy?" Willy asked with as much gruffness his high-pitched voice could produce.

"Nothin'," Josiah said.

"Don't lie to me, boy. Now, tell the truth, shame the Devil and you might not taste my whip. Dependin' on what you said."

Josiah set a round on the stump, took careful aim and split it down the middle.

"Boy!" Willy screamed. "I am talkin' to you!"

"But I ain't listenin' to you," Josiah said.

"Maybe you'll listen to this," Willy said, uncoiling his whip. "You boys don't seem to respect nothin' else."

Josiah lowered his axe and turned to face Willy just as the whip snapped and wrapped around his right arm. Josiah grabbed the whip with his left hand and yanked the whip from Willy's hand.

"Now you done it, boy," Willy said, fumbling for the holstered pistol. Next to the whip, it was his prize possession. "Mr. Crenshaw don't stand for no trouble makin' niggers."

Willy finally pulled his pistol, but Josiah already had a hold of Willy's leg and dragged him from his horse like a limp deer carcass. Willy hit the ground with a thud that took his breath and knocked the pistol from his grip. Josiah kicked it as far away as he could. He picked up the whip.

"Don't you dare, boy," Willy gasped, finding just enough air to form the words. "Your black ass is already on the way south to pick cotton. Use that whip and you'll be one dead nigger."

"Don't matter much, do it?" Josiah said, picking up Willy like a sack of potatoes. Willy kicked and cursed but could not break Josiah's bear hug grip.

"Put me down, you black bastard, or you will die!"

"Ain't listenin'," Josiah said. "Not to you. Not to nobody. Not no more."

"Josiah," Noah yelled, running up along the row of brine pots he had been stoking. "You is in enough trouble. Put that white man down."

"Aint' listenin'", Josiah said, carrying Willy towards the brine pots.

Josiah's bear hug had Willy's arms tight to his side, but his feet kicked like a lynched rustler's.

"Don't you do it, Josiah. Don't you go and do it!" Noah yelled, realizing what Josiah intended to do. The brine pots were at full boil. "Hannah wouldn't want this,"

"Hannah be gone," Josiah said, still carrying Willy towards the brine pots, slow and steady with the pace of an execution walk.

"She be in your heart, Josiah. She always be in your heart. She not really gone. She tell my woman how much she love her man. She wouldn't want her man dead over killin' no white trash, now would she?"

At that, Josiah stopped. He could see Hannah, feel her gentle hand caress his face to make the worst day at the salt works melt away like lumps of brine. She would tell him that his spirit was too strong to be a slave. Mr. Crenshaw could lease your body, she said, but he didn't own your soul. Wait, she said. Wait. Someday your body be free like your soul.

Hannah vanished as Willy squirmed out of Josiah's arms like a frantic pig. He hit the ground still kicking and crawled towards the splitting stump that held an axe. Josiah showed no signs of stopping him. He was looking past Willy, past the boiling brine pots and the cluster of the trees that were almost cleared.

"Josiah," Noah said. "You gotta run. They do more to you now than just send you to the cotton fields. Get away before…"

Willy had the axe and was limping towards Josiah.

"You black-assed bastard son of a bitch," Willy said. "I don't care what Mr. Crenshaw says about not hurtin' his property. You are one dead nigger!"

A horse was ridden up hard behind Willy. He could hear it snort to a skidding halt. He half-turned to look, still keeping one eye on Josiah. It was Mr. Crenshaw and Willy did not like the look on his face.

"Put that damn axe down," John said with the authority he had thought he was losing. Sometimes he could still surprise himself. "Now!"

"But…," Willy sputtered.

"Now!"

Willy dropped the axe and glared back at Josiah who stared at Willy without blinking.

John had his Colt Paterson aimed at Josiah and slowly cocked the hammer. John knew he was not the best shot, but the target was large and close enough for him to feel confident he could at least slow the nigger down with the first shot, with four in reserve. He had heard that a new

Colt, the Walker, was available now to the Army, and they were using it in Mexico. Certainly his son-in-law was carrying one. John heard it weighed nearly five pounds and could easily take down the most rabid Mexican with its thirty-six caliber shot. But for now, his ten-year-old Paterson would have to do against this nigger.

"Boy," John said, pointing his pistol at Josiah's heart, "you have most definitely overstayed your welcome and overtaxed my patience. I hope you enjoy picking cotton. Who knows? You might even see that ugly woman of yours. Of course, she will most likely be even less desirable after her new master and overseer have their way with her. What was her name? Hannah, I believe."

"That's right," Willy said. "Hannah. I remember. Always thought it was too pretty a name for a nigger that looked like one of them travelin' circus monkeys."

Josiah started walking slowly towards Willy.

"Stop, boy," John said. "Do not test me. I will shoot."

"I ain't listin' to nobody," Josiah said.

"Maybe you will listen to this," John said, pulling the trigger. The pistol exploded. He missed.

Josiah knocked Willy hard to the ground and picked up the axe. John re-cocked and fired again, hitting Josiah in left forearm. Before he could re-cock, Josiah pulled him from his horse by his long coat. He let go of the pistol as he hit the ground. Josiah picked it up and tossed it aside. He stood over John, the axe raised in his unwounded arm as if preparing to split a log.

"Kill me and you die too," John said.

"I done told everybody," Josiah said as he started to swing the axe. "I ain't listenin' no more."

The shot startled Josiah. The bullet tore into his back just below the left shoulder blade. He lost aim of the axe. It went deep into John's left leg, six inches below the knee. Bone snapped and splintered like kindling as the sharply honed blade cut in. John drew a breath and held it. He was not going to scream out in front of a nigger. As Josiah pulled the axe up, another shot hit him in the lower back, lodging in his spine. His legs gave way as he crumpled to the ground.

"Get the nigger off of me," John screamed, releasing his breath.

Willy rolled Josiah off John's legs. He was still clutching the axe. Willy pulled it out of his hand with some effort.

"You are bleedin' bad, Mr. Crenshaw," Willy said.

"Make sure the nigger's dead," John said.

Josiah was lying on his back, his eyes half-opened.

"The bastard is still breathin'," Willy said, pointing the pistol at Josiah's heart. He didn't like to see headshots, even if it were a nigger.

"Hannah," Josiah whispered, then closed his eyes.

Willy pulled the trigger.

"What did the nigger say?" John asked.

"I don't know," Willy said. "I wasn't listenin'."

"Bandage this leg before I bleed to death. Use your shirt, filthy as it is," John said to Willy. "Then dispose of the body. I do hate to lose such a strong buck. He would have brought a fine price in Memphis."

"Don't worry none, Mr. Crenshaw. He probably wouldn't have made it to market. He was like a wild horse that can't be broken. Shootin' this nigger was probably the best thing we could do for you, and for him."

"Maybe you are right, Willy," John said, suddenly remembering his new overseer's name. "Now, stop this bleeding. I would rather not lose the leg."

Part Two

Thirteen

Beulah felt she had kept the promise Devlin insisted she make years before, doing what she needed to save Betsy and herself from being sold south to pick cotton or cut sugarcane. Beulah had taken Devlin's words to heart and bowed her head to all white folk, making sure Betsy did the same even if it took a kick to her shin. She looked away when spoken to and played the obedient house slave. She could polish silver to make mirrors of butter knives. Her pies were as renowned in Memphis as her mother's had been at Hickory Hill, especially her apple, which had won blue Ribbons for Mrs. Cruickshank at the First Baptist Church, the pride of Memphis with its new brick buildings erected on Second Street between Washington and Adams.

Beulah was biding her time until it was right. She had birthed her boy child, Seth, and was raising him with a kindness he took as natural while Beulah knew it was a rare thing in this world troubled by Lucifer. Seth was born six months after Mr. Cruikshank bought her and Betsy at the auction and brought them home to his wife like two bunnies in a basket for Easter. His wife had been requesting new help since Cornelia caught the Cholera and left her without a cook or housekeeper. Clara Cruickshank had tried desperately to save Cornelia, threatening her own life by tending to her, insisting that Dr. Paynter treat Cornelia, something he had reluctantly done by bleeding her and prescribing purges. Nothing helped. Dr. Paynter said he was not surprised Cornelia had contracted the sickness. Cholera was a disease born in the filthy living conditions of the Negro and the recently arrived Irish, Dr. Paynter reminded Clara. Pastor Cleary had preached the Sunday before Cornelia died that the current Cholera outbreak was the wrath of God for breaking His commandments, each sin the Pastor would describe with great zest in the smallest detail before beseeching his congregation to pray for forgiveness and deliverance. Clara had prayed but Cornelia continued to fail, wasting away even as Dr. Paynter bled her. Cornelia died on a Sunday morning while Clara was attending Pastor Cleary's fiery service that would have woke the Devil sleeping off a productive Saturday night.

~ ~ ~

Frederick Cruickshank carefully clipped the end from his cigar and placed it in the Carrera marble ashtray on his pipe stand, removed a match from his waistcoat pocket and struck it to life with a manicured thumbnail. He rolled the cigar as he drew flame into the moist tobacco, filing his library with a pungent cloud of smoke that drifted towards the filigree copper ceiling. He heard the front door open and close. Clara was home from church, early. He stubbed the cigar out and set it gently in the ashtray, rose painfully from his leather chair favoring his gouty foot and limped to slide the library's pocket doors closed behind him. Clara was not fond of his cigar smoke, regardless of how much he said he paid for his Cabañas imported from Cuba.

"Short service?" he asked, assisting Clara out of her heavy winter shawl. It could be cold on the ride to the First Baptist Church, even in the best carriage.

"No," Clara said, untying her bonnet. "Pastor Cleary was as exuberant as ever. I left early. I was anxious to see how about Cornelia."

"Cornelia is dead," Frederick said without a pause. "She apparently did not survive the night. Soon after you left for church I could hear wailing coming from her cabin. It made my skin crawl. Shrill cries like those of a banshee. It must have been her daughter, since she was soon knocking on the front door to inform me…"

"I must go…"

"You will do nothing of the kind, Clara. Our business with Cornelia is done. She was a fine house slave and served us well for many years. But it is not your place to grieve for her."

Clara looked at Frederick with astonishment. "You grieved for days after Otto died."

It still pained Frederick to think of losing Otto. He had never had a better bird dog, an English Setter with a naturally soft mouth but the gumption to stand his ground against bobcat and black bear when cornered.

"Otto was family," Frederick said.

"Otto was a dog," Clara said.

Frederick took a step towards Clara, his right hand clenching into a first. With effort, he let it relax.

"Cornelia was a slave," he said. "Nothing more."

"We shall never replace Cornelia."

"Don't speak such nonsense, Clara," Frederick said. "My new bird dog has proven adequate, if not equal to Otto. But he may be, given time. We have an abundance of slaves passing through Memphis, considering the expansion of cotton fields in Mississippi. I have first pick of the slaves, being it is my auction. You will have a fine house slave. She might take a little training, like Franz has.

It has taken longer for him to learn not to bite into the pheasant, but he is improving. And there is something to be said about training a new dog, or a new house slave, to meet your needs, to do your bidding. Very satisfying. I am confident that soon you will forget Cornelia."

Clara made no reply. She was holding back tears for the years she and Cornelia had shared. Frederick is a man, she reminded herself. To him a hunting dog merits more affection than any slave.

"Slaves are children that never grow up," Frederick continued. "They require the white man to do their thinking. They cannot be treated as equals. That would be blasphemy against the Bible, Clara."

Clara was thinking of Cornelia. Her daughter would be washing her body now, dressing her in her Sunday best, preparing her for burial. Burial. Clara had no idea where slaves were buried in Memphis. She was embarrassed she did not know. Cornelia had been with her for many years. Ever since she and Frederick sold their tobacco farm in Virginia and moved to Memphis. Slaves who died on the farm were buried in fields behind their cabins. There must be a cemetery for slaves somewhere in Memphis. She would find out. Frederick had buried Otto in Clara's garden, removing a bed of her prize English roses. He had masons build a small mausoleum; had a plaque carved with a sentimental quote from Robert Burns. Cornelia deserved as much respect. Clara would not discuss it with Frederick. For once, she would follow her heart.

"Clara," Frederick said. "Clara. Are you listening to me?"

"Listening," Clara repeated. She wasn't.

"Good," Frederick said, taking the word to mean she was. He continued. "More acreage is being committed to cotton in the south every day. More cotton brings a higher demand for slaves. No telling how much plantations buyers will pay for my slaves. The future looks bright,

Clara. Cotton is King and I serve the King as its proud nobleman!"

"I'm going to help Cornelia's daughter," Clara said, walking towards the door. "I can't even remember her daughter's name. Isn't that sad?"

"Clara," Frederick said.

"I'll make dinner when I return," Clara said, closing the door behind her.

Frederick stared at the shut door. Otto had obeyed him. So does Franz. Where had he gone wrong with Clara?

~ ~ ~

Frederick had brought Beulah and Betsy home from the auction as a surprise for Clara. He had not told her beforehand that Devlin had recommended the twins, one of them with child, born of and raised by a house servant who had taught them their skills and good manners. Frederick would also never tell Clara that they had been sold into slavery from Illinois, a so-called free state, taken from their mother and sold to lessen their master's debt. They were slaves now. In a slave state. Their history started the day they moved into Cornelia's quarters behind the house and assumed her chores. The twins appeared submissive and docile, had no flogging scars to betray inbred willfulness. They possessed good teeth, clear eyes and strong limbs.

Frederick had also surprised the slave dealer, a filthy river rat who called himself Frank, by taking his first offer without a haggle. Frederick did not like the tedious game and money was no object to him, since he had seen the lot in the pen and knew his profit would be handsome. The two girls were young enough for Clara to keep for years with the bonus of a baby she could spoil as the child they had never been blessed with, as long as she remembered they were slaves and treated them accordingly.

~ ~ ~

"Your boy is growing so fast," Clara said, wistfully remembering when she would open her arms for Seth to run into her embrace. He called her ma'am now and kept a distance. Clara's husband assured Seth knew his place. "How old is Seth?"

"He be seven," Beulah said, wiping her forehead with the back of her hand, trying not to dust her face with flour. She turned the pie dough over on the board, dusted it with more flour, and began rolling it thin and into a perfect circle.

"Seven. Astonishing. My, the years are fleeting. You do have a way with pastry," Clara said.

"And you keep your fingers out of it," Beulah said to Seth, who had come into the kitchen from the yard, tore a piece of pie dough from the perfect round and savored it like a pull of taffy.

"I chopped all the kindlin'," he said, licking his fingers.

"Now, what Betsy got to do if you be takin' all her chores?"

"I like choppin' wood. Look," Seth said, pushing back his sleeve to expose his arm. Beulah squeezed his bicep.

"You be strong as…" Beulah stopped. She almost said Rueben. Her mother's man who looked after her and Betsy as if they were his own after their father, Silas, was sold south to the cotton fields, so long ago Beulah remembered nothing of him but the name some white man gave him. Mr. Crenshaw said he needed the money, but Beulah knew, for Mr. Crenshaw, there was something he hated about watching a family of Negroes raising children and going about their business like they were good as white folks. It made him angry. And nothing seemed to give him more pleasure than selling Negroes, one at a time, to break those families up. And here was something in Rueben's dignity that caused Zeke to kill him one day out of meanness. But Zeke be dead now, shot through the head by a slaver, Beulah remembered. And that be comforting. "Rueben."

"Who Rueben be?" Seth asked, rolling his sleeve down.

"A kind man I once know," Beulah said. "And strong as an ox."

Beulah looped the dough over the rolling pin, picked it up from the board and carefully placed it over the pie dish filled with apple slices dusted with a fortune of exotic spices. Beulah reckoned she could live for months on what Mrs. Cruickshank spent to make this one pie. Beulah could feel herself slipping into what Devlin called her glower, a fancy word for allowing her face to betray the dark moods she usually hid with the pleasantries of a simple fool. Devlin told her never to reveal her cleverness so she had adopted a perpetual smile and cultivated the compliant qualities of the weak-minded. But her true nature begged for air and sometimes rose to the surface without bidding. Yes, Mrs. Cruickshank had treated Seth like a grandson since he was born, especially since she had never had children of her own. But Beulah also knew that as soon as Seth was old enough, Mr. Cruickshank would be taking him to auction and selling him south, to make money, to deprive her of her child and to show Clara that Seth was nothing but a slave. Beulah was biding her time, but time was running out.

"Betsy, aren't you finished polishing that silver yet?" Clara asked. Betsy was sitting at the pine-topped kitchen table, holding a three-pronged salad fork, gazing out the window.

"No, ma'am. I got the forks to finish," Betsy said, wiping silver polish from the utensil with tarnish-blackened rag.

"Get a clean rag," Clara said. She sighed as she usually did, dealing with Betsy. It amazed Clara that she was Beulah's twin. They bore little physical resemblance and even less when it came to work. "The silverware needs to be finished for setting the table. We have an important dinner guest tonight."

"Yes'm," Betsy said. "I be done in plenty of time."

"Betsy."

"Yes'm?"

"New polish rag?"

"Yes'm."

"I be grateful you and Mr. Cruickshank keep Betsy and Seth and me together," Beulah said, balancing the pie plate on her fingertips and cutting off a ring of dough. She set it down, pinching the edge of the crust to seal it, then cut slits in the top to vent the steam from the bubbling apples. It was ready to bake, as soon as she lit the shaved kindling to ignite the splits Seth had chopped and the wood oven reached temperature. "No one know better than me how lazy Betsy be."

"There have been times when Mr. Cruickshank…" Clara began, then thought the better of it.

Beulah could feel her face falling into its glower again. She went to the stove and lit it, blowing on the flame to spread it through the shavings. The kindling sticks caught with the crackle of seasoned wood. She shut the firebox and adjusted the draft, letting smoke circulate through the oven on its way out the chimney. Beulah's mother had taught her well, even though Patsy had always felt her daughter was not paying attention. Beulah longed now to be scolded by her mother. Her mother had been her life. Now Beulah was clinging like a prisoner of war to thoughts of escape, if only to see her mother one more time, if her mother was alive after more than seven years. And yes, she would take Betsy with her and Seth, dangerous as it would be. Her mother had always expected Beulah to watch out for Betsy. They were twins, but Beulah had grown older in a way that Betsy never would be. Now it was time to prepare her dumplings for Mr. Cruickshank and his dinner guest. Patsy also thought Beulah hadn't paid attention when she demonstrated the making of her prize dumplings, but she had. Every detail. Pie and dumplings. Since being sold down river by Mr. Crenshaw, that was all Beulah had left of her mother. Pie and dumplings, and the sound of her voice as she scolded Beulah, and the same gentle lullabies she had used to soothe Seth to sleep when he was a baby.

~ ~ ~

"These were the most delectable dumplings I ever tasted," Jonah Johnson said, leaning back from the dining table to pat his substantial belly.

"No one makes them like our Beulah" Clara said to her dinner guest. "I hope you saved some room for her apple pie."

"I most certainly have, ma'am. And I assume it is equally delectable."

"If not more so. Then brandy and cigars in the study with Mr. Cruickshank, I assume" Clara said, directing her comment towards Frederick who had picked up his bowl and drank the remaining chicken broth from the dumplings like a saucer of coffee, setting the bowl down then dabbing his lips with his linen napkin.

"Yes, ma'am," Jonah said. "Your husband and I have some mutual undertakings to discuss."

"And brandy is a fine lubrication for the machineries of commerce. But now, some of Beulah's apple pie, which is, I assure you, Mr. Johnson, just as delectable as her dumplings," Frederick said before letting out a loud belch.

Beulah overheard the dinner guest's praise from the kitchen. She couldn't help but smile. She had heard Mr. Crenshaw say that about her mother's dumplings back at Hickory Hill. She had very few fond memories of Hickory Hill, or of Mr. Crenshaw, but praise for her mother's cooking was one of them.

Beulah went to the windowsill where her pies were cooling. They were ready to serve. Picking up the first of the three pies, she saw Devlin coming in the back gate and down the yard. Chickens scattered as Seth ran to him with joy, as if seeing his father come home from the fields, although he had never known his father, or many men, mostly being raised his short life by his mother, her sister and Mrs. Cruickshank. Seth sensed there was something besides the color of his skin that made him different, and that the affection Mrs. Cruickshank showered on him was not free. He had overheard Mr. Cruickshank say to a neighbor that little Pickaninnies were useless until they were old enough to be sold. Seth asked his mother what Pickaninnies were and she had told him they were beasts of burden, like mules. Seth didn't like overhearing Mr. Cruickshank, it made him feel as if he had done something wrong and would be whipped with a sapling stick, never knowing what it was he had done to deserve it. His mother never spanked him. One look of disapproval from her was worse than any switch, and a smile was better than any piece of her apple pie, usually an uneaten slice scraped from the plate of one of the church ladies after a Sunday gathering, since gluttony was a sin, although their husbands may not have been reading the same Bible.

"Your boy certainly is growing," Devlin said, taking a bare-knuckler's stance and pretending to box. Seth bobbed and weaved away from a phantom blow and punched Devlin in the stomach as he had been taught. Devlin bent over in mock pain.

"He must take after his father," Devlin said. His mother being so petite."

"Petite?"

"You are no Mammy, Beulah. How old is he now?"

"Old enough to do his chores," Beulah said. "Seth? Go chop some wood for the breakfast cook fire."

"But…" Seth began.

"Mr. Doyle and me gots to talk," Beulah said, sensing that he had come for more than a slice of pie.

"Yes'm," Seth said, heading for the woodpile. He picked up the axe and looked back with a scowl.

"That boy do have a mind of his own," Beulah said.

"I wonder where he got that? Maybe from his pretty mother."

Beulah was familiar with the ways of men. Every one of the salt workers at Hickory Hill had considered himself to be the bull elk worthy of his own harem. Devlin's words made her wary, the way he talked kindly to her and seemed to want nothing more. She never could figure Devlin out. He was different. Even for a white man, he was different.

"You is outta luck if you be lookin' for dumplins'," Beulah said. "Ain't none left. Not the way Mr. Cruickshank and his guest be eatin' tonight. There be pie. I always bake more than…"

"No," Devlin said. "I had my supper. I want to talk to you."

"What you want to talk to me about?" Beulah asked. "Somethin' bad happen?"

"Not yet. But…"

"Mr. Cruickshank meanin' to sell us, ain't he?" Beulah asked. That was always her first and worst fear. She had sensed the foreboding. Even Mrs. Cruickshank had changed in the way she treated Seth. Like she was practicing for when he was gone.

"It seems so. The slave market is so good I have overheard him telling Mrs. Cruickshank it is not profitable to keep you three as house slaves when he can sell you all south and make a tidy profit. And now that Seth is getting old enough for the fields…"

South. Beulah's blood froze at the unspoken word. She had vowed never to say the Devil's word out loud. It was like conjuring up Satan. She had done her best keeping

Seth from hearing the word since he was born. If someone ever did utter the word in front of Seth and he asked what it meant, Beulah would act as if she had never heard the word before and had no idea of its meaning. South. It was an evil curse; another name for Hell.

"Mrs. Cruickshank would never let that happen to Seth," Beulah said, but she wasn't convincing herself.

"Frederick Cruickshank is the master," Devlin reminded her. "He indulges Clara, but business comes first. I have heard him say that many times. Selling slaves south is his business and a dealer has made him an offer for you and Seth and Betsy he feels he cannot turn down."

"What dealer?"

"Jonah Johnson. A representative for a sugar cane plantation in Louisiana. He was invited to dinner tonight. You made dumplings and baked the pies for him. He tries to act the gentleman, but his coats miss buttons and his shirts fray at the cuffs and his ties have not been in style in years. He attempts proper speech, but his words cannot help but betray his station. He is one step removed from trash. He is here to finalize the purchase. Mr. Cruickshank has instructed me to deliver you. The plantation he contracted with is desperate for sugarcane cutters."

Beulah was too horrified to speak. She just slowly shook her head, looking at Devlin like a quizzical dog waiting for a command.

"Tomorrow morning we are to leave. For dealers, speed is of the essence. However, I am not taking you to Louisiana. Do not tell Betsy this, but I am taking you up river. North."

"North," Beulah repeated. North. That blessed word like a promise of salvation, a treasure stored up through despair now plummeting from heaven, a prize she had come to believe she would never win. "We is goin' north."

"Beulah," Clara said, bursting into the kitchen. "The men want their pie.

"Yes'm," Beulah said with a touch of repentance. "Me and Mr. Doyle was talkin' 'bout...how much Seth be growin'..."

"The pie, Beulah? The men have business to discuss."

"Yes'm," Beulah said, glancing at Devlin. Business. The business in which she and her son and her sister were to be bought and sold like bales of cotton, bundles of cane, plow horses, split apart like the kindling Seth was chopping in Frederick Cruikshank's yard...

"Pie?" Clara repeated.

"Yes'm," Beulah said. "I be slicin' it now."

Fourteen

Elias knew he could break the bronco, but he also knew the boys didn't like it when the nigger made it look too damn easy. He would give them a show.

"Ready, boy?" Abel Picket asked, pulling the Mustang towards the corral fence with the rope Hackamore harness. As the Mustang crashed against the fence, Elias found the gap and dropped onto the saddle, taking the rope from Abel and pulling it tight to his waist. The Mustang spun in a leaping circle towards the center of the corral.

"That nigger knows how to ride," Jack Gallagher said to Abel.

"Better'n any runaway slave I ever seen," Abel said. "Most niggers ain't never been on a horse, much less broke a Mustang."

Elias gave sway to the sorrel stallion as it turned and reared, attempting to fling him from his back like he was a mountain lion that had dropped off a canyon ledge. Old Bear had been a good teacher. Do not resist, he told Elias, do not force. Nahahevoha will tire himself and join you under your guidance. But he will fight giving up his savagery to those who believe that they can be his master by being more savage. Even if he is broken, as the whites say, by a cruel rider, his hate will never diminish. He will show this hate in his eyes as he looks to the far hills, and as his ears twist forward, not listening, only responding to kicks from spurs and yanks on the bit that leaves the sharp taste of cold iron on his tongue.

Elias was singing a prayer Old Bear had taught him, a song of praise to Nahahevoha, Sacred Dog, what the whites called horse. Before Maheo'o sent Sacred Dog, Hotame, little dogs, pulled the drag sleds, wore the packs and saddlebags, helping to follow the Hotoa'e` across the plains. When Sacred Dog appeared from the south, five generations ago, creatures the Cheyenne had never seen, their lives soon intertwined like the roots of short grass—impenetrable and fused as one growth. Old Bear taught Elias that his pony needed praise. His pony liked it when Elias spoke of him to others around the fire, telling of how brave he had been running down the buffalo, ignoring its horns, bringing Elias close enough for the kill shot. Old Bear had told Elias to tell his pony about himself, his victories and his defeats. The pony will understand and the bond will be complete.

"Don't know how he stays on them Mustangs," Abel said. He was perched on the corral railing, prepared to bolt if the thrashing hooves aimed at his head. He took his sweat-stained hat off, leaned back and slapped it on his dusty chaps. "The nigger ain't human."

Elias held steady, holding the rope rein tight enough to remain seated but loose enough to assure the pony that his intentions held no violence. The pony responded, each kick less vicious, each circle turning slower. Elias released the tension, his hand relaxing on the rope, but firm enough to provide a gentling control. He finished singing the song as the pony shook his main, gave one last snort and settled down to a trot, once around the corral. Elias nudged him to the fence where Abel and Jack stood, not trying to disguise their astonishment. Jack jumped down into the corral.

"Toss me the rope," Jack said. "I'll take him now."

Elias knew Jack would be the one to force in the iron bit and buckle the belts. Elias understood that it must be done, if the pony was to be useful to the Cowboys, although he had come to prefer the Cheyenne way, without a saddle, running the wild ponies into deep river water and letting them buck until they grew tired to form a union of human being and horse, cooperation instead of conquest. He handed the rope to Jack, dismounted and stoked the Mustang's neck. Elias left the corral and walked back to the bunkhouse. He was hungry.

~ ~ ~

Driven south by the Sioux, the Cheyenne had renounced any crop plantings that bound them to the earth. They followed where the sacred buffalo lead, scornful of the whites that travelled across the prairies in rolling lodges, covered with stiff blankets, pulled by short-haired buffalo with long horns. Moons before, the hairy-ones had appeared, one at a time, seeking beaver from woodland rivers, hunters so dirty it was difficult to tell their color. But more would come to take their place, men who believed that the buffalo were not sacred and only good for hides to sell to other white men far to the east and across a great water as their stripped carcasses rotted to become food for vultures and flies. The recently arrived whites sought after the shining dust and would kill for it, would die for it, claiming ownership of the holy hills and rivers that held it, even though the earth could not be possessed any more than the thunderheads that blessed all with rain could be purchased or persuaded with strings of ponies. To these whites, all things were dead. The earth, the animals and especially human beings who were not white were already dead to their cruel eyes. Old Bear had told Elias that since the white man believed this, they could pile buffalo bones up in hills to bleach white as their skin in the sun with no shame. They could rub out Cheyenne villages of women, children and old man and feel no shame. To the white man,

Old Bear said, death was a starving dog that needed much food.

Old Bear was Medicine Man and War Chief. As a child he felt the Spirit that walked in the short grass and in the sun that rode across the sky. He heard the Spirit singing over the lodges on the wind that cleared the clouds for the stars and the moon. He heard the Spirit whispering in the flowing waters that refreshed his blessed Human Beings and their thirsty ponies. And he heard his name the Spirit gave to him, and his purpose. He was Old Bear, ancient and strong, surviving long winters to rise again each spring to teach the young.

But for all his power, wisdom and knowledge, Old Bear had no defense against the enemy that had crept from lodge to lodge on fox paws, circled his camp with the silence of a hawk, searching with keen eyes, seeking out prey to attack with devastating speed.

Elias and Caleb were living among the Cheyenne, traded to Old Bear's tribe by the renegade Shawnee who had captured them for a few ponies, when cholera first attacked with the tenacity of a wolf pack culling a herd of antelope. It took the infants and the aging first, the woman and the children just as the white soldiers did, but it also took the warriors, the strongest Human Beings who had never known defeat and had collected coup like Everlasting Plants and bark for medicine. Nothing yet had worked to defeat this invisible enemy. Old Bear called the braves who were still untouched by this evil to his lodge. He had a plan.

"Howling Hawk," Old Bear said to the young brave sitting to his right, first in a circle of warriors, his face lit by the dancing buffalo dung fire. "How many coup have you collected?"

Howling Hawk sat tall, his face stern to prevent the pride he felt from being revealed in the fire's flickering light. "Many, Old Bear."

"Our new enemy is a coward, but very clever," Old Bear began. He paused, looking deep into the flames. He knew his young warriors were growing restless, but they required a patience they found difficult. They had much to learn and it was for him to teach.

"Old Bear..." Howling Hawk began, regretting his interruption when Old Bear turned his stare from the fire to him.

"Howling Hawk," Old Bear continued, gladdened to see the shame the young warrior could not hide on his face. "Your name is well deserved. Your cry fills the hearts of enemies with fear and your skill with the war club and lance proves those fears to be true. Because of these things, you are worthy of what I ask."

Howling Hawk leaned back, thankful of the tribute, but wary of what Old Bear might propose.

"Stand," Old Bear commanded. "Go, bring back your war lance. I will purify you and your weapon with smoke rising to the Spirit. Then I will tell you what you are to do."

Howling Hawk left the lodge uneasy. What was it Old Bear would have him do? Old Bear was Medicine Man as well as Warrior Chief. His powers were legend. But recently, the young warriors were talking among themselves that Old Bear was showing signs of age. Factions were forming. Some defended him; others thought it was time for Old Bear to give up being Warrior Chief. Let him mix the roots and powders. Let him chant for rain and victory. But there would be no victories if he lost the confidence of his warriors to lead them into battle. And it was beginning to happen. Old Bear was becoming an old woman sickened by the sight of taken scalps.

Howling Hawk pushed aside the buffalo hide door and crouched into his lodge. It was empty. The fire was old and dying. He and Sweet Water had no children, yet, but still he was looking forward to teaching his oldest boy the ways of the bow, the club, the lance, and the coup. Girls would be for Sweet Water to raise and teach the ways of the Human Beings. But with the shape of her hips, he had overheard the older women gossiping that Sweet Water should bear him many strong sons. He was smiling as he picked up his lance, appreciated its balance and recalled gaining the deep battle scars that resisted the honing of its edge he performed after each fight. His victories were many. He carried it back to Old Bear's lodge.

Smoke swirled up to where the lodge poles met, drawn through the vent by a steady wind. Howling Hawk handed the lance to Old Bear who examined it as if he had never seen it before. He stood and gestured for Howling Hawk to come closer. Howling Hawk obeyed. Old Bear may be failing as a warrior, Howling Hawk thought, but his Medicine had only grown stronger as he sang to the Spirit and the smoke from the sacred fire twisted towards his hands that held the lance, hesitating, swirling around like dogs begging for affection, carrying the earth's scent, strong and intoxicating. Old Bear's chants faded. Old Bear offered the war club to Howling Hawk who received it as a newly-born son. At first he failed to recognize the lance. Something was not the same. But the scars were similar, although they looked deeper, more defined, fresher.

"Lame Fawn..." Old Bear began. More words did not come.

Howling Hawk looked up from admiring his war club. Old Bear was rigid. Howling Hawk knew that Old Bear's wife, Lame Fawn, had been fighting the invisible enemy for days. Now he could see in Old Bear's eyes that the invisible enemy had won its coup. Any doubts Howling Hawk felt about Old Bear's ability to lead dissipated with the smoke that no longer lingered on the lance but drifted straight towards the sky.

"Put on your war paint," Old Bear said. "Wear your best war shirt. Mount your bravest pony and ride three circles towards the sun around the lodges. Your cry must be strong. You must startle the Great Spirit into paying attention if he has turned away from Human Beings and has lost interest in us. If the sacred war lance will not defeat the invisible enemy we must wake the Great Spirit to beg forgiveness for whatever we have done to anger him. The evil he sends is like no other. Even the Blue Coats show their faces as they slaughter our women and children and old men. This enemy remains hidden."

Howling Hawk felt the weight of what he was being asked. Old Bear's grief for Lame Fawn had made it impossible for him to challenge the invisible enemy in battle. His medicine remained strong but not his body. Howling Hawk was to be the new Warrior Chief.

"You have been chosen, Howling Hawk," Old Bear said. He pointed to his War Bonnet hanging from a lodge pole over his buffalo hide bed. It was nearly tall as Howling Hawk, a headdress trailing eagle feathers woven with shimmering beads, ribbons of blue cloth and yellow insignias. "Wear it as you defeat the invisible enemy. My sister, Walks Beside, is preparing Lame Fawn. I must go to her now, but I will watch your ride."

Old Bear stooped through the low door. Howling Hawk followed, hurrying to his lodge with leaping strides, struggling to compose his flailing energy into a compact strength, not letting the War Bonnet's holy feathers touch the ground fouled by pony and dog.

"Spotted Horse," he said to Elias, using the Cheyenne name Old Bear had given to him when he and Caleb became members of the tribe three winters before. "Bring my war pony and prepare him for battle."

"War Party?" Elias asked. He was sitting on a blanket outside his lodge, restringing his buffalo-hunting bow, testing it like a fiddler tuning strings.

"Old Bear has honored me with his War Bonnet. I am now War Chief. I am to kill the invisible enemy, alone."

"It is an honor you deserve, Howling Hawk. I will fetch your best war pony."

Howling Hawk smiled and began striding towards his lodge. He stopped and called back. "Spotted Horse. How is Mud Dog?"

Old Bear had also given Caleb a Cheyenne name. Mud Dog. It suited him. He only took baths if he fell in the river and after his capture and trade to the Cheyenne, his loud and rowdy ways fled inside and he became subdued as a beaten mongrel, sullen and silent so that when the sickness took him down, few noticed at first. He refused any medication, lying on his fouled buffalo skins, sleeping or watching the smoke of the fire Elias set and tended rise and escape.

"He wants to die," Elias said. Howling Hawk nodded.

"He knows it is his time. You have a good heart, Spotted Horse. Not many men would tend to another as you have."

"He has no woman," Elias said. Howling Hawk nodded. He did not know if Spotted Horse was like other black-skinned men, since Spotted Horse and Mud Dog were the first to live with the tribe. He had heard they were often not worth the contrariness they showed when told to work. The Crows made better slaves. But Howling Hawk had come to like and admire Spotted Horse. Especially his way with ponies. Old Bear had seen something in Spotted Horse, too. Instead of turning the two Shawnee renegades away, he traded three ponies for the two black-skinned men they were bartering. He later told Howling Hawk that the one who came to be called Spotted Horse had the spirit of a warrior, and Howling Hawk agreed. He could not say the same for Mud Dog. He avoided horses the way he avoided work. When he talked, thinking he could speak like Humans, it was the yelp of a hound. Spotted horse had been eager to truly learn the Human tongue. Soon, the tribe was forgetting he was a slave, or even that his skin was Black. He was a Human Being as the other remained a Mud Dog.

"I will fetch your pony while you prepare," Elias said.

Howling Hawk nodded and strode off to his lodge. His steps were longer. His heart pounded but his face kept the grim determination that had carried him victorious through many battles. He did not expect to die, but if he did, it was a good day for it.

Howling Hawk could hear his pony stamping its hooves outside his lodge. He was anxious as his pony to face the enemy. He had applied war paint to his face slowly and with precision—the red lightning zigzag across his forehead, flash of the Thunderbird's eyes, bringing power and speed to the warrior; the red handprints diagonal from one cheek to the other across the mouth, the source of energy and countless coups in hand to hand combat. His pony wore the same paint. Howling Hawk had instructed Elias how and Spotted Horse had applied the red hands to the pony's shoulders and the lightning over his eyes with the blood-red intensity of the warrior. Spotted Horse was not yet Cheyenne, Howling Hawk thought, but he was becoming one.

Howling Hawk burst out of his lodge, handing Elias the feathered war lance. His eyes looked away to something in the distance. He mounted the pony with a contained rage. Elias handed him the pony's rope bridle and then the lance. Howling Hawk never looked at Spotted Horse. He pulled the pony back. It reared in a half circle in a maneuver Elias felt would cause him to slide from the pony's slick back. He reined the pony down, observing the sun as it rose above the lodge where Mud Dog lay dying. He nodded to Elias, raised his lance and released a whirlwind of war cries. His pony knew the moment, surging into full gallop through the camp before turning to circle the lodges. Those well enough to stand walked out to watch the sight of

Howling Hawk prodding his pony into full charge around the village, his lance stabbing and slashing at the invisible enemy, his cries waking feverish babies into wails.

"Spotted Horse," Old Bear called to Elias.

Old Bear was standing straighter, Elias thought. His burden was lighter.

"Come, Spotted Horse," Old Bear said to Elias. "Lame Fawn is at rest. Let us watch Howling Hawk defeat the Invisible Enemy.

Elias followed Old Bear between the lodges to the open plain of Buffalo grass. He could hear Howling Hawk on the far side of the village; his war whoops and the pounding hooves of his pony. A strange heat flushed Elias' face. Howling Hawk's cries were more than human. Elias felt the presence of a vengeful healing as if the earth had begun tilting back into balance. Howling Hawk rounded the far lodge. Elias' eyes could not leave Howling Hawk's painted face. It was resolute, almost arrogant, blazing, yet distorted with the horror of a dreadful dream.

Howling Hawk's pony galloped with the urgency of battle, thundering towards where Elias and Old Bear stood. Watching transfixed, Elias saw a camp dog appear between two lodges. It snarled, baring its teeth at the approaching pony, its matted fir the color of dung. It lunged towards the pony with unexpected power and speed, snapping at the pony's hooves. Howling Hawk broke his trance, leaning to stab his lance at the dog. The pony reared back, its legs thrashing the air before smashing down. The dog yelped once and fell silent under the hooves. The pony reared up again, Howling Hawk fighting for control with the hand not grasping the war lance. The pony lurched away from the bloody dog, stumbling and falling. Howling Hawk released the lance, grabbing at the reins. The pony tumbled on its right flank, frantic, crushing Howling Hawk under its full weight, struggling up to resume a lame trot around the lodges. Old Bear turned and walked back to his lodge, seeing the broken war lance that had pieced Howling Hawk's heart. Elias could not move.

~ ~ ~

"Caleb," Elias whispered, leaning over his friend who looked shriveled as a slab of dried buffalo.

"Mud Dog," Elias whispered. Caleb opened his eyes.

"Is I dead?" Caleb asked? "I feel dead."

"You ain't dead," Elias said. "But you is still very sick."

Caleb began a coughing fit that lasted a full minute. Elias helped him roll to his side.

"Thought you told me that wild buck was going to kill...what you call it?" Caleb asked after regaining enough breath to speak.

"The Invisible Enemy."

"That be it," Caleb said. "Well. Did the buck kill it?"

"It killed him," Elias said. His grim face told Caleb it was not a joke.

"He be dead?"

"Dead."

"You told me Indians got strong medicine," Caleb said.

"Maybe before the white man come."

"Thought we was done with masters," Caleb said. "Thought we be free of 'em."

"They be the Devil, Caleb. If'n they can't whip us like beasts to do their work, they send their disease to kill us. Same with the Cheyenne, Old Bear tell me. Ain't no Invisible Enemy before the white man came. Cheyenne never get the cholera, or the pox before the white man. Never lost their spirits to whiskey. Now..."

Elias' voice trailed off as Caleb rolled on his back, his breathing rattling to a gurgle, slowing to stop. His unblinking eyes stared towards the opening where the poles crossed and the cloud-mottled sky accepted the smoke from the lodge's dying fire.

~ ~ ~

"Elias," Abel Pickett repeated, louder. "You gone deaf, boy?"

Elias looked up, his spoon still hovering over the empty tin plate. "No sir, Mr. Pickett," he said. "Just thinkin' 'bout..."

"You spend too much time thinkin', boy. Don't do no one no good. Just get you all confused like. Bet you thinkin' bout them redskins, ain't you?"

"They was my family for three years, Mr. Pickett. Until the cholera took 'em all." Elias said. "Treated Caleb and me better'n..."

"Can't complain 'bout the way you been treated round here, now can you boy? We took you in when you showed up with that string of Cheyenne ponies. You was near dead and skinnier than a fence rail. Pukin' and shittin' like a newborn."

"That what I been told," Elias said. His memories of how he got from Old Bear's village to the ranch jumbled and mixed-up as a fever dream.

"I know you been treated bad, boy. Seen the old welts on your back. But you don't think I'm dumb enough to run off my best bronco buster I got just 'cause he's a nigger, do you?"

"No sir, Mr. Pickett."

"Now you finish with your grub, get your black ass back to that corral. We got another bronco for you to bust. Hear tell he's a meaner son of a bitch than the last one," Abel said.

Fifteen

"Michael. Michael!" Elizabeth said, shaking her husband. "Wake up. You will frighten the children again."

"I shall have no Rackensackers in my Company!!" Michael yelled as he sat up in bed. "Advance…"

"Michael," Elizabeth repeated. "You are home. The war is over."

Captain Michael Kelly Lawler first led his company from Shawneetown to guard the supply route from Vera Cruz to General Winfield Scott's Army during the Mexican War. After the fall of Vera Cruz his company was discharged and he returned to Equality. Later he was asked by Governor Thomas Ford of Illinois to organize a company of riflemen and served in the campaign to take Matamoros, Tamaulipas. That was more than seven years ago.

"Wars are never over," Michael said. "Battles are won, or lost. But the war never ends."

Elizabeth nodded as if she understood. She knew her words would be of no comfort to her husband. He was lingering in Mexico, still commanding his troops and would never fully return home. She prayed there would be no more wars since she knew Michael would be first to volunteer. Michael could not resist the call of duty, to God or to the country his father had wed his family to like a new spirited wife after his first had passed from a long and wasting sickness. His family would need to be understanding of his duty, Michael would tell Elizabeth and the children. Elizabeth would never understand.

Michael pulled the quilt back and sat on the edge of the feather bed. It was too soft. He missed his army cots and sleeping rolls spread on the sun-hardened ground of Mexico. He felt smothered, drowning in the down pillows. He loved his wife and children. He was a good husband and father. He was good at business and even tolerated Elizabeth's father who disapproved of his religion and most everything he did, except making money for his financial endeavors. But, by God, if another war broke out, and there was always talk of the states fighting each other over the right to expand slavery into the territories, he would be first to recruit troops and volunteer. He was an Irish warrior, first and foremost. He searched for his slippers. The floor was cold as the ground outside that lay dusted with the first snow of the season that was still falling.

"Michael…" Elizabeth began to protest his getting up so early, then thought the better of it. He will start the fire, she thought. At least the house would be warm when she got up to assist Ruth in the kitchen. She knew there was nothing she could do for Michael. He fought his demons alone with toil and sweat and the complications of commerce. Less time to think, he would tell Elizabeth, as long as my hands and my mind are busy, which meant he often took chores away from Ruth, like starting the morning fire. It was one of the reasons Ruth was the only house help. She cooked and cleaned and assisted with raising the children, but Michael did most everything else.

Michael trudged through drifts to the outhouse for his morning duty, still wearing his nightclothes. He enjoyed testing himself with the elements, ignoring the chill that penetrated his silk robe and cotton nightshirt as he had thrived on desert heat while other soldiers fainted. He finished his business and returned to the warm house, refreshed. The fire he had set blazed in the fireplace. Ruth was up and beginning to kindle a fire in the stove. Michael would wash, shave, dress, have breakfast and coffee, kiss Elizabeth and the children goodbye and ride into town. As the sun rose higher behind a thick covering of cloud, he could see it looked like more snow, but that would not keep him from his work. His horse understood that and did not protest any weather. He seemed to enjoy the challenge as much as Michael.

~ ~ ~

"What are you doing in town on a day like this, Captain Lawler? Thought this snow would've kept you home?"

"You are new, Mr. Smith, and unaware that I never let a little inclement weather impede commerce. Just take my horse to the Livery Stable, Mr. Smith. I'll get the fire going today. And make the coffee." Michael said, dismounting.

"Yes sir, Captain Lawler," Bobby Smith said. Bobby liked the way the Captain called him Mr. Smith, even though he was just sixteen, the new office boy hired to stoke the pot-bellied stove and sweep the floor, make the coffee and deliver messages. Bobby took the reins and led Michael's horse away.

Not too bright a young man, Michael thought as he unlocked and entered his cold office. But Bobby has proven loyal and there was no greater quality in a man than loyalty. Bobby follows orders without question. He would make a good soldier. Michael caught himself. Elizabeth constantly reprimanded him for speaking in military terms. But he saw no harm in it since, as he would tell her, life is a series of battles in a war against many tenacious advisories. Elizabeth would ignore his proclamations and begin a conversation about the children, but he knew he was correct. The war never ends.

~ ~ ~

"Mr. Lawler," John Hart Crenshaw said to Michael as he entered the office, swiveled on his wooden leg and closed the door to the snow that swirled in behind him. His crutch thumped on the floor planks as he moved towards the coat rack. John was the only one in town who did not call Michael Captain Lawler, making a point of emphasizing the word Mister. He removed his broad-brimmed hat, whacked it against his good leg to remove the layered snow and hung it over Michael's imported Derby on top of the coat tree.

"Let me help you..." Michael began, sliding his chair back from the desk to stand.

"No need, Mr. Lawler," John said, leaning the crutch against the wall and removing his buffalo skin coat. "I am not a cripple. One leg is just slightly shorter than the other. Didn't think you would make it to town today."

"You say that every time it snows," Michael said, guarding against letting the irritation he felt color his conversation. "Never once have I missed a day of work."

John retrieved his crutch and hobbled solemnly to his side of the partner's desk, attempting to conceal any difficulty he had in maneuvering on his peg leg. The partner's desk had been John's idea. He wanted to keep his eye on Michael Kelly Lawler, the man who possessed the audacity to elope with his daughter, descendant from pagan stock, professing a religion superstitious as the voodoo his darkies pretended was Christianity. John sat across from Michael, picked an envelope up from his desk, slit it open with the folding, silver-handled pen knife he kept in his vest pocket, slid out the letter and unfolded it with exaggerated formality.

"One hundred and twenty-nines dollars," John said.

"Beg your pardon?"

"The last debt I owe on the salt works. I shall pay it, tomorrow, and the business will be another man's headache."

"A wise decision, Mr. Crenshaw," Michael said.

"Maybe," John replied. "That is what my banker acquaintances tell me. Of course, they think of themselves, first. But then, what businessman doesn't?"

Michael was amazed at John's openness. Their conversations seldom were more than grunts and commands from John and nothing about his feelings.

John was surprising himself as well. Selling the salt works was causing him to take deeper stock in his life, caused by more than the recent conversion of his property to agriculture that forced him to move his family back to Hickory Hill from town, than by the loss of the income that had built his empire, or even the loss of his leg. John had never been an introspective man. He left that to the over-educated with too much time on their hands. His hands were always busy building a life others could envy. He had never looked back, or questioned his methods, until now.

"Ever heard of the New Madrid earthquakes?" John asked.

"Before I was born," Michael said. "But I have read of them."

"I was fourteen," John began. "We had moved there three years before. 1808. Five years before that, Tom Jefferson had purchased the Louisiana Territory from Napoleon who needed the cash to pay for his wars, a lot of good that did the Emperor."

"Waterloo," Michael said, still amazed. John had spoken more words to him already today than he usually did in a month, or two.

"Waterloo," John affirmed. "And a good lesson. Start to believe you are invincible and somebody will come along to prove you wrong."

Michael was further amazed that John was referring to losing the salt works, in a veiled way, but still unusually forthcoming for a man loathe to admit any mistake or misstep.

"Where was I?" John asked.

"Louisiana."

"Missouri," John corrected. "New Madrid is in Missouri, now, after the Louisiana Purchase was divvied up into territories and states. We moved there from the Carolinas after my father's father died. Family said our cabin straddled the North and South Carolina border. Could be. The family also said my Great Grandfather signed the Declaration of Independence, like Sina's family said they were related to President Zachary Taylor. Regardless, some family stories can be put to use, true or not."

"You were living in New Madrid during the earthquake?"

"Yes. In the Missouri Bootheel. A place called Nigger Wool Swamps. At fourteen I found the earthquakes …exhilarating. They livened up my humdrum life. The earth was no longer solid. It shook for days, weeks. You couldn't tell the difference between day and night. The Mississippi River flowed in both directions. People were running in the streets. Chimneys were falling and I heard later that farther north a crack in the ground opened up so deep no bottom was visible. I suppose some were peering down to see if demons were dancing in the dirt to celebrate their devilish mischief. Certainly, church attendance increased, in the churches that remained standing. After the earthquakes, we moved across the Mississippi to Kentucky for a few years, then later followed the Saline Trace, an old Indian trail turned wagon road, to the Ohio River crossing at Flynn's Ferry into Illinois and starting a farm on the east side of Eagle Mountain in 1813."

"You must have been content to finally find a home," Michael said.

"Nothing good lasts. That is life's first and hardest lesson. Father died the next year, leaving a widow, three daughters and six sons. But, there was land. And land is everything," John said. The statement seemed final, as if embarrassed by how much he had revealed.

"Coffee is ready," Michael said. "Would you like a cup?'

John nodded. The sound of the percolating coffee reminding him of boiling brine pots. Now he was growing crops on his land like Cain, fruits of the earth God had found unworthy. Nothing good lasts, John reminded himself. Life's hardest lesson that he was still learning.

~ ~ ~

On October 2, 1817, John Hart Crenshaw married Francine "Sina" Taylor. They settled less than a mile away from John's home. Being the eldest son of a family that had lost its father, William, to drowning on December 12, 1814, John had toiled at the crude salt refinery at Half Moon lick since he was eighteen to support his mother and siblings. Now he was almost twenty, had a wife and the prospect of future children to support.

In 1829 the government decided to sell off the salt lands to raise money for a new State of Illinois prison. Individuals were given the right to purchase the land they had been working, and John Hart Crenshaw did. Over the following years he added to his empire of salt, eventually owning several thousands of acres, a sawmill and three furnaces for processing, amassing a fortune to the point at which he was paying one-seventh of all the taxes being collected in Illinois.

A steady flow of workers was required to perform the backbreaking and brutal labor in the salt mines, drawing in only the most desperate white men, down on their luck. Slaves filled the gap. Although slavery was illegal in Illinois, slaves could be leased for one-year terms in the salt lands of Gallatin and other counties. And, besides leasing, there were other ways John Hart Crenshaw could secure workers.

As the salt works in the saline's continued to develop, slave labor, cynically and thinly veiled behind the technicality of leasing increased in Southern Illinois, as did the profit, as well as the incentive for kidnapping free slaves for sale. Good businessmen became dependent on these easy sources of revenue, a craving like whiskey to which the white man had introduced the Indian. By the 1850's John Hart Crenshaw, along with other gentlemen of property and means who had no moral objections to the Peculiar Institution, feared business failure without free labor. They would spread stories of how slavery was dying a death of attrition, unnecessary in the modern age, and would soon be assigned to the halls of history like powdered wigs and knee britches, repeating these fictions with knowing winks and nods to each other like participants in secret Free Mason ceremonies only shared with the initiated.

Now that John had sold the salt works and his new agricultural endeavors no longer required the use of many leased slaves, it did not mean that trading in that dark flesh could not still assist in the support and well-being of his family. The trans-Atlantic slave trade had been abolished in 1808, but that did not stop the darkies already on the continent from breeding, or being bred like prize horses and plow oxen.

Even while being concerned that the law could lead to Free Blacks being kidnapped, President Filmore had signed the Fugitive Slave Act while warning he would use Federal Troops to enforce returning runaways to their rightful owners, but still claiming, "God knows that I detest slavery, but it is an existing evil, for which we are not responsible, and we must endure it, and give it such protection as is guaranteed by the constitution, till we can get rid of it without destroying the last hope of the free government in the world."

It was a confusing time of shifting loyalties, and John Hart Crenshaw was going to take every opportunity to profit by it.

~ ~ ~

"You are an abolitionist, are you not, Mr. Lawler? John asked, his desk chair creaking as he leaned forward.

"I am an American," Michael replied. "I am a Unionist who fears my country is being torn apart..."

"Your country? You were not born on this soil, Mr. Lawler, as I recall."

"I was brought here as a baby, as many Americans were."

"My family..."

"I am married to your daughter, sir. I know something about your family."

"And I know something about your family," John countered. "This country was built on the Bible. On hard work..."

"Of others?" Michael intervened. "Built on the backs of Negroes stolen from their native lands? Built on the backs of Negroes bred in this continent after enlightened politicians outlawed their transport from African shores? Built on the backs of free Negroes kidnapped and returned to slavery..."

"No such thing as a free Negro," John said. "If they don't have a white master they are just fugitives from civilization. Jesus might take their souls, but white men will always own their bodies, in this country, so called freedmen or not. So, I ask you again, Mr. Lawler. Are you an abolitionist?

"If you are asking me if all men should be their own masters, then I am an abolitionist."

John Hart Crenshaw leaned back in his chair. The only sound in the office was the tick of the regulator clock's pendulum swinging back and forth on the wall. He picked up documents from his desk, shuffled them like oversized cards from a poker deck and put them down as if expecting someone to cut.

"As I thought, Mr. Lawler," John said. "As I thought."

~ ~ ~

"Your father was very... plain-spoken today," Michael said to Elizabeth, struggling for the right word as he allowed Ruth to take the heavy great coat he had unbuttoned, caked snow falling to the kitchen floor that had accumulated on his ride home. Ruth heaved it over the hook by the door to dry.

"Plain-spoken?" Elizabeth asked, stirring the soup on the stove Ruth had made with a long-handled wooden spoon.

"Yes. He has never spoken as much to me in the office. He asked me if I was an abolitionist," Michael said. "He knows where I stand. I believe there were other memories on his mind. Maria Adams. And her children. The public manner of the incident still bothers him."

"Father was acquitted," Elizabeth said sternly, hoping to end the discussion. "And it was a very long time ago."

"There are still suspicions..."

"Captain Michael Kelly Lawler. Father and I may have our differences, but he is not a kidnapper. He would never break up families and send then into slavery for profit."

"Of course not, Elizabeth," Michael said, even though he was one of those who harbored suspicions, knowing it was possible John Hart Crenshaw had been acquitted because he was innocent but it was more likely due to his financial and social position. "They were unsubstantiated rumors. But something was bothering your father today. I have never seen him so..."

"Plain-spoken?"

"Something more," Michael said. "You do know your father has never forgiven me for forming the Vigilantes to protect the Negro families from the Regulators who were trying to force all Negroes out of Gallatin County after the trial?"

"It was a very long time ago," Elizabeth repeated.

"Yes, it was," Michael said, but recalling to mind the accusations that had hounded John Hart Crenshaw for more than a decade.

Charles and Maria Adams worked as indentured servants at Hickory Hill in 1842. Gossip speculated that John had men in his employee abduct Maria, seven of her children and keep them in hiding until they were sold for $2000 to Lewis Kuykendall who in turn took them across the Ohio River and delivered the family into slavery. Kuykendall and the victims disappeared, leaving only a mysterious I.O.U for $2000 discovered in county records. John was found not guilty of any involvement. Shortly after, Charles Adams and other men confronted John with weapons on the road. They were swiftly jailed. Weeks later, John's mill burned down at the cost of more than $20,000. Negroes were blamed. The Illinois Republican, a Shawneetown newspaper, demanded all coloreds be out of the county within a week.

Michael understood that being a free state did not shelter Illinois from the coming tempest. The warning signs were everywhere, fat drops of rain splattering in the summer dust. Winds were rising and the skies across the river over Kentucky and over Tennessee were growing darker. The approaching storm would respect no boundaries on a map.

"I am a Unionist," Michael said, returning to his argument like a defense lawyer who had been interrupted by the objections of a belligerent prosecutor. "I believe the greatest threat to our precarious Democracy is slavery administered by the affluent gentlemen of the South who use human bondage to procure profit, then drape a veil of gentility over their Peculiar Institution, and calling on God's Word to justify it…"

"Michael," Elizabeth interrupted.

"Yes. I am an abolitionist," Michael said, knowing he was only confirming what Elizabeth , and her father, already knew.

Sixteen

The winter was cruel, even if only a trace of snow had fallen, and the freezes were few in Memphis. Nothing like the winters Beulah and Betsy had known in Illinois. The Chickasaw Bluffs sheltered Memphis from the winds of the Mississippi, it was said. The cruelty lay in the waiting. The hiding. The fear of discovery and punishment if caught for daring to believe they could be free.

Devlin had secreted Beulah, Seth and Betsy in the Burkle Estate on North Second Street in Memphis that some called Slavehaven, but only in whispers. He had promised to return soon and travel with them north. But first, he needed to return to Mr. Cruikshank and convince him he had nothing to do with their disappearance. He would put all his Irish cleverness to work concocting a tale of being brutally accosted by highwaymen who kidnapped Beulah, Seth and Betsy, leaving him near death as the side of the road. Devlin was confident his blarney was sufficient to sell the story.

"We is in the underground," Betsy said. "But there ain't no railroad."

"Ain't no railroad," Beulah agreed. "But Mr. Devlin say we be takin' a steamboat north soon as the weather gets better. Then a real railroad. He got it all worked out. When he gets back, we…"

"How long that be? He gone a mighty long time. I's tired of livin' in this root cellar like a turnip."

"Can't say, Betsy. I lost track of time. But, I trust Mr. Devlin. Never trusted no man before, but I do him."

Beulah looked towards Seth who was asleep in the candlelight on a makeshift cot. A root cellar was not a good home, she thought. But better than a cane-cutting shack somewhere in Louisiana.

~ ~ ~

Jacob Burkle was a German immigrant who came to America fleeing conscription into Bismarck's Prussian military and had become the gentleman owner of a stockyard and bakery north of downtown Memphis. Jacob arrived in the United States in 1848, the year of revolts against European monarchies that started in Italy, soon spreading to France, Germany and the Austrian Empire. Europe was in turmoil. Grain harvests were poor, potato blight hit Ireland and typhus ran rampant. America beckoned.

Jacob built his manor house in 1849. It overlooked the stockyards and the Mississippi River three blocks away. His estate occupied the north edge of the Gayoso Bayou, which separated it from Memphis, preventing overland travel from downtown. The house could only be reached by taking roads to the east and looping back toward the river. And between the house and the river, grew a dense stand of trees. The isolation offered more than a retreat; it offered freedom. Jacob's devout Lutheranism and the misery he had witnessed in Europe as the poor struggled against the forces of the entitled had given him a great distaste for the institution of slavery, seeing it as an extension of the feudalistic chains from a darker age. Jacob decided to unlock as many shackles as he could.

~ ~ ~

"Here be your supper," Naomi said, coming down the cellar stairs with both hands tightly holding the tray that was covered with a linen napkin of conspicuous quality. "Don't wanna spill nothin'".

"Heard from Mr. Devlin?" Beulah asked. Taking the tray.

"Mr. Burkle don't keep no runaways longer that need be," Naomi said. "When Mr. Devlin come back, you be gone."

"Naomi!" a voice called from the top of the stairs. "You get yerself up here. The Mrs. Burkle has chores need doin'."

"Well ain't you the bossy one, Mose? You got two arms and two legs and none of them is broke."

"Don't do women's work. Chickens need feedin' and there be eggs to get."

"He ain't white and he ain't kin," Naomi said to Beulah. "But that don't matter none. It just be the way a man treats a woman who ain't his mama."

"Naomi?" Mose yelled.

"I's comin', Mose. Don't want to break my leg on these here stairs."

To conceal being a conductor on an Underground Railroad Line, Jacob Burkle had bought Naomi and Mose at a Memphis slave auction. He owned them, but treated them as if they were family, promising that he would eventually help them get to Canada. He kept that promise later, sending them on the same route he described to Devlin. When they were safely across the border. He ran an advertisement in the *Memphis Appeal* offering a reward for two runaway slaves he knew he would never have to pay.

Betsy took the tray from Beulah, put it on the wooden table and removed the linen napkin.

"Smoked venison," Betsy said. "I's gettin' a likin' for this meat. And cornbread. Just need a slice of Mama's pie. Or yours, Beulah."

"When we get to Canada."

"Where be Canada, Beulah?"

"It be north. Devlin say we be safe there. No Night Riders. No cotton fields or cane breaks. No slaves. Get there on a steam boat and a railroad."

"How we do that, Beulah?"

"Devlin say Mr. Burkle bribe the steam boat Captain with a sack of gold coins."

"We worth a sack of gold coins, Beulah?"

"Yes, Betsy. You and me and Seth be worth a big old sack of gold coins. Now you go wake Seth up. It be time to eat."

~ ~ ~

Devlin had little trouble convincing Frederick Cruickshank that highwaymen had robbed him of Beulah and Betsy and Seth. The bruises and cuts he had inflicted on himself helped. It was an occupational hazard of delivering slaves to their new owners. Night Riders would often turn free agent to steal back the slaves they had sold to sell them again. It might eventually cost them their lives, as the thievery had caught up to Zeke, but the pittance they were paid for their services provided a living barely better than the darkies they trafficked, and that made taking chances worthwhile. Frederick shrugged off the loss, asking Devlin to never tell Mrs. Cruickshank about the abduction, then told Devlin that another flatboat was arriving that afternoon with more cargo. Devlin assured Frederick Cruickshank he would be at the dock to deliver the new slaves to auction, then limped down the street towards the landing before turning north in the direction of the Burkle Estate. It was time for Beulah, Becky and Seth to head up the river.

~ ~ ~

Devlin arrived at the Burkle Estate just after dark, using every precaution to assure he had not been followed on his roundabout route. The next morning Mose showed him the tunnel dug from the root cellar, extending into the thick woods of oak, cypress and tupelo that separated the house from the Mississippi. There would be a riverboat Captain expecting them dawn the next day. It would be hard travel to the river once they entered the forest. Devlin assured Mose no one would complain, except maybe Betsy. Mose handed Devlin a sack of gold coins from Mr. Burkle to pay the Captain.

"Gold coins for your safe passage to Cairo, Illinois. Then Canada," Devlin said, showing Beulah the sack. "We leave at first light in the morning."

"Cairo?" Beulah said. "I heard that name before."

"Not far downriver from Equality, I believe," Devlin said. "And Hickory Hill."

Beulah winced at the sound of the name. Hickory Hill. It made her remember Mama. She could feel the tug as Mama combed her matted hair for church, scoldin' her to sit still. She could smell Mama's apple pie bakin', a pie she knew she could never make as good. And she could hear Mama callin' her and Betsy in for supper as the sun be goin' down, Mama askin' what they talked about sittin' under that old elm for so long. There be Night Riders soon as it be dark, Mama told her. They take girls like you and Betsy to sell south for pickin' cotton all day in the sizzlin' sun. Ain't no shade elm for talkin' under down south, Mama said. Beulah always thought Mama was just tellin' boogeyman tales, like the man who carried naughty children away in a sack slung over his back, voodoo stories to scare Beulah and Betsy into bein' good, until Zeke carried them away, not in a sack, but a wagon. Mama. You was right.

"Mama..."

"No, Beulah. I know what you're thinking. If you tried to see your Mama back in Hickory Hill, you and Betsy and Seth would be captured and lose any chance at freedom. I have no doubt about that. We must stick to the plan. Steam boat to Cairo, then railroad…"

"Underground?" Betsy asked.

"Not this time," Devlin said. "The Illinois Central Line to Chicago."

"Chicago be in Canada?" Betsy asked.

"No," Devlin said. "But that is far as the railroad can take us. And, there is a man in Chicago who owns a company that makes railroad cars. A very rich man. You will be his…servants."

"No!" Beulah began.

"No," Devlin agreed. "The man is a figment of my fertile imagination."

"What do that mean?" Betsy asked.

"The man does not exist. I am using him as the excuse for travelling with two such attractive ladies and a boy of color."

"It just be a story," Beulah said.

"That is correct," Devlin said. "I will tell people that you and Betsy and Seth were freed when the master of the sugarcane plantation you lived on in Louisiana died. He bequeathed…gave you to his brother in Chicago, as servants. To the rich man who makes railroad cars and lives in a magnificent mansion in the best part of the city. I don't recall the man's name…"

"Because you ain't made it up yet?" Beulah said. "It still be in your…imagination?"

"And there it will stay. Unless someone insists while we are on our travels to know his name. One will come to me."

A boat whistle blew, piecing the dawn silence. The fugitives and Devlin walked slowly to the river.

"No haste," Devlin cautioned. "We do not want to arouse suspicion."

"Who see us?" Betsy asked. "The sun just comin' up."

"Need I remind you of Night Riders?" Devlin asked.

"No," Betsy said, slowing her walk. "I knows Night Riders."

Devlin handed the Captain standing on deck at the top of the ramp the burlap sack of coins. Devlin nodded to the Captain. The Captain returned the nod, looking at Beulah, Betsy and Seth who followed behind, heads down. As far as the Captain was concerned, Devlin was delivering three house darkies to their new home. They wouldn't need to hide among the boxes of ceramic dishware, two crated pianos, bales of cotton and wool, crates of seed corn and potatoes, barrels of beer, stacks of bricks, lumber and raw logs for building, a breeding bull, a breeding ram and three mules that crowded the deck. The sack of gold coins assured they would not be treated as slaves. They were heading north to Chicago, Devlin assured the Captain. They were to be servants for Carl Shultz, the name Devlin had just concocted for the imaginary railroad car builder, knowing from his Irish curiosity-fueled newspaper reading that many immigrants living in Chicago were from Germany. The Captain nodded, gently cupping the burlap sack like the voluptuous breast of the dance hall girl he left in Memphis, the breast she would not let him touch, no matter how many whiskeys he bought. The Captain slipped the burlap sack into his peacoat pocket, climbed to the bridge, took the wheel and shouted to the deckhands below, "Let go the lines from the dock and bring them on board." The rising sun rippled on the river. The air was sharp with the keen taste of late winter and a possible sweetness of early spring, the brightening sky clear of cloud. Last night's sunset had been red. This was going to be a fine day.

Seventeen

Elias had settled into his life as a cowboy busting broncos and herding cattle with a determination that made memories of Hickory Hill and his life with the Cheyenne distant as disturbing dreams that dissolve with the dawn. His horseman skills on Chief had overcome the color of his skin. He had become an experienced ranch hand given due respect. He held his own in bar brawls and was a favored customer of cattle town parlor ladies, ignoring the women in the street preaching social purity to the customers entering and leaving the houses who called out patrons names if recognized, especially gentlemen of power and position. Elias was never singled out, coming and going as it pleased. And please him it did. To foes of the great social evil he was just another cowboy falling to the temptation of the nearly-nude tarts airing their wares on the front porch with the doors wide open. Elias was just another dusty cowboy, which the other cowboys at the ranch began calling him, Dusty, a name he preferred to Boy, or nigger, although he was still partial to the name Spotted Horse that Old Bear had given him when he was a Cheyenne, before Cholera killed his adopted tribe and made him a cowboy.

"Dusty," Jack Gallagher called out to Elias. "Cut that steer off. We can't afford to lose a another head. You lollygagging again?"

Elias pulled hard to the right on the reigns. Chief responded without protest, not as quickly as he did a few years before, but fast enough to block the Longhorn and return him to the herd.

"Good work, Dusty," Jack said. "Gettin' to be about time to bed these sons of bitches down for the night. Not much light left. Looks like this creek runs through a meadow up yonder."

"I'll ride back and let Abel know," Elias said.

"You do that, Dusty," Jack said. "Just pay attention. Your mind's been wanderin' like that creek recently. Dangerous for a drover."

Elias nodded and urged Chief around the herd towards the rear where Abel Pickett was riding drag, eating enough dust to cough up and plant a garden. Elias had learned to respect, even admire the Longhorns. This had not been their home. Their ancestors had been brought to this land like Elias. They were the products of the accidental breeding of escaped Spanish cattle and cows from early American settlers mixed with fugitive English Longhorns. In the wild they had few enemies. Native tribes preferred the taste of buffalo and never hunted the wild cattle, finding more uses for the buffalo hides, bones and dung than for the Longhorn leather. Wolves shied away from the cantankerous cattle. As the buffalo were killed off to near extinction, grasslands from Mexico to Canada were opened to feed the Longhorn, their only predator the cowboys who rounded them up, corralled and branded them. Since the Gold Rush of '49 there had been a market for cattle in California. The demand was beginning to slow as the gold fields were mined out. But Homer Heaney, owner of the Double H Ranch, was in need of money and it was worth one last drive to the coast. Elias was glad to join the drive. Once it was over, or somewhere along the way, he was determined to leave this company of cow hands.

Kansas was becoming more and more unwelcoming as settlers moved in to fence off Longhorns from their natural feed for homestead farms. And, the fact that the settlers were mostly white and hostile to Elias' general appearance did not make things better.

Bleeding Kansas. Like Indian Summer before, Elias wasn't sure at first what the words meant, hearing them spat out in saloon fights like insults to a rival's kin. But he soon learned what the words meant. Every time a new territory in the west petitioned for statehood, the two factions dividing the country fought over it like the last chuckwagon biscuit after a hard day on the trail. The Missouri Compromise of 1820 determined that all new states above Missouri's southern border would enter free. The Compromise of 1850 admitted California as a Free State and ended slave trade in the District of Columbia while allowing settlers in the territories of Utah and New Mexico to decide the question of slavery by vote. But it also strengthened the Fugitive Slave Act, enraging people of the North who were obligated by a law upheld in the Supreme Court to catch and return runaway slaves to their rightful Southern owners. When Nebraska and Kansas both applied for statehood in 1854, it threw a wrench into the cogs of the government's gears. Their geographical location would ban slavery, so the South balked at the imbalance, a shift towards freedom giving Northerners the upper hand. Fearing secession and Civil War as real possibilities, Congress passed the Kansas-Nebraska Act, repealing the Missouri Compromise and allowing the people living in Kansas and Nebraska to determine the slavery issue through voting. When Missourians crossed the Kansas border to illegally vote for slavery, war broke out. Elias was glad Homer Heaney ordered one last Longhorn drive to California. Elias was done with the Double H. He was done with Kansas. He would play Dusty for the time being. He would tolerate Jack Gallagher, Abel

Pickett and the other drovers without revealing his intentions. But Elias had other plans for Chief and himself. He had heard talk of a place of forests and rivers wilder than the Mississippi. A place called Oregon. A place as far as he could get from John Hart Crenshaw and Hickory Hill and Bleeding Kansas where people killed each other for the right of returning him to chains.

"Mr. Picket," Elias yelled to Abel through the dust and din raised by the longhorns. "Mr. Gallagher say we beddin' the herd down in that meadow up yonder."

"Gonna be nice to get out of Kansas, Dusty," Abel said. "Might just stay in California. Gold's mostly gone, but I hear it's God's country. Too many angry men with guns around these parts."

"I be ridin' back now to my flank," Elias said.

"You do that, Dusty. Enjoy the ride. I believe tomorrow you'll be drag, and you are welcome to it."

Elias didn't reply. He rode back to his flank position where he kept the heard from spreading out and losing forward momentum. Riding drag would be good for leaving the heard, hidden in the dust, Elias thought. He and Chief would head northwest on the Oregon Trail while the herd veered south to Sacramento on the California Trail. No Conestoga wagon, or farm implements or tools to clear land or pull stumps, just a solitary Negro and his horse, a freedman of his own making, reconciled to being called Dusty, or Elias, Boy or nigger, as long the name callers understood that no one owned him or ever would again.

Eighteen

"My name be Robert Wilson. But I's mostly called Uncle Bob. Or just Bob."

The new arrival from Kentucky stared at Bob as he stood on the porch of Hickory Hill. She had never seen such a tall, muscled or black-skinned man. But his broad smile that exposed healthy rows of teeth calmed her fears.

"Take the young lady to Patsy's cabin, Willy," John Hart Crenshaw said, the porch boards creaking as he positioned himself beside Bob, his armpit aching even after Sina has sewn on more quilt scraps to pad the support. It had been years since he lost it, but from time to time John still felt pain in the leg he no longer had. Willy had saved his life, stopping the bleeding after John has been attacked by a salt worker with an axe, but he could still barely tolerate him. Willy was white trash only slightly better than the sneak thief Zeke he had replaced, but John's honor as a gentleman made him feel he still owed Willy a debt and until it was repaid, he would reluctantly endure Willy's crudeness, his foul language, and his smell. Afterall, Willy fetched the leased slaves from Kentucky to work Hickory Hill, and he took them back to the river to sell when expenses running the farm that replaced the salt works grew unsustainable. And Willy did the jobs with no sign of disloyalty, yet.

"Wait," John said to Willy who had the girl firmly by the upper arm, leading her to the cabin she was to share with Patsy. Willy spun her around to face John. "What's your name?"

"Don't rightly know," she said, neither in arrogance nor submission. "Depended on my master."

"I am not your master," John said. "I have leased you."

"I's free?"

"You work for me, as long as I say."

"Then I be your slave," the girl said, a flicker of light flaming out in her black eyes. "And you be my master. My name be whatever you say it be."

"Martha," John said, recalling the scripture passage read at the last Methodist Service. "Martha was the busy one. You will be busy, too."

"Martha," the young girl repeated. "Never been a Martha before."

"Come on, Martha," Willy said, tightening his hold on the young girl's arm. "Time to meet your bunkmate."

"Well, Bob. What do you think?" John asked.

Bob's grin widened, revealing more perfect teeth. "I knows my job, Mr. Crenshaw. And I knows it ain't to think."

"You like your job, don't you Bob?" John asked, patting Bob on his broad back as he repositioned himself on his crutch. He was longing to sit down to take the pressure off the stump where the leather straps securing his wooden leg dug into the tender flesh. Even the new leg he had gone all the way to Washington to buy and have fitted caused pain.

"Yes, I does. Truly I does like my job, Mr. Crenshaw."

"Let the new girl settle in with Patsy for a few days. Then, go introduce yourself."

"I do that, Mr. Crenshaw," Bob said, his grin dissolving into a look of determination. "Soon as the new girl be settled in."

~ ~ ~

Robert Wilson was born January 12, 1836 in Richmond, Virginia, the year that the Battle of the Alamo was fought and lost to Santa Anna and Texas declared independence from Mexico, its Constitution legalizing slavery. The year that P. T. Barnum exhibited an African slave named Joice Heth, claiming she was the 161 year old nursemaid to George Washington. The year that Samuel Colt patented the revolver, the first sidearm to be fired multiple times before reloading. The year that Charles Darwin returned to England after his five year voyage on the HMS Beagle and began formulating his origins of species and the year that Martin Van Buren was elected the 8th President of the United States, continuing Andrew Jackson's forced march of Indians west of the Mississippi, down the same Trail of Tears.

Born into slavery, saddled with his master's European surname, Bob had descended from a proud line of Mandingo, a mostly Muslim tribe that migrated west down the Niger River, immigrants labeled foreigners by local tribes and told to "Go home", becoming prey for the slavers, the Portuguese and Dutch, the French and British who worked the "white man's grave coast", bringing Yellow fever and malaria with their ships and chains.

The Mandingoes were prized by the slavers for their majestic stature and stamina, and Bob stood well over six foot, weighing more than two hundred pounds at an early age. He was a magnificent specimen of youthful vigor and confidence, groomed like a prize bull which he took as his calling, traded from master to master as his reputation grew. He was purchased by John Hart Crenshaw on his trip to the Capital City of Washington to acquire a new wooden leg, accompanied by his brother, Robert, for the grand cost of five thousand dollars. With the salt works sold, and John relying only on farming for income, the resale of leased and kidnapped slaves and their offspring back into slavery had become vital to his ability to maintain Hickory Hill and retain the style of life to which his family, and he, had grown accustomed. The addition of an impressive breeder like Bob would only increase his profits.

~ ~ ~

'What be your name?" Patsy asked the girl, after Willy pounded on her cabin door and left her on the porch like a sack of spuds.

"Be Martha, now," the girl said. "Least that what I told. My name change from master to master."

"Mr. Crenshaw ain't your master," Patsy said, not really believing what she said. "This be the free state Illinois."

"Then we leave anytime we want?"

"No. You leased."

"What that mean?"

"It mean you work for Mr. Crenshaw as long as he say so."

"Sound like bein' a slave to me."

"Sure do," Patsy agreed. "Whites use big words to deny they be sinnin', and all the while claimin' to be Christian."

"I thought you said there be no slaves in…Illinois."

"Never mind what I said. No more of this talk…Martha. That be a fine name."

"Ain't really mine. The new master give it to me."

"Keep up that master talk and you be sold downriver to pick cotton. Or maybe cut cane like I do once. You most likely be dead the first day in the field, how puny you be.

"I…"

"You be a house nigger like me," Betsy interrupted. "We work for Mr. and Mrs. Crenshaw, in the big house, cookin', cleanin', whatever they say. No better job at Hickory Hill. No better job for any nigger. 'Cept maybe Uncle Bob."

"I seen him on the big house porch. Huge as a horse. Never seen a nigger so clean. What he do? He a house nigger, too?"

"He be comin' over in a few days to introduce hisself. You find out then," Patsy said. "You need somthin' better to wear. Mrs. Crenshaw not like to see house niggers lookin' like field niggers. Still got dresses left that was my girls. You 'bout the same size. Might as well get some use out of them."

"You got girls?"

"They be gone. But that none of your business," Patsy said, making it clear any more talk about her girls would be ignored.

~ ~ ~

Patsy liked Bob. He was friendly, free with smiles, respectful of her and the other leased Negro women who had come and gone from Hickory Hill. He could quote the Bible and said that someday he was going to be a preacher. But Patsy knew what his job was now. And what it had been before Mr. Crenshaw had brought him to Hickory Hill. It was not to labor doing farm chores, not cutting and stacking wood for the cooking fires now that Cyrus had passed, not tending to the horses, the job Elias had left behind when the salt works closed and he ran away with one of Mr. Crenshaw's best stallions. And it was not spreading the Word of the Lord.

One day after dinner, on a balmy evening of fireflies and crickets, not long after Bob had arrived at Hickory Hill, Patsy was sitting in her front porch rocker, watching the moon rise over the hills that hid the river, the now barren hills that once were forested with the Slippery Elm, the White Ash and the Oak that had been sacrificed to boil down salt. She was thinking about her lost girls,

Beulah and Betsy, whose disappearance had left a hole in her heart time had not healed.

"Evenin' ma'am."

"Bob. You scared the livin' lights outta me."

"Sorry, ma'am. I's just out for a stroll on this fine night and I seen you rockin' on the porch and it made me miss my mama."

"And I be missin' my girls," Patsy said before she could catch herself. She didn't often speak of her girls.

"You got young'uns?"

"Did. They be gone. But, that be water so far downstream now the bridge done collapse."

Uninvited, Bob climbed the cabin steps and leaned against the porch railing.

"I's sorry," Bob said. His voice soft and sympathetic. "Guess we all be losin' more'n we gain."

"Heard you wantin' to be a preacher one day. You got the gift, for bein' so young."

"One day I be a preacher" Bob said. "But I's got a lotta sinnin' to repent for first."

"We is all carryin' a hefty burden of sin," Patsy said. Mine be losin' my girls, Patsy thought, even if others say it ain't her fault. Ain't no preacher words will ever take that weight away.

"My burden bigger'n most, ma'am." Bob said.

"Patsy. I ain't no ma'am."

"You look too much like my mama for me to call you by your name," Bob said.

"Ma'am'll do. Don't believe I ever been called that before. Was there somethin' else y'all wanted to talk about?"

Bob stood up and started pacing the porch. He stopped and turned to the yard.

"Ain't that fat moon somethin'?" Bob said. "Lights up the land like a torch. Same moon that followed us all the way here from Virginy."

"It be somethin'", Patsy said. "What you want to talk about, Bob? Dawn comes early and there be biscuits to bake for breakfast."

"Sorry, ma'am. Never talked to no one 'bout this before. But if I doesn't, I feel I might bust."

Patsy had heard the gossip. Bob slept in the attic of Hickory Hill, with his own outside stairs leading up the back of the house. He had the run of the Hickory Hill and didn't do a lick of work. His hands were clean and uncalloused and he carried himself with a little too much pride. The expectation, or even hope by some of the field niggers, was that Bob's fall would be hard and soon.

He was a nigger's nigger, Bob told Patsy in the low tone of a confession. He was a stud. A buck. His services had been sold from plantation to plantation like a prize bull to increase the slave population.

"Every master I had told me it be in the Bible, that slaves is to obey. Paul said so. And if I want to be a preacher someday I's to believe what God say or burn in hell. Well ma'am, I don't want to burn in hell so I do what my masters say."

"Somethin' else botherin' you, ain't it?"

"People say what I do be a sin. Don't feel like no sin. I do what the masters say. I ain't never hurt no girls. But if I keep doin' what I's doin' can I still be a preacher?"

"We is all sinners, seem to me,' Patsy said. "Probably good for a preacher to be a sinner, knowin' what he preachin' 'bout. Ain't no way nobody got a right to judge. That be God's job, not people. If bein' a preacher be what you want, preach. Don't matter how many young'uns you stud."

"It do say in the Bible, 'Be fruitful and multiply'. But maybe that just be for the Hebrews."

"I got biscuits to bake for breakfast in the mornin', Bob. I's mighty tired," Patsy said, rocking up from her chair.

"Goodnight, ma'am. People do say I talk to much…"

"Talkin' be fine, if you know what you talkin' 'bout. Most people don't. They like sheep bleatin' at each other. I got the feelin' you ain't no sheep, Bob. You come back and talk anytime you like. Maybe introduce you to the new girl, Martha."

"We met…" Bob began.

"Ain't no sin, Bob. Remember that. You only doin' what God and the master say."

"That be right," Bob said, still feeling sinful. "And someday I be a preacher."

~ ~ ~

"Boy," Willy yelled at Bob. "That ain't your job."

"Who chop the wood now Cyrus be dead?" Bob asked, swinging the axe into the chopping block.

"It ain't you," Willy said. "Plenty of other niggers to chop wood. You know what you need to be doin'. You been with the new bitch yet?"

If Willy hadn't had a whip looped over his shoulder Bob might have objected to him calling Martha a bitch. He didn't.

"Plannin' to," Bob said.

"You turnin'…soft?" Willy asked with a scum-toothed grin.

Bob pulled the axe out of the block and set up another round, splitting it with a ferocious swing. "I do my job," he said.

Willy grasp the whip, his fingers tingling with the urge to use it. He hated uppity niggers who acted like they were good as him. Bob was the worst. A pampered stud thinking he was special.

"Remember you are just a nigger," Willy said, spitting saliva on his bristled chin.

"If I be forgetful," Bob said, setting up another round to split, "I sure you remind me."

~ ~ ~

Bob pulled the bucket from the well, splashing cold water on his face to remove the slight sheen of sweat that wood chopping had left. He checked his hands for splinters and his nails for dirt. He was proud and carful about his appearance, how clean his overalls and shirts were, not patched at the knees or ripped at the elbows. He palmed a gulp of the water, then rubbed his teeth with his index finger. His teeth were his prize possession, the first thing people noticed about him, besides his towering height and muscles that rippled out of his rolled-up shirt sleeves. Bob's teeth were strait, white and he had every one God had given him. The ladies liked his smile and he was on his way to try it on the new girl.

~ ~ ~

Pink and purple crocuses bloomed along the porch of Patsy's cabin, but Bob did not know their name. Or the names of other flowers sending shoots out of the spring beds. No one had taught him. He climbed the stairs and knocked on the door. It was early evening. Supper was done, the sun was down and Patsy would have finished her house chores in the big house. Bob knocked again. The door opened at crack, Pasty's face gleaming in the light of the kerosene lamp she carried.

"Evenin', ma'am. It be Bob."

"So it be," Patsy said, opening the door, waving Bob in with her free hand. "Don't get many visitors. Specially this time of the evenin'. And now that I got Martha to look after, I's thinkin' 'bout Night Riders."

"I"s sure they don't be kidnappin' girls right outta cabins," Bob said.

"I ain't so sure," Patsy said

Every time someone came to her door, Patsy opened it with the hope it was news about her girls, no matter how long they had been gone. Or with the hope that her girls would be standing on the porch, wanting hugs and bursting with stories of their capture and escape.

"I's thinkin' you after Martha," Patsy said.

"Yes'm," Bob said with a touch of shyness.

"It be your job, Bob," Patsy reminded him.

"Yes'm," Bob said. "It be my job."

Nineteen

Beulah stood at the paddlewheeler's railing. She could hear it's engine pumping like the heartbeat of Jonah's whale. She could feel it in her hands as she held the rail, watching the bow part the river into frothing wakes lit by kerosene lamps swaying on a string of poles along the deck and the moon reflecting from the river's glassy surface. She remembered the preacher telling the story. How Jonah tried to run and hide from the Lord. He was a shirker, the preacher said, refusing to do the Lord's will. And the Lord called up a vengeful storm that threatened to sink the ship that Jonah thought would be his escape. And the crew of the ship threw Jonah overboard to save their own lives, knowing Jonah had offended the Lord, tossed Jonah into the sea where he was swallowed by the great fish before being vomited onto dry land after he repented. Beulah felt she, too, was living in the belly of the whale with her son and sister. And she had prayed for salvation, asking God what she had done to deserve exile from her mother, why she was stolen and sold into slavery to bear her child in a strange land, because if she knew what wickedness she had committed in the eyes of the Lord, she would repent. Tonight Beulah was thinking about her mama and how her sin might be believing she should be free and trying to run from a slave's true fate.

"I can always tell when you have your mother on your mind," Devlin said, leaning against the railing beside Beulah. "It's that look an Irishman has when missing his Ma across the sea."

"You miss your mama?" Beulah asked, not looking at Devlin.

"My mother lies buried in the hard soil and rock next to Da, behind the cottage my family made believe was our home, even though it was rented from a British landlord. Da never owned a damn thing in his entire sad life. But few Irishmen do. Don't feel sorry," Devlin said before Beulah could speak. "We Irish wash sorrow down with stout pints. We wear grief like a tattered overcoat and feed the mangy hound of misery well that follows us to the grave. I ramble on, don't I? Another burden the Irish carry, the gift of gab, like a stone smoothed from handling we take out of our pockets and kiss, hoping it will hold back the devilish silence. As I was going to say before I so rudely interrupted myself, I have been pondering long and hard about our travels. I know you harbor thoughts of taking your mother from the clutches of Mr. John Hart Crenshaw. It might just be possible."

"But you said…"

"Yes. I know. Too dangerous. But Murphy's Law states everything that can go wrong likely will, the Luck of the Irish it's called, so adding one more thing to go wrong won't make much difference."

"How we do it?"

"I have been doing some enquiring with the deck hands. Most are boys from the Old Sod and one produced a fine bottle of uisce beatha."

Beulah looked puzzled.

"The Water of Life. The Brits butchered its name to Whiskey because they could not wrap their stiff tongues around the good Gaelic. I understand American

Government Agents call it Fire Water when they distribute it to the Indians so they won't notice they have been cheated on their reservation food rations. There I go rambling on again. As I was saying, I was discussing with the boys about the river heading north. Beyond Cairo on the Ohio River, just past the old outlaw stronghold of Cave-in-Rock, there is a landing called Shawneetown…"

"Shawneetown?" Beulah interrupted. "I heard the river slavers sayin' that name. The rickety dock they tie their boat to was near. They scared to go near town, I hear them sayin'. Christian townsfolk say slavery Satan's work and slavers just devil's helpers. It be a long time ago, but I ain't forgot one thing about what they say, or do. Like how that one slaver shot Zeke in the face."

"Who's Zeke?"

"Be Mr. Crenshaw's Overseer and Night Rider what brung us to the slavers. He grabbed me and Betsy when we's sittin' under the talkin' elm, like Mama called it, when we shoulda been helpin' her with supper in the big house. Zeke come up and point a big pistol right at us. Done shove us to a wagon where George sit holdin' the reins, lookin' down like he be real sad. We scared, knowin' Zeke'd kill any Negro for no reason. He done it lots a times. It be rainin' real hard on the road and the wagon slip down the bank and break up in the river, nearly drown us all, almost killed the horse. Thought Betsy be dead, in the river…"

"So you do know the way from the river, near Shawneetown, to where your mama lives?" Devlin asked, interrupting Beulah's telling of the kidnapping before she was overcome by reliving that night's terror.

"I does," Beulah said as if taking an oath in court.

"It won't be easy."

"Ain't found nothin' in life yet that be easy," Beulah said.

"Fair enough, Madame," Devlin said. "Before our endeavor is complete, freeing your mother, I will need to make further inquiries as to how to proceed north. After all, my job remains delivering you, your son, your sister and now, apparently, your mother to your new employee, Mr. Carl Schultz, in Chicago, even if he is a figment of my fertile imagination."

The boat gave a shudder, as if reacting to the undertaking Devlin had pledged to Beulah. The tremor suddenly stopped, then the chug of the pistons driving the paddlewheel fell silent. Deck hands ran towards the boiler room hatch. The boat began turning towards shore, caught in a swift current without the power to steer where the mile wide river had narrowed and the current increased. Steam billowed up from the engine room hatch, then burst into a violent cloud of vapor, pitching crew back fifty feet into the air, onto the deck or into the black water. Devlin could hear the screams as splinted wood deck planks flew like jagged arrows. He turned his back, sheltering Beulah from the volley of shards. One caught him in the calf, not deep. This time, he was a lucky Irishman.

"We must find Seth and Betsy," Devlin yelled over the hiss of the steam. He grabbed Beulah by the hand and pulled her towards the bow. The deck tilted to starboard as water rushed into the hole the explosion had torn. A second blast knock Devlin and Beulah down. As they struggled up, the boat sank more towards the stern. They crawled through the cargo, over crates of shattered ceramic dishes, bales of cotton, wool, and barrels of beer still lashed to the deck. They found Betsy and Seth in the river, clinging to a crated piano, barely visible in the light of a single kerosene lantern swinging on a pole near where the piano had crashed through the railing.

"Hang on," Devlin yelled.

"I can't swim!" Betsy screamed.

"I can," Seth yelled to Devlin.

"Then help Betsy."

The boat shuddered again, another detonation

surging steam and splinters of the deck a hundred feet into the air, lurching Devlin and Beulah into the river. The kerosene lamp on its pole followed them, hissing out, the night now only lit by the moon that was being swallowed by drifting clouds.

Devlin frantically paddled towards where Beulah floated, clutching a bundle of lumber.

"I can swim," Beulah said. "I taught Seth."

"You are full of surprises, Madame," Devlin said, grabbing hold of the same floating planks.

Devlin surveyed the damage. He could see no other survivors, except a bleating ram struggling against the current. Scalded bodies of deckhands floated face down among scattered wooden boxes. Farther back he could hear the bellow of the breeding bull he had admired earlier that day, keeping his distance, the massive Shorthorn restrained by a nose ring and halter, tethered to an iron loop screwed deep in the deck. In a few minutes, the bellowing stopped. And in a few minutes more, the entire boat sank below the surface in a final sizzle of steam, its only remnants cargo that had broken free. Devlin and Beulah swam to the piano crate. It was marked with a delivery address in St. Louis. It was floating well, but the river would never take it to St. Louis, New Orleans being a more likely destination, if it survived the more than five hundred mile journey. Seth had climbed up to lie on top of the piano crate. Betsy's fingers tore into cracks, still half-submerged in the river.

"Is anyone injured?" Devlin asked.

"I hate the river," Betsy said

For once in his life, Devlin was at a loss for words. He could see Beulah's eyes blinking in the darkness, determined yet pleading.

"I don't care about me and Betsy," Beulah whispered. "But save my boy. Seth don't deserve to drown in the river."

"None of us do," Devlin said. "There was a jolly

boat on deck. Called it a currach back home. Sturdy little boat for fishing. If it survived…"

"I see it!" Seth said.

The jolly boat's lines were tangled with other floating debris. It was slowly turning in a circle where the current swirled into eddies, deflected by a curving point of land. Devlin could see the jolly boat was dangerously close to being swept down river in the main flow.

"I can get it," Seth said, diving off the piano crate.

"Seth!" Beulah cried.

"He'll do fine," Devlin reassured.

"He better," Betsy said. "I hate the river."

Seth swam to the jolly boat, catching the side and throwing his leg up and over like mounting a horse bareback. Four oars were still lashed inside, and a sail. He untied two oars, slipped them over the horn oar locks and began rowing."

"Where did your boy learn that?" Devlin asked.

"Memphis. Seth love the river. Told him if he spend too much time in the water he get web feet like ducks. He know all about boats."

"He certainly can row. From what the boys told me while we were sharing their bottle, Cairo is close. A riverboat exploding should bring out the salvagers. We just need to survive long enough for them to show up. I saved out some gold coins from the bag I gave the Captain. I'm sure he's dead and the rest of the money lies on the bottom of the river. So he won't mind. We can use it to bribe or buy or talk our way to Shawneetown. Shouldn't be hard for an Irishman."

"Climb on," Seth hollered, extending an oar as the jolly boat drifted up to the piano crate. "I see lights comin' this way on the river."

"Salvagers," Devlin said. "They smell blood in the water before sharks.

Betsy grabbed the oar first, pulling herself towards

~173~

the jolly boat.

"I hate the river," she said, sputtering as water splashed into her mouth.

"Not fond of it, myself," Devlin agreed. "Next time we shall take the train."

Twenty

"I want to hear no more talk of war, Michael Kelly Lawler," Elizabeth said. "Of all people, I would think you have had your fill. You relive battles in your dreams most nights. And you reenlisted when you could have stayed home with your family. Reenlisted to lead your precious 3rd Regiment, mostly farm boys looking for adventure and escape from the plow horse…"

"Elizabeth," Michael said, cutting her off as if she had taken the name of the Lord in vain. Seldom had Michael seen Elizabeth so agitated, or daring to question his decisions. "No doubt there will be armed conflict between the States. The slavery issue cannot be resolved with compromise when a territory like Kansas petitions for statehood, is provided with the right to choose their own destiny, and pro-slavery Border Ruffians raid from Missouri to assault and murder anti-slavery Free-Staters."

"Politics and business," Elizabeth said. "I take no interest."

"When the war comes it will pound on our front door and not be refused entrance. We are surrounded by slave states. We have leased slaves working the fields. Patsy…"

"Patsy is family," Elizabeth said.

"Whose daughters disappeared one night, most

likely sold down river for profit."

"Do not even suggest my father has been involved in such affairs. He is a gentleman and Methodist Elder."

Elizabeth had heard all the rumors. She knew that her father had been tried and acquitted of kidnapping and selling freed slaves. But that was many years ago and her father refused to even discuss the stories as being far below his dignity. Since then it had only been malicious gossip spread by jealous town businessmen and nosy farmer's wives looking for juicy stories to swap at quilting bees.

Michael loved Elizabeth, loved their children, his country and his God. But he had always been treated with contempt by those who did not share his faith. He was a Papist. As Protestants supposed, Michael prostrated himself to the Pope in Rome, prayed to plaster statues of the saints, worshiped Mary like she was the equal of God, wreaked of incense and believed the communion wafer really was the flesh of Jesus and the wine His blood. Michael was a Catholic to them who errantly held that good works could get him into heaven and was surrounded by righteous Protestants, including his father-in-law, who considered him belonging to a religion no better than the nigger's voodoo they brought from the jungles of Africa. But thoughts of conversion to Martin Luther's or John Calvin's heresies to make life easier, to better his business opportunities or to fit in had never crossed Michael's mind. He could no more convert to a religion that denied the one true faith than he could deny that he had been born Irish in Ireland. But immigrant or not, Catholic or not, Michael was American to the depths of his soul. Those who loathed him for his faith and origin had no better claim to the land than he, most having recently disembarked on a new continent's shores hoping, as his family had, to escape hunger and hatred, or being decedents of those who had. Michael observed that it was a very human trait to seek out strawmen, scapegoats, pariahs—Indians to settlers, Negroes to poor whites, Irish Immigrants to British, and Catholics to Protestant. The list is long as human history. But Michael had proven and distinguished himself in the Mexican War, leading troops without discrimination. His reputation was for being hard on everyone, regardless of origin, delivering discipline, order and the vengeance of God against the disloyal. He was Captain Michael Kelly Lawler and he would return to war when called by his country, if the cause be just. Especially if it were in support of ridding his country of the evil of slavery that ate at America's core like apple maggots. Michael's hope was that joining a Crusade against human bondage would ease his mind of the shame that had haunted his sleep for years.

~ ~ ~

President James K. Polk had prodded the United States Congress into a Declaration of War against Mexico on May 12, 1846 after a skirmish between American and Mexican troops in the disputed area along the Rio Grande led to twelve American deaths. President Polk proclaimed that the "cup of forbearance has been exhausted, even before Mexico passed the boundary of the United States, invaded our territory, and shed American blood upon American soil." Congress declared war, despite opposition from northern lawmakers who feared the creation of more slave states. No official declaration of war ever came from Mexico.

Ulysses S. Grant, a young lieutenant in the Army during the Mexican war later said, "For myself, I was bitterly opposed to the measure, and to this day regard the war, which resulted, as one of the most unjust ever waged by a stronger nation against a weaker nation. It was an instance of a republic following the bad example of European monarchies in not considering justice in their desire to acquire additional territories."

And a young Whig Congressman from Illinois, Abraham Lincoln, questioned both the motive for the conflict and how it began, asking for evidence to prove the skirmishes that killed troops of the US Army and provoked the war even took place on American soil.

Michael was fully aware of why he enlisted in the fight. His smoldering urge to prove he belonged, his desire to demonstrate his patriotism overpowered questions of military morality. At least until he returned to his farm at war's end, came back to his family, his business dealings with his father-in-law, reacquainting himself with the Negro field hands and house-help of Hickory Hill legally leased from a bordering slave state and his conscience began calling his name in the silent moments, in the darkness of nights too cold even for the down quilts imported from Cincinnati as it will for Catholics—cradle, convert or fallen away. Michael had heard the rumors, descriptions of the atrocities committed by American troops on Mexican peasants. He had seen first-hand the treatment of his fellow Catholics by their so-called superior officers that drove some to desert, feeling the sting of that barbed lash on the flesh of his decency.

~ ~ ~

Armies may march on their stomachs, a sentiment attributed to Fredrick the Great, or Napoleon, but just as likely to have been uttered by a starving French soldier retreating with rag-wrapped feet through the snows of a Russian winter. But mostly armies run on rumors, Captain Michael Kelly Lawler thought, gossip growing in the ranks like gangrene, swelling the enemy to Goliath proportions, or shrinking their own strength to the dimensions of the stone in David's sling, although size is obviously not always the deciding factor.

But one rumor from the conflict between Mexicans and Americans was true, and it sat sourly on Michael's belly. It was the story of a fellow Irishman, John Riley of County Galway, born just four years after Michael saw the light of day in County Kildare, Sean O Raghailligh before his name was Anglicized while serving in the British Army, emigrated to Canada and then to the United States, Michigan, where he enlisted in the US Army, going on to train West Point cadets in artillery. Only shortly after his arrival, John discovered that the hatreds and the bigotries of the Old World had been a shipmate that sailed with him to the New. Resentments against any newcomers had been growing long before the deluge of refugees that flooded America with the Irish during and after the famine. Michael felt the intolerance first hand and had read about them in the papers, the destruction of Philadelphia Catholic churches in what came to be known as the Bible Riots of 1844. Earlier, angry mobs had burned down a convent on the outskirts of Boston. The contempt for Catholic immigrants continued to fester as their numbers grew. Jobs were at stake, and everyone knew the grubby Papists would work for less than any Christian man, sometimes for less than a freed nigger.

In 1836, American squatters lost the Battle of the Alamo, a Spanish Mission in Mexico. Later, the settlers in Texas, led by Sam Houston, using the battle cry, "Remember the Alamo", defeated Santa Anna and the Mexican Army, declaring themselves an independent republic. Texas sought annexation by the United States, but both Mexico and antislavery forces in the United States opposed its admission into the Union. It wasn't until 1845 that Texas joined the Union as the 28th state, tipping the balance of power back towards the slave states, making the Mexican-American War inevitable.

In 1845, influential columnist John L. O'Sullivan wrote in *Democratic Review* "...our manifest destiny (is) to overspread and to possess the whole of the continent which Providence has given us for the development of the great experiment of liberty..."

Manifest Destiny. Providence. God-given. Preordained before Columbus or Cortez, before Lewis or Clark, before Daniel Boone or Jim Bridger that Americans were to possess all the lands from the Atlantic to the Pacific. At first John L. O'Sullivan disapproved of the Mexican–American War in 1846, but he came to believe that the outcome would be beneficial to both countries, and especially for the spread of republican democracy.

John Riley was not as certain. He saw the war as little more than a further oppression of the poor, as clear evidence of the ruling class being willing to kill for lands occupied by those they determined to be inferior, ever eager to invade territory occupied by peasants who practiced beliefs they felt no less pagan in ritual than the bloody Aztec religion that had been replaced by the Jesuit, the Franciscan, and the Dominican conversions, and finally the Protestant ruling class that was not above using an army of Papist immigrants they despised to do their dirty work.

Nativism raged in 1840's America. Publications were filled with woodcut illustrations of ape-like caricatures named "Paddy and Bridget". It spread like cholera in a Cheyenne village and nowhere were reprisals against the foreign born more severe than in the army where recent immigrants, especially the Irish and the German, were punished more severely for infractions than the native-born troops, a favored punishment being the excruciating pain of "bucking and gagging", in which a soldier was tightly bound and gagged for hours. And of course, no Catholic services were offered and the penalty would be severe for troops caught secretly seeking out priests to receive the sacraments. Michael Kelly Lawler saw this abuse and felt a lingering guilt that he had escaped the harshest treatment only because he came to America as a child and most of the old sod had washed away in the seasons that had followed, although the scent of benediction incense still clung to him and could be detected by the sensitive turned-up noses of the gentry.

~ ~ ~

As war with Mexico menaced in the spring of 1846, desertions from the American Army grew. There were the age-old reasons of rancid rations, dysentery, boredom, scorching sun and torrential rains. But for others it was the love of a Mexican woman or for the Irish Catholics the beckoning toll of church bells from the village of Matamoros across the Rio Grande or the sight of Mexican priests splashing holy water on their army's cannon that made immigrant recruits who were too recent to be naturalized citizens question their loyalties—they were soldiers expected to die for a country in which they could not vote. Taking advantage of these sentiments, Mexicans secreted pamphlets through the ranks urging troops to desert, to join the Mexican cause as Catholic comrades in arms where they would be given bonuses, free land and citizenship. John Riley was among the first to take this offer, claiming later it was "on the advice of my conscience." He had obtained a pass to attend a Catholic mass near camp, but dove into the Rio Grande and swam into infamy, deserter but not traitor, since the war had not officially begun.

John Riley's experience and training gained him a commission in the Mexican Army where he organized fellow deserters and other soldiers of fortune into an skilled artillery company, his Legion of Strangers, later becoming the celebrated St. Patrick's Battalion, the *San Patricios*.

At the Battles of Monterrey, Buena Vista, and Cerro Gordo, John Riley and his men proved gallant fighters against their former tent-mates. By August of 1847, U.S. regiments under the command of General Winfield Scott, Old Fuss and Feathers, were poised ten miles from Mexico

City, preparing to storm the Halls of Montezuma. John Riley attempted to counter with circulars that appealed to "my countrymen, Irishmen" to honor their "common bonds of religion and Ireland's long kinship with Spanish-speaking Catholic nations…", pleading with them to desert the American Army and join the Mexicans. The pamphlet never made it to American camps.

On August 20, 1847, John Riley and his St. Patrick Battalion of over 200, including 142 Irishmen defended the fortified monastery at Churbusco. They fought until their ammunition was exhausted. Intervention by an American officer was all that prevented the Battalion from total annihilation, although the assumption was all would be hung. 85 were captured, including a wounded John Riley.

72 would face court martial. General Winfield Scott would personally review each case. To the shock of his Army, Scott reduced John Riley's punishment to whipping and branding, a two-inch "D"—for deserter—seared into each cheek, the brander applying the second upside down in his haste before being marched off to military prison with the few of the St. Patrick Battalion who escaped the gallows.

The Treaty of Guadalupe Hidalgo ended the war. John Riley and the remaining members of the St. Patrick Battalion were freed. John Riley returned to the Mexican Army, promoted to colonel, later honorably discharged, migrating to the port of Vera Cruz on the Gulf of Mexico some claiming he married into a wealthy family, or with the intentions of sailing back to Ireland, where he had a son. He died in 1850 and was buried in the general Vera Cruz cemetery before disappearing from history. But not from Michael Kelly Lawler's memory. John Riley was a fellow Irishmen, persecuted for holding unpopular beliefs. Willing to sacrifice what little he had for his God, but not for the country that treated him with no more respect than the English had given him back or Ireland, or Americans gave the Negroes picking their cotton.

~ ~ ~

Elizabeth's father often remonstrated Michael's tendency to share more than he should with his wife. Her mother knows very little about my life in commerce, John would tell Michael. Sina doesn't want to know, he said. She understands that business of any sort is man's work. Michael didn't argue with these whiffs of wisdom that drifted across the partner's desk, mingled in the clouds of smoke from John Hart Crenshaw's cigar, a smoldering refugee from the Mexican war when US soldiers developed a liking for the darker, richer tobacco preferred in Latin countries, the cigarros that exploded in the use of the cigar by Gringos. Michael seldom smoked, but he did share most of his life with Elizabeth, as long as it did not disturb her female's delicate ability to bear the cruel brutalities of the world. Accordingly, he would never share with her some stories he had heard during the war with Mexico, verified by multiple witnesses on both sides of the armed conflict, of the barbaric acts committed by American troop he never thought to be in their nature. One incident that Michael never forget or forgave involved Arkansas volunteers who had assumed the role of guerrillas, killing any Mexicans they encountered, man, woman or child, in or out of uniform, and a Christmas Day raid on a ranch in Agua Nueva that lead to robbery and rape and murder. When an American was killed in retribution, the Arkansas cavalry took revenge. They rounded up civilians, nearly thirty Mexican men, and committed the massacre in front of their wives and children with techniques they had mastered during the Indian Wars. Samuel Chamberlain, an Illinois volunteer, described the scene: "The cave was full of volunteers, yelling like fiends, while on the rocky floor lay over twenty Mexicans, dead and dying in pools of blood, while women and children were clinging to the knees of the murderers and shrieking for mercy…nearly thirty Mexicans lay butchered on the floor, most of them scalped. Pools of blood filled the crevices and congealed in clots."

~ ~ ~

"You may be correct, in some aspects," Michael conceded with the resentment he always felt when forced to even partially agree with his father-in-law as they sat at the partner's desk, the darkening sky and chill that crept into the office indicating the day's business was nearly done. "Although Elizabeth has convinced me that she is not the member of a weaker sex, women can be more susceptible than men to the ravages of emotion created by calamities, such as war."

"Which is why Sina's greatest worries as my wife have been about raising children, managing the household help and the budget, although she is unaware of everything I do to secure the funding. Cigar?"

John pushed a wooden box of Cuban Pantages, the almost obscenely long and fat rolls of tobacco leaves provided him by grateful business associates after successful deals, across the partner desk to Michael. John prided himself on never having to buy them. The box was almost empty when Michael opened it to remove one of the last pungent cigars John would only smoke after he had outsmarted a competitor.

"Aren't you having one?" Michael asked, running the Pantages under his nose, glorying in the heady scent.

"After you," John said.

Michael replaced the cigar in the box and shut the gold-inlaid lid, realizing he would have been participating in a John Hart Crenshaw victory ritual if he lit it, capitulating to his father-in-law's premise that women should always be kept from knowing too much.

"My throat is somewhat sore," Michael improvised. "Any further irritation might bring on the grippe."

John nodded a knowing smile, took a cigar from the intricately carved wooden box, snipped the end with a pair of silver cigar scissors and ignited the moist tobacco with a flourish of flame from a long wooden match, taking many puffs to bring the smoke.

"War is coming," John said, picking bits of tobacco from his tongue. "Buchanan is a useless president. Millard Fillmore may have run as a Know-Nothing, but James Buchanan is even more ignorant. He will do nothing if the Southern States secede. And mark my words, they will secede."

Michael had heard the tirade many times before, confused as usual as to where his father-in-law's loyalties lay. John Hart Crenshaw lived in a free state that would never leave the Union but had built much of his fortune on leasing slaves to labor in his salt works. Maybe that's America, Michael thought. All men are created equal. They just aren't treated that way when there is profit to be made.

John leaned back in his swivel desk chair, its springs screeching like a rusted gate hinge. He blew a long column of smoke towards the ceiling, then two perfectly formed rings.

"When the war begins," John said, "I assume you will be among the first to volunteer."

"That is Elizabeth's fear," Michael said, realizing he had once again broken his father-in-law's rule of never considering the wife's opinions in business, or in war. "But, duty is duty."

"And a woman's duty should be only to her husband... and her children," John said, the pause indicating that to father-in-law, Michael thought, his offspring were afterthoughts.

~ ~ ~

"Tired?" Elizabeth asked as she assisted Michael out of his great coat. It was too heavy for her to hang on the hook by the door to dry, saturated from the sudden shower that dampened Michael's ride home from town. She handed it to Michael.

"Yes," he said, hanging his coat on the hook. "Weary might be a more appropriate word."

"Martha has dinner ready to serve. Patsy has trained he to be a fine cook and house servant," Elizabeth said. "And she is such a good mother to Enos. Too bad Bob left Hickory Hill before Enos was born."

"Elizabeth…" Michael began. Elizabeth nearly let out a gasp, knowing she had spoken the unspeakable, Michael not needing to finish his sentence.

"And she is so much more agreeable than Ruth." Michael said, knowing Elizabeth would most likely never mention Bob's name again.

Martha had replaced Ruth as their house servant. Ruth had suddenly taken ill with a fever and had not responded to Dr. Hasting bleedings, only growing weaker, unable to eat or drink.

"We should speak kindly of the dead," Elizabeth said.

"Ruth did make a fine stew," Michael said. "After dinner, could we talk?"

"You sound troubled, Michael."

Michael considered, then said, "We can talk about it after Martha's fine dinner. What has she prepared?"

Elizabeth listed the dishes like a menu from an elegant restaurant in St. Louis. Michael wasn't listening. He was making his own list of what to discuss with Elizabeth. What to tell; what to conceal. Followed by, he hoped, a good night's sleep with no nightmares.

Twenty-One

"Oregon Territory ain't no place for you, Dusty. They have laws making you people illegal," Jesse said, holding the reins steady to keep the oxen team in check.

"How I be illegal?" Elias asked. "I's a man just like any other."

"Not in Oregon Territory. Ain't got no slavery out there, but they don't want no niggers...Negroes, neither. Don't want nobody who ain't white."

~ ~ ~

The 1850 Donation Land Act, written by Oregon territorial delegate Samuel R. Thurston, which President Millard Fillmore signed into law on September 27, 1850, granted 320 acres of free land to white male American citizens, as long as they lived on it and cultivated it. If the male settler was married, his wife was granted an additional 320 acres as encouragement to families to settle. Passage of the act resulted in eight thousand Anglo-Americans claiming three million acres of land from 1850 to 1855, as well as a population increase of 300 percent. This also meant that the number of white settlers now exceeded the entire Native population of the region.

However, thousands of women living in Oregon Territory could not qualify for land because they were married to Natives, Pacific Islanders, Chinese, Negroes, British, or French Canadian men. And to emphasize the need for keeping Oregon Territory white, Samuel L. Thurston argued: "I am not for giving land to Sandwich Islanders or Negroes. The Canakers (Pacific Islanders) and Negroes, if allowed to come there, will commingle with our Indians, a mixed race will ensue, and the result will be wars and bloodshed in Oregon." During a congressional debate, Thurston stressed the supposed affinity between Negroes and Natives, claiming that that the few Negro residents in Oregon "preferred to rove with Indians, encouraging them to acts of hostility against the whites instead of settling down and laboring like the settlers."

~ ~ ~

"I's done my time boilin' down salt, ridin' with the Cheyenne, bustin' broncos and drivin' longhorns," Elias said. "I's just lookin' for a parcel of land to work and a pasture for Chief. He done enough work in his time for ten horses. Don't know why it be so hard to settle down and be left alone."

"Just bein' a Negro is enough to anger most white folk. You never gonna change their minds. I hear some politicians talkin' about sendin' you people back to Africa."

"Africa? How can I go back to somewhere I never been?"

"Can't say," Jesse said. "But I do know we got miles to go before sundown. This bunch been lollygaggin' around the fort long enough. Every day counts, even if the tenderfoots complain about me drivin' 'em too hard. Trip's been flat and easy land since St. Joe. Greenhorns got no idea how much it could cost to get to their Promised Land."

"You been to Oregon Territory a-fore?"

"Hell, this is my third trip," Jesse said. "Missouri River to the Willamette Valley, leadin' wagon loads of sodbusters."

"Why's you not stay in the…Promised Land?"

"I ain't the settlin' kind. Not much for cuttin' down trees or plowin' stumpy fields or feedin' hogs. Oregon got too much rain and ain't enough sun for my likin'. Anyhow, figure when I finally have a plot of land the only thing planted on it will be me and my tombstone."

~ ~ ~

Elias had planned to help drive Homer Heaney's herd of longhorn with Abel and Jack along the Oregon Trail until they turned south on the California Trail towards Sacramento. At that point he would split to the northwest, alone with only Chief as his companion, living off the land and his wits like had learned from the Cheyenne. But this layover at Fort Kearney and his talk with Jesse troubled him.

Elias had gone unnoticed at Fort Kearney, a bustling post along the Oregon-California Trail that provided food and mail service east and a resting place to emigrants camping in the wide Platte Valley around the fort in the newly organized Nebraska Territory. Elias was just another trail-filthy drover passing through and only stopping long enough for his horse, his longhorns and him to be sufficiently watered and fed. He had become convinced he could disappear into the trees of Oregon Territory, clear a patch of his own and let the rains wash away his past. But talking to Jesse made it clear that although Oregon Territory was against slavery, but they had no room for the race that had suffered as salves. Elias had been going to ask Jesse if he could tag along with the wagon train, just him and Chief, trading his trail skills for biscuits and beans, hardtack and jerky until they arrived in Oregon Territory But now, his mind was troubled. Maybe he would finish the drive to California as Dusty, then decide who he was, and what he would do. There was talk of war, free states against slave. California was a free state and as far away from slave states as possible. Elias had been wrong about Oregon Territory, which claimed to be a free state. Would California be any better? He was going to find out.

"Thanks, Jesse," Elias said, taking off his hat to shade his eyes from the sun that had risen above the wagon.

"What fer?

"Settin' me straight on Oregon Territory. I's decided to finish the drive and see 'bout California. You stayin' in Oregon Territory this time?"

"Hell no," Jesse said. "Maybe. Kinda like lettin' circumstance make up my mind. Seems like my plans don't never work out."

"Must be 'bout the same for most. They is lyin' to themselves it they is thinkin' otherwise."

"Well good luck to you, Dusty. You will need it wherever you go, all things considered."

Jesse yelled back to the line of wagons behind his to follow and shook the reins. The oxen lurched forward, showing little strain in pulling Jesse's lead wagon, beginning their slow and plodding pace that would take the greenhorns to their Promised Land.

Elis put on his sweat-ringed hat after waving goodbye to Jesse and went to look for Abel and Jack. Although whiskey had been banned from military outposts, there were always some spirits to be traded for with cordial members of wagon trains. Even if only a jug of grandma's elderberry wine. Abel and Jack were not particular. They never knew Elias had intended to veer off to Oregon Territory at the California Trail junction. And he was never going to tell them. Elias would let circumstance make his decisions. For now, he was headed to California with Abel and Jack and a herd of cantankerous cattle. But, circumstance could change.

"Where you been, Dusty?" Abel asked, carrying a sloshing jug he passed to Jack, then leaned against the sod wall of a lopsided structure that passed as the fort supply store.

"Care for a pull?" Jack asked, holding the jug out to Elias.

"Don't drink whiskey," Elias said. "Like a cold beer to wash down the trail dust. But no whiskey.".

Elias had seen how whiskey inflamed the white man's hatred towards his brother leased slaves at the salt works in Illinois, towards his brother slaves in Kentucky, how the white man used whiskey to make slaves of his brother Cheyenne, slaves to a new and powerful evil spirit they had no way of fighting.

"When you're done with that jug," Elias said. "let's get Mr. Heaney's longhorns to California before they get any skinnier."

Twenty-Two

"Much obliged, Captain," Devlin said, counting out coins he had saved for an emergency from the sack he had given the Captain of the ill-fated riverboat for passage that was now being salvaged. The riverboat exploding was certainly an emergency. The gold glittered in the salvager's torchlight as Devlin dropped the coins into his hand. "This should pay for delivering us to Shawneetown, Captain Crispin, is it?"

"It is. And it will. And thank ye for fetching the piano," Captain Crispin said. "It should bring a fine price. Would've floated to Memphis if your Negro boy hadn't hogtied it and rowed it to shore."

"Not my Negro, Captain. I am just delivering him, his mother and his aunt to Hickory Hill, not too far from Shawneetown, I understand. To a gentleman named John Hart Crenshaw," Devlin said, careful to protect his true intentions.

"Name don't sound familiar. But Ted'll help you get to this Hickory Hill, once we finish salvaging and get to Shawneetown. It ain't too far up river from Cairo. We make most all ports headed north."

Beulah, Betsy and Seth were huddled around a large fire the salvagers had built on the river bank for light, trying to dry their clothes and cut the shivering chill. Devlin squatted next to Beulah who had hunched as close to the fire as she could without bursting into flame.

"Captain Crispin said he will have one of his boys, Ted, take us to Hickory Hill when we dock in Shawneetown. He was grateful that Seth rowed in the piano. And a few gold coins were also persuasive. He warned me about Night Riders and kidnappers along the river. I told him we were indebted for Ted's guidance and protection."

"You trust him?" Beulah asked.

"We do not have much choice," Devlin said.

~ ~ ~

Shawneetown faced the Ohio River, for good and for bad. The good was easy transport on the merging rivers that ran through the heart of the continent: the Missouri, the Wabash, the Ohio, the Mississippi and countless tributaries, all the waters that combined to flow past Shawneetown, leading to the Gulf and the seaport of New Orleans. The bad was that rivers rarely respect the boundaries of their banks, leaving Shawneetown at the mercy of wandering water. It was also at the mercy of the changing times.

Shawneetown was plotted to be the "Gateway to the West". And it had a history. The Lewis and Clark Expedition, sent by President Thomas Jefferson to find "the most direct & practicable water communication across this continent for the purposes of commerce", passed the mouth of the Wabash River near the future Shawneetown in November of 1803. The Marquis de Lafayette, the last surviving French general of the American Revolutionary War, made a grand tour of the then twenty-four states from July 1824 to September 1825. He visited Shawneetown in May of 1825, greeted as a national hero who had helped create the nation, as though "Washington himself had risen from the grave," a citizen said. Legend is that Lafayette saw a man in shabby clothes standing in the doorway of the room where Lafayette was speaking in Shawneetown, reluctant to greet the General who rushed to the old man when he recognized him, embraced him, and fell into long conversation of how his friend was a revolutionary soldier who had saved Lafayette's life during the war. And as legend goes, when a delegation from the newly-chartered village of Chicago visited Shawneetown in 1833 they were told by the visitors that Chicago was too far away from Shawneetown to ever amount to anything. The Second Bank of Illinois, built in 1840 at the cost of $86,000, signaled Shawneetown's importance as a river town built and booming on agriculture, coal iron ore and salt mining. In future years there would be a decline as local resources were depleted, railroads spread and floods threatened Shawneetown's very existence, the great flood of 1937 finally driving the town three miles inland to higher ground.

But as Devlin, Beulah, Betsy and Seth approached Shawneetown on the river, days of decline were far in the future. It bustled with boats loading and unloading, allowing the salvage crew to land and disembark their human cargo without drawing attention. Even though Cairo, further south, was the hub of the Underground Railroad in Southern Illinois, other stations were strung north along the rivers.

"Not far out of town there's a small farm, run by the Widow Alice with the help of a couple of Negroes. Alice is a Station Master on the Underground Railroad. I deliver passengers to her when I can," Ted said in a hushed voice as he tied the boat to the dock. "The boys'll be busy unloadin' the salvage and hagglin' with the dealers in town for good prices, then tryin' to drain the taverns of all whiskey and beer. Anyway, I know where we can hire a cheap buckboard and horse and I'll drive you to the farm. Shouldn't take long to get you folks there. No one asks questions about men leadin' a group of Negroes round these parts."

"We are in your debt, Ted," Devlin said, shaking his hand. "We'd be floating out to sea with the piano by now if it hadn't been for you and the other boys."

"No debt," Ted said. "Got a piano out of the deal. Not often we find a Steinway bobbin' in the river, carryin' passengers. Now, let's get you to the Widow Alice. There's plenty more salvaging for us to do up and down the river. Some fools always blowin' up a boat, or runnin' aground. Keeps us salvagers busy."

~ ~ ~

"Eyes down," Devlin reminded his band of refugees as Ted hired a wagon and horse at the livery. "Remember. I am a dealer delivering you as leased slaves. Draw no attention. And please, kind lady…"

"I know," Beulah snapped in a whisper. "I is a slave and it ain't my place to look no white man in the eye."

"Maybe in Chicago," Devlin said. "But not here. And not now."

Ted led a horse out of the stable and began harnessing it to a buckboard in a line of three wagons that all looked as old and tired as the grey gelding.

"I'll take you as far as the Widow Alice's farm," Ted said, tightening buckles without turning to talk directly to Devlin. "Then, you are on your own. I'll return the horse and wagon to the livery stable."

"Understood," Devlin said.

"Thank you, Mr. Ted. For your…kindness," Beulah said averting her eyes, practicing her slave manner as Devlin insisted, looking up to see Ted's hard expression soften.

~ ~ ~

The late afternoon sun slanted sharp shadows across the farmyard where chickens pranced and pecked for leftover feed, scattering as the Widow Alice led the refugees to the house after Ted dropped them off, waved goodbye and hurried back to Shawneetown before dark.

"No rain tomorrow, my old bones tell me," Alice said. "Get some rest tonight before…"

Alice Ward did not finish her thought, always careful not to speak of plans where they might be overheard, even if there were only chickens to hear them.

Alice Ward was a widow, left a small farm when her husband, Samuel, died two winters before from the Yellow fever. But she was not alone. She had Jesse, a free man of color and his wife, Peggy, to help with the chores, which were never ending. There was a small orchard of apple, pear, sour cherry and plum to tend and fruit to preserve. Potatoes, turnips and beets to be dug for the root cellar. A patch of corn to cultivate that fed the pigs and a smokehouse for ham and links. A milk cow. A mule for plow or wagon. Some goats, a chicken coop for eggs, two cats for the river rats and an aging hound that barked at foxes stalking the henhouse even if he was too old to put up much of a chase. With little left over to take to market, money was scarce, but there was not much Alice and her help couldn't make, mend or repair to reap a good life from the fertile earth. And to feed her soul, Alice had become a Station Master on the Underground Railroad, her farm a depot, Jesse and Peggy conductors and agents, folks from Shawneetown generous stockholders providing passengers tickets on the tracks leading to northern terminals. Night Riders knew Jesse was handy with a shotgun and pistol and skirted Alice's farm in search of easier prey.

"I believe I might have met your mama," Alice said as they climbed the steps to the porch. "Isn't her name Patsy?"

It had been so long since Beulah heard her mama's name spoke it hardly sounded familiar.

"Yes, ma'am," Beulah said. "That be the name one of her masters give her. How you know my mama?"

"Years ago now, just passing through on the road to Shawneetown for supplies. But something about the depth of her grief touched me. I have never forgotten her. The horse pulling the wagon she was riding in had thrown a shoe and was going lame. The driver stopped at our farm for help. Samuel was alive then, and told Jesse to help with the horse. Jesse is a good blacksmith and had them on their way in no time. But the driver was quite a talker. A white haired Negro man. Patsy didn't say much, but the man made up for it, Patsy looking pained by the details of his story. While Jesse worked on shoeing the horse, the old man introduced me to Patsy and told of how her girls, Beulah and Betsy, were taken by Night Riders from Hickory Hill. I knew of Hickory Hill. As I knew of John Hart Crenshaw. You might say we are competitors."

"Competitors?"

"He enslaves Negroes for his own profit while I work hard to set them free."

"Like undoin' wild horses hobbles and openin' the corral gate?"

"Something like that, Beulah. That is a very pretty name. I believe it means "married" in Hebrew."

"I ain't married, ma'am, but I does have a boy, Seth. And a sister, Betsy."

"You can call be Alice."

"Yes, ma'am."

"Just remember, Beulah. You and your kin are not wild horses, or plow horses, or animals of any kind. You are God's children as much as any minister in the pulpit."

"I remember that. I truly will," Beulah said, feeling a certain pride she feared might be sinful.

"I have been talking to Mr. Doyle about your plans to rescue your mother from Hickory Hill…"

"I know it be dangerous," Beulah began.

"Foolhardy," Alice said. "Reckless, rash, risky and imprudent. And exactly what I would do in your place. I have been foolhardy since Samuel died. Be foolhardy, Beulah. God blesses the foolhardy. He doesn't want you to hide your freedom under a bushel or bury it in the ground."

"Ma'am?"

"I do have a tendency to preach," Alice said. "Now, it's time for supper. Peggy is an excellent cook. Then a good night's sleep and in the morning you and Mr. Doyle can…"

"Be…foolhardy?"

"You must be hungry," Alice said, smiling.

"That I be," Beulah said, following Alice into the farmhouse. Betsy and Seth were already in the kitchen, watching Peggy stir a pot of something savory bubbling on the stove. "That I be."

~ ~ ~

The mule resisted as Devlin tugged the harnesses into place and tightened the straps.

"A wee bit early in the morning for you, is it now, boy," Devlin said.

The mule shook his head, snorted and settled down.

"There you are. Just going for a little drive this fine morning. You'll be back in the barn and on your feed by sundown," Devin said, hoping it was true. It was nearly ten miles from Alice's farm to Hickory Hill to rescue Patsy. Then the same distance back without being detected. Beulah said Alice called the plan foolhardy, but was in favor of it. Might not be strong enough a word, Devlin thought. But then, his life had never been a bed of roses, and you often get pricked when picking a beautiful bloom. Devlin lead the mule from the barn and finished harnessing him to Alice's farm wagon, sturdy and suitable to the job at hand. Alice was standing on the farmhouse porch. There was a chill in the air, but no frost. The sky was overcast, but without the smell of rain, or snow. A good day for travel, especially on the well-maintained road between Shawneetown and Hickory Hill, once a thriving salt works, but now a farm struggling to support the Crenshaw family and leased slaves. Many freight wagons filled with sacks of boiled-down salt had once rolled along the road to the river port, and coffles of shackled slaves leased to mine the salt shuffled in the dust or mucked in the mud from the river to Hickory Hill to work the salt. Even with the salt mines closed, Devlin was confident he could explain to any curious fellow traveler where he was going alone with a Negress in his farm wagon pulled by a mule. And, he could just as easily explain why he had two on his return trip to the river. His Blarney had never let him down before and there were no omens it would now.

Beulah came out on the porch, holding a steaming cup.

"Coffee, Mr. Devlin?"

"Don't mind if I do," Devlin said, bounding the stairs with the agility of a lumberjack hopping logs rafting on a river.

"Careful," Beulah said. "It be boilin' hot."

"It is delicious," Devlin said, taking a sip. "Ready for our adventure?"

"Been up for hours," Beulah said. "Just the thought of seein' Mama…"

"We need to get there first. Dress warm."

"Mrs. Alice give me a winter shawl. She done told me the same thing. Dress warm. No one never told me that before. Only Mama."

~ ~ ~

The sun rose at their backs as the mule pulled the farm wagon with Devlin and Beulah at a steady pace towards Hickory Hill, then was swallowed by the overcast of a waning winter. The snows had melted, the mud left dried to wagon ruts and the road deserted at such an early hour. Devlin had no need for his Blarney to satisfy the curiosity of strangers, or fear of the Night Riders that only rode under the cover of darkness, then scurried out of sight like potato bugs exposed to the light under overturned stones. The trail was theirs alone until Hickory Hill loomed high on a hill in the distance, and to the right, shacks where Beulah said she had lived with her mother and Betsy so many years before. Smoke rose from its river stone chimney.

"Look familiar?" Devlin asked, pulling back on the reins to bring the mule to a halt.

"It do," Beulah said.

"Where do you think your mother would be?"

"This time a mornin', breakfast bein' done, she probably back in her cabin. If Mr. Crenshaw be at work, Mama done in the main house 'til supper need fixin'. Probably mendin' and sewin', without the vegetable garden to tend."

"Then to Mama's cabin it is," Devlin said, directing the mule towards the row of shacks along a creek. "First, we hide the wagon best we can in the bush and go on foot. Where would the rest of the…help be at this hour?"

"They's workin' the salt when I be here."

"Apparently your Mr. Crenshaw is out of the salt business. He's taken up farming…"

"Ain't my Mr. Crenshaw," Beulah snapped.

"I meant nothing by that, Beulah," Devlin said. "I am only trying to keep us from being discovered. Too cold for farming, and less help would be required than when salt was being worked. We will take our chances and assume they are doing some kind of chores away from their cabins at this time of the morning. If so, we can get in, rescue your mother and return to the Widow Alice's undetected."

Beulah hadn't totally allowed herself that hope, but it was starting to rise in her like the sun glowing just below the horizon of a cloudless sky. To see Mama. To hug and kiss Mama. The idea of her family all being free was not a thought she could dwell on without fear of it vanishing like a sweet dream at dawn.

"There it be," Beulah said as they approached the cabin. They had seen no one since leaving the hidden wagon and mule. Except for smoke curling from the chimney, the cabin appeared abandoned, the unpainted clapboard siding even more weathered grey and splintered than Beulah remembered, roof patches looking like sores on a mule's rump. The stairs sagged and creaked as they stepped onto the porch that groaned even louder under their weight.

"Hard to sneak up on anyone..." Devlin began. The door swung open.

"Far enough," a woman's voice called out from the doorway. Devlin and Beulah's eyes were focused on the barrel of a shotgun pointing at them.

"Easy now," Devlin said. "You wouldn't want to shoot your daughter, now would you?"

"Ain't got no daughter," the woman said.

"Mama?" Beulah said, taking a step closer, the porch boards screeched like an owl diving on a mouse. The shotgun lowered.

"Beulah, could that be you?"

"It be me, Mama. It be me," Beulah said, running to the doorway.

"Now before you drown each other in tears," Devlin said to a hugging and sobbing mother and daughter, "we need to be on the road back to the Widow Alice's farm."

"Leave? You just got here. Why you leave so soon..."

"Mama. You don't understand. We come to take you away. Betsy and your grandson Seth be waitin' at the Widow Alice's. We all goin' north. Chicago, Mr. Devlin say."

"Betsy alive? And I got a grandson? My head be spinnin'," Patsy said, wiping her tear-wet face with her apron.

"Gather what you can carry," Devlin said to Patsy.

"We need to be back at Alice's farm before dark."

"Ain't got much," Patsy said.

"You still got that winter shawl?" Beulah asked. "It be cold and you need to dress warm."

"That be what I always tell you," Patsy said.

"I remember," Beulah said.

"I got a grandson," Patsy said. "This mornin' I ain't got no children and now I got two daughters and a grandson. God do work in mysterious ways."

"Yes he do," Beulah said, hugging her mother.

"Now, let go of me so I can get my shawl. I got Betsy and…"

"Seth," Beulah said.

"I got Betsy and Seth to meet," Patsy said. "Seth be a good name. A real good name."

"Ladies. Best we get to our destination before dark."

"Mr. Devlin be right," Beulah said. "They be Night Riders prowlin' like bobcats once the sun go down. Time to leave Hickory Hill, for good."

~ ~ ~

"Where you get that shotgun, Mama?" Beulah asked as Devlin drove the wagon out of the brush and they climbed into it. "Never seen you with no gun before. Mr. Crenshaw'd whip you bad if he ever caught you with a gun."

"After you and Betsy was took, I…borrowed it from the Mr. Crenshaw. He got so many fancy huntin' guns he don't miss one."

"That be stealin', Mama," Beulah said. "Preacher'd say it be a sin."

"Mr. Crenshaw stole my girls," Patsy said. "Nothin' I stole of his could…"

"Even the score," Devlin said.

"Don't matter none now. I done left the scatter gun in the shack," Patsy said, taking Beulah's hand. "Done got my girls back. And a grandson."

Devlin shook the reins to speed the mule best he could on the road that showed no traffic. Still hidden in the thick overcast, the sun had passed noon.

"Ladies, unless there are unforeseen mishaps, we should be pulling into our train station before sundown."

"Train station?" Patsy asked.

"Underground," Devlin said. "Beulah will explain."

Devlin spurred the mule on. They had been fortunate so far, but he wasn't sure how long his Irish luck would hold back.

~ ~ ~

The Irish luck held back from Hickory Hill to the Widow Alice's farm, the few wagons and riders they passed paying little attention to a white man driving a buckboard with a cargo of niggers, looking somber, averting their eyes, most likely going down to the river and south to the cotton fields.

"That's Alice's place on that little rise," Devlin said to Patsy. "Hopefully, there will be a nice warm supper waiting for us."

The mule had kept a steady pace, delivering on Devlin's promise of arriving by sundown, a relief to Devlin who knew that any travel after dark would have called down the Night Riders like a pack of starving wolves descending on a herd of blizzard-bound buffalo.

Devlin drove the wagon into the farmyard and towards the barn, the mule nodding its head, anticipating its feed bag. Alice had come out onto the porch to greet the new arrivals.

"Miss Alice," Devlin said, helping Patsy and Beulah down from the wagon. "May I introduce you to Miss Patsy."

"You must be anxious to see Betsy again," Alice said. "And to meet your grandson."

"I is, Miss Alice. It be too much to believe."

"Believe," Alice said. "Seth is just as anxious."

Twenty-Three

John Brown rode from jail to the gallows sitting on his coffin made of black walnut in a wagon drawn by two white horses. It was just before eleven o'clock on the morning of December 2, 1859. More than one thousand troops lined the field to protect the gallows in Charles Town, Virginia, where the fierce abolitionist was going to die.

John Brown's plan to seize weapons from the United States Armory and Arsenal located in Harpers Ferry, Virginia, where the Potomac and Shenandoah rivers met, to arm Negroes, igniting a slave rebellion, had failed. After a thirty-six-hour standoff, Brown and his twenty-two men, including his sons, were captured or killed by State Militia and U.S. Marines led by Colonel Robert E. Lee, assisted by Captain J.E.B Sturart.

He was tried and convicted of conspiracy and inciting insurrection and treason against the State of Virginia. Fearing further uprising by Brown's supporters, the Governor sent part of the Corp of Cadets from the Virginia Military Institute as protection for the execution, including a professor of natural history named Thomas Jackson, later known as the Confederate General Thomas "Stonewall" Jackson, to be eye eyewitness to the death of the man who had written a note in his cell before leaving for the gallows: "I, John Brown, am now quite certain that the crimes of this guilty land will never be purged away, but with Blood. I had, as I now think vainly, flattered myself that without very much bloodshed, it might be done." It would take more bloodshed than John Brown could have ever imagined.

~ ~ ~

John Brown stood on the gallows, straight as a cadet in a West Point parade ground inspection, his long white beard blown by a noon hour wind that foretold a storm, Moses at the shore of the Red Sea ready to raise his staff, if his hands had not been tied behind his back.

Robert Wilson stood in the crowd gathered for the execution. He was a head taller than most.

"Watch," Earl Brighton said, poking Robert in his ribs.

John Brown had been standing on the gallows for a full ten minutes with the white hood over his head, unwavering, silent, waiting. Finally, the rope was cut that released the trapdoor. He fell less than a yard, his knees still above platform, his arms rising up his back, hands clenched before falling in slow spasms until John Brown's body swayed lifeless in the breeze.

"That's what happens to nigger lovers and those that try to defile the natural order," Earl said.

Robert Wilson had heard this all before. Niggers had their place and anyone trying to change that, nigger or white, would pay the price, even if it came to war between the States to keep the right to own slaves. Even if you didn't own slaves but worked for those who did. Some things can never change.

Robert Wilson. Uncle Bob. Bob. He wasn't a field slave, or a house slave, or really a slave at all, but he still wasn't a free man of color, either. Since leaving Hickory Hill his services had been sold like a stud stallion, travelling from plantation to plantation, wherever the slave population was dwindling while the amount of work increased, a missionary spreading the faith of the Southern Gentleman, the culture of gentility, the God-ordained society of nobleman to serf, master to slave. With the slave trade illegal, a good breeder was the best alternative. Bob was the best. He prided himself on treating the women with kindness. They were going to be mothers, mothers of his children, and mothers deserved respect.

"How many places have you studded?" Earl asked as they walked away from the gallows.

"Last count I believe it be seven."

"Lucky seven," Earl said.

"I been lucky," Bob said, thinking of how his special service had kept him out of the fields, given him the best food and drink and constant praise for his accomplishments, even if the women did have something to do with it.

"And today's another lucky day for you, Bob," Earl said, slapping Bob on the back as if there were headed to a tavern for a beer. "Daddy tells me a new girl should be arriving later this afternoon. Fresh from Maryland. House slave. Young and unsullied and ready to breed. Yes sir, it's your lucky day, Bob."

"Sure is, Mr. Earl. My lucky day," Bob said, forcing a grin, his head bowed to diminish his height that tended to anger Earl and other white men. "My lucky day."

~ ~ ~

Bob had been treated as special since he was born. He was a big baby at birth, nearly killing his mama.

"You ripped me like a bloody sheet when you was born," she told him when he was old enough to understand. "And you come out cryin' like I's the one that hurt you. But you be Mandingo. Big and strong. You meant for something special."

As he grew, Bob slowly came to realize that Mandingo was a tribe from a distant place called Africa he'd heard old slaves whisper about at Sunday meetings before the preachers led his ragged congregation in songs about heaven.

"How come you gotta die to be happy, Mama?" Bob asked one Sunday leaving church.

Bob's mother looked at him as if he had taken the Lord's name in vain.

"Preacher say slaves be happy when they die and go to heaven," Bob continued. "Is heaven in Africa, Mama?"

"What made you say a thing like that? Heaven ain't nowhere on this earth. The devil made sure of that when he tempted Eve with that apple. She disobey God and she trick her husband into disobeyin' God and that brought pain and death into the world."

Bob stopped asking questions. If he kept it up, he knew his mama would be telling him he was too young to understand. But he understood. If you disobeyed, you suffered. God wanted obedient servants and the rebellious ended up in hell. Must be a lot of slaves in heaven, Bob thought, except for the runaways, since they just run straight into the arms of Satan.

~ ~ ~

Bob didn't like to remember how he got from his mother's protection to riding in the wagon beside Earl Brighton, the son of an owner of the Virginia tobacco plantation he was being brought to as a stud with the reputation of producing new generations of strong slaves from his Mandingo blood. He didn't recall the name of his new plantation, some fancy name to make it sound more than the dirt farm it was. He didn't remember the names of the other plantations or owners that had sold his services from Illinois to Virginia like a prize bull, but he couldn't help but remember that night at Hickory Hill that changed his life and began his wandering like a Hebrew lost in the desert. It haunted him like dreams of his mama being sold when she was still young enough to pick cotton and he was old enough to begin his life as a stud.

~ ~ ~

"Goodbye, Mr. Nash," John Hart Crenshaw said. "Be careful on your ride. I warned you about my brandy."

"It was delightful," Benjamin Nash said, mounting his horse with controlled precision. "Napoléon may have miscalculated by attacking Russia in winter, but his brandy remains excellent. As was dinner."

"Patsy never disappoints," Francine Hart Crenshaw said, standing on the porch beside her husband, supplying subtle support as he wobbled slightly on his crutch. "Good evening, Mr. Nash."

Benjamin Nash waved as he turned his horse towards the road. If he hurried, he could be home on his farm before twilight turned to total darkness.

"Dreadful," John said, closing the front door.

"Dinner?" Elizabeth asked.

"That man," John said. "I do not know why I feel obligated wasting a good meal on him."

"Business?" Elizabeth asked.

"I didn't think you cared about business," John said.

"I do when it gets you so upset."

"I'm not upset. Maybe a little," he confessed. "Nothing another glass of brandy won't cure."

John Hart Crenshaw hated Benjamin Nash. He was a banker and in John's book, no better than a petty thief. But the money he controlled was necessary in sustaining John's farm commercial enterprises that had replaced the salt works.

"You look very tired," Elizabeth said. "You need a good night's sleep."

"I must let Patsy's roast beef digest first," John said, "tender as is was. Then one more brandy…"

"John."

"I know," John relented. "Fewer cigars and less brandy. Doctor's orders for a longer life. But, if all the enjoyments are eliminated, what is the purpose? And it won't grow my leg back."

"I'm going to see if Patsy needs help in the kitchen," Elizabeth said, smiling as she turned to the front door, knowing John would do what John did, her counsel taken as readily as he would take advice from a field hand.

"I'll be in after my cigar," John said, reaching into his coat pocket and heading for the porch. "It's such a pleasant evening."

~ ~ ~

Benjamin Nash nearly slid backwards off the saddle as he pulled hard to rein his horse. A Negro woman had walked into his path from behind the last cabin in a row of servant quarters, as those from polite society would call them.

"Hey. Watch where you're going," Benjamin yelled. "You almost got trampled."

"Sorry, sir," the girl said. "I's just hurrin'. Got to help Patsy clean up supper…"

"You are a sassy little nigger," Benjamin said, catching a glimpse of her face revealed by the first colors of sunset in the wispy clouds over the cabins. Her nose betrayed the delicacy bequeathed by a string of white masters. Her complexion was light with faint freckles, her body still slim with youth, a slight bulge of the pickaninny she was carrying in her belly starting to show and her back straight, not bent from years of picking cotton.

"Slow down, girl," Benjamin said. "What's your name?"

"Martha," she said. "I's late…"

"Martha. That's a nice name," Benjamin said, dismounting, feeling the last glass of brandy in his legs as he found his balance. He gave his horse a slap on the rump to move it out of the way. "Nice name, Martha. Very biblical."

"I…" Martha began before Benjamin grabbed her by the arm. "I be with child."

"Well good for you," Benjamin said, pulling her closer. "Then it's best you don't struggle."

She was young, just the way he liked them. She had spirit, but suspected she would give easy to protect the baby. He pushed her dress up, admiring her firm thighs, then looked her at her face, expecting fear. Her expression was fierce. It enraged him. He slapped her, hard. Martha returned the slap with the back with her free hand. Benjamin released her arm in shock before his brandy-fueled anger fanned into fury. Martha ran, but Benjamin's rage compensated for his age. He caught her and threw her to the ground, straddled her and began tearing at her dress.

Benjamin Nash had never heard such a scream. It possessed a wildness that chilled him with the primal fear of having offended some vengeful god. He put his hand over Martha's mouth, attempting to silence her. She bit his hand. He pulled it away, bleeding. The scream wouldn't stop. Some force pulled him from her, stood him up and turned him around to face the biggest Negro he had ever seen, a shining blackness outlined by the red glow of the setting sun. The scream stopped.

"Get your damn hands off me, nigger," Benjamin said with the confidence of a white banker. "It's not your place to interfere."

"Bob, let go of him," a man called, coming down the row of cabins.

Bob turned, one arm crooked around the banker's throat. There was enough daylight left for Bob to recognize Willy the overseer, pointing his revolver at him. Martha had struggled up from the dust, moving away to lean against a cabin wall. Her face was stern; her eyes dry.

"Now, you let go of that man, Bob. I ain't never whipped you before, but you hurt a white man and I will beat you near death and Mr. Crenshaw won't stop me."

"He was rapin' Martha," Bob said. "And she be with my child. My child."

"Don't matter none," Willy said. "He's a white man and you is a nigger."

"Ain't right. Just ain't right."

"Lots of things ain't right," Willy said.

"And you can't change them this way, Bob," John Hart Crenshaw said. He had heard Martha's scream while finishing his cigar on the porch and come to investigate, curiosity overriding any pain produced by his wooden leg and crutch.

"He be rapin' my Martha, Mr. Crenshaw," Bob said. "And she be with child. My child."

"I assure you I concur that Benjamin Nash is scum. Don't know a banker who isn't. Living off the hard work of others. Nothing but leaches. I like you, Bob. I always have. I was told you were the best stud when I bought your services in Washington City and you are. But I can't allow one of my niggers to hurt a white man. It's contrary to everything sacred."

"So is rapin' Martha," Bob said, his massive forearm still locked around Benjamin Nash's neck, the banker's toes struggling to touch the ground.

"Let go of Mr. Nash," John said, "and we'll forget this ever happened. I am certain that Mr. Nash's cooperation can be purchased. He's a banker. He puts a price on everything."

Bob looked at Martha. She nodded. Bob began releasing his grip when Benjamin Nash bit deep into Bob's arm that jerked tighter around the banker's neck in painful reaction. The snap sounded like a woodsman stepping on a dry twig in a silent forest. Benjamin Nash went limp, crumpling to the ground when Bob opened his arm, floppy as one of the ragdolls Martha would make for the children of the leased slaves working Hickory Hill's farm, the children that would be sold when Mr. Crenshaw was low on money. Willy cocked his revolver.

"Put the gun down, Willy," John said.

"Bob broke the banker's neck," Willy said. "I'm getting' the whip…"

"Forget the whip."

"The nigger needs a lesson…"

"Listen to me, Willy. I'll only say this once. Strip Mr. Nash of anything valuable. Bury his pocket watch, wallet, money and coins where thy can't be found. Put him on his horse and dump him on the road close to town and away from Hickory Hill. Set the horse free. It needs to look like a highwayman robbed and killed him in a struggle."

"But…"

"Shut up, Willy. Take care of this situation and you will be well compensated."

"Why you doin' this, Mr. Crenshaw?" Bob asked.

John asked himself the same question. Putting his reputation at risk for a nigger was nothing he thought he would ever do. But now he was willingly involving himself in covering up a murder, even if the victim was only a banker.

"You are too good a stud for some mob to lynch," John said, knowing there was more to it than the potential loss of a valuable property. His relationship with Bob felt like a friendship, something he hadn't thought was possible with a nigger. Bob fancied himself a minister of sorts, able to repeat scriptures to the other niggers he had memorized without the benefit of reading. As a Methodist Elder, John was acquainted with the Bible and became fond of hearing Bob's primitive understandings of God when they talked on the porch waiting for another Negress to be delivered for breeding. God truly does move in mysterious ways, John thought as Bob looked up at him, thankful for saving him from Willy's whip, or the mob's rope.

~ ~ ~

"Rumor has it you killed a white man back in Illinois," Earl said to Bob who was sitting on the wagon seat beside him as he drove to the tobacco plantation and Bob's new situation. He continued to be curious about Bob, even if Bob demonstrated a firm resolve to keep his past secret. The field workers and house slaves were of little interest to Earl other than being useful property on his father's plantation, but Bob was special. Earl admired Bob's profession, and was maybe just a little bit envious.

"My job be makin' babies," Bob said.

"No working in the field for you, right Bob?" Earl said, poking Bob in the ribs. " No cutting up those big soft hands picking cotton or weeding tobacco, right Bob?"

"Never have," Bob said.

Bob had travelled from plantation to planation like a freedman, carrying letters of passage he protected with his life, a notarized document explaining to those who might stop him that he was not a fugitive slave or a desperate runaway but that he was in fact in transit to a new job, his services sold to a new master, having journeyed safely without escort many times, a loyal, reliable and faithful servant to his masters and their God. He had never been whipped, wore no scars on his broad back and was seldom mistreated, except for the separation he suffered from the mothers of his many children, hundreds, the way he told it, which he accepted as part of his trade, as when he left Martha behind at Hickory Hill in Southern Illinois with and unborn child, working his way to Virginia with letters of transit, including the yellowed letter from Mr. John Hart Crenshaw of Hickory Hill, carried now to a plantation where tobacco was king, not cotton or sugar cane or salt.

"There's a war coming," Earl said, his voice becoming solemn. "You know that, Bob? Agitators and abolitionists like John Brown are determined to start one. Yankees have been looking to take Dixie down for years."

"Don't care none 'bout politics," Bob said. "Ain't got nothin' to do with me."

"You're a nigger, Bob. It's got everything to do with you. Yankees pretend they're against slavery, but they're just using freeing the niggers for a reason to invade the South and steal our wealth. If they do that, my Daddy goes broke. And who knows what free slaves will do. Revenge on their masters, most likely. Like that nigger preacher Nat Turner a few years back. That was what John Brown wanted. A slave rebellion to hack up the white people. Are you listening to me, Bob?"

Bob was thinking about Martha. By now the baby was born. Most likely a boy, since Bob's reputation was for producing male children, due to his imposing stature. And all this talk about war and Yankee invasions and freeing slaves was also making Bob think about what kind of world was coming. If slaves had no masters, what would they do? How would they live. What kind of white man would hire a Negro? What kind of white man would want to work alongside a Negro? Ain't never seen no white man boilin' down salt or pickin' cotton, Bob thought. And if there be no slaves, they wouldn't need no more studs. What would this new world of freed slaves be? Heaven on earth, or a different kind of hell? Bob let those thoughts fade with memories of Martha. He was heading to a new plantation and no talk of war or Yankee invasions or freedom was going to keep him from doing his duty to master and God.

Part Three

Twenty-Four

~~1861 The Civil War

"You are forty-six years of age, Michael."

"And still in my prime," Michael Kelly Lawler said, tugging the Captain's jacket he had kept from the Mexican War around his substantial girth, the brass buttons far from reaching the holes. "This one is out of date. I'll be issued a new uniform."

"You can't even buckle your sword."

"Then I shall sling the scabbard over my shoulder."

"It is not a wife's place to be contrary," Elizabeth said, "but maybe there are better ways to defend the Union than on the battlefield, even if you still are in your prime."

"I owe it to my country, and I owe it to God," Michael said, struggling out of his coat.

"I know better than to disagree with a stubborn Irishman," Elizabeth said. "I assume you have already been making arrangements."

"Since Abraham Lincoln was elected President and South Carolina seceded," Michael said. "And years before that. This storm has been brewing since the first Africans were brought to this continent in chains.

~ ~ ~

As strongly as Secessionists argued that the coming war was about states' rights, or Northern Aggression, citizens of Southern Illinois knew the truth. It was about owning slaves, a right some assumed to be God-given, allowing them to expand slavery into the new territories that would one day fulfill Manifest Destiny by completing the United States of America from Atlantic to Pacific. It was a quick slide down the slope to abolition, slavery supporters argued, from permitting settlers in the territories to vote on slavery to the banning of the institution where it already existed. It was an obvious Northern plot to bring plantation owners to their knees by flooding cotton fields with European filth released from Eastern city slums who would demand exorbitant wages for harvesting cotton that niggers would pick for chitlins, corn-husk beds and dirt-floor cabins.

On December 20, 1860, South Carolina seceded from the Union. Five days later, 68 federal troops stationed in Charleston, South Carolina, fled to Fort Sumter, an island in Charleston Harbor. The North considered the fort property of the United States government. The people of South Carolina believed part the new Confederacy.

The commander at Fort Sumter, Major Robert Anderson, although a former slave owner, remained loyal to the Union. With 6,000 South Carolina militia ringing the harbor, Anderson and his soldiers were cut off from reinforcements and resupplies. In January 1861, as one the last acts of his administration, President James Buchanan sent 200 soldiers and supplies on an unarmed merchant vessel, *Star of the West*, to reinforce Anderson. It quickly retreated when South Carolina artillery started firing on it.

On February 18, 1861, Jefferson Davis was inaugurated as President of the Confederate States of America, in Montgomery, Alabama. On March 4, 1861, Abraham Lincoln took his oath of office as President of the

Union in Washington. Weeks passed, pressure grew for Lincoln to take action on Fort Sumter. Lincoln had a dilemma. Fort Sumter was running out of supplies, but an attack to fortify the fort would appear as Northern aggression. States that had not seceded might be driven into the Confederate camp. Yet Lincoln could not allow his troops to starve or surrender and risk showing weakness.

Finally, Lincoln negotiated a deal with the Governor of South Carolina allowing provisions to be shipped to Fort Sumter, sending no arms, no troops, no ammunition — unless, South Carolina attacked. But Davis could not allow the fort to be resupplied, deciding he had no choice but to order Anderson to surrender Sumter. Anderson refused. At 4:30 AM, Aril 12, 1861, Confederate artillery batteries, under the command of General Pierre Gustave T. Beauregard, opened fire on Fort Sumter with over 3,000 shells in a three-and-a-half day period. Anderson surrendered. The Civil War had begun.

~ ~ ~

The day After Fort Sumter fell, the news reached Uniontown, Kentucky, only a few miles north of Shawneetown. Cannons were fired off by jubilant secessionists to celebrate. Echoes could be heard in Shawneetown. Secretary of War Edwin Stanton called for all loyal states to raise troops for the preservation of the Union. He asked Kentucky. The Governor refused. He asked Illinois, their Governor did not. And, although John Hart Crenshaw had backed efforts in the past to make Illinois a slave state, and having profited and continuing to profit from slavery, he decided to support the Union cause, although maybe not as strongly as his son-in-law.

In May of 1861, Michael Kelly Lawler recruited the 18th Illinois Volunteer Regiment and was appointed its first Colonel. The 18th was mustered into service by Ulysses S. Grant, Captain on the staff of the Illinois adjutant general. Lawler was an Irishman of quick temper, attempting to enforce strict military discipline of new troops who tended more to drunkenness and brawling.

The Mexican War had proven to Michael his suspicion that duty and honor were as rare in this world as avarice, lust and a love for the bottle were abundant, although those devilish traits were tempered by a widespread slothfulness that often prevented the worst from happening. Michael had a low tolerance for fools and was dedicated to the proposition that discipline was the cure for all manners of stupidity.

By August of 1861, with his troops still training in Illinois at Camp Mound City, Colonel Michael Kelly Lawler had grown impatient with Army procedures and decided to implement his own measures. He commenced supervised fist fights to settle disputes, threatened to personally knock down any soldier who disrespected his command, and gave prisoners in the stockade gifts of whisky laced with syrup of ipecac to emphasize the righteous glory of sobriety. He pushed his authority to its limit when he appointed a Catholic Priest to be Regimental Chaplin, disregarding the protests of the Protestants who were the majority under his command. In August of 1861, he ordered and carried out a summary hanging of one of his troops who had shot and killed a fellow soldier in a drunken rage without superiors' approval. He was court-martialed and convicted of overstepping his authority, but soon restored to his position on appeal, since it was the opinion of his superiors that he was just the kind of officer the upcoming war would need. It was deemed that Colonel Michael Kelly Lawler's understandings of duty, honor and discipline were required, unorthodox as they were, if the Union was to be saved.

Twenty-Five

The easy gold was gone, dug and panned by 49ers or snatched by claim-jumpers attracted like crows to shiny objects. Immigrants from the Orient crowded into Chinatowns, wayfarers who had arrived in search of fortune only to be run off the gold fields by whites, reduced to earning money from laundries and bath houses, apothecaries and Chop Suey joints to send home to widowed mothers and destitute relatives or to fund bringing their families to America where the streets were not paved with gold but were in fact muddy and stinking with horse dung. But opportunity floated on the air like glowing paper lanterns released into a balmy evening breeze.

Min Li had heard all the stories about the Gold Mountain of California as a young man in China. Mostly from merchant sailors in his hometown of Guangzhou, the terminus of the Silk Road, one of the first ports open to barbarians like the Portuguese and Dutch, the English and even later, to the Americans. When Min Li was a child, the British, behind the façade of fighting for the right of free trade, bombarded Guangzhou and started the First Opium War, although the Empire upon which the sun never set's intention all along had been to gain the monopoly of selling opium to the Chinese, a war which they eventually won, ending the Qing Dynasty's Mandate of Heaven they had held since 1644 when they had invaded China from beyond the Great Wall. China was now another jewel in the British Crown.

Min Li remembered the deep humiliation and shame suffered by his parents at the hands of the barbarians. He had gawked at the bizarrely-dressed strangers in the streets, disgusted by their smell and their toothless smirks. He was perplexed by the uncivilized language they spoke and the way they disrespected his mother and father with commands that sounded like dogs barking, yapped by the foreign sailors as Min Li's parents stood frozen in their wet market stall.

"Chinaman," one of the sailors yelled and Min Li's father. "You runnin' a meat market or a zoo?"

Min Li did not understand the English sailor's words, but he felt the arrogance as if he were a cook from a rich house shopping for live chickens, wearing the eminence of his employer's stature like the Emperor's Dragon Robe.

"You got a problem, boy?" the sailor asked Min Li who stared back into the pale blue eyes, their whites the only clean patches on a filthy face covered with the growth of a scraggly beard. "I'll take that chicken."

Min Li's father stepped between the sailor and Min Li who held a fattened chicken, sensing the sailor had no intention of paying for it. The sailor punched Min Li's father straight in the nose without warning. Blood gushed. He fell, crumpling like a loose pile of clothes on the laundry floor. The sailor snatched the chicken from Min Li's arms, then push him back with the strength built from years of hoisting mainsails. Min Li crashed into his mother and they both fell to the muddy earth of the stall. Min Li helped his mother up while the sailors leisurely strolled away, pausing at other stalls to examine their exotic wares. The chicken flapped its wings, desperate to escape the sailor's grip, falling motionless and silent as the sailor wrung its neck like a washrag. He threw it on the ground and gave it a kick, laughing with his companion as if they had just shared a particularly nasty Limerick.

"Father," Min Li said, kneeling. Blood had pooled but the flow had stopped. Min Li's father's eyes were open but he did not see. His nose was flat, pushed back. He was dead.

~ ~ ~

Min Li's mother did not live long after the loss of her husband. And Min Li had no stomach to continue the wet market on his own. He was a young man with ambition and no family. California beckoned and there was nothing to hold him back. He was free to pursue wealth without sending most back to China. His grandparents succumbed to the plagues long ago and aunts, uncles and cousins were scattered to the Provinces by floods, War Lords and other pestilence. Sacramento, Min Li had heard, was a port that thrived on miners and their needs. Even if the gold belonged to someone else, they would be willing to part with some of their treasure for clean clothes or food. And there was a thriving Chinatown there, second only to San Francisco. Being an only child, his mother had taught him the important skills of laundry and cooking. When he got to Sacramento he would decide which would make him a rich man.

~ ~ ~

Min Li had never been to sea before. He had not eaten in days; his stomach would not allow him. His only experience on the water before had been the river with his father, fishing from a flat-bottomed boat, catching carp and trout and freshwater eels to sell in the family wet market. His only concern then was not tumbling into the river as he hauled nets onto the boat. Now a few chopsticks of boiled rice drove him to the Clipper ship deck, leaning over the railing with little concern if he fell into the rising and falling sea or not. It did not comfort Min Li that he was sailing on the quickest vessel ever constructed by man, *Challenger*, that could transport more than five-hundred passengers, tea and other cargo from China to San Francisco in as few as thirty-three days, covering as much as two-hundred miles per day. That would be nothing more than a month of misery to Min Li, not a great achievement of ship design and construction. But today, a monsoon from the northwest working its way across the China Sea had slowed the Clipper's progress until a favorable tack was found, and the monsoon passed, and the seas fell into slow swell, the perfect storm for sea sickness.

"Not a sailor?" Chen Wu, another of the two hundred Chinese men immigrating to California aboard the Clipper, asked as he joined Min Li at the ship's railing.

"No," Min Li said, turning to dry heave towards the sea.

"You need water," Chen Wu said.

"I have had enough water for two lifetimes."

"If you can't eat, you must drink."

"So, you think you are a doctor."

"I am," Chen Wu said. "As my father and his father before him."

"I am in exalted company," Min Li said.

Chen Wu bowed, put his arm around Min Li's shoulder, guiding him towards a water barrel lashed to the mizzen mast.

"I'm not thirsty," Min Li said.

'Yes, you are," Chen Wu said, tipping the barrel's lid back, dipping in the ladle and handing it to Min Li. "I know. I am a doctor, as my father and his father before him."

~ ~ ~

"Celestials," Chen Wu said. "That is what they call us."

"Celestials?"

"We are the first people in America who did not

come from Europe, or Africa. We are held in awe for our exotic ways or ridiculed for our "pigtails" and strange clothes. The boss men like how hard we work, and for less pay, because we are not Christians. But our ambition often angers the Americans we work with, thinking we are trying to "show them up", as they say."

"You know much about California," Ming Li said. "You have been there before?"

"This is my second voyage. My mother died. I returned home, bringing what I had earned in the goldfields to share with the family. Not a fortune to me, after years in America, but a fortune to the family. I saved out enough for return passage and to buy back my laundry in Sacramento."

"You said you were a doctor."

"I am. But I cannot make a living as one in California. I provide herbs and medicines for the Chinese and wash the gweilo's wool underwear for gold."

"Wool?"

"Yes. Even in the hot weather they wear wool."

"I am going to Sacramento. Tell me more about it."

"Before the Americans, the Spanish conquered the land and forced the natives into labor, and to believe in their god. The river the town is on is also called Sacramento."

"What does it mean?"

"Sacrament. A ritual. In the Spanish religion they eat the body and drink the blood of their god."

"I am not a fool," Min Li said. "You can keep your fanciful tales for the more gullible."

"Very well," Chen Wu said. "I do have a reputation for…"

"Knowing everything?"

"Yes," Chen Wu said.

"Well deserved."

"I am humbled," Chen Wu said, stepping back to offer an honorable bow. "You have brought a considerable sum with you on your journey, have you not?"

"Why…"

"Your manner of dress. The wicker baskets that stow your belongings. Your demeanor."

"Talkative *and* observant."

"It can be an advantage. Being observant, not talking. Although that can be an advantage, too. As a distraction."

"You want to distract me into doing what?" Min Li asked, wary but intrigued.

"If you have the means I would consider you as a partner, once I buy back my laundry in Sacramento. The Americans underestimate us, especially when we are washing their woolen underwear. We have time to discuss my proposal before we make port in San Francisco. And, it will keep your mind off thinking about your stomach. Hungry?"

Min Li felt queasiness growing as Chen Wu began discussing the dinner menu, boiled rice with remnants of vegetables and a dribble of chicken broth.

"You look green as a head of bok choy," Chen Wu said.

Min Li turned and ran for the railing.

Twenty-Six

"It's all your fault, nigger!"

Elias reined Chief to an halt outside the Golden Palace saloon. A man on a black horse covered in sweat and burrs leaned over its shaggy main to give what Elias supposed the rider intended to be an intimidating glare. Elias knew his best option was to continue down the street to the bathhouse, an establishment he had been looking more forward to than the saloon after months on the trail. A cold beer, a fragrant lady and a deck of cards could wait. Now, so could a bath. The rider pulling his pistol demanded Elias' full attention.

"Ain't carryin' no gun, sir," Elias said. "Sign back there say no firearms in town."

"Who read it to you, boy?"

"I can read," Elias said.

"Well, we got ourselves one smart nigger here, Gideon," the rider pointing the gun at Elias said to the man beside him who was attempting to mount his horse. He had obviously more than quenched his thirst at the saloon and the man pointing the gun spoke with a whiskey slur. "Then you heard about the war goin' on?'

"I heard," Elias said.

"You killed my brother."

"Hold on, mister," Elias said. "I ain't never met…"

"Shut up, nigger. Don't matter none you never met my brother, Clyde. You killed him just the same. You and your kind. You started the war."

"How I start the war?"

"Just bein' a nigger. Without niggers there'd be no war. And without this goddam war my brother wouldn't be dead."

"Come on, Enoch. The nigger ain't worth it," Gideon said.

"You one lucky nigger. My brother Gideon here saved your life. Just git your ass outta town," Enoch said, continuing to glare at Elias, slowly uncocking and holstering his pistol before spurring his horse into the street.

"What be his trouble?" Elias asked Gideon.

"Happens when Enoch sees a nigger," Gideon said. "Never shot one, but the whisky makes him talk big. Our brother Clyde rode off to join a Confederate Militia soon as the fight begun. Didn't make it to the war. Got caught cheating in a poker game somewhere in Nevada. Clyde was a lousy cheater and never much of a draw."

"I thought California be a free state," Elias said.

"Lots of folks out here side with the Rebs," Gideon said, a gleam sparking in his bloodshot eyes. "Lots of us don't hanker to niggers. Don't like redskins or greasers or Chinamen neither. Don't need no slaves 'round these parts to do our own work. So niggers can go just back where they come from. No place for 'em in California. This is God's Country and God's Country is white."

Elias had heard all this before, whites talking about niggers to his face like he was invisible. Go back where I come from? What do that mean? Even President Lincoln had talked about sending freed slaves to some strange African country to avoid a war. And other politicians thought the slave problem could be solved by sending them to Central or South America because it was hot, and everyone knew slaves thrived in the heat where the lazy races lived.

What Elias was sure of, the white folks had come up with their own ideas and knew nothing about what Negroes thought or felt or wanted. They considered them children. And not very bright ones. Elias knew he was not a child. He was a man. But he had no more idea where his home was than the white folks did. He knew it wasn't Africa, or some steamy jungle island in the Caribbean. Home for Elias had not been Kentucky where he was born a slave. It hadn't been Hickory Hill, even if Mr. Crenshaw had treated him better than most of his leased niggers because of Elias' skills with a horse. It wasn't with the Cheyenne, although he had learned much from the elders and admired their ways before cholera killed his adopted tribe. The closest he had come to finding a home was on the ranches and the cattle trails as a cowboy, accepted for his knack for breaking the wildest bronco, roping steers and as a drover, riding drag without complaint, driving Texas Longhorns to markets. Elias being a runaway slave meant nothing to the other cowboys in the bunkhouses or when they circled around mesquite fires on the range to trade lies and plates of grub. Now that Mr. Heaney's herd had been delivered to the stockyards on the outskirts of Sacramento to be slaughtered to feed the growing population of merchants, businessmen and the more refined gentry who had replaced the 49ers and roughshod miners, Elias was looking for work, and maybe a real home.

Elias looped Chief's reins over the hitching post in front of the Celestial Baths and dismounted, unbuckling and slinging the heavy saddlebags over his shoulder. Everything he owned in the world was in those bags. A Chinaman sat in a wicker chair on the boardwalk in front of the baths, swatting away flies with a painted fan without the intent to kill.

"You met Enoch and his brother Gideon," the

Chinaman said. "I am sorry. Enoch is a poor representative for our community. He threatens to gun down every Negro he encounters after a few whiskies."

"Not this Negro," Elias said, pulling back his duster to reveal a holstered revolver.

"Did you not read the sign coming into town? No firearms."

"Y'all forget," Elias said, letting his duster fall back to conceal the gun. "Niggers can't read."

"Inscrutable," the Chinaman said. "My name is Min Li. I am the proprietor of this humble establishment."

"Cowboys called me Dusty, but I's done eatin' trail dust. Call me Elias, like Mama did. I needs a bath."

"Most cowboys do. This way, Mr. Elias," Min Li said, opening the door. "The water is hot and the lye soap is strong."

"You talk good for a Chinaman," Elias said, entering into the hushed darkness of the Celestial Baths. Fragrant smoke drifted on the still and steamy air of the room. A sudden drowsiness flooded Elias.

"As fits the situation," Min Li said. "For you, I am master of your primitive tongue. For others, I am fresh off the boat from China. A Coolie fated to do the hard labor. For survival, it is often best to remain mysterious. Exotic. Humble. Inscrutable."

"What do that word mean?" Elias asked.

"Concealing my true face," Min Li said. "Letting Americans think I am just a heathen peasant. Pardon me, Mr. Elias, I am delaying your bath and it will be my honor to provide you with one. Do you have clean clothes in your saddlebags?"

"Cleaner'n what I have on. Wash 'em in rivers and creeks when I gets the chance, while takin' cold baths."

"No cold baths here," Min Li said. "I also own the laundry next door," Min Li said. "We can accommodate all your needs, well, most of them, at fair prices."

"Obliged, Mister...?"

"Call me Min."

"Obliged, Min. Never met a Chinaman like you."

"And you are an unusual cowboy, Mr. Elias," Min Li said, bowing.

~ ~ ~

"Mr. Elias..."

"If I can call you Min, you can call me Elias."

"Elias," Min said, bowing, "I trust you are refreshed. Was the water hot enough?"

"Hot enough to boil potatoes. Lucky I still got my skin on."

"Bathing customs are very different in America and China," Min said, not going into details, but remembering his first impression of Americans as he arrived in San Francisco, the repugnant human stench, the disregard and even contempt for personal cleanliness.

"This is some bathrobe," Elias said cinching the belt tighter. "Ain't felt nothin' like it."

"Silk," Min Li said. "Woven from the cocoons of the mulberry silkworm..."

"Worms?" Elias said, loosening the bathrobe belt, then retying it, remembering he was wearing nothing underneath.

"Woven from their cocoons. Legend has it that long ago, while the Yellow Emperor's wife was sitting under a mulberry tree having tea, a cocoon fell into her cup and began to unravel. From that, Empires have risen and fallen."

"What this animal be?" Elias asked, rubbing his hand over a large patch of golden embroidery against the crimson background of the robe. "Looks like a worm with legs and wings."

"A dragon," Min said.

"That Emperor's wife have...dragon's, too?'

"Mythological creatures," Min said.

"That a Chinaman word?"

"No. Just means it's a tall tale, a story to teach a lesson."

"What be the lesson a…dragon teaches?"

"Avoid large flying worms that breathe fire," Min said, noticing the puzzled look on Elias' face. "I brushed your clothes best I could."

"Obliged," Elias said, taking the neat stack from Min.

"The rest of your clothes have been laundered and are drying. They will be ready this afternoon."

"Think I'll get dressed and mosey over to the saloon, now that Enoch and his brother be gone."

"You be careful, Elias. Plenty of other folks are just as mean as Enoch in this town."

"I been dealin' with folks hatin' me for bein' born since, well, since I be born," Elias said.

~ ~ ~

"Beer," Elias said to the man behind the bar of the Golden Palace Saloon. Elias felt uneasy. This was his first venture into a saloon without being in a crowd of cowboys just off the trail who would be so dark with dust that the color of his skin blended in. Now, fresh from the steaming waters of the Celestial Baths, his skin shimmered like crow feathers as it caught the little light penetrating the filthy front windows. "Beer?"

The barkeep kept cleaning dirty glasses with an even dirtier rag, his back turned to Elias. Boots scuffed on the sawdust-scattered floor behind him as the doors swung shut.

"Boy!"

"I's called Elias," Elias said, turning his head towards the man he recognized. "Enoch."

"No nigger got the right to use my name," Enoch said. "To you I am "Sir"."

"Don't recall you doin' nothin' to earn bein' called

"Sir", Enoch. Beer?" Elias said, turning back to the barkeep who was still diligently ignoring him.

"Nigger!" Enoch yelled. "Git off'n that stool!"

Elias saw Enoch coming in the cracked bar mirror. Enoch threw off his duster and lunged towards Elias who dodged off the stool, grabbed Enoch by the scruff of his greasy neck and smashed his face against the bar. Enoch crumpled to the floor, knocking over a stool and the brass spittoon that emptied its contents on his pants. He would be out for a while.

"Beer?" Elias asked again.

"Don't serve beer to no niggers at the Golden Palace, boy," the barkeep said.

"I ain't no boy and I ain't no nigger. I be Elias," he said, pulling his revolver, cocking it and laying it on the bar, his finger on the trigger. "And I be thirsty for a cold beer."

The barkeep leaned over the bar to look at Enoch who was sprawled on the floor, gurgling blood through his broken nose. There was no one else in the saloon to back him up.

"You better be gone from town before Enoch wakes up," the barkeep said, pouring a beer, scraping off the suds and smacking it on the bar in front of Elias..

"Obliged for the beer" Elias said, taking a coin from his pocket, flipping it on the bar, draining the glass and smacking it back down on the bar. "It coulda been colder."

~ ~ ~

"Your clothes are ready. They are in your saddlebags," Min Li said to Elias. "You will be leaving soon?"

"The barkeep said I should."

"Trouble?" Min Li asked as the front door smashed open. A bloody Enoch staggered into the Celestial Baths. Gideon stayed on the boardwalk outside the Baths, holding a rope in one hand. In the other hand he held a revolver.

"Ain't no guns allowed in town," Elias said to Enoch. Motioning towards Gideon and the pistol on Enoch's hip.

Enoch pulled his revolver and shot a hole in the sawdusted floorboards six inches from Elias' boot. Neither men moved.

"I know the Sheriff," Enoch said. "He'll understand."

Min Li maneuvered to slightly behind Enoch. No one paid attention to the Chinaman. Before Enoch could cock his revolver for another shot, Min Li kicked it out of his hand. The gun hit the floor, spinning like a toy top. Enoch stared in surprise until Min Li struck him across the throat and he fell gasping to the floor. Min Li picked up the gun.

"Follow me," Min Li said, leading Elias through the baths where a man lay back in a steaming tub, smoking a cigar, his sweat-stained hat hanging on a wall hook over a green silk gown and above a pair of dusty, pointed-toe cowboy boots. He stood up suddenly, water splashing out in a flood.

"Pardon us," Min Li said, pushing Elias towards the back door. "The alley will take us to the laundry. We can get your saddlebags. Then to the livery stable. Before Enoch fully recovers, we'll be out of town."

"Why…?"

"No time. Follow me."

~ ~ ~

"Where's the nigger and the Chinaman?" Enoch sputtered, his voice still hoarse from the blow to the neck.

"Took off out the back door," Gideon said.

"Help me up," Enoch croaked.

"The Chinaman's laundry," Gideon said, struggling to pull Enoch up, his legs giving little support. "Bet that's where they're headed. Probably got hatchets or other weapons hid there."

"This time," Enoch said, "I kill the nigger, and the Chinaman, and be done with it."

"Sheriff'll understand." Gideon said, rolling the rope over in his hands and testing the knot. "Self-defense."

"Just helpin' him clean up the town," Enoch said, smiling, gaining his footing, feeling his nose that still oozed blood. "You can let go of my arm now, Gideon. Let's go."

~ ~ ~

Elias paid for Chief's brief stay at the livery stable then bought the cheapest horse and tack for Min Li, who saddled and bridled the horse like an experienced rider.

"You sure you want to do this?" Elias asked. "Only money I got is left over from the cattle drive. What I ain't already spent."

"I gathered some belongings from the baths and laundry," Min Li said, shaking a sack that jangled with a rich ring. "I knew this day would come."

"Better git", Elias said, mounting Chief. "I's sure Enoch and Gideon'll be lookin' for us."

"Like hound dogs," Min Li said, mounting his sway-backed bay.

"And we are the coons they want to tree and skin," Elias said.

Riding into the street, Elias could see two men outside Min Li's laundry. Enoch and Gideon. They were both raising pistols. Puffs of smoke were followed by the cracks of gunpowder explosions and the whiz of two bullets passing and splintering into the livery stable doors.

"Their aim is off," Min Li said, "but it would be prudent to do as they wish and begin our journey."

"You do speak good for a Chinaman," Elias said, urging Chief into a gallop. Min Li urged his bay on to match Chief's stride.

"What will happen to your baths and laundry?" Elias asked, glancing over his shoulder to see Enoch and Gideon recede in the distance, more puffs of smoke drifting as they emptied their revolvers in a futile attempt to bring down the nigger and the Chinaman.

"My business partner, Wang Shu, has been prepared for this day. He knew I was growing restless. Sacramento was never my home. Wang Shu is ambitious and will be very successful with the bath and laundry. Someday he may feel as I do today."

"Where we's headed now?" Elias asked.

"There is a new railroad being built that will run from the Pacific to the Atlantic Ocean" Min Li said. "And it starts right outside of Sacramento. We'll just follow the new tracks."

"Jobs on the railroad? I is tired of cattle and dust."

"And I am tired of laundry, and giving white men baths," Min Li said. "I understand they are hiring Chinamen and…Negroes. Twenty-six dollars a month, Sunday's off."

"Must be hard work," Elias said, slowing Chief to a trot and then a walk. Min Li did the same with his bay. "Like the salt works back at Hickory Hill. Too hard for white men. Used slaves…"

"No slaves on the railroad," Min Li said. And if the war continues to go in the favor of the Union, as it is, emancipation will be more than a piece of paper. Slavery will be a thing of the past, like wagon trains when the railroad is completed."

They both fell into a silence as Sacramento faded in the distance on the road along the river so many had hoped would make them rich. Most were broke or dead. Min Li had said the dragon meant good fortune. Elias had stuffed the silk robe from the bath into his saddle bag. For the first time in his life, Elias was feeling lucky. And in a few days, they would both be working on the railroad.

Twenty-Seven

Brigadier General Michael Kelly Lawler, commander of a brigade in the Second Division of the XIII Corps, tried to pull his sword from its scabbard looped over his shoulder since it would not buckle around his three-hundred pound girth with his left hand, but his hand would not close around the hilt. A year ago, near the Tennessee-Kentucky border, during the assault on Fort Donelson that opened up the Cumberland Gap for the Union, a musket ball had passed through his left forearm, severing muscles. During bombardment of the fort he had also sustained injures to his head and ears, leaving him with some deafness. He had returned home to his farm to recuperate but never fully recovered, losing the use of his forefinger and thumb and, being left-handed, was required to learn using his right hand to write, a difficult and still frustrating endeavor. It did not prevent him from rejoining the Union cause, which was now Vicksburg, high on a bluff overlooking the Mississippi, halfway between Memphis and New Orleans, still in possession of the Confederacy with its commanding batteries that denied the Union free run of the river. Taking Vicksburg would fulfill General Winfield Scott's original Anaconda Plan he had proposed at the war's start, squeezing, strangling and choking the South with blockades by river and sea, allowing no cotton to be traded from the Confederacy to Europe to finance the war or goods shipped in to feed the fledgling country.

On the morning of May 17, 1863, Grant's army camped ten miles from Vicksburg, facing a Confederate army that held strategic placement on the Big Black River, a bayou jumbled with fallen trees and bordered by improvised barriers of stacked cotton bales from surrounding plantations, covered with dirt by rebel details, soldiers war-weary and dispirited and no match for Grant's troops who omens of victory in the blood-red sun rising over the swamp.

Astride his horse that he could only mount with great difficulty, a solider under his command later said, and when he had mounted, it was pretty hard on the horse, Brigadier General Michael Kelly Lawler pulled the sword from its sheath with his right hand with difficulty, swung it over his head and pointed across the mud-brown bog to where the Confederates massed, tired but confident that their numbers and position kept them safe from a Union charge, dug in behind the mile-long wall of earth-covered cotton bales that skirted the shallow bayou filled in with felled trees, their sharpened branches pointing towards the Yankees. After an artillery exchange, hidden in a swale his troops had spotted that was capable of concealing his attacking force, Michael was stripped to his shirt sleeves in the midday heat, forty-eight years old, rotund but a rough and ready soldier who often recited his favorite Tipperary saying to arouse his troops, "If you see a head, hit it." Across the bayou there were many heads, all wearing gray caps, begging to be hit. Michael ordered his men to fix bayonets and with his own variation on the Rebel Yell, kicked his mount into the bayou, armpit deep in places, his four regiments of Iowa and Wisconsin volunteers wading in behind him as minie' balls buzzed by and hit the water like mad mosquitoes. Unnerved by the Union troop's daring, a risky maneuver Grant would never have ordered, many rebels immediately stuck cotton on their bayonets in a sign of surrender.

It was a rout. In three minutes, with the loss of 199 casualties, the Union brigades had captured 18 cannons, 1421 stands of small arms, and over 1700 Confederate prisoners while losing only 27 men killed.

Panicked rebels fled towards the Big Black River in a stampede, burning the main bridge in their retreat, come drowning in terror as they attempted to splash to the other side. Grant did not argue with success, however it was accomplished, and later said, "When it comes to just plain hard fighting, I would rather trust old Mike Lawler than any of them."

The burned bridge was replaced in a day by three temporary bridges constructed with wood from torn down farm houses and barns in the area. That evening Generals Grant and Sherman sat on a log by the Big Black River in the glow of a pitch pine bonfire, watching their troops march across the new bridges to camp, a sight Sherman would later describe as being "a fine war picture."

During the general assault on Vicksburg that followed on May 22, 1863, troops under the command of Brigadier General Michael Kelly Lawler were the only Union forces to enter the Confederate works at the Railroad Redoubt where they planted the flag of the United States of America. Vicksburg was Union territory, the Mississippi was free and the stranglehold on the Confederacy was complete.

Twenty-Eight

"Use your spit, boy," Brigadier General Raleigh E. Colston said. "And put your back into it. I want to see my face in those boots."

"Yeah, Suh," Bob Wilson said. But even using extra polish it was getting harder to return shine the leather lost in a line of battles, dulled by dust, muck, and blood. "I do my best."

Bob liked General Colston. He had a peculiar accent, not the usual southern drawl of the other officers. He was born in Paris, France, Bob had heard from other camp slaves. He was the adopted son of a Duchess, who was divorced from a cavalry general who had served under Napoleon Bonaparte and remarried Dr. Raleigh Edward Colston, an astonishing scandal in a Catholic country. When of age, the young Raleigh was sent to America to live with an uncle in Virginia to study. Prodded to join the Presbyterian ministry by his uncle, Raleigh preferred the military life, entering the Virginia Military Institute in 1843 and graduating in 1846. He taught French and Military Science at the Virginia Military Institute after graduation and commanded a group of Virginia Military Cadets who served as guards at the hanging of the firebrand abolitionist, John Brown, Bob Wilson being in the crowd of observers.

With Virginia's secession in 1861, Raleigh volunteered and was commissioned as a Confederate Colonel in the 116th Virginia Infantry. He was promoted to Brigadier General the same year and given the command of the District of Newport News, Virginia, during the Battle of Hampton Roads when the ironclads Monitor and Merrimack fought to a draw in 1862.

In April of 1863, Raleigh commanded a brigade under Stonewall Jackson who recommended him because they had been fellow professors at the Virginia Military Institute. Now, on May 2, 1863, General Colston would lead one of the divisions involved in Stonewall Jackson's flank attack on the Union Army's right flank in what would come to be known as the Battle of Chancellorsville.

"This be the best I can do, General," Bob said.

"I have a dress pair," General Colston said. "I'm sure the Yankees won't mind if this pair is a little dull. Help me on with them, Bob."

"Yeah, Suh," Bob said, bringing the boots to where the General sat, smoking a long cigar that filled the tent with its foul cloud.

"History will be made today, Bob," the General said, lifting his leg while Bob straddled it to slip the boot on and pull it up under the creased uniform pants leg that was saved for parade dress or important battles in which death was a possibility, even for Brigadier Generals who led their troops from the rear.

"My sword, and my hat," the General said, standing to adjust his coat that Bob had brushed to a sheen. It fell nearly to his knees in a grand scale.

Bob fetched his sword and buckled it around the General's waist, once slim, now the generous cut of his coat concealing the inevitable spread of a gentleman nearing forty, then fetched his prize possession, a hat similar to the one worn by General J.E.B. Stuart that was made in Paris and adorned with a similar black ostrich plume. Bob placed it on the General's head in a slow, ceremonial fashion. The General examined his image in the mirror Bob kept spotless that hung from a tent post over a shaving stand and the porcelain bowl Bob had emptied of its soapy water and dried to a gleam. Brigadier General Raleigh E. Colston was ready for battle.

"Tidy the tent while I'm gone, Bob," General Colston said, as he always did before leaving for battle. "Then make yourself useful around camp."

"I always does, Suh."

"I know you do, Bob. I get nothing but good reports about you. When this war is over I hope you find a good home."

"I's not one to settle down," Bob said, knowing the General was considering the only outcome of the war would be a victory by the South that would continue slavery in the Confederate States of America and that the good home he was hoping Bob would find would be a plantation. "I been doin' some preachin' lately…"

"I hear you are very elegant, for a…"

"When the spirit gets in me," Bob interrupted. He knew the General would feel real bad if he let the nigger word slip out. Bob also knew that the General considered him to be more like a loyal hunting hound than a grown man. But the General had never laid a riding crop on him, even when Bob broke his favorite shaving mug, a crime for which other masters would have taken the whip to him as punishment for being clumsy.

~ ~ ~

Bob had come to be in General Colston's service by way of Captain Earl Brighton, son of the Virginia tobacco plantation owner Bob had been bought to stud for. Earl had volunteered for military duty soon after Virginia seceded. If Robert E. Lee is in the fight, Earl told his father, so am I. Earl was commissioned a Captain in the 116th Virginia Infantry and convinced his father he needed to take Bob with him as his batman, his servant, his camp slave. After some heated debate as to Bob's net worth as a breeder on the tobacco plantation, and value if his services were sold to populate another plantation, Earl finally convinced his father that Bob would never be in harm's way. He wouldn't be a soldier on the battlefield, he would never carry a gun or be shot at by Yankees, he would be a camp slave, doing the menial jobs that freed the Confederate troops to carry on the cause of freedom. Bob wouldn't shoulder a musket. He would dig the latrines, tote the water, cook the meals and shine the boots. Anyway, Earl assured his father, the war would be over by Christmas. Bob had no say in the matter, but was always ready to move on, leaving behind children in various stages of development who would grow up to pick crops like tobacco, or be sold for profit, if the Confederacy won the war, as Earl assured him it would, because God was on their side. If Mr. Lincoln's Army won the war, however, Bob's children might just live free, emancipated, the word he heard other slaves whisper, a word from a proclamation, a piece of paper Mr. Lincoln signed that said all slaves living in the rebel states were free, whether they knew it or not. Bob hoped it was true and that the children he left behind on a string of plantations would soon be free and grow up to plow their own fields, to plant and harvest their own crops they could keep and not be forced to share with any master.

Thoughts of his children living free made Bob smile as he smoothed wrinkles from the wool blanket on the General's cot, then brushed the spare uniform he had taken from the General's trunk, then sat in the folding chair to polish the General's best pair of boots, even though the leather was unscuffed and only dusty, the General having not worn them since the parade inspection when the 116th had first tented and prepared to meet Major General Hooker's Union Army of the Potomac near Chancellorsville in Spotsylvania County, Virginia, whose goal was to capture the Confederate capital of Richmond. General Hooker had replaced General Ambrose Burnside after his disastrous defeat at Fredericksburg the previous December. Mr. Lincoln was still looking for a General who would fight, and win, as he had been for years. Bob always polished the General's dress boots and brushed his spare uniform when he went to battle, the General telling Bob it was his responsibility to make sure he looked his best if Bob needed to take his body home, as good camp slaves were required to do, as he had done for Captain Earl Brighton, taking his body back to his father's tobacco plantation before returning to the 116th.

~ ~ ~

Bob recalled that day the 116th tented. Captain Earl Brighton was agitated. Itching for battle and glory, untested, he bellowed orders like a salty First Mate at Bob who needed little instruction, and less motivation. After the inspection, after dinner, while Earl was enjoying his Cuban Cabañas cigar and his second glass of Old Crow, he began talking to Bob like a drinking companion, although Bob didn't drink, rambling on, his tongue lubricated by liquor.

"Remember when I picked you up near Harper's Ferry to take you to my Daddy's tobacco plantation?" Earl asked, waving at Bob to refill his glass.

"Sure does, Suh," Bob said, nearly emptying the bottle of bourbon into Earl's glass. "Long time ago."

"Not that long," Earl said. "You had studded your way from Illinois to Virginia, travelled free and not got yourself killed. Quite an accomplishment."

"I still got my letters of transit back to the one Mr. Crenshaw give me at Hickory Hill," Bob said, pulling folded papers from his shirt pocket. He opened the newest one like a delicate silk lace handkerchief to reveal a precious jewel. "When I leave one plantation, sold to another, it be written down on a new letter of transit tellin' where I's been and where I's goin'."

"You be careful with those papers, Bob."

"Oh, I am, Suh," Bob said, folding it with the other letters and slipping them back into his shirt pocket, gently patting it like a small child's head. "They be my life saver. They be how I walked busy roads during the daylight so's everyone seen me and I could show them my letters if needs be. After dark, Night Riders woulda just laughed, teared them up, clapped me in chains, sold me, or lynched me for walkin' 'round like I be free."

"We watched John Brown being hung, didn't we, Bob?" Earl said, not really interested in Bob's travels.

"Yes, Suh."

"You know who else was in the crowd, watching?"

"No, Suh. I surely does not."

"Our Frenchie Brigadier General Raleigh E. Colston. Professor Colston was at the Virginia Military Institute at the time, with a group of cadets serving as guards. You know who else was in the yard, Bob?"

"No, Suh."

"Thomas Johnathan "Stonewall" Jackson," Earl said.

"Ain't that somethin'?" Bob said. "All of us in the same place."

"Do you believe in fate, Bob?"

"Don't rightly know what that be, Suh," Bob said, although he did. Bob had learned from his mother at a very early age that there was nothing more aggravating to the masters than being a smart nigger.

"Means that events have already been plotted out in our lives. That there is a divine reason for everything that happens. Means that no matter how hard we try, we cannot deny God's Will."

"It be fate that me and you and the generals all be at John Brown's hangin'?"

"I merely speculate," Earl said, attempting to drain an empty glass.

"What be the...divine reason?" Bob asked, emptying the last of the Old Crow into Earl's glass. He had never heard Earl talk this way before.

"John Brown was a town crier shattering the genteel evening with the news that Yankees were agitating to begin the destruction of the South and would use niggers to do it. Not talking about you, Bob. You're not an agitator. You know your place. It's the niggers who think they are as good as a white man. And that just goes against God's creation, Bob. You being a preacher should know that."

"Slaves, obey your earthly masters with respect and fear, and with sincerity of heart, just as you would obey Christ," Bob recited the first Bible verse he had committed to memory from St. Paul's letter to the Ephesians, the one verse that every travelling preacher at every plantation Sunday service Bob had ever been to preached in his sermon, expecting his flock to answer with an enthusiastic "Amen!"

"And it proves that abolitionists are ungodly, acting contrary to God's word," Earl said, his face flushing in rebel fervor. "The will of God, John Brown's fate, was to hang for the sin of abolition as a warning to others that slavery is a holy institution and God will seek vengeance on those who would destroy it."

"You sound like a preacher yourself, Suh. You surely does," Bob said, picking up the empty Old Crow bottle and putting it in the wooden barrel with the other empties.

"Just speaking the truth, Bob. I'm going out for some fresh air," Earl said, taking a deep draw on his cigar. Have my cot ready when I return. I am tired."

"Yeah, Suh," Bob said, hating to be ordered to do what he was already going to do.

"I won't be long," Earl said, stepping out of the tent and tangling with a team of horses pulling an empty supply wagon.

"Look out!" the driver yelled at Earl, too late.

Earl threw up his arms to protect his face, jamming the lit end of the Cuban Cabañas he held between his fingers into the left lead horse's eye. The horse reared in startled pain, its hoof catching Earl under the chin. Earl fell backwards, stunned. The horse's hooves came down on Earl's chest as it bolted forward, the driver pulling the reins back hard enough to gain control. He tied the reins off on the wagon seat, set the brake and jumped down. Earl lay motionless between the stamping horses on his back, a hoof print pressed into his chest.

"The damn fool," the driver said as he pulled Earl's lifeless body free of the horse team and towards the tent where Bob had emerged. The light from the open flap illuminated Earl's face. The skin still bore the redness of many whiskies, but was beginning to pale. His eyes were open as Bob knelt down to close them. "He walked right into my horses."

"Fate," Bob said, standing to brush the dust from his knees.

"This damn fool stinks like a backwoods still," the driver said, nudging Earl with the toe of his boot as if he were the carcass of a deer killed by a cougar. "Blind drunk."

"I's goin' to go tell General Colston what happened," Bob said.

"You do that, boy. I ain't takin' no blame for what this damn fool done. Walked right in front of my team..."

"Fate," Bob said, interrupting the drivers tirade. "God's will. Can't do nothin' 'bout it."

"Sure, boy. You go tell the General all about what you saw. Ain't my fault. You tell him that. Ain't my fault..."

The driver's words drifted away into the Virginia night mingled with the sounds of frogs announcing their desires in a nearby pond. Bob wondered if the Captain will be surprised to find out there are niggers in heaven, if that where the Captain be spendin' eternity.

~ ~ ~

Bob could see his face in the shine he had put on General Colston's dress boots, proud of his accomplishment. He slid the boots into their burlap storage sack, opened the General's trunk and gently laid them down like putting a baby in a bassinet for an afternoon nap, nestling them between the neatly folded spare uniform, the spare trousers and shirts, the lye-bleached long johns and artifacts of comfort from his family and plantation the General felt he needed to accompany him to war, from battle to battle. Especially important were the letters from his wife, Louise, the envelopes addressed in a flowing script. Bob had slipped a few from those envelopes in the General's absence to read, touched by the General's wife's eloquence in expressing her sentimentality towards her husband, but saddened by her attitudes towards the inferior races, as she wrote, who had caused this dreadful war by their mere existence.

After Captain Earl Brighton died under the hooves of the supply wagon horse, and he delivered his body home for burial, General Colston had taken Bob on as his batman, his servant, his camp slave. Bob had grown accustomed over the years to being traded like a prize stallion, first for breeding purposes, now to dig latrines and shine boots. But, there were good masters and bad masters. General Colston was a good master. He was the kind of master that the defenders of the Peculiar Institution pointed to as a benefit of being held in captivity. General Colston was kind by nature. Although he firmly believed that the Negroes in his service were as inferior to him as the horses that pulled the supply wagons, he believed their abuse would lead to resentment and a reduced capacity for work. He was kind to Bob because he wanted his boots to shine. Bob knew that. Good master that General Colston was, he was still a master, and Bob was still a slave.

~ ~ ~

News filtered back that the battle had not gone well for the 116th. In two days of fighting, the division had lost more than 30% casualties. General Robert E. Lee felt that General Raleigh E. Colston had been painfully slow in directing his men into action. He was the least experienced of Lee's Generals and it showed. General Lee relieved him of his command on May 20th.

On May 31st, Bob packed his meager belongings in a carpetbag he borrowed from the General. I ain't goin' to study war no more, Bob told himself. And he was never going to be a plantation stud again, either. Recorded as a discharge from the Confederate Army in the War Records as slave desertions often were, Private Robert Wilson of the 116th Virginia Infantry slipped out into the surrounding wilderness, a camp slave not worth pursuing, presumably headed to Union lines where he could carry a gun and fight for his freedom. But Bob had never fired a gun in his life. He felt the urge to preach. He wanted to share his belief with his fellow Africans that they were more than mules hauling supply wagons and more than servants shining their master's boots.

Twenty-Nine

"Chicago is the windy city, just like you say, Mr. Devlin," Beulah said as he helped her down from the train, the brim of her bonnet flapping like a flag, secured under her chin with a tight bow.

"Blows in from the lake," Devin said. "Lake Michigan."

"You forgot about me, Mr. Devlin," Betsy said, holding out her hand, waiting for Devlin's assistance.

"You know I could never forget you, Miss Betsy. You wouldn't allow it."

"Ain't that the truth," Beulah said.

"What about your mama?" Patsy said, standing at the top of the steps, holding Seth's hand. "Ain't nobody goin' to help this poor old woman off the train?

"You ain't old, Grandma," Seth said. "But I help you down. The last step be a long one."

"Thank you, Grandson," Patsy said. "You be a real gentleman."

"Mama taught me," Seth said. "Like she taught me how to read."

"Hush now, Seth. Don't be sayin' that round strangers," Beulah cautioned.

"Your mama is right," Devlin said. "Chicago is not

bad as Memphis, but just because there is no slavery here doesn't mean Negroes are treated much better."

In 1853, the Illinois General Assembly adopted the "Black Laws", proclaiming that no Negro from another State could remain in Illinois for more than ten days before subject to arrest, jail, a $50 fine and forceful removal from Illinois. If unable to pay the fine, the sheriff was directed to auction the Negro to the highest bidder willing to pay the fine and court costs. The Negro was obliged to leave Illinois after working off the debt. If not, the fine was increased $50 for each infraction. This was among the harshest laws restricting Negro inhabitants in the nation, and in the State that nominated Abraham Lincoln to be President in Chicago in 1860, provided the Union Army with thousands of volunteers when war broke out and was home to General Ulysses S. Grant who, as President of the United States, proved a strong advocate for Negro rights as the nation reconstructed following the Civil War.

Leading up to the war, Negroes resisted and navigated around the "Black Laws" as best they could, building a small population of tradesmen, house servants and seamen on the steamers that moved lumber, coal, iron ore, wheat, corn and other crops from midwestern farms across the Great Lakes to markets in the East and ports in Canada and out to the Atlantic Ocean. But the "Black Laws" were not repealed until the end of the Civil War and on the day Devlin, Beulah, Betsy, Seth and Patsy arrived in Chicago on the Illinois Central Railroad, the laws remained in place, leaving Devlin to invent the subterfuge he was delivering a family of Negro servants to the mansion of a wealthy shipping baron.

With the Widow Alice's help, it had been simpler than Devlin had feared to find passage on the Illinois Central Railroad, his easygoing manner and forged traveling papers securing seats in the last coach where the black smoke belching from the engines stack drifted down and in through any open window. They had arrived, a little sooty and very tired, at the Great Central Station along Water Street, the terminus of the longest railroad line in the world, in possession of the letter of introduction given to Devlin by the Widow Alice that indicated the location of the townhouse he was to take his passengers and the name of the station master who would assist him in booking passage for them on a steamer running up Lake Michigan, into Lake Huron and docking in Canada.

~ ~ ~

The townhouse was down Michigan Avenue from the station, he had discovered, by asking the conductor who was clearing all passengers from the train in preparation for departure, checking his pocket watch between giving Devlin directions.

"The new Terrace Row. About a mile. You can walk, or ride an omnibus. But that takes money," the conductor said, looking up from his pocket watch to assess Devlin and the Negroes in his company.

"My dear man," Devlin said, "do I look destitute?"

"All aboard!" the conductor yelled without answering Devlin.

"Where would we find an omnibus, sir?" Devlin asked.

"Through the station then out onto Michigan Avenue. There will be a line of them waiting to pick up passengers. Chicago is very proud of its omnibus service. Or you could walk. Only about a mile."

"My ladies are weary from their train journey," Devlin said. "They do not need to walk a mile."

"Suit yourself, if you've got the money."

"I assure you…"

"All aboard!" the conductor yelled again and passengers shuffled towards the train stairs carrying carpet bags and cardboard suitcases lashed with rope and belts, wearing the worried looks of wartime travelers, well-dressed ladies herding well-dressed children like playful puppies, men pulling pocket watches from their vests on long chains festooned with fobs of gold coins to assure themselves they were on time and Union soldiers in patched uniforms heading back to battle.

Omnibuses lined Michigan Avenue as the conductor had said. One driver looked directly at Devlin and nodded.

"I believe we have been summoned," Devlin said to Beulah. We are taking that omnibus.

"Mr. Doyle," the driver said to Devlin when they reached the carriage. I have instructions to drive you to your destination."

"How…?"

"Everyone in. The wind had died down. Looks like we might be in for a little sunshine."

"Thank you, sir," Beulah said.

"Always my pleasure," the driver said. "We must be going."

"Seth," Beulah said. "Get yourself into the wagon."

"Omnibus, Mama. It be called omnibus. That what Mr. Devlin say."

"The exuberance of youth," Devlin said.

"Like you say, Mr. Devlin, that boy keep drawin' attention to hisself like he do he might be usin' that exuberance to be pickin' cotton," Beulah said.

~ ~ ~

The ride was teeth-rattling down the cobblestones of Michigan Avenue, the omnibus carriage pulled smartly by two lively greys.

"Once the slave states seceded," Devlin said to Beulah, "hunting down runaways in a hostile country didn't make much sense. And in Michigan, they don't really mind much if Negroes keep going to Canada. But you are right, it is best take no chances and draw no attention. Our goal is to get to Canada."

"Then what we do?" Seth asked Devlin, sitting as

close as he could to his Grandmother.

"Ain't sure what we do when we get off the boat," Beulah said. "But there be no masters in Canada to tell us how to do it."

"First, we get to Canada," Devlin said.

The driver brought the carriage to a stop in front of Terrace Row, between Congress and Van Buren Street, facing the Lake Michigan Breakwater, eleven connected four-story limestone-faced homes completed in 1856 that only the wealthiest of Chicago could afford. It suited Devlin's story that he was delivering a black family of servants to a rich ship owner and few would ever believe the old money Aubrey family home would be a waystation on the Unground Railroad.

"Thank you, my good man," Devlin said, flipping the driver a coin, hoping it was enough to cover the ride, but too proud to ask the price of the fare.

"My pleasure," the driver said, tossing the coin back and tipping his cap. "Just get the ladies, and gentleman, to Canada."

Devlin tipped his cap, feeling tears forming. He rubbed his eyes as the driver drove away, scolding himself that this was no time for Irish sentimentality. He envied Beulah's grit.

"Come ladies, and gentleman," Devlin said. "Let us meet our benefactor."

"Ain't seen nothin' like it," Betsy said, gazing up at the four stories of limestone that gleamed in the sun that had broken through the clouds. "Like somethin' the Hebrew slaves built in Egypt 'fore Moses set them free."

"It is impressive," Devlin said. "It's what rich white people build to let you know they are rich. Up the stairs, now."

They climbed the steps to the wide stoop and the tall, double red doors. Devlin checked the address and the name from the letter Alice had given him once more, then pulled back the heavy brass knocker and struck it down three times. After a pause, the door swung open to reveal a man dressed in simple finery who took a moment to examine the refugees, then said, before Devlin could state the group's intentions, "This way. Mrs. Aubrey has been expecting your arrival."

They followed the butler down the entrance hall, past a large mahogany coat tree and hat stand. Devlin caught his image in the massive mirror. He took off his cap, running his fingers through his tangle of hair, whacking his newsboy cap on his coat and trousers, producing a cloud of travel dust that settled on the oriental rug runner that ran the full length of the hall. The butler turned to give Devlin an irritated look, then ushered them all into an expansive living room with a tall ceiling of intricately embossed tin squares. An elegantly attired lady sat beside a marble fireplace, a large model of a sailing vessel, fully rigged, the only decoration on the mantle, the fire crackling as if it had been freshly set. She was crocheting on one of two couches facing each other in front of the fireplace, its silky pink upholstery displaying patterns of brocaded roses among the tufts, the curvaceous silhouettes of the carved walnut arms and back mixing the masculine and the feminine. Voluptuous chairs and chaise lounges covered in silk and velvet filled each corner, accented with carved tea tables. Curios along the wallflower-papered walls displayed delicate porcelains and crystal. Devlin had entered a new world he only dreamed existed. It was a great distance from the fields of blighted potato in Ireland to the slave pens of Memphis, employed as purchasing agent for a master who treated the transactions as no more significant than buying and selling goats to standing in a Victorian mansion in Chicago hoping to help set those slaves free.

"Mr. Devlin, Madame. And…"

"Thank you, Meeks," the lady said to the butler, putting the doily she was crocheting down on the lap of her dark pink embroidered dress that complimented the couch. "I am Mrs. James Aubrey."

"Alice Ward said you could help us. I have a letter…" Devlin said.

"There will be time for that, Mr. Doyle," Mrs. Aubrey said, standing, taller than Devlin had expected. "You must be hungry."

"I's starved, ma'am," Betsy said.

"I am sure you are," Mrs. Aubrey said. "The train journey must have been exhausting."

"Smokey, too," Seth said. "What's for supper?"

"Mrs. Grady has roast beef, potatoes, gravy and carrots, I believe, waiting for us," Mrs. Aubrey said. "We eat simply here."

"Ain't nothin' simple 'bout roast beef and taters," Beulah said.

"And I loves carrots!" Seth added. "You got pie?"

"Indeed we do," Mrs. Aubrey said. "Mrs. Grady makes the best apple pie."

"Not better'n my mama's," Beulah said, smiling at Patsy.

"That be a long time ago," Patsy said.

"I's sure they got apples in Canada," Beulah said.

"We can discuss your future journey after dinner," Mrs. Aubrey said. "Now, everyone to the dining room. I'm starving."

~ ~ ~

After Mrs. Grady had cleared the dining table of the dishes, Seth was leaning on his mother's shoulder, sound asleep.

"Mrs. Grady. Would you put Seth to bed. The rest of us have plans to make."

"I ought to…," Beulah began.

"Mrs. Grady has had plenty of experience with children," Mrs. Aubrey said. "She raised six before losing her husband to the typhus and coming to work for me."

"Seth," Beulah said, gently awakening him from her shoulder. "You go with Mrs. Grady. She put you to bed. I be there after we…make plans."

Seth nodded, yawned, rubbed his eyes and followed Mrs. Grady.

"You got room for all of us, Mrs. Aubrey?" Beulah asked.

"Only Mrs. Grady, Meeks and I rattle around these four stories. And our visitors, like you, pausing on their journeys. More rooms than I ever knew what to do with. Didn't have children, but Mr. Aubrey felt it was fitting and proper for a man of his means and position to live in such…opulence. And he liked to make me happy, although I kept telling him my happiness had little to do with the authenticity of paintings hanging over the fireplace. It is always nice when I have travelers staying with me on their journeys, although I do understand you must be anxious to reach your destination."

"Our destination," Devlin said. "We have made it from Memphis to Chicago and know from Alice Ward that our final objective is Canada. We just don't know where, or how."

"It was safer for all involved to keep you in the dark, until now," Mrs. Aubrey said. "Tomorrow evening you will all board the passenger steamer *Pilgrim*. You will be met by an associate of mine, First Mate Arthur Wesley. No one will question your presence. You will sail up Lake Michigan and down Lake Huron to the Canadian town of Sarnia. We have contacts there that will help you settle. Quite a few Negroes have taken up farming near the town of North Buxton, not far from Sarnia."

"Without masters," Patsy said. "Praise Jesus."

"Yes," Mrs. Aubrey said with the fervor of prayer. "Praise Jesus."

~ ~ ~

The refugees spent the night and the next day at Mrs. Aubrey's in great anticipation. Seth could barely contain his excitement, running up the stairs to the second floor and sliding down the bannister into the entrance hallway.

"Seth," Beulah scolded. "This ain't our house."

"I know, Mama. But I ain't never seen no house like this before."

"It be nicer than Mr. Cruickshank's house in Memphis, or Mr. Crenshaw's 'fore that," Beulah said, regretting she had spoken their names out loud, like conjuring devils in a voodoo ceremony her mama talked about seeing when she was cutting cane on a sugar plantation in Louisiana. "Now don't go messin' up them nice clothes Mrs. Aubrey done give you. We need to look good for the boat tomorrow. We ain't slaves no more."

"We ain't?"

"Not when we get to Canada. Ain't no war. Ain't no slaves."

"They got outhouses inside like Mrs. Aubrey? And hot water that runs out of pipes?"

"Don't rightly know, Seth," Beulah said. "But I don't care if we sleep in the barn with the horses and share their water trough when we's get there, as long as we's free.

"Mrs. Aubrey has been telling me about our destination," Devlin said, walking into the hallway as Seth ran up the stairs for another slide down.

"Seth," Beulah scolded.

"The exuberance of youth," Devlin said.

"My," Beulah said. "You do look like a gentleman."

"Emma thought it would be best if I blended in with the other businessmen in Chicago when we go to the boat this evening. She had Meeks get some new attire for me"

"Fine," Beulah said. "Just fine. Who be Emma?"

"Emma is Mrs. Aubrey's first name."

"Gettin' friendly?" Beulah asked with a teasing smile.

"Now Beulah," Devlin said. "Remember that I am Irish. The Irish are friends with everyone."

"Uh huh," Beulah said. "And there ain't nothin' wrong with bein' friendly with a rich widow. How old you think she be?"

"Never you mind, Beulah. Just business. I came to get your approval of my ensemble."

Devlin buttoned his long brown frock coat over the plaid vest that matched his pants, adjusted his tie and put on a top hat that coordinated with the color of his coat.

"My, my, my," Beulah said. "Ain't you somethin'"

"I take that as a compliment," Devlin said, removing his top hat and bowing to Beulah. "I must say that your dress is very becoming."

"Mrs. Aubrey…Emma, took it right outta her wardrobe and give it to me. Feel like I should be goin' to one of them balls Mr. Crenshaw used to have at Hickory Hill to show off for the visitin' preachers and politicians."

"We're attending a more important event than a dance. Beulah," Devlin said. "When this party is over, you and your family will be free".

~ ~ ~

Devlin was standing on the stoop of Emma Aubrey's townhouse, admiring the view of the breakwater that protected the shore from Lake Michigan that appeared to be wide as the Atlantic, as a two-horse barouche carriage drove up to the curb. The driver set the brake, secured the reins and bounded up the stairs.

"Mr. Doyle? I am Connor Walsh. I have come to get you and your party safely aboard the steamer *Pilgrim*."

Devlin pumped his hand as if greeting a long lost brother.

"Do I detect a bit of the old sod?" Devlin asked.

"The accent or the breath," Connor asked with a wink.

"A wee bit of both."

"Came from County Sligo. Left during the Potato Famine, my younger brother, Dooley, and me. The rest of the family had already starved. We survived the Coffin Ship but I lost track of Dooley in New York City. He was the wild one. Probably joined up in one of those gangs. Or he's dead. I worked my way across this great land, endin' up in Chicago. Was a seaman on schooners and steamers runnin' cargo and passengers on the Lakes. Now I'm helpin' Mrs. Aubrey with what she calls her Sojourners. Excuse me, Mr. Doyle. I'm not usually so free with my sad and sorry life's tale. Maybe its hearin' the lilt of fellow Irishman's brogue, or it might be that second pint of stout I had at O'Leary's Pub that loosened my tongue. And a fine pub it is. Pity we don't have time to raise a glass or two before leavin', but…"

"Best we get to the dock," Devlin said. "I will not feel secure until my charges are all safely on the boat and the shore is at our stern. I have been troubled by the ease at which we have had getting here first by wagon and then on the train. I only hope the luck of the Irish saves itself for another day."

"Since your travelin' companions are obviously not Irish, chances are their luck will hold."

"There might be some truth to that, Connor. We have come all the way from Memphis to Chicago without incident. Why should anything happen in the few more miles to the docks?"

"It is my job to assure nothin' does happen. People are mostly involved in this bloody war. A fine dressed group of Negroes followin' a white gentleman to a steamer is not an unusual site in Chicago. I assure you, sir, the worst is behind you."

"I'll get the…sojourners."

~ ~ ~

"Goodbye, Mrs. Aubrey," Patsy said. "Ain't got the words to thank you enough for bein' so kind to me and my family."

"Emma," Mrs. Aubrey corrected. "I hope we have become friends during your short stay, Patsy."

"You done give us faith…Emma. We's known white folks before pretendin' they be nice, but they just do that to get what they want. They mostly believe we ain't nothin' but dumb animals."

"You and your family are no animals, Patsy."

"We sure ain't," Seth said.

"Beulah," Emma said. "You take care of that boy. I believe he will grow to be quite the man."

"I do that," Beulah said, taking Seth's hand.

"And Betsy, when you get to Canada, there will be a good life waiting for you, of that I am certain."

"I hope so, Mrs. Aubrey. I's real tired of livin' this one."

"You are doing a wonderful thing, Mr. Doyle," Emma said to Devlin.

"I have done nothing more than you have done for hundreds of souls seeking freedom. Sojourners, Connor tells me you call them. I'm no savior. I just followed the tracks someone else laid from depot to depot. I was only a conductor relying of an army of agents to show me the way to your station."

"You talkin' 'bout the Underground Railroad, ain't you?" Betsy butted in. "Why, there be a time, Mrs. Aubrey, I believed there be a real train underground…"

"Time to go," Connor Walsh said as he began gathering the small carpet bags Emma Aubrey had filled with items she knew each of they would need on their journey.

"Mama, look at that!" Seth said, running down the stairs to examine the carriage, climbing in and rubbing his hands over the red leather seats. "Look at this, Mama!"

"The exuberance of youth," Devlin said to Beulah.

"Seth, you be quiet now," Beulah said, hurrying down the stairs to the carriage. "Hush now, boy. I don't want to hear another word from you until we's off the boat in Canada. You hear me?"

"I does, Mama. It just…"

"It just nothin'," Beulah said, climbing in the carriage. "Now move over and hush."

"Yes, Mama," Seth said with the remorse of a repentant.

"May I assist you down the stairs?" Devlin asked Patsy.

"I just take your other arm, if you don't mind none," Betsy said.

"Of course," Devlin said, crooking both arms. "Shall we catch the boat to freedom?

"Boat to freedom," Patsy said, squeezing Devlin's arm harder. "That do sound good."

~ ~ ~

"There she be," Connor said, pointing to a steamer with the name *Pilgrim* neatly inscribed on her bow. "She's a package and passenger screw propeller. Staterooms above and cargo below. Shipped out on a few of those myself."

"We's ridin' in a stateroom?" Patsy asked.

"Yes, ma'am. Mrs. Aubrey ain't rich for nothin'. She sends her sojourners to freedom in style."

"I say she do," Beulah said.

"That's First Mate Arthur Wesley at the top of the gang plank checkin' his pocket watch. You have more than an hour before the *Pilgrim* sails, but Arthur is a man known to fret. The sun's down soon. I'll drop you off and head back to Mrs. Aubrey's. I don't like bein' on the streets after dark. Bullies and bums everywhere near the docks."

Connor secured the horses to a hitching post along the dock. The *Pilgrim* rose and fell gently against its moorings as waves lapped in from Lake Michigan.

"Mama..." Seth began as he jumped down from the carriage.

"Hush now," Beulah said. "Once we's on the boat you can jibber and jabber all you want. Now, pick up your own bag. Don't let Mr. Welsh do all the work."

"Yes, Mama," Seth said, lifting up two carpetbags to prove his growing strength and carrying them to the bottom of the gangplank, looking back for approval. Beulah pretended not to notice.

Beulah had let the others go ahead, admiring the steamer that was coming to life from the oil lamp glow as twilight settled, a red lamp marking the port side, a steady green lamp marking starboard, white lamps marking the stern, and golden lamps strung along the passenger decks, all swaying and shimmering off the lake at dusk. Beulah's family was gathered at the bottom of the gangplank, Devlin talking to Connor Walsh, too involved with conversation to notice Beulah was not among them.

"Well, well, well" a young man said, revealing himself from behind the carriage horses. Another young man with the look and swagger of a tough followed. "A darkie all by herself."

"It's our lucky night, Johnny," the other tough said.

"Right you are, Billy Boy," the other tough replied."

Beulah glanced across the dock, thinking she might have a chance to make a dash to the steamer gangplank.

"Be lively now, Mr. Welsh." First Mate Arthur Wesley called down from the deck of the *Pilgrim*, pulling his watch from its pocket, examining it with a fretted frown before snapping it shut. "Bring your company aboard. We shove off in less than an hour."

"Like clockwork," Connor said to Devlin, elbowing him in the ribs.

Betsy was first up the gangplank, followed by

Patsy, Seth holding his grandmother's hand like a proud suitor.

"It has been a pleasure," Devlin said to Connor, shaking his hand. "If I'm ever in Chicago again, I will take you up on that pint."

"Agreed," Connor said. "I must get back to Mrs. Aubrey's carriage and horses before they vanish…"

A muffled scream drew Devlin's attention across the dock in time to see Beulah being dragged behind the carriage. Devlin felt the fool for not noticing Beulah had not joined her family, too busy talking about the old country with Connor. He ran across the dock in a panic, Connor following.

"Shut your mouth," Johnny hoarsely whispered to Beulah. "You should be grateful any man is payin' you attention, considerin' how ugly you are."

Billy circled, sniggering, anticipating his turn that would come only after the most aggressive hyena had satisfied his hunger. Beulah pulled her mouth away from Johnny's filthy hand and bit into the flesh to the bone. He pulled back with a yelp. Beulah's teeth had drawn blood. He stared at his hand, then punched her Beulah in the face with a blow that knocked her to the dock, dazed, fighting for consciousness. Johnny dropped on her, tearing at her clothes with wild frenzy. Beulah clawed at his face, but Billy pinned her arms.

"Let her go," Devlin said, Connor standing beside him.

"You boys come for your share?" Johnny asked, ripping Beulah's blouse enough to expose a breast. "There's plenty for all of us."

"Let the lady go," Devlin said.

"Lady?" Johnny sputtered. "You must be blind, or daft."

"I'm Irish," Devlin said. "Let the lady go."

"Or you'll hit me with your shillelagh?" Johnny

laughed. "Micks and niggers are ruinin' Chicago. Worse than wharf rats."

"Then you won't mind letting the lady go, considering your feelings about Negroes."

"They are good for one thing," Johnny said. "But then, you probably already know that."

Beulah raised her head enough for her teeth to find Johnny's hand she had not bitten, leaving another set of tooth imprints. He pulled a knife from his boot and brought it to her throat until she released his hand. Johnny froze, hearing the distinctive clicks of a pistol hammer being cocked. He turned to see Devlin pointing a .36 snub nose Army issue at him.

"Some call it a Belly Gun," Devlin said. "supposedly because it can be neatly concealed and carried behind a trouser belt. In your case, I'd like to think the name describes a gut shot and the slow, agonizing death you will suffer if you do not release the lady."

"All right, Mick. This nigger ain't worth dyin' for," Johnny said. "See? No harm done. I'm puttin' the knife back in the boot."

Johnny bent down, slowly moving the knife towards his boot, then knelt and threw the dagger underhand at Devlin. The blade penetrated deep through Devlin's plaid vest and white shirt, below the heart, missing ribs, missing the lung. The Belly Gun exploded. Johnny fell forwards, clutching his gut, the Belly Gun bullet had found an artery and blood was pooling like a puddle in a rainstorm. It was not going to be the long death Devlin had promised. Billy freed Beulah's arms, stood and ran down the dock without looking back.

"You're bleedin'," Conner said to Devlin.

Devlin looked down, feeling the dagger for the first time. His knees wobbled as he pulled it out, blood ruining his new vest.

"Never mind," Devlin said, pulling a letter from his

unbuttoned frock coat pocket. "Give this to the First Mate. They are the instructions on what to do when the family gets to Canada."

"Aren't you goin'?" Conner asked. "They need you. There must be a ship's doctor..."

"They will do just fine without me now. The family needs a fresh start, not someone who just killed a man bringing the law down on them. That kid that got away is likely telling the coppers all about how I jumped them and killed his buddy. Get Beulah to the boat. I'm sure they heard the shot. Make up a good story."

"They are goin' to wonder where you went," Connor said, helping Beulah to her feet. She was clutching what her torn blouse around her, her eyes unfocused, struggling for balance.

"Like I said, use the Irish in you. Kiss the stone. Make me heroic, if you like. It's a small wound. I'll be fine. Just tell them goodbye for me."

Devlin moved back into the shadows, watching Connor guide Beulah to the steamer and up the gangplank. He could see the commotion on the deck, Patsy comforting her daughter, Seth looking over the railing, calling Devlin's name, and First Mate Arthur Wesley snapping his watch open and shut before ordering deckhands to prepare to shove off. The gangplank was raised. Connor walked back to the carriage, rolling Johnny's body behind a stack of broken cargo crates. Devlin turned and walked towards the breakwater, not waiting for the steamer to sail. Beulah and her family would soon be free and that was what mattered. And, staunching the blood that still oozed into his plaid vest.

Thirty

The day of the Confederate surrendered at Vicksburg, July 4th, 1863, an Army surgeon, examining Brigadier General Michael Kelly Lawler, determined him to be suffering from hepatitis and diarrhea. He was given leave and did not return to service until August. In December he was diagnosed as disabled with fever and advanced years at the age of forty-nine. He was sent home to Illinois to convalesce. In Equality, his doctors recommended an extension of leave due to continuing poor health, compounded by tonsillitis and bronchial inflammation, eventually returning to the field in February of 1864. He was sent to Louisiana to head a division during the Red River Campaign with the goals of taking Shreveport, controlling the Red River to the north, occupying East Texas and confiscating as much as a hundred thousand bales of cotton from the plantations along the river. But the outcome was a Union failure, extending the war by diverting troops from the more crucial objective of capturing Mobile, Alabama.

After the end of the hostilities, Michael Kelly Lawler received a brevet promotion to Major General from President Andrew Johnson in 1866, a reward for his gallantry and courageous conduct, but with no increase of authority or pay. He was assigned command of the East District of Louisiana at Baton Rouge, where he bought a cotton plantation before selling it after being appointed as government shopkeeper in San Antonio, Texas where he remained for two years, buying and selling horses. Michael Kelly Lawler returned to Equality in 1868, at the age of fifty-three, to his farm, to his family and to the raising of horses, plagued by stomach conditions for which his doctor prescribed the chewing of tobacco, although Michael had never before used tobacco in any form. War injuries haunted him, his arm, his hand, deafness and what the doctors called softness of the brain for which in the end, even tobacco was not a cure.

~ ~ ~

"President Ulysses S. Grant," Michael read from the front page of the Chicago Tribune he had delivered to his office every day. "Those words still astonish me."

"I do not see why," Sina said. "The country was very grateful for his leadership in preserving the Union under President Lincoln."

"Most were grateful," Michael corrected. "Certainly not John Wilkes Booth and his conspirators."

Michael Kelly Lawler had returned to his farm the year Ulysses S. Grant was elected president. Michael's journey home from the war had been long and circuitous, leaving Elizabeth suspicious as to his reasons for staying away from home. She was certain that he loved her and his children, but he also felt a strong desire to serve his adopted country, having twice raised troops first for the Mexican and then for the Civil War.

"You have nothing left to prove," Sina said, slowly rocking in her chair in front of the fire that Michael had set and lit, having dismissed the extra Negro servants when he returned from the war that allowed Elizabeth to maintain the farm during his long absences. The doctors were right. His fighting days were over. Only in his mid-fifties, he felt

~268~

old. He had redirected what was left of his energy to raising horses as his Irish kin had done in Kildare to race on the spring grass of the curragh, although he would never mount one of his stud thoroughbreds, even for a walk or a canter.

"Prove?" Michael asked.

"That you are an American," Sina said.

"Why would I…"

"Michael. You recruited troops for the Mexican War. You did the same for this last bloody war, returning after being wounded, after being sick, at your age."

"My age?"

"You have put many more years on your body than birthdays," Elizabeth said.

"Starting when I volunteered for the militia during the Black Hawk War."

"You have never spoken of that, Michael."

"You were only twelve at the time. I was a man of…seventeen."

"Handsome in your uniform, I am sure," Elizabeth said.

"We wore our own clothes, but were issued guns. The regular army had a low opinion of us, often for good reason. Farm boys had great courage, until being shot at by Indians with excellent aim. Many boys just hightailed it back to the farm. No I didn't, if that is what you are thinking."

"I would never think that, Michael. You are a very brave man, Michael," Elizabeth said. "Being seventeen would have made no difference."

Michael rose from his leather chair, picking up the poker, then pausing before stabbing the logs on the fire.

"Strange that I never mentioned being in the Black Hawk War to you," Michael said

"I am sure you had your reasons," Elizabeth said.

"You are correct about my desire, my need to prove that I belong. That I am worthy. With all the accolades, the promotions, even praise from General Grant himself, there were those who could never respect me because I was a Catholic from Ireland."

"Father finally accepted your...convictions," Elizabeth said.

"Because I added to his profits, did not abuse his daughter and gave him grandchildren. To him I am still a Papist and will burn in hell. To your father that is the final tally," Michael said, returning the poker to its stand and sitting in his leather chair. The fire was burning down, its progress from log to ember telling time as accurately as the clock on the mantle.

"I am very tired, Elizabeth."

"But before bed," Elizabeth said, "tell me about when you were seventeen."

"What do you want to know?"

"After all these years I can tell when something is bothering you more than indigestion."

"And contrary to the doctor, chewing tobacco does not help. It is a vile and disgusting habit of which I will no longer partake. I was proud to fight in the Black Hawk Wars, when I was seventeen. I was looking for adventure, but found little, never seeing real combat. But the misery of the marching, the endless training because we were green volunteers, the heat, the insects and the foul food made me feel grown-up, even if I never killed an Indian. I never questioned at the time that Black Hawk and the Sauk tribe were fighting for their own land and that their only crime had been breaking a treaty of dubious intent."

"Mexico?" Elizabeth prodded, encouraging her husband to speak freely about the wars he still fought in nightmares.

"We never talked much about this before."

"Your stomach has been telling you to talk about it all these years," Elizabeth said.

"Maybe you are correct," Michael said, falling into his usual silence, watching the fire retreat from flame to ember.

"Duty," Michael began. "Strong enough to pull me away from my wife and family. Do women understand this about men?"

"Women know of it," Elizabeth said. "But we do not truly understand. We do not understand it any more than we understand why violence is how men settle differences."

"My country called and I answered," Michael said.

"I never did understand why we went to war against Mexico," Elizabeth said.

"Greed. The desire that our country run from sea to sea. Manifest Destiny. General Grant spoke out against it, too. So in the end we took their land, as we have taken the Indians land and left them with pitiful reservations often far from their ancestor's homes. But, the Civil War was different. This country's very existence was threatened. And slavery was the issue. It was my Christian duty to do all I could to destroy that tradition of bondage."

Elizabeth agreed with her husband, taking a stand against her father who had become rich exploiting the enslaved, using them to build his wealth under the guise of legally leasing them from slave states for his salt works, a practice Elizabeth never condoned. Her father chastised her for marrying a Catholic out of her Methodist faith who agreed with her distaste for slavery, but she never wavered.

"You fulfilled that duty," Elizabeth said. The children and I were patient, enduring your long absences, knowing all the while you were truly doing God's work. And now, the slaves are free and the country is united."

Michael nodded, but with little conviction. He had stayed in the South long enough after the war to see that it would take more than a Proclamation or the North winning a military victory to truly free the Negro. Gangs a whites were already riding and lynching to keep Negroes in what they considered their God-ordained place. It took federal troops to prevent the worst of the atrocities, but how long would they remain?

"Slavey is ended, that is true," Michael finally said. "But, is the country united? I fear the war has even more deeply divided the country. The South is resentful. To them the war was not to protect slavery and extend it into the territories, but a war of aggression with the North's intent of destroying southern economy and their traditions. Their culture."

"No one will believe that," Elizabeth said.

"They already ready are, Elizabeth. It is comfort to many in the South to remember the pre-war days as genteel, scented with orange blossom when the slaves were protected and treated like the children they were, happy and contented to work for their benevolent masters."

"And they blame the North for destroying that life?"

"Yes. President Grant has pledged to protect the Negroes, and their new life of freedom. But for how long is anyone's guess. How's your father?" Michael said, feeling the need to change the subject. His stomach was beginning to feel a queasy.

"Not well," Elizabeth said. "He is failing."

During the Civil War, John Hart Crenshaw had sold Hickory Hill and moved to a new farmhouse closer to Equality. Without the salt works, he had begun investing in lumber interests, railroads and banks years before, even as he retained skepticism for other bankers, retaining enough of his wealth to live in comfort with his wife, Sina.

But now in 1871, at the age of seventy-four, he was experiencing a growing weariness like the sleepiness after a big dinner. Shadow pain was a constant throb in his leg stump. Walking with his crutch had become excruciating. He left business concerns to his younger associates and spoke less and less to Sina. He spent much of his day sitting in front of the fire reliving his life, finding most it commendable, although somethings of what others might call sins were beginning to bother him.

"I don't know how much long father has," Elizabeth said. "I believe he is resigned to death and he is content."

"He has never been one to question his actions," Michael said.

"He never will," Elizabeth said. "Or at least he will never admit to others that he does."

"No stomach complaints or nightmares," Michael said.

"None," Elizabeth said. "Just the sleep of an innocent baby."

~ ~ ~

John Hart Crenshaw was dying; Sina was stoic. She was not unfamiliar with death, losing children, parents and friends frequently in a time when bleeding and mustard plasters were the doctors best defense against dreadful diseases they did not understand. Sina understood her husband's disease. He was old and the Lord was calling him home.

"Your Father would like to see you, Elizabeth," read the note that a servant had delivered. Elizabeth showed Michael the note her mother had written.

"It must be very important," Michael said, handing the note back. "I'll take you to the farm."

Sina was waiting on the farmhouse porch as Michael reined the carriage horse to a halt. Sina came down the steps and approached Michael while he was tying off the reigns.

"Michael," Sina said. "John would speak to Elizabeth alone. It might be best if you and I wait in the parlor. He was adamant."

Michael nodded agreement, helping Elizabeth down from the carriage and escorting her into the farmhouse where he turned into the parlor while Elizabeth followed her mother. John had his reasons and on his deathbed they should be respected.

"How much longer?" Elizabeth asked her mother.

"Soon," Sina said. "Only God knows for sure, but soon."

"Do you know what Father wants of me?"

"No. But it seems very important to him."

Father," Elizabeth said, entering his bedroom that was darkened by thick curtains, filtering most but not all the afternoon sun. The scent of ointment and sweat hovered over the bed as she leaned in to kiss her father on the forehead. For once he did not resist. His flesh was cool.

"Daughter," John said without opening his eyes. "You came."

"You are my Father."

"There were times you might not have said that."

"Not now."

"Because I am dying."

Elizabeth took her father's hand. No words were needed.

"You remember Patsy, who ran away during the war?" John asked.

"Of course I do. You raved about her dumplings. And apple pie. She was one of the best…servants you ever had."

"She had two daughters. Twins."

"Beulah and Betsy. They disappeared one night. Night Riders, most likely. Patsy never recovered until the day she ran off. Can't say that I blame her. She probably went looking for her girls."

"The girls didn't disappear," John said, his voice taking on a seriousness beyond his grave condition. "I sold them."

"You sold them?"

"I sold them because my business was failing."

"Father…"

"The twins were mine."

"Of course, Patsy was a leased slave..."

"No. Beulah and Betsy, Patsy's girls, were my children."

"Your children?" Elizabeth said, releasing his hand. "You sold your own children."

"They were niggers and I needed the money," John said.

Elizabeth looked at her father. He seemed to shrink into the damp bedsheets, growing smaller, his hand trembling as he pulled them tighter under his chin. Tears were forming in his eyes. Elizabeth had never seen John Hart Crenshaw cry.

"Elizabeth," John said, his voice trembling like his hands. "I have never regretted anything I did in my life, until now. I have done many things others may have found vile, but I had my reasons, mostly to provide for and protect my family, my children, like you Elizabeth."

"But Beulah and Betsy were your children..."

"They were Patsy's children and..."

"You have no answer now, do you father? No defense for this most disgusting action. You called me here as an act of repentance, didn't you? You want my forgiveness. You think it will wash away your sin and the hurt you inflicted on your own children and their mother?"

"Elizabeth..."

"It is my Christian duty to forgive you, Father. But I only hope God is more sincere in his forgiveness that I can be."

Elizabeth bent over the bed and kissed her father on the forehead, turned and left without looking back. Her mother was in the parlor, talking to Michael.

"What did your father want to tell you?" Sina asked.

"He wanted to say goodbye. I did," Elizabeth said, fighting back tears she didn't feel her father deserved. "Take me home, Michael."

"Should we wait with your mother?"

"The Methodist Elders will be here soon. And his other children. I believe there is no more I can do."

"You have made your peace?" Michael asked.

"Yes," Elizabeth said. "In our way."

~ ~ ~

John Hart Crenshaw died on December 4, 1871. He was Seventy-four. He was surrounded by his children, Methodist elders and his wife, Sina, who softly sobbed. He was buried in Hickory Hill Cemetery just northeast of the home he once owned. His wife, Sina, died on September 14, 1881 at the age of eighty-two. They had ten children, five of them living to maturity.

Michael Kelly Lawler died the next year on his farm, July 26, 1882 at the age of sixty-seven. His wife, Elizabeth, who outlived him by almost twenty-six years, died on July 4, 1908, at the age of eighty-eight.

Thirty-One

Elias and Min Li had hired onto the Central Pacific Railroad as it lumbered towards the Sierra Nevada Mountains. Ground had been broken in Sacramento in January of 1863, the year of Gettysburg, the year of Vicksburg, and finding workers had always been an issue. Constructing the Transcontinental Railroad required thousands of laborers wielding picks and shovels, hammers and explosives, black powder, and later, the volatile nitroglycerine. There were no steam shovels or earthmovers. No tunneling machines. No power drills. No diesel lifts. No pile drivers. The Central Pacific Railway would be hand-made and carved from granite mountains. Work was slow in the beginning, since the company at first only wanted white workers. In a year and a half the line was barley thirty-one miles from Sacramento at an elevation below a thousand feet. Only a few hundred white men had responded for the initial call for workers and when there were rumors of new gold strikes they just walked off the job.

With the dwindling and unreliable white work force, management had considered radical solutions. There was talk of enlisting captured Confederate soldiers, or transporting in freed slaves, or even Mexicans. Eventually,

Chinamen like Min Li, although shunned by the white population as inferior in culture and physical stature, were welcomed and appreciated for their endurance and willingness to work. And Negroes like Elias, although rare in California, were also accepted, since with the muddle of war, no one cared if they were free men or escaped slaves as long as they worked as hard as the Chinamen.

At first the Central Pacific Railroad only hired a few Chinese on the lower grades, but they worked out so well they hired more and more until by 1865 there were three thousand working the line, mostly recruited from those already living in California, like Min Li. More were to come. They were paid about a dollar a day, twenty-six per month, with one day off per week. Less than a white worker, but the race-based difference was common practice for all jobs, and the earnings were much more than they ever made in China, making the impending Sierras the true Gold Mountains.

The route to meet the Union Pacific Railroad was straight forward. Start near Sacramento, then summit the High Sierra at Donner Pass before crossing the Great Basin desert through Nevada to meet up somewhere in Utah. But little was known about the mountain range terrain and geologists and engineers were making up their solutions on the go as track was laid with no detailed plan or blueprint outside of the final destination. Surveying the route continued while the army of Chinese workers advanced into the high country where the winters would prove the worst of the century, the granite leveled and tunneled with pick and shovel and the Chinese expertise with the gunpowder their ancestors had long before invented.

"I thought Mr. Crenshaw's salt works was hard," Elias said to Min Li, gripping the sixteen foot section of steel rail with all his strength, the only Negro on a gang of Railroad Chinese.

"But you are not a slave," Min Li said from just a

few feet ahead of Elias, his slight body seeming to have little trouble moving the weight of the iron rail.

"Maybe I not be owned," Elias said, "but I is workin' for twenty-six dollars a month. Got paid forty dollars a month as a drover, when we gots the cattle to market, if'n we did."

"I thought you were tired of eating dust."

"Right now," Elias said, grunting to bend as the gang lowered the rail onto the cross ties, careful to keep his fingers from being crushed, wiping sweat from his face with a wet neckerchief, "dust might taste awful good."

~ ~ ~

September, 1865. The Civil War had ended in victory for the Union and the freeing of the slaves, but the death of Abraham Lincoln had placed the Reconstruction of the country in the hands of Andrew Johnson, Tennessee born and bred, slave owner and inclined as President to allow the southern states free rein to rebuild themselves in their own fashion, as long as they pledged loyalty to the Union, paid their debts and upheld, in theory if not practice, the abolition of slavery. This Presidential Reconstruction of leniency led directly to the "Black Codes", designed to limit the liberties of four million freed slaves, laws that required them to sign yearly labor contracts and if they refused, they could be arrested, fined and forced into unpaid labor.

Elias and Min Li knew nothing of this as the Central Pacific Railroad reached the newly-named town of Colfax, fifty miles from Sacramento, 2500 feet in elevation, approaching the steep mountain of Cape Horn, an obstacle formidable as the foreboding sea passage at the tip of South American it was named for, but an obstacle that had to be surmounted if the railroad was to be completed.

Cape Horn was a mile below the summit, below the snow line with a breath-taking view of the American River some 1300 feet below, but with a sheer granite face leaving no ledge to lay tracks.

Elias watched as Min Li and a gang of Railroad Chinese dangled from ropes secured around their waists, lowered down the near-vertical cliff, ropes looped around Ponderosa Pines that ringed the upper rim, to hammer in drills, finding seams in the granite where explosives could be set, sometimes four-hundred strung at a time, connected by fickle fuses to blow away enough rock to allow gangs to clear a level path for the tracks.

"I am not a superstitious man…" Min Li had begun saying to Elias before leaving camp with his gang to drill and set black powder charges on Cape Horn.

"But…?" Elias said, encouraging Min Li to continue.

"But," Min Li said, "I do not wish to be a Hungry Ghost."

"You believe in ghosts?" Elias asked.

"I said I am not superstitious. But I am not disrespectful. My ancestors believed is such things. To them, unhappy ghosts are responsible for much of the misery of life. They can cause illness and accidents and even death as they wander, homeless. Who am I to contradict them?"

Elias' puzzled look spurred Min Li on.

"Dying in a foreign land is bad," Min Li said. "But not as tragic as to die and not have your bones returned to the soil of your ancestors. If this does not take place, one becomes an abandoned soul, a wild, lost and Hungry Ghost."

"Bones?'

"Where spirit resides."

"Sounds like superstition to me."

"And where does your Christian soul reside?"

Elias began to answer, than realized he couldn't.

"All religions are superstitions, to other religions," Min Li said.

Elias didn't have an a answer. He was a Christian because his mother had been a Christian. His beliefs were her beliefs, a faith that said there was hope and salvation for slaves after death. Preachers offered an eternal Heaven as reward for a short lifetime of hell on earth and it made sense to Elias and gave comfort. He had no idea there were other religions that offered different ways to happiness, that Min Li was influenced by the local deities from his ancestorial lands that combined ancient Taoism with a more recent Buddhism. Railroad Chinese would build temples and altars as soon as they arrived at a new construction site, honoring those who had gone before and the many who would soon join them.

"Last August," Min Li continued with the distant look of an elder reciting a list of ancestors leading back to the Shang Dynasty when King Tang overthrew the tyrant Jie of the Xia Dynasty, creating Chinese culture and building the Great Wall to hold back the Barbarians, "at Camp 20, when Speaker of the House Colfax came..."

"The man they named the town after? Ain't much of a town."

"Yes. The Railroad Chinese had a festival. It was a Hungry Ghost Festival, held on the fifteenth day of the seventh lunar month."

"You Chinamen sure is sky watchers," Elias said.

"Some are," Min Li said.

"I remember the fireworks," Elias said. "And everythin' lit up with candles and kerosene lamps. Piles of food..."

"And the one big demon made of paper scraps and cloth, blown to bits to end the festival, representing the evil spirits that cause accidents and all misfortune. Gone for another year, or so it is hoped. The festival also honors the Hungry Ghosts, the Chinese spirits wandering this strange land, the bones lost in black powder explosions, cave-ins, landslides, snow avalanches, raging rivers..."

"Bones," Elias said.

"Yes. Bones and the spirits that require returning to their land of birth."

"Thought you said you ain't superstitious," Elias reminded Min Li."

"But I respect of my ancestors beliefs, Elias," Min Li said.

Elias nodded, but could not relate to having ancestors going back any farther than his mother. His was a world with few fathers in which it was best for slaves to think of only their mother as the beginning of life, not clinging too hard even to her since the auction block always threatened as a Negro boy grew tall and strong. Images of Elias' mother drifted in his thoughts but as the years passed her face had blurred and her voice faded into a faint whisper.

"Elias," Min Li said.

"Sorry. You sound like you want me to do somethin' for you."

"I still have gold hidden. Not a fortune, but enough to get my bones back to China, with enough left for you to purchase some land, raise cattle…"

"Told you I's tired of the dust."

"The dust taste different when it's your own."

"Why you talkin' like this. It be bad luck to talk 'bout dyin'."

"It is worse luck to die without preparation. Americans act like they are going to live forever. They pretend death does not exist. Chinese understand that death is part of life."

"I ain't no American," Elias said. "I's African. Bein' a slave, I learned all about death."

Min Li nodded. The bond he had felt with Elias had grown stronger.

That evening, after a long day that had included blasting granite for Min Li, shoveling and hauling rock for

Elias, they sat around the fire outside their camp tent. Min Li told Elias where he had hidden the gold coins he had saved from his bath and laundry businesses, and other profits he had accumulated from various financial ventures on his trip from China to Gold Mountain. He also introduced Elias to Railroad Chinese in camp who were familiar with the cost and the methods of shipping bones back to China.

"I am indebted to you, Elias."

"I don't believe nothin' is goin' to happen to you, Min Li. You too…"

"Inscrutable?"

"Tricky. You too tricky to let sneaky Mr. Death get ahold of you."

~ ~ ~

"No gold in these mountains. Just stubborn rock," Min Li said, probing the granite face for a crack, a crevasse to penetrate with his six-foot pole drill, flared and flat tipped at the end, searching for a natural seam. Finding a likely split, a nearly mystical skill he possessed, Min Li yelled back to Elias, "OK!"

"Hold 'er steady," Elias said, raising his eight pound sledgehammer and striking the end of the drill with a jarring precision. After each strike, Min Li rotated the drill a quarter turn before Elias struck the drill again, and again, and again, the drill penetrating the hardened ancient lava a few inches at a stroke. In an eight hour shift a hole of only two and a half feet deep might be drilled my multiple gangs in this fashion, but deep enough for charges of black powder to crack and crumble the granite into blocks and rubble to be hauled out when the dust and smoke settled and dumped down the mountain in small landslides, repeated for days and weeks and months as the Railroad Chinese cut through the Sierra Nevada Mountains for a dollar a day.

~ ~ ~

Forty fierce storms raged across the Sierra Nevada Mountains in the winter of 1866-1867. The Railroad Chinese became full-time snow shovelers, tunneling networks to connect camps with work sites. Many workers were lost to avalanche, buried until exposed by the spring thaw, and even finished tunnels often requiring gun powder to break through the ice that had sealed them shut.

The Central Pacific Railroad blasted and dug fifteen tunnels through the Sierra Nevada Mountains in all, eleven tunnels being excavated that winter, seven bunched two miles east of Donner Summit that required massive amounts of black powder, sometimes as many as five-hundred kegs a day, a mixture of saltpeter, sulfur and charcoal, pulverized, mixed and rolled into cakes to dry. It was first brought to California by 49ers to speed up their quest for gold. There were no factories to produce the explosive in California, so miners relied on shipments from the eastern United States and European countries. The Civil War made black powder a scarce commodity. To fill the need, John Baird, a miner from Kentucky along with financial backers opened the Powder Works Factory near Santa Cruz in 1864, a company that employed 275 Chinese, considered experts in handling the explosive. Within the first year the factory produced 150,000 twenty-five pound powder kegs.

Black powder was expensive, however, and each explosion left behind thick and lingering smoke that required time to dissipate, slowing work. The answer was nitroglycerine, discovered by Italian chemist Acanio Sobrero in 1847 and perfected by Alfred Nobel in the early 1860's. It had more explosive power than black powder, left less smoke and broke the rock into larger fragments, making the clearing of the rubble quicker. But it was also unpredictable and dangerous, especially in transport and storage. As a solution, British chemist James Howden set up shop near Donner Lake, producing one-hundred pounds of nitroglycerine a day in a shed surrounded by red flags as warning, the finished liquid product transported to the tunnel excavations by Railroad Chinese with the ritual solemnity of carrying ancestral bones for burial.

Min Li had proven to be the most reliable carrier. The bosses knew his name and admired his calm dedication to the job, transporting the nitroglycerine to the tunnel, sliding the cardboard cylinder into the drill hole, lighting the detonator fuse and retreating to a safe distance before the explosion so he could live to repeat the process.

"I appreciate their admiration," Min Li had said to Elias one evening outside their canvas tent after a successful day of explosions, warming by the fire, camped close to the excavation site of Tunnel #6, the Summit Tunnel, first to employ nitroglycerine. "But I might live longer without it."

"Don't go talkin' that way," Elias said. "I don't want to be carryin' your bones all the ways back to China."

"If something goes wrong," Min Li said, "there might be some dust, but no bones. Nothing left but a Hungry Ghost haunting the Sierra Nevada Mountains."

"Now don't you go talkin' that way, Min Li. It be bad luck"

"Are you getting superstitious, Elias?"

"Ain't never claimed I weren't. I's African," Elias said, unable to conceal his grin.

~ ~ ~

The Summit Tunnel was unique. Besides being the highest, crews tunneled from both the east and the west to meet in the middle. And a shaft had also been drilled down from the top of the summit to meet the grade, allowing crews to tunnel both ways from the center, four faces to the same tunnel, all requiring drilled holes into which to place the unstable nitroglycerine to ignite with equally fickle fuses.

"Boss say we might break through today," Elias said, drinking his morning tea that Min Li had steeped. Since Elias started eating Min Li's cooking and drinking his tea, he had not been sick. At first, Elias could not stomach the Chinese food. Since leaving Crenshaw's salt works, and after his years of living with the Cheyenne, Elias had become accustomed to the cowboy grub of beans and beef jerky and sometimes roasted potatoes, washed down with any drinkable water that could be found along the trails, and beer when they got to town. Now he ate rice and fish and vegetables and the water was boiled for tea. The Chinese rarely got sick. The white men suffered most from dysentery and still ridiculed the Chinamen for washing their hands and daily baths.

"Possibly," Min Li said, pouring the rest of the tea into a tin coal miner's lunch pail that he would drink the rest of the day as it cooled instead of water. "If the engineers have calculated accurately."

"I hope so," Elias said. "Nothin' I hate worse than haulin' big rock outta a dark hole."

"And I wouldn't mind giving up carrying and exploding nitroglycerine, even if it is an honor," Min Li said.

~ ~ ~

"This might be the last one," Luke Stearns, the foreman, said to Min Li as they entered the tunnel, light from kerosene lamps glittering from the granite surrounding them, a wooden box carried steady in Min Li's strong hands, each step taken as if in a holy procession.

"I lit incense this morning," Min Li said, taking another steady step, then another.

"Praying to them Hungry Ghosts?" the foreman asked.

"Praying not to become one," Min Li said.

Chinese workers parted like the wake before the bow of a fisherman's sampan and crowded to the sides of the tunnel. No one spoke. No one breathed until Min Li and the foreman had passed down the tunnel towards the blasting site. A hole had been drilled to the proper depth at the end of the rounded tunnel, carved from the granite, measuring sixteen feet high and sixteen feet wide. The rest of the job was up to Min Li. The workers hurried towards the entrance, knowing the distance they needed to be for safety when Min Li denotated the nitroglycerine.

Luke carried the kerosene lantern that provided the only light this deep in the tunnel, reflecting from the smooth granite like moonlight off a breeze-rippled bay. As foreman, Luke Stearns had been put in charge of a gang of twenty Railroad Chinese, not for his experience as a railroad man, since he had none, but for the color of his skin: white. The gang and grown to over fifty, although some had been lost to avalanche, snow storm, rock slide and faulty fuses.

"Right here, boy," Luke said to Min Li. Luke raised the lantern to expose the drilled hole. "I'll leave the lantern and see you outside, Lord willing."

"Thank you for your confidence, Boss."

"You ain't let us down yet, Min Li," Luke said, his voice softening to reveal a touch of respect. "You boys are the best."

"Pay would be better than praise," Min Li.

"I don't want to hear none of that strike talk. You ain't white and you ain't Christian. You get paid what you deserve," Luke said, his voice growing hard as the rock that surrounded them.

Min Li knew better than to argue. To Luke, paying Chinamen equal pay would be the same as giving it to niggers. God knows, Luke would say, white men are worth more than black men or yellow men and that ain't never goin' to change.

"OK, Boss. I'll bring the lantern."

"You better," Luke said. "Or it'll come outta your

wages."

Min Li waited for Luke to be out of sight. Min Li did not like doing his job, any part of it, while being watched like a child buckling his own sandals for the first time. Now that he was alone in the glow of a single kerosene lantern, he began setting the charge.

He opened the wooden box he had been carrying, slowly removing cloth packing to expose a cardboard cylinder with a fuse protruding from one end. He understood the cylinder's contents. Inside was the nitroglycerine, encased in another cardboard container, surrounded by rock. Above the nitroglycerine, a load of gunpowder igniter and above that, a preload that the fuse ignited. The fuse should give him time to light it and run to safety. He had now survived many of these explosive excavations and had no doubt he would survive this one, but to be prudent, he said a prayer to his ancestors, and a prayer for the Hungry Ghosts who might be looking over his shoulder as he prepared to light the fuse. Min Li lit the fuse, grabbed the lantern, and ran.

Min Li could hear the usual sputtering of the fuse, but it sounded different. It was louder. Faster. He turned to look back as the sparks raced towards the gunpowder ignitor. It was going to blow early. He turned and dove to the floor of the tunnel. The kerosene lantern shattered into flames as the entire tunnel erupted.

~ ~ ~

"Am I a ghost?" Min Li asked. No one heard him. He was lying on a cot in a canvas tent. He was alone. He hurt. Everywhere. He struggled to sit up. There was a small table by the cot and sitting on the table, a ceramic teapot with a wicker handle, embossed with a blue dragon, and one ceramic cup with the same design. The teapot was still steaming. Through the slit of the tent entrance he could see that it was morning, not long after sunrise. He could recall the sound of the sputtering fuse, feel the force of the explosion rush over him as he lay prostrate on the tunnel floor, but nothing else. He poured himself a cup of tea, steeped to the correct strength. It was still hot. He took a sip. He was not a Hungry Ghost. Elias entered the tent.

"You been out cold since we carried you to the tent," Elias said. "Yesterday afternoon. Everyone thought you be dead."

"I lit incense. I wonder if they will pay me full wages for the day?" Min Li mused, pouring another cup of tea. "You brewed this perfectly. You learned well."

"How're your bones?" Elias asked. "I was afraid I be carryin' them back to China."

"My bones seem unbroken," Min Li said, "although the flesh is bruised. I should be able to work today."

"I's not goin' to argue. You Chinamen don't seem to feel no pain."

Min Li smiled, not contradicting Elias, a Negro, repeating the white man's notion that Chinamen weren't quite human, didn't feel pain the same as a white man, didn't feel pain like a river trout didn't feel the hook, like the worm on the hook didn't feel pain, that Chinamen could work longer and harder because they weren't civilized Christians, not quite human.. Min Li knew the real difference. A Chinaman just didn't complain. Life was not fair or unfair. Life didn't care. You made your own life, whether it was growing rice near Guangzhou, digging gold from the fields of California or by blowing holes in mountains to lay railroad tracks you'll never ride in a country that despises your difference.

"It is the tea," Min Li said, pouring the last cup from the pot. "Much better than whiskey, or beer. Your head never hurts the next morning. Much easier to work."

"That explosion that near killed you broke through," Elias said. "We be clearin' the rock out today. We's reached the summit."

"Long way left to go," Min Li said.

"That be true, but once we's outta these mountains, we hit what they call the Great Basin and can start layin' track fast, the way them lazy Irishmen been doin' on the Union Pacific all along."

"I hear they had some troubles with the Indians."

"It be Indian land, after all," Elias said, remembering his days with the Cheyenne, thinking that if not for the cholera, he might have been one of those braves attacking the iron horse as it divided his prairie, brought death to the buffalo and delivered more homesteaders.

"You lived among the Indians," Min Li said, reading Elias' pause.

"Cheyenne," Elias said. "They called me Spotted Horse, 'cause I's good with the ponies. And when I's herdin' cattle the boys called me Dusty. I does prefer Elias. That be what my mama named me."

"You lived as many lives as most Railroad Chinese, Elias," Min Li said. "What are your plans when this railroad is built?"

"Too long off to figure now," Elias said. "Just thinkin' 'bout today, clearin' out the rubble you made to finish the tunnel. Not thinkin' 'bout what next when this railroad be done."

"Wise man, Elias. Fewer worries that way."

"That be my thoughts," Elias said. "What be your plans?"

"First, I hear the Chinese are scheming to strike for equal wages. I doubt management will give in to any demands from foreigners with pigtails, but I admire the effort. Might help others in the future, if nothing else. So I will do my part."

"Just don't let the goons make you a pile of bones I gots to carry back to China."

"I will do everything in my power to remain among the living, for my sake and yours," Min Li said. "Most likely I'll head back to San Francisco. There is much more opportunity for a Chinaman on the coast than in Utah."

"Utah?"

"The Central and Union Pacific are on course to meet up somewhere near Salt Lake City. Not many Chinamen in those parts."

Min Li was making Elias think about his own life, his future, even if he didn't want to. The railroad would end and so would his job. The Civil War was over, slavery was abolished, but he was still a Negro who had lived among the Cheyenne. He knew the hatred of those who despised him for the color of his skin would not go away because the Confederacy lost their cause, or even when every Indian was confined to a reservation. Hate was his heritage. He felt it less when he was a cowboy among men who respected his skills with horses. Cattle drives were ending, but ranches were springing up all across the West and there was always the need for experienced hands. He had told Min Li he was sick of eating dust on the trails, that his name was Elias, but he didn't really mind being called Dusty. It was better than nigger.

"You be done lyin' around the tent, Chinaman?" Elias asked, punching Min Li in the arm. "There be more rock to drill and mountains to blow up."

"Careful with the bones," Min Li said, rubbing his arm where Elias punched him. "Let's finish this tunnel.'

"Then on to Utah," Elias said, handing Min Li his coolie hat.

"Then on to Utah," Min Li agreed, opening the tent flap for Elias. "After you."

"You Chinamen is sure polite," Elias said.

"It is a curse," Min Li said, bowing, smiling, and following Elias out of the tent and towards the Summit Tunnel, #6.

Thirty-Two

"Devlin Doyle," Connor Walsh called out to the man leaning on the gaslight post just blocks from the dock where the *Pilgrim*'s crew was heaving off the bow and stern lines, the steamer's deep-throated whistle declaring departure for Canada. "If you're tryin' to keep hidden from the coppers you are doin' a pitiful job."

"Connor," Devlin said. "If I were a praying man, you would be my answer."

"I'll take that as a compliment," Connor said. "Let me help you to the carriage. If the coppers find you, you'll bleed to death in a cell tonight and be planted in potter's field tomorrow, just one less bleedin' Paddy in the world."

"I…" Devlin began before feeling his legs buckle and the light from the lamppost grow brighter at the center and darker around the edges.

"Whoa, now," Connor said, leaping from the carriage's driver's seat just in time to keep Devlin from slumping to the sidewalk.

"These clothes are ruined," Devlin said, lifting his bloody hand from the wound that continued to ooze.

"And elegant enough attire for that tough who run off to remember when he tells the coppers how you killed his poor, innocent hooligan friend," Connor said, nearly carrying Devlin to the carriage and depositing him in the passenger seat. "Now, you stop bleedin'. I am takin' you to Mrs. Aubrey's. She has the right to see what you've done to that expensive suit of clothes she bought you."

Devlin moaned, and passed out.

~ ~ ~

"Meeks," Emma Aubrey said to her butler. "We are going to need some new clothes for Mr. Doyle."

"Of course, ma'am," Meeks said, dropping Devlin's white shirt, soaked scarlet with his blood, into the pile with his suit jacket, plaid vest and pants. His frock coat had flown open during the attack and escaped the knife but was soaked in blood nonetheless. "It was a very dapper outfit."

"You have exquisite taste, Meeks," Emma said, knowing how to please his pride. A happy Meeks made for a much happier household.

"Thank you, ma'am. After lunch I will go shopping."

"The knife apparently hit no vital organs or arteries. The bleeding has stopped and his fever is mild. But Mr. Doyle will need time to recuperate. And clothes to wear."

As a Station Master on the Underground Railroad, Emma Aubrey had tended to more than her fair share of wounds. She knew from experience that Devlin Doyle might not be out of the woods, since there was always the possibility of infection, but he was near the clearing in the forest.

"Yes, ma'am," Meeks said, picking of Devlin's bloody clothes in a loose bundle. "I will take these to the incinerator."

"Thank you, Meeks. Tell Mrs. Grady she can bring lunch. I believe broth and tea for Mr. Doyle."

"Of course, ma'am," Meeks said, holding Devlin's clothes arm's length from his butler attire like a bachelor carrying a soiled baby in need of a fresh diaper. Devlin began to stir.

"Mr. Doyle," Emma said. "Welcome."

"Emma," Devlin whispered.

"No need to speak, Mr. Doyle. You can stay with us as long as you need to recover."

"I have no money…"

"I do," Emma said. "We'll worry about finances after you are well. Mrs. Grady is bringing her delicious chicken broth. My Jewish friends tell me it can cure anything."

"A knife wound?"

"They would lead me to believe.

Mrs. Grady entered the bedroom after a polite knock at the partially closed door.

"Your medicine has arrived, Mr. Doyle," Emma said, taking the tray from Mrs. Grady, setting it on the table beside the bed

"I'm not hungry," Devlin said.

"Eat first," Emma said. "Sometimes your brain isn't hungry but your stomach is. Can we help you up?"

"I can do it," Devlin said, struggling to sit without success.

Emma nodded to Mrs. Grady. Both took an arm at each side of the narrow guest bed and gently sat Devlin up, placing pillows to keep him upright. Emma sat the tray with the bowl of soup across Devlin's lap. He attempted to pick up the spoon. It fell from his shaking fingers to the enameled tray, bouncing onto the chenille bedspread. Mrs. Grady picked the spoon up, wiped it on her apron and handed it to Emma.

"And I don't expect you to feed me," Devlin protested. "I am not a child."

"And I am not your mother. But I do expect you to obey as a good patient for a nurse," Emma said. "Now, Mr. Doyle, open your mouth. It is time to take your medicine."

~ ~ ~

As Devlin was recovering from his knife wound in a bedroom usually reserved for passengers on the Underground Railroad at Terrace Row, Emma Aubrey had shared the good news that Patsy, Beulah, Betsy and Seth had arrived safely in Canada and been taken to the farm community of ex-slaves, North Bruxton, in Southwestern Ontario. Devlin's job was done, the long journey from Memphis to Chicago completed with only one hitch, his stabbing by the hooligan. But his wound was healing without infection and he was growing restless, feeling well enough now to accompany Connor Welsh to O'Leary's Pub for a pint.

"It's called the Irish Legion," Connor said, taking a slow sip from his pint, savoring the heavy bitterness of the stout favored by himself and his fellow countrymen. "Recruited by Father Dennis Dunne of St. Patrick's church."

"All Irish?" Devlin asked, intrigued.

"At least three quarters, I hear."

"Well that would be a rowdy bunch. Both for Johnny Reb and for their own commanders."

Father Dennis Dunne was born in 1824 in Queen's County, Ireland. His father was Patrick Dunne and his mother was Amelia Maloney Dunne. When he was young, he came with his parents to Chatham, New Brunswick, Canada, moving to Quebec where he studied for the priesthood, being ordained in 1848 for the Diocese of Chicago. He was pastor of St. Patrick's Church at 700 West Adams Street when it was built in 1856 and founded the St. Vincent de Paul Society in Chicago to assist the poor and needy during the financial Panic of 1857. And in 1862, he organized the 90th Illinois Infantry; the "Irish Legion" or "Father Dunne's Regiment", out of patriotism but also to rebut the accusations that the Irish Catholics did not support the Union cause, especially because they were fearful that freed slaves would work for lower wages and replace them doing the menial jobs they were forced to take as unskilled immigrants, made all the worse by bigotry because of their faith.

"Some might call you a Skedaddler," Connor said, his pint nearly empty. He was considering ordering another.

"Now what would that be?" Devlin asked, draining his pint. What little pain he had left from the knife wound was gone with the stout.

"Father Dunne gave a speech the other day to shame those able-bodied Irishmen who would run away from the draft to Canada and live under what he called the "blood stained felon flag of Great Britain" rather than do their duty to defend the United States. He suggested that hangin' might be a fine punishment for the betrayal of their adopted country."

"Not sure Father Dunne needed to taunt shame out of Irish Catholic boys. It starts with their mothers, is passed on to the nuns then confirmed by the priests and bishops."

"That it is," Connor said, tossing another coin on the bar that got the barkeepers attention. Connor pointed to his empty pint.

"You know this...Father Dunne?" Devlin asked.

"Pastor of my parish. St. Pat's is just over on Adams Street. Walkin' distance from here. And other Irish pubs. We didn't leave everythin' back in the Old Sod."

"Shouldn't you be wearing a uniform, then?"

"Mrs. Aubrey thinks the job I'm doin' now is just as important as bein' shot by a Johnny Reb. I am not one to argue."

Devlin had been contemplating what was to come next, lying in Emma Aubrey's goose down bed as he healed, sipping Mrs. Grady's broth, then eating her chicken soup with matzo balls. Jewish dumplings, she called them. A friend's recipe. It could cure the grippe and slow down consumption, he was told. Through the window, opened to allow the invigorating air to flow into his bedroom from the lake, Devlin could hear the mournful steamboat whistles declare arrivals and departures and trains rattle up and down Michigan Avenue, taking soldiers to war and occasionally, bringing Negroes to freedom.

Since fleeing Ireland as the middle son, escaping the famine and oppression of English rents, leaving his older brother Davey to cultivate land he could never own, his younger brother, Finian, buried in the priesthood and his parents dead or dying, Devlin had survived on the brutal streets of Manhattan Island, worked his way west down the rivers on cargo flatboats, finally to Tennessee, falling into the slave trade because the money was good. Now he was nearly healed after being stabbed while delivering Negroes to freedom. Not a hero. Not a savior for sure, as he had told Emma Aubrey when she praised his bravery. Just an Irishman who understood bondage and how it ravaged the soul as surely as famine did the body. Not a savior for sure, but maybe he was seeking his own salvation that had nothing to do with heaven, hell or time served in purgatory to purge a multitude of sins. His transgressions read like a lengthy list of slaves for sale in a Memphis auction market, something with which he had been all too well acquainted. Accompanying Patsy's family to Canada, at least to the steamship, had been a penance, Our Fathers and Hail Marys. But he still felt in need of making a sincere Act of Contrition.

"Is it still possible to volunteer?" Devlin asked, having been lost in his own thoughts and interrupting Connor's story about a lass he had recently met at the Great Central Station along Water Street.

"Volunteer?" Connor asked, having forgotten he even mentioned Father Dunne and his Irish Legion after his third pint.

"The Irish Legion," Devlin said. "Are they still taking volunteers."

"Can't see why they wouldn't be," Connor said, trying to drain his empty glass. "Wars need fresh bodies like…"

"Irishmen need another pint," Devlin suggested.

"Good idea, Devlin," Connor said, tossing another coin on the bar. His empty glass disappeared and a full one took its place. "I'll take you to see Father Dunne tomorrow, if you like. I know everyone in Chicago. Everyone that's someone."

"I bet you do, Connor."

"Now," Connor said, taking a long drink from his pint and wiping foam from his lips with the back of his hand, "let me finish tellin' you about that lass I met at the train station. And listen this time."

"I will listen," Devlin said, "as long as you take me to see Father Dunne tomorrow."

"I'll take you to see Father Dunne tomorrow. If you want to get yourself killed preservin' the Union that treats you no better than the slaves the war is supposed to be freein'. That's dandy with me. Now, about that lass. Flamin' red hair. Wearin' an emerald green dress that would have gotten her arrested in Dublin…"

Devlin slowly turned his empty pint, watching remnants of the stout's foam head sink to the bottom of the glass, thinking about salvation.

~ ~ ~

Devlin was performing his penance. He volunteered for the 90th Illinois Infantry, the Irish Legion, eventually marching more than 2600 miles with Major General William T. Sherman's XV Army Corp, fighting through seven Confederate states, from Chattanooga to Atlanta to Savannah on their march to the sea.

Following the capture of Atlanta and the burning of anything his Army didn't need, or the Confederate Army could use, General Sherman suggested a daring strike into the Heart of the Dixie. His troops would no longer rely on supply lines. They would live off the land, marching through Georgia to Savannah, destroying anything of value to the rebel army they fell upon. Modern warfare was born as it was taken to the people, destroying their will to resist, burning their houses and farms after looting for food, tearing up railroad tracks and downing telegraph lines to slow rebel troop movement and communication. Sherman's Army met little resistance.

All along the march, a mood of imminent victory infiltrated the Irish troops, unspoken for the fear of Irish Luck, but adding a lighter lilt to the brogues of the many recent immigrants and a quicker step on the long march. But by the time they reached the outskirts of Savannah, they were in need of supplies, down to half-rations of coffee, sugar and hard tack as the pickings from the land had grown slim.

Just anchored off the coast, Admiral John A. Dahlgren's fleet waited with the needed rations and mail for the troops that had not been delivered in more than six weeks. But Confederate fortifications in Savannah prevented Sherman from linking up with the fleet, in particular, Fort McAllister, its large cannons blocking traffic on the Ogeechee River, preventing resupply from the ships floating offshore. The small sand fort had survived months of bombardment from the sea, day-long salvos of 350 pound shells from the 15 inch cannon that bristled from the ironclad gunboats, but remained defiant, the projectiles only moving the sand around that the Confederate defenders and slaves quickly put back in place. Sherman's solution was a frontal attack, and the 90th Illinois Volunteers would be part of the charge.

Fort McCallister had been fortified to withstand a thirty-day siege, but its eight large cannon facing riverside offered no defense on the three landsides. Ditches fifteen feet deep, seven feet across, moats, had been dug, and in front of the moats, abatis, cut trees with sharpened branches were placed pointing towards attacking troops as a barrier, and behind the abatis, torpedoes, the "infernal machines", buried land mines, artillery shells with friction matches that were detonated by the weight of a soldier's boot.

"The Rebs are pretty near done, ain't they, Sgt. Doyle?" Private Quinn asked, nervously swaying back and forth, clutching his brightly polished Springfield 1861 rifle musket as the 90th Illinois stood ready, just an open field between them and the fort, waiting for the signal to attack. Devlin had warned him that the shiny barrel of his gun was an easy target for Confederate sharpshooters, but Private Ewell Quinn, son of an Irish immigrant family and a recent stock yard worker in Chicago was so proud of his weapon he said he didn't mind if a Johnny Reb with a keen eye admired it. In contrast, Devlin had let the metal of his rifle musket tarnish mottled as southern soil, incapable of reflecting the hottest sun.

"Best not to tempt fate with talk of victory before you've fired a shot," Devlin said. "This is the Irish Legion."

"I didn't know you were a superstitious man, Sgt. Doyle. The Luck of the Irish, is it? You always seemed so…worldly."

"My Da believed it was good luck if a bird shite on him," Devlin said, remembering. "And Ma kept a candle burning in the window throughout Christmas time to welcome the Holy Family. If it went out, which it occasionally did, our family would be cursed with bad luck for the entire next year. It was as good a reason for any to explain her life of tragedy. Am I superstitious? If I am it is to honor my parents."

"And did a bird ever shite on your Da?"

"Not to my knowledge, and since he was never known to be a fortunate man…"

"Fix bayonets!" the Lieutenant coming down the line ordered.

"Bayonet," Devlin said, elbowing Ewell in the arm who was gazing across the open field towards the Rebels earthen fort.

The best riflemen could reload and shoot about three times a minute. The officers carried handguns. For the volunteers leading the charge, the bayonet was their last best chance at surviving when the combat became close and hand to hand.

"Sorry," Ewell said, sliding the bayonet into place below the muzzle. It was shiny as the rifle metal, having never been stained with blood. So far in the his battles as a member of the Irish Legion, from Vicksburg to Savannah, Ewell had not stuck a single Reb with his bayonet, or had proof that any of his shots had hit their target.

"What you asked before," Devlin said, "the Confederacy is nearly done. The war would have been won long ago if we would have had Generals like Grant and Sherman from the beginning."

"Let's take the fort, boys!" the Captain hollered, waving his saber.

"Good luck," Devlin bellowed to Ewell over the din of the trumpet and the regiment's answer to the Rebel Yell as they began their run to the fort, led by the standard bearer waving the Irish Legion's green flag embossed with the Golden Harp of Eire. The Confederate's sporadic return fire suggested the fort was meagerly defended, depending more on artillery, sharpened sticks and land mines for protection. The Irish Legion reached that line of protection in minutes.

"Careful," Devlin yelled to Ewell as they worked their way through the sharpened tree branches and into the ditch that ringed the earthwork walls. "Watch your step."

~ ~ ~

"You are one lucky Irishman," a blurry form hovering over Devlin said.

"Did we take the fort?" Devlin asked, reaching up

to feel the bandage that covered his left eye, the right beginning to focus. The man speaking was a Union doctor, his white coat splattered with blood like a butcher.

"Took it in fifteen minutes. You boys should be proud."

"I don't recall a thing," Devlin said, "after I told Private Quinn to be careful about the torpedoes."

"That is what put the grapeshot and shrapnel in you left side and almost took out your eye. I am glad for once I had a patient not in need of amputation."

"Private Quinn?"

"He stepped on the land mine. Not so lucky."

"I was lucky," Devlin said.

"We have removed all the metal we could find. You are bandaged and there is nothing to do now but watch for infection while you heal. The eye might take longer."

Devlin nodded. His ears were still ringing, pain stabbed his left leg and side, and he never in his life had such a headache.

"The Luck of the Irish," Devlin mumbled.

"What's that?" the doctor asked, not sure if he had heard Devlin right.

"Have you ever been shite on by a bird?"

"I believe Sgt. Doyle is delirious," the doctor said to an orderly passing with a bucket full of bloody rags. "Keep watch on him tonight. Be diligent for the smell of gangrene in that leg. We may still need to amputate."

"Yes, doctor," the orderly said, tossing the bloody rags into a growing pile in the corner of the field hospital tent.

"Keep the candle lit. Don't let it go out," Devlin whispered before losing consciousness.

~ ~ ~

Fort McCallister was occupied by Union troops, including the Irish Legion, vital supplies beginning to flow in from the ships at sea.

Major George Wayne Anderson had commanded the 250 Confederate troops left to defend the fortification. Once captured, he felt the wrath of General Sherman who called the land mines placed around the fort weapons of murder, not weapons of war, naming it a less-than gentlemanly tactic. General Sherman personally ordered Major Anderson to join the detail with other captured Confederate troops to clear the land mines.

Union troops occupied Savannah in late December, 1864 after a brief siege; the march to the sea was accomplished. Sherman announced his success to President Lincoln in his famous telegram, "I beg to present you, as a Christmas gift, the city of Savannah, with 150 heavy guns and plenty of ammunition, and also about 25,000 bales of cotton." Congratulating General Sherman, President Lincoln wired back, "What next?".

The "what next" was uniting with General Grant's army near Richmond to engage the Confederate Army of Northern General Robert E. Lee and to do that, Sherman's army would march north through the Carolinas. The winter season was bad, roads were nearly impassable, but the army that had marched across Georgia to the sea felt prepared to go wherever General Sherman would lead them, this time to Colombia, South Carolina.

Most, Including General Sherman, thought there would be a hard fought battle for Columbia, possibly the last big battle of the war. But Confederate forces in South Carolina were divided and small, and the general in charge of those forces, Gen. Pierre Gustave-Toutant Beauregard, was ill, a reporter writing that Beauregard—who four years earlier had commanded Confederate forces that fired on Fort Sumter—was suffering from "melancholy." As with Savannah, Confederate troops strategically retreated with hopes of joining General Lee for the final defense of Dixie.

On February 17, 1865, in the last months of the Civil War, much of Columbia was destroyed by fire while

Union troops occupied under the command of General Sherman who blamed the high winds and retreating Confederate soldiers for firing the more than four thousand bales of cotton which had been stacked in the streets as barricades in a city constructed mostly of wood. Sherman denied ordering the burning, though he did order militarily significant structures destroyed. But his reputation after Atlanta did nothing to bolster his denials. Witness accounts by local residents and newspaper reporters spoke of the burning as revenge by Union troops for Columbia's and South Carolina's roles in leading Southern states to secede, the state of Fort Sumter and the first shots of the rebellion, although it was likely Confederate troops lay waste to the city as they evacuated in an attempt to leave nothing of value for the Yankees. Hostilities remained even as the fighting was ending.

~ ~ ~

Devlin read about the exploits of the Irish Legion in the *Chicago Times* with his one good eye. The city was proud of the way they had distinguished themselves and so was Devlin. He wished he had been there when they marched into Washington and paraded in the Grand Review of General Sherman's Army to celebrate victory and honor the troops. But he was already back in the Windy City by then, recovered as much as possible, using his experience of the rivers, sympathy that he was a wounded, surviving member of the 90th Illinois Volunteers and his friendly Irish persuasions to land a job on the steamer *Pilgrim* that still ran the route to Canada, although no longer a connection on the Underground Railroad. First Mate Arthur Wesley was now Captain and remembered well the night of Devlin's stabbing. He was glad to know Devlin had survived the attack, and the war, and welcomed him aboard, noting that the eye patch gave Devlin the devilish appearance of a Caribbean buccaneer.

The eye had gotten infected. Doctors packed it with bromine-soaked dressings, bandaged it and hoped for the best. The infection receded, but the eye could not be saved. Added to that, a limp from a shrapnel wound from the land mine that had done damage to his left knee. The leg remained stiff, but it did not keep him from performing his duties as the newly commissioned First Mate on the *Pilgrim*. And any of the pain his wounds might still cause were quickly remedied with a stout or two with Able Seaman Connor Walsh. Devlin had found Connor still sitting on his favorite stool at O'Leary's Pub, hunched over the bar, nursing a Guinness when he returned to Chicago after his discharged from the Irish Legion. Devlin had talked Connor into joining him on the *Pilgrim*, now that the Underground Railroad had been dismantled and Emma Aubrey no longer required Connor's services. A good job. A good friend. The war won. Slavery abolished. There was only one thing left Devlin needed to do to make his penance complete and he would do that on the *Pilgrim's* next run to Canada

~ ~ ~

Captain Wesley had maneuvered the *Pilgrim* to berth with his usual aplomb in the port of Sarnia, Ontario, Canada, at the southern tip of Lake Huron, last stop before returning new cargo and passengers to Chicago. He leaned on the rail by the gangplank, lit a match and puffed his pipe to life.

"North Buxton is about sixty miles south, as the crow flies," Captain Wesley said.

"Too bad I can't hop a crow," Devlin said, repositioning his eye patch.

"Considering what passes for roads," Captain Wesley said. "The eye still pains ya?"

"Can't in truth say it doesn't," Devlin said. "The knee gives me greater fits. I suppose being a sailor was a questionable choice of career, considering how the cold and damp of the lakes can stiffen me up like an old Salty Dog. I'm hoping time will heal what ails me. Until then, a stout, or two."

"I can attest to the medicinal qualities of Guinness," Connor Walsh said, joining them at the rail. "You ready for your shore leave, Devlin."

"Indeed I am. My duffel bag is packed and I am grateful to you Connor for arranging my transportation."

"North Buxton was the end of the line for many of Mrs. Aubrey's Underground Railroad passengers," Connor said, "like Patsy and her family, so I knew people on the Canada side who could help. And I still know people."

"I will be standing on the pier when the *Pilgrim* returns, Captain," Devlin said. "I best be going. Looks like my carriage awaits, thanks to Connor."

"No Irish Goodbye for me," Connor said, grabbing Devlin's hand and pumping it like an un-primed well pump handle. "Like Da used to say to his pals in the pub, "May the hinges of our friendship never grow rusty."

"No chance of that, with the proper pints of lubrication," Devlin said, swinging the duffel bag over his shoulder, walking down the gangplank to the waiting carriage and stopping to wave a final farewell to Connor and the Captain.

"Think Devlin will come back?" Captain Wesley asked Connor, tamping the tobacco down with a gnarled finger and relighting his pipe.

"I'm no gypsy fortune teller," Connor said. "But if I were a bettin' man, which I am, I would put the odds at fifty-fifty. Now if you don't mind, Captain, it is time for my shore leave."

"Just don't miss the boat," Captain Wesley said. "Without Devlin you'll be filling is as First Mate, if you think you can handle the job."

"Handle the job?" Connor said, not going into detail of his earlier days, before working for Mrs. Aubrey, when he was a seaman first on schooners, then on sidewheelers and screw steamers, hauling cargo and passengers from the St. Lawrence Seaway to Chicago, being shipwrecked once in a sudden winter storm on Lake Superior and surviving. "Yes I can."

"Good," Captain Wesley said. "I'll hold ya to that. You have friends in Sarnia?"

"I know people," Connor said.

"I'm sure you do," Captain Wesley said. "I'm sure you do."

~ ~ ~

North Buxton was founded in 1849 by the Irish Presbyterian Minister, Reverend William King and 15 former American slaves, Underground Railroad refugees, and abolitionists. They cleared the land and established farms on 50-acre plots. By the 1860's, the settlement boasted a general store, two hotels, a post office, a sawmill, a brickyard, a grist mill, a pearlash factory for the manufacturing of soap and glass and three integrated schools.

"The erasers are all clean, Miss Doyle.

"Thank you, Jennie," Beulah said to the young girl who had come into the schoolhouse after pounding the felt erasers into clouds of chalk dust on the porch. Her black dress had turned grey in the process.

"You had better go back to the porch and brush yourself off. Your mother wouldn't like me sending you home looking like a dirty dust mop."

"Yes, Miss. Doyle. I'll do that on my way home. See you in the morning, Miss Doyle."

"Be sure you practice your multiplication tables, Jennie. You are a little weak with the times eights. Arithmetic is important."

"Mother will help me after supper."

"And read some of your family Bible to her. Any passage will do. Reading is as important as arithmetic."

"Yes, Miss Doyle, see you in the morning," Jennie said, opening the school door and running into a man standing on the porch who appeared ready to knock, leaving her outline in chalk on his black Greatcoat. "Sorry, sir. Goodnight, Miss Doyle."

"Nothing to be sorry for..." Devlin began but the little girl was gone before he could finish his sentence. He looked up to see Beulah drop the papers she was sorting at her desk. They fluttered to the floor like autumn leaves.

"Mr. Doyle?" Beulah said.

"Miss Doyle?" Devlin asked.

"Your eye."

"I still have a good one," Devlin said. "Now, what is this about being Miss Doyle."

"We were told you were alive, and gone to War."

"I do know that," Devlin said. "But I don't know how you came to be Miss Doyle."

"It was Seth's idea. We had no family name when we arrived in Canada. And had no intentions of adopting Crenshaw. Or Cruickshank. Seth proposed that we name ourselves after you. I hope you don't mind."

"I am very flattered, Miss Doyle. The name suits you. Beulah Doyle. A teacher. With impeccable English, and an Irish name."

"Arithmetic. Geography. Penmanship. I have been busy studying as much as my students while you were away fighting to end slavery."

"Indeed you have, Beulah. I may still call you Beulah?"

"If I can call you Devlin."

"You already have my last name. Using my first seems appropriate."

"Let me lock up the school and I'll take you to the farm to meet the rest of the Doyles . They will be delighted.

~ ~ ~

"A teacher and a landowner," Devlin said with some astonishment, walking past fields of sweet corn, patches of tomato and carrots, and potatoes. "Praties."

Beulah looked at Devlin, puzzled.

"Potatoes," Devlin said. "Praties is what we called them in Ireland. Our lifeblood, and our death. But yours look robustly green and healthy."

"Ontario is a kind place to grow all sorts of crops," Beulah said. "Or I've been told. I teach. Hank takes care of the farming. And Seth. Betsy, too. The kitchen belongs to Mama."

"Hank? He drove me here?"

"Yes. I'm not married, if that's what you're thinking. My last name is still Doyle. Hank's last name is Briggs. Not that Hank hasn't been persistent in trying to persuade me to marry him since we arrived in North Buxton. Hank came to Canada the year before we did, thanks to Mrs. Aubrey. He met us at the dock when the steamboat landed and drove us here, as he did you. Sixty miles."

"I know," Devlin said. "My knee was stiff before the ride. I am still recuperating. You must have spent the night at that frightening house along the road, about halfway?"

"Hank thought it was funny to tell ghost stories."

"Probably the same stories he told me. The house and surroundings made them…believable."

"We moved into the farmhouse on this property," Beulah continued. "Hank added to the toolshed to make himself a comfortable cabin. Mama cooks, Betsy feeds the chickens and the pigs. milks the cows, tends the tomato patch. Seth is as strong a farmhand as Hank. You'll be surprised how he's grown."

"You have made yourself a family," Devlin said.

"New Buxton is a community of families, not all of them related, except by the common bond of slavery."

"And now there is no slavery."

"On paper," Beulah said. "But, how many generations will it take before the wounds heal? Not just the scars of the whip, but the resentment of whites for Negroes thinking they could be the equals of their old masters. And there is always the old fear of freed slaves taking revenge."

"So I take it you are not returning to America any time soon?"

"Why? We have three schools in North Buxton. They are considered good enough that white farmers send their children. It is something in which our community is extremely proud. Good farmland. We are surrounded by friends who shared the same shameful bondage and survived the brutality to flourish. This is our home."

"Why return to America indeed," Devlin agreed. "You have a lovely place here, Beulah. You deserve it. You and Patsy. Betsy and Seth. You all deserved the best life."

"We have it here," Beulah said. "I never did thank you for all your help. All the way from Memphis…"

"Yes you did," Devlin said, "Just look around. You have made this life, something to pass on to future generations."

"I'm not married," Beulah said, smiling. "But there is Seth."

"Mr. Devlin!" Seth called out, running down the rutted farm road towards them. He was waving a garden hoe like a battle standard.

"Your boy has grown," Devlin said.

"Seth has a girl from the neighboring farm. He's been inviting over for Mama's dumpling dinners…"

"Mr. Devlin," Seth said, breathless, shaking hands with a strong, farmer's grip. "Never thought I'd be seein' you again."

"Wanted to see how your family was doing. Very well, from the looks of it. How do you like farming, Seth?

"It be…"

"It is," Beulah corrected.

"It is our land," Seth said. "What we grow we eat and we sell the rest. Ain't no one…"

"Isn't anyone," Beulah corrected.

"Oh, Mama!"

"Not easy having a teacher for a mother, is it? I bet you know your times tables."

"I does…I do," Seth said, correcting himself.

"Mama and Betsy are preparing supper by now," Beulah said. "Let's go surprise them with Mr. Doyle, Seth."

"How long are you stayin'?" Seth asked.

Devlin looked at Beulah and paused before he answered.

"As long as he likes," Beulah answered for him. "Have you ever thought of taking up farming, Mr. Doyle."

"Not until now," Devlin said. "That cold and damp on the lakes has been seeping deeper into my bones. Drying out on land might be a good change."

"We can always use more hands," Beulah said.

"Even with only one good eye and a gimpy knee?"

"Yes," Beulah said.

"What happened to your eye, Mr. Devlin?" Seth asked.

"No time for war stories now, Seth. Let's go see your grandmother and aunt. I wonder what's for dinner?" Devlin said.

"I do know she made an apple pie. Our own apples," Seth said with pride.

"The best pies I have ever tasted," Devlin said.

"So, Mr. Doyle," Beulah said as they started walking up the road towards the farmhouse, "what have you been doing for the past few years?"

"That's a dangerous thing to ask an Irishman," Devlin said.

"This family has never been one to run from danger," Beulah said.

"Indeed you have not," Devlin agreed. "Well, let me begin when I got stabbed by the hooligan on the dock…"

Epilogue

Thirty-Three

~~1948 Elgin State Hospital, Veteran's Colony, Elgin, Illinois

"Bob. You awake?"

"Yeah, Suh. I's still breathin', and surprised each mornin' I wake up to see I's still alive."

"I hear you had a birthday party on my day off," Phil Maynard said, drawing back the room's curtain to the pale but harsh light of a January morning on the grounds of the Elgin State Hospital, the Veteran's Colony, Elgin, Illinois, about thirty-five miles northwest of Chicago. "How old are you now, Bob?"

"Catchin' up to old man Methuselah," Bob said. "One hundred and twelve years old."

"Unbelievable," Phil said.

"It be true," Bob said. "1836. Mama done told me. You might not know your Daddy, child, she said, but you will always know what year you was born. 1836. I never forgot. It be 1948 now and that makes me one hundred and twelve years old."

"You must have seen a lot in all those years," Phil said.

"Yeah, Suh. I seen more than was good to see. And the older I get, the more I remember what I seen, whether I wants to or not."

"Get anything nice for your birthday?"

"Yeah, Suh. A big cake. Three layers. Devil's food. Never did like that fluffy angel food. Ain't nothin' to it. I like the dark chocolate, black as like I is," Bob chuckled. "Someone snuck in a bottle of hootch and the orderlies mixed it in the punch. Had a few sips myself, even though I always been temperance. I think the Lord will look the other way once, considerin' my age. And since I be one hundred and twelve years old, I don't think there be any fear of it shortenin' my life none. Help me sit up, Phil. My rheumatiz is makin' me stiffer every mornin'. I gots some presents, too. Remember that half-dollar the governor give my back in '41?"

"I wasn't working here then, Bob," Phil said. "I didn't start working at Elgin until after the war. The Second World War."

"I remember that war," Bob said, although it was true he was forgetting recent events and orderlies names more and more. He remembered Phil's name. He liked him. Bob could tell you the name of every leased slave on Mr. John Hart Crenshaw's Hickory Hill from a century ago, both when it was a salt works and then when it was a farm. But last night's dinner menu could be a mystery. "Fightin' the Hun, again. And the Japs."

"That's the one," Phil said. "After I came home from the Pacific I lived in Chicago and needed work. Elgin offered room and board in the Veteran's Colony. I've been working here for almost two years. Thought I'd be moving on in a hurry when I started, but I enjoy the company of other veterans."

"Ain't none left from the Civil War at Elgin 'ceptin' me," Bob said, suddenly feeling the chill of outliving everyone.

"Fewer and fewer survivors left anywhere, Union or Confederate. It was a long time ago. Over eighty years, if my arithmetic is right."

"Seems like yesterday, sometimes. Like I sayin', the governor, he give me a half dollar back in '41 for tobacco. That be my one vice. I do like my pipe. But I never spent the half dollar. It be my good luck piece, give me by Governor Dwight Green of Illinois hisself. But I lost it. Don't want to think nobody stole it. The governor, he heard about me losin' the half dollar and sent me a new shiny one for my one hundred and twelfth birthday. I ain't spendin' this one, neither. Or losin' it. It be in that drawer in the table by the bed. I use it to mark my place in my Bible."

"Are you hungry, Bob? Breakfast is being served in the kitchen…"

"You know I ain't one for breakfast, Phil. My stomach don't wake up till noontime. Help me to the commode and then you can fetch me a cup of coffee."

"I'll bring you the coffee after I make my morning rounds. Shouldn't take long. If you don't mind, I'll bring a thermos and we can continue our talk."

"I'd like that, Phil."

"Now, let's get you out of this bed, to the commode and dressed. Then I'll bring the coffee."

"Black," Bob said. "None of that cream or sugar."

"Black. None of that cream or sugar," Phil repeated, knowing that Bob believed not drinking milk or eating sugar had contributed to his longevity.

Phil was looking forward to another session, listening to Bob as he recounted his life over cups of coffee. Phil felt he was the keeper of the chronicles that so often passed without being shared, disappeared with the death of those who lived them, taken unspoken to their silent grave. Phil felt compelled to keep Bob's story alive, if only to share with strangers at a bar over glasses of beer.

~ ~ ~

"You are the best dressed man in Elgin, Bob," Phil said, setting a thermos down on the small table Bob used for eating when he was too tired or his arthritis made it too painful for him to walk down to the dining room. Bob's private room also had a single bed, a small bathroom with toilet and shower stall and a kitchen area with counters, cupboards, a single sink and a hot plate. Phil retrieved two cups and saucers from the cupboard, careful not to drop them. Elgin State Hospital's budget did not always cover broken dishes.

Bob wore a white shirt, a dark blue, shoulder-padded, double-breasted suit coat, dark blue pleated pants, and a striped yellow and blue silk tie. He unscrewed the thermos top and began pouring the steaming black coffee into the two porcelain cups Phil had gently placed on their matching saucers.

"To life," Phil said, raising his cup to Bob. "A toast my Jewish buddies in the Solomon Islands would make, with canteens water, before he hit the beach. L'Chaim, in Hebrew. I got pretty good at pronouncing it by the time we landed on Iwo Jima. Anyway, I came to hear your story, Bob. I know mine."

"I already told you 'bout me bein' a stud nigger at different plantations 'cause they made slave ships from Africa illegal," Bob said, pouring coffee from his cup into its saucer, lifting it to his mouth, blowing to cool it and sipping.

"Yes, you did," Phil said, not wishing to hear those stories repeated, still feeling the repulsion over Bob being used to increase the enchained population like a thoroughbred stallion. "And we've discussed the Civil War."

"Just one thing I wants people to know," Bob said, putting the saucer back down on the table. "I was not no Rebel soldier. I was a camp slave to my master who was the soldier. The officers treated me like a slave 'cause I was a slave. They afraid to put a musket in my hand to fight 'cause I might uprise again' and slaughter 'em all like Nat Turner. They be always whisperin' about Nat Turner like he be a Hoodoo Man. No, suh. I just shined boots. I dug latrines and delivered dead officers back to their family plantations. But I never shot a gun at no Yankee. I's hearin' people now sayin' slaves must've liked bein' slaves 'cause they fought for the Confederacy. Damn lie, Lord forgive me. Damn lie. Negroes hated slavery. They didn't fight for it. Plantation owners wanted slavery. They still be usin' slaves to pick cotton today if'n they could get away with it. Robert E. Lee fought again' his own country to keep slaves in chains, claimin' he be fightin' for Virginny. Damn lie."

"And after the war?" Phil said, sensing Bob's growing anger. Phil didn't want to be the cause of a one hundred and twelve year old man's stroke.

"It be a big country," Bob said. "I gots myself a Bible and learned my letters, since it weren't against the law for a Negro to read after the war. But some things were the same. Most white people hated me for being a Negro and bein' big made 'em madder. So I kept movin'. Workin' farms. Preachin'. Staying far away from that old Jim Crow Dixie. 'Course Yankee's not that much better'n the way they treat Negroes. Best if we stay to ourselves, they'd say, and do the dirty work. I been doing the dirty work since General Robert E. Lee surrendered to General U.S Grant in that farmhouse. I hoped by now it'd be better for those children I made. Can't say it be any better. Maybe someday. That what bein' a preacher taught me. Hope. Don't do no good to despair. They always be hope. So here I be. One hundred and twelve years old. Livin' in the Veteran Colony of the Elgin State Hospital, still talking 'bout things I done last century. I'm getting tired, Phil. I hate gettin' so tired. Like one foot it the grave. 'Course I probably got both legs up to my knees sinking into that fresh dug earth," Bob said, laughing at his joke. "Think I's goin' to take a nap, Phil. Can you leaves the coffee. I sure like a cup after my nap."

"Of course, Bob. I'll check back later."

"I's obliged, Phil," Bob said. "Don't know why you want to hear my stories, bein' a young white boy and all."

"I'm not that young," Phil said. "But compared to one hundred and twelve..."

Bob lay down on the unwrinkled bed he had made with hospital corner precision, careful not to rumple the spread, careful not to crease his one good suit, head straight on the firm pillow.

"If I think of anything else you want to know," Bob said without turning his head, "we can talk about it next time."

There were plenty of next times, Bob constantly remembering new details from the past hundred years. And Phil was eager to listen, sucking up incidents and accidents in Bob's life like a red-bagged Hoover vacuum. The meetings of coffee and recollections continued until April 11, 1948, as lilacs bloomed in the dooryard of the Elgin State Hospital as they were when Abraham Lincoln was assassinated eighty-three years before, something that Bob clearly remembered and recalled for Phil. Bob died early on that Sunday morning, just after midnight.

~ ~ ~

Bob was buried in the cemetery north of the hospital grounds with a simple carved stone marker bearing his name, birth and death dates. Three months later, on July 26, 1948, President Harry S. Truman issued and Executive Order that abolished discrimination in all American Military Service "on the basis of race, color, religion or national origin". It was the law when Phil Maynard was called up as a Marines Reserve to serve in the Korean war, only five years after World War Two. Remembering Bob, Phil regaled his Negro Marine buddies with stories of Bob as a slave stud, and being a camp slave who was never trusted to carry a musket in the Confederate Army while they crouched in foxholes under mortar fire from the North Koreans before the taking of Bloody Ridge and other battle hills. Phil would continue to pass Bob's tales on to others in hopes that someone would do the same for him one day, weaving him into the tapestry of humanity, sometimes a dull length of brown yarn, other times a shining strand of brilliant color.

Made in the USA
Las Vegas, NV
15 January 2021